The Many Tortures of Anthony Cardno

EDITED BY ANTHONY R. CARDNO

This is a work of fiction. All characters and events portrayed herein are either products of the author's imagination or are used fictionally. Any resemblance to persons living or dead is purely coincidence (except for resemblance to Anthony Cardno—that was planned).

Editing: Anthony R. Cardno
Proofing: Anthony R. Cardno, Teresina Jonkoski
Design and Layout: Bear Weiter
Cover and interior art: Bear Weiter, Marlyse Comte

Published by
Talekyn Press
21 Sunset Inn Road
Lafayette, NJ 07848
www.anthonycardno.com

ISBN: 978-0692250587

Printed by CreateSpace

Table of Contents

"We are a race of musical liars, and who you are may depend on who's singing your song. Many's the tree-spirit come tripping out of yesterday to find itself a saint today and rudely surprised by the change."

—PARKE GODWIN, FIRELORD

Foreward: I'm Not a Nice Guy: Really

ANTHONY R. CARDNO

It really is all Brian White's fault. I know in his Introduction to this volume he tries to paint me as a nice guy, but he's the one who offered Tuckerizations at such reasonable prices as part of his Kickstarter campaigns. And who am I to pass on giving someone the opportunity to eviscerate me in print?

Because I'm really not a nice guy. People think I am, because I back Kickstarters and donate money to charity events and because I tweet and post on Facebook about stories you should read, small press publishers you should purchase from, unsigned bands you should listen to. I don't do all of this promotion for other people because I'm nice.

I do it because I'm selfish.

Look. It's this simple:

If I tell you about a Kickstarter project? It's because I want the project to succeed so I have something new to read or watch or listen to. It's not about wanting those authors, movie-makers, or bands to succeed. Or if it is, it's so I can name-drop them in casual conversation. Because I'm not only selfish, I'm all kinds of vain.

If I tell you to buy books from a small press publisher? It's because I want them to stick around long enough to publish me. Because I'm not only selfish

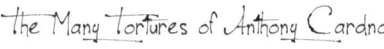

and vain, I'm avaricious.

If I tell you to support a cancer-based fundraiser like the American Cancer Society's Relay for Life or Ronald McDonald House? It's because I've had cancer, I've lost friends to cancer, and I want them to find cures before I relapse or I lose any more friends to that disease. Because I'm not only selfish, vain, and avaricious, I'm scared.

Okay, you caught me.

This really isn't all about me, even though the stories in this book are. Every one of you reading this knows somebody who has fought cancer, or at the very least knows somebody who knows somebody. We're all connected that way.

I am a colon cancer survivor (2005); Michelle Moklebust is a breast cancer survivor. As we were making the final adjustments to this book, we learned that Jay Lake passed away, just a few days before his 50th birthday, after a protracted battle with the same colon cancer I had. Jay's family is still around to deal with the aftermath. Because cancer is not a solitary disease. Every author in this collection has been impacted by cancer, intimately or distantly.

And that's the real point of this collection: raising money to support the research, patient outreach, and family support that the American Cancer Society provides. Because we lose too many people every year to cancer, and it needs to stop.

In February of 2005, my mother died from lung cancer; in September of that year I was diagnosed with colon cancer, followed by surgery and chemotherapy. Every year since then, one way or another, I have participated in my home-town of Mahopac, New York's Relay For Life event. Some years I've walked, some years I've done book-signings. Every year I donate.

When Brian White and I joked about the "seven tortures of Anthony Cardno," I knew right away this was another way for me to give and give back. All of the authors involved have donated their stories. Bear Weiter has donated the cover and interior art and formatting chores. Other friends have promised to donate time promoting the book.

But you know why they're doing it, right?

Not because they're nice.

Because who can resist the urge to torture me in print?

Or, for that matter, who can resist reading about it?

To which I can only say: thank you, my friends. For putting up with me, for keeping me humble, and for making this project possible.

Enjoy the following 22 stories and songs. I know I did.

Anthony R. Cardno
Lafayette, NJ and other places
April, 2014

Introduction: Who is Anthony Cardno?

BRIAN WHITE

Who is Anthony Cardno? A human rights activist? A shy little boy learning to stand up for himself through the power of a story? An evil professor? A drunk so far gone he will empty his guts on sacred ground?

Well, yes. He is all of these things, and many more, as you will find as you read this collection. Anthony Cardno is sometimes depraved, sometimes righteous, or somewhere on the spectrum in between. Human, in other words.

That's the fictional Anthony Cardno. As far as I know, the real Anthony Cardno has never harnessed the power of zombies, communicated with ghosts, or visited exclusive restaurants on distant planets. What I *do* know is that Anthony is an enthusiastic and generous supporter of creative projects and people. He is someone who is always looking for ways to help. (Take this book, for example, and the good it is doing for the American Cancer Society's Relay For Life.) And he is a good friend.

I first met Anthony during the Kickstarter for the first issue of my magazine, *Fireside*, in early 2012. He picked a Tuckerization reward for the story by Christie Yant. Don't know what Tuckerization is? Well, this whole book is an exercise in it. Tuckerization is when a real person's name is used in a fictional story. The name comes from Wilson Tucker, a science fiction writer who would often put people he knew into his stories.

So Anthony picked that reward, and Christie wrote a story called *Temperance*. A few months later, we did the Kickstarter for Issue Two. And Anthony popped in again, this time with Damien Walters, who wrote *Scarred*. Anthony and I chatted a bit after that, and he said he was going to try to get into every issue of Fireside. (We were planning on being a quarterly at the time.) I thought that would be cool, actually, a little nugget for repeat readers to find. We've met in meatspace a few times, and I am really happy to be able to call Anthony my friend. We also connected on Twitter, and he is among a group of friends who are funny, smart, and always ripping on me. It's pretty great.

Anthony appeared again in Issue Three, in Mary Robinette Kowal's story *The White Phoenix Feather*. This is probably Anthony's least flattering appearance in Fireside. Kind of a jerk, really. After that we switched to a monthly format, so the idea of being in every issue didn't work out, but Anthony showed up again in early 2014 in a story by Adam P. Knave, *The Brutal and the Simple*, and will be back in 2015 in a story by Stephen Blackmoore.

Somewhere in all of this, because he kept seeming to come off badly in the stories, I joked he should do an anthology and call it *The Seven Tortures of Anthony Cardno*. But that joke sparked an idea, and, like I said, Anthony is always looking for ways to help. He came up with the idea of this charity anthology. And, because Anthony has so many creative friends, it ended up with a lot more than seven stories. There's even some where he looks good, but I do think he gets tortured just about as much as he deserves.

We begin with the story that started it all in the first issue of Fireside *magazine. Christie very graciously took on the task of making me a character even though at the time she knew precious little about me. She was nervous about how I'd respond to the first line of the story; it remains in my mind one of the best opening lines I've ever read. Since this story, Christie and I have become fast friends. And to think, it all started with a far more alcoholic version of me puking ...*

Temperance

CHRISTIE YANT

It wasn't the worst bender of Anthony Cardno's life, but it was the first that he had ended in a cemetery, vomiting into an open grave. His head throbbed; his mouth tasted of dust and sickness. He didn't recall how he came to be here; he remembered the wagon that had carried him away from Santa Lydia where he had quickly worn out his welcome, but he didn't know which direction it had taken him and couldn't guess where he might be now. As long as it wasn't San Francisco, he'd probably be all right.

His flask lay out of reach, at the bottom of the freshly dug hole. He tried to roll over and rise, but his stomach rebelled, leaving Anthony to pray his usual prayer on mornings like these: *Never again, O Lord, if only you'll make it stop.* But the Almighty had heard it all before, and Anthony's stomach evicted its contents right into the grave. There was a ringing in his ears, and it wasn't until the heaving stopped and he could breathe again that he heard the voices, angry and dismayed, and saw the rest of the scene before him: the grim marble markers that stretched out in rows all around him; polished leather shoes and long black skirts; the shaggy hooves of horses and the narrow wheels of a hearse wagon; and the shocked faces of the recently bereaved.

He tried to get to his feet but vertigo and drink still had him, and he tumbled

over the side. He felt a rib crack as he landed hard at the bottom of the grave.

"I apologize," Anthony said, the words coming out slow and muddy. "I apologize for disturbing your peace." He retrieved his flask and did his best to rub the sick off it before tucking it back inside his coat.

"Get him the hell out of there." The man who spoke stood out of view, but two young men—twins, by the look of them, with sun-faded hair, rolled sleeves, and ruddy, smirking faces—each reached a hand down and hauled him painfully over the side.

"What town is this?" he asked and spit the sour bile that still lingered in his throat. "What day?" Those assembled stood in affronted silence.

A man stepped forward, stately and well-dressed in black hat and overcoat, a white flower in his lapel. An important man, by the look of him, but with a meanness in his eyes that reminded Anthony of his father.

"The wrong place, on the wrong day." Anthony detected the familiar note of escalation in the air.

"I'll just be on my way, then." Anthony took several careful, uneven steps toward the track that led down the hill and toward the gates that he could just see beyond.

"Not just yet." The man nodded at the pair who had pulled Anthony from the grave, and they moved in with swift menace. Each twin seized an arm and together they dragged him along, past the women who gasped and whispered behind their gloved hands, and out to the road where a row of buggies waited to carry the grieving home.

"Right there's fine." The boys dropped Anthony to the ground. "Stand up." Anthony climbed unsteadily to his feet. The man stepped up to him and stood too close. "You stink of drink."

"I meant no harm, sir."

"My sister's children will remember this day for the rest of their lives. So will I."

And then he was caught again, held by the beastly twins while this man felt through his coat and searched his pockets, scattering his few belongings in the dirt. He had a moment of real fear when the man tossed his watch, and his attempt to pull away and go after it was rewarded by a sharp punch to the gut. The search continued until the man found what he was looking for.

The man pulled Anthony's flask out of his inside pocket and held it up for all to see; then he pulled the stopper and poured the precious contents out into the dirt.

The Many Tortures of Anthony Cardno

"I'm the mayor of this town, and I don't want to know you. Get your things, and get the hell out of my sight."

The mayor and his cohorts turned their backs on Anthony and started back toward the grave site. Anthony collected his things — pocket watch and watch-maker's tools, unharmed; flask, empty; coins and notes, gathered and accounted for, despite the tremor in his hands.

"You asked what town this is," the mayor called back over his shoulder. "You're in Temperance. You might not care to linger."

❀

Temperance, California—there would be no relief for him in this town. Dry as a bone, surely, and righteous as hell about it.

The road into town was muddy and pitted with tracks, and the high winds whipped his face, cold and smelling of the sea. He twisted his ankle painfully before he'd gone a quarter mile; he limped past fields of plants cultivated in careful rows and past the dark-skinned Japanese immigrants who tended them. They took no notice of the dejected stranger trudging his way toward town, where maybe he could find a room for the night before boarding the steamer to San Francisco.

People were forever sending Anthony away from wherever he was. Bodie, Omaha, Leadville—he'd been through and driven out of them all. He'd go wherever they pointed him, generally, as long as it wasn't toward home. He had reached the edge of town when he heard the slow, clip-clop crescendo of approaching horses as the funeral party returned from the hill. The party would overtake him soon; humiliation made his cheeks burn despite the cold. He shivered and quickened his pace toward the nearest shelter, a sturdy brick building with no sign to identify its purpose.

A door in the front stood wide open, but Anthony could see nothing in the darkness within. He took a step inside and was assailed by the heat. A furnace burned bright in the corner, and he recognized the trappings of a foundry: scrap metal in one pile, finished hinges and gadgets in another. He took a seat on a rickety stool and within minutes the chill had finally left his bones, for what seemed like the first time since he'd been shut out of the comfort of his father's house.

He pulled his watch from the safety of his coat pocket; it had been in the family for three generations. He'd had to buy his tools back three times now, but

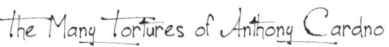
The Many Tortures of Anthony Cardno

somehow Anthony had never lost the watch, nor sold it, nor had it stolen, nor gambled it away. He could say the same for nothing else in his life.

He opened the case with a soft click and held it to his ear. It was hard to hear above the roar of the furnace and the wind in the rafters, but the smooth *tick-tick* sound it made comforted him.

A sound from behind him made him jump to his feet. He expected to find the foundry owner, ready to accuse him of trespass and chase him out. Instead, he found a young woman on her hands and knees in a pool of light from a source he could not see, feeling around on the dirt floor and talking under her breath. Her hair was a dark brown and styled in a peculiar fashion: cropped boy-ishly short across the brow and the rest pinned back and curled under, falling only to her collar. What he could see of her dress was plain and shorter by far than was decent, but despite her apparent lack of modesty there was nothing slatternly about her—rather, he immediately felt as if he knew her. Her nose turned up just slightly at the end, and he knew that scowl she wore—of course: She was the very image of his sister Anna, who he hadn't heard from since he began his wanderings three years ago.

Her hands searched frantically, and though she spoke too low for him to make out the words, he recognized the tone—the panicked pleadings of some-one who is in a great deal of trouble.

He cleared his throat. The girl looked up at him, hazel eyes wide with sur-prise and fear.

"I'm sorry, I didn't mean to startle you," he said.

"Shit," she said. He reconsidered his early assessment of her.

"I beg your pardon?"

"You're not supposed to be here!" That much was true; she had caught him trespassing and would now surely summon the smith, and Anthony would find himself once again at the wrong end of a fist.

"I'll just be going, then," he said.

"Sssh!" She gestured urgently for him to be quiet and looked back over her shoulder. She glared at him, shook her head, and then she scrambled backward and disappeared into the shadows. A moment later the unseen light source winked out.

He crept forward to see where she might be hiding, but the corner was com-pletely empty. The girl was *gone*.

A loud crash came from the opposite end of the open room—a second door swung open, and the shape of a broad, bearded man filled the doorway.

The Many Tortures of Anthony Cardno

"You there!"

Anthony ran. Out the door and back to the road, his ankle sore and the pain from his cracked rib shooting through him like a bullet, but he did not stop. The man shouted after him. Anthony's pounding pulse and the rasp of his own labored breath filled his ears. It was only when his pace slowed and he was able to catch his breath that he realized the man had been shouting, *"Did you see it?"*

He was exhausted and in pain, and now he found himself spooked and uneasy as well. What *had* he seen, exactly? He wondered if she'd really been there at all. It wouldn't be the first time his mind had played tricks on him.

Right now he needed shelter, a room for the night, a hot meal, and—God help him—a drink.

◆

The front room of the hotel was a single open space, with a small check-in desk at the front opposite a lounge area and staircase, and past that, a few scattered tables and chairs. The room seemed over-sized for its purpose, as if in the planning of it the proprietor expected to seat a hundred instead of the two men who sat at the back of the long room. Another bitter reminder of his circumstances, there was no bar along the wall; just a pair of batwing doors in the back, probably leading to the kitchen. A wood stove just past the front desk warmed the room, and the scent of something meaty simmering in the kitchen made Anthony's mouth water.

One of the gentlemen at the far end of the room rose when Anthony closed the door behind him—a dark-haired, mustachioed gentleman in sleeve garters and an apron, clearly the hotelier. The other, a short, bald man looked as if he'd just come from a funeral—which, Anthony realized with a sick feeling, he probably had.

"That's the one," the short man said. The proprietor raised an eyebrow and Anthony's hopes for a safe haven sank. He turned to leave, but the door swung open again and he found himself facing the man he'd most recently run from: the metalsmith.

"You," the man said, and grabbed his arm above the elbow, where painful bruises from the morning's manhandling had blossomed. "Tell me, did you see it?" So he *hadn't* imagined it. Anthony nodded. "Did it speak to you? Come sit, and tell me what it said." He allowed himself to be pulled deeper into the room, and took a seat at a table. "Now tell me."

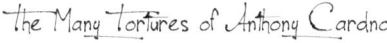

"About the girl? Who is she?"

"That's no girl. Or if it is, it's surely the ghost of one." The man extended a scarred and calloused hand for Anthony to shake. "Mike Epple." Anthony started to introduce himself, but Epple continued before he could get a word out. "You heard it speak? What did it say?"

"Nothing that I could make sense of."

Epple hushed him as the hotel owner approached. "Harmon," he said to the man.

"Mike." Harmon nodded toward Anthony. "This a friend of yours?"

"We're acquainted. Just discussing some business."

"What kind of business are you in? Apart from making a mess of other people's."

Anthony shifted uncomfortably in his chair.

"Timekeeping," Anthony said. "Watch repair."

The bald man, silent during this exchange, stood and donned his hat. "I'll leave you to your—guests," he said. The front door scraped closed behind him with a sound that set Anthony's teeth on edge.

"What are you serving tonight?" Epple asked. The proprietor crossed his arms across his chest and gave him a hard look. "Harmon, have mercy. We've seen what no man should, and we need ourselves a damned drink. And whatever you've got in the pot for supper. I'm buying." He clapped a pair of coins on the table. Harmon collected the coins and retreated through the doors to the kitchen.

"That's very generous—"

"What do you think it wants of me?" the smith interrupted, clearly agitated. "I've tried to be a godly man."

"I think she may have lost something," Anthony said. "She didn't seem threatening."

"Demons never do."

Harmon returned with two bowls of stew and a pair of glasses, each with a finger of something amber and sharp. "You carrying on about your ghost again, Mike?" Harmon pulled up a chair and produced another glass.

Epple pulled something from his pocket and set it on the table. "I found this in the foundry. Maybe it was hers before she died, and that's why she haunts me now."

He handed the thing to Harmon, no bigger than a button. Harmon examined it briefly before passing it to Anthony.

The Many Tortures of Anthony Cardno

"You didn't make that, Mike?"

"Nah, I couldn't possibly. It's too fine."

It was a polished brass lapel pin, skillfully cast and intricately detailed. The design was of a clock face: Roman numerals, one through twelve, and the hands marking the time at quarter to six. All the way around the edge were words picked out in careful relief: Temperance Society for Historical Preservation.

"Like the Ladies' Society, I suppose," Harmon said. "But we haven't much in the way of history here in Temperance. Town's only six years old."

The door flew open and the two townsmen swiftly disappeared all three glasses under the table and onto the floor with a practiced ease. Framed in the doorway stood a tight-lipped woman of middle years, with an air of importance, and of menace.

She passed through the lounge and was followed by a dozen more women, each with something in her hands: rolling pins and broom handles, canes and clubs. They gripped and brandished them like weapons.

"Mrs. Finncutter," Harmon said, hands up in a placating gesture, "what's got your ire up this evening?"

"Good evening, Mr. Harmon." She sniffed at the air and wrinkled her nose in disgust. "For your own safety and that of your guests I suggest that you leave us to God's work, and the work of the Ladies' Society of Temperance."

"I can't imagine what you mean, ma'am. I like to think I'm doing God's work by giving shelter to those who need it."

"This house is well-known to be unlawful, Mr. Harmon—a house of sin and temptation. You've been warned; the consequences are your own." At her signal the women charged past: two tossed the contents of the front desk, two more marched up the stairs presumably to search the rooms, several more went straight to the kitchen, and beyond it, the stable. Soon the sound of barrels and bottles being shifted and overturned could be heard in the back room.

"You've no right!" Harmon's face was red as a beet as he watched his hotel destroyed. Anthony wondered what he should do; trying to stop them seemed foolhardy. Epple seemed to share his confusion. Harmon made a move toward the kitchen, where the sound of crates being upended could be heard, but just then two men stepped into the room: the bald fellow who had left not long before, and, to Anthony's deeper consternation, the mayor. The bald man, still in his mourning clothes, held a rope in his hands. Harmon froze where he was.

Triumphant shouts of "We've found it!" came from the back. Anthony started to edge toward the front door, hoping to escape further violence.

"Stay right where you are." The mayor leaned against the front desk and searched his coat pocket, and found what was he was looking for. "I'm surprised to find you here. I took you for a drunk, but not an idiot. If you were smart, you'd have been on a steamer to San Francisco by now." He produced a pipe and box of matches. "But as you're still here, I want you in particular to see this." He struck a match and touched it to the bowl of his pipe. He puffed at it with the leisure of a man sitting in his own study, rather than overseeing the wreckage of a fellow man's livelihood.

A cask was rolled out from the back by two of the women and uncorked in the middle of the room. The brandy spilled out onto the wooden planks of the floor, the smell so strong it made even Anthony choke. Where it didn't pool it trickled down between the floorboards.

They made short work of it. When it was all over the chairs were in splinters, three illegal casks of spirits had been spilled out onto the floor; the barware was smashed and the food stores ruined. The Ladies Society of Temperance left without a word, and the mayor's rope-wielding associate with them.

With the last witness to the night's calamity gone, the mayor walked a wide circle around the stunned proprietor and hapless guests, glass crunching under foot, careful not to step in the puddles of liquor that covered the floor.

"It's a shame," he said, and puffed on his pipe. "I took you for better, Harmon. You knew the law, and you knew you was breaking it. Can't rightly blame the ladies for defending the town sensibilities. Still—" He kicked a broken chair leg aside. "—it's a shame."

He reached the front door and crouched down, pulling the matches from his pocket once again. Anthony's mind clamored to make sense of what was happening—*He's the mayor, he can't do this*—as the man struck a match.

"Good night, gentlemen," he said from the doorway, and held the match to brandy-soaked floor and stepped outside.

The spirits caught fire and the floor bloomed with bright blue flame, wending its way across the boards toward them. Anthony pushed past Harmon and ran for the kitchen. This seemed to jostle him from his stricken daze and he quickly loaded Anthony's arms with wet towels. The two of them did their best to smother the flames and keep it from reaching the walls.

"I've got it," Mike called, carrying two full buckets, which he emptied onto the remaining flames near the front door. The three men stood side by side, watching the water drain away between the floor boards.

Something glinted on the floor beneath a settee across from the front desk.

Of course, Anthony realized—the peculiar pin that belonged to the ghost girl. It must have been kicked clear across the room in the chaos.

He got on his hands and knees and reached for it. He could see it as clearly as if someone were shining a lantern on the space beneath the sofa, though where the light was coming from he couldn't guess.

The light spread steadily outward—the otherworldly lantern lit first his hand, then the floor around it, and continued to grow. Anthony scrambled backward, trying to escape it, but the circle of light grew too rapidly, and as it enveloped him the room around him changed.

Music: loud, raucous, festive music, and laughter. He was on the floor in a sea of people, tapping their toes to the rhythm. Colorful, bare-legged girls danced with men all dressed alike, in khaki trousers and shirts. A banner hung from the back wall in patriotic red and blue, bearing only the meaningless initials "U.S.O."

A few people looked at him oddly and moved away, but one young man looked him over and laughed.

"I didn't know this was a costume party, chief. You came dressed as my grandpa!"

"Under the floor," he could hear Mike calling from the shadows beyond the light, "the liquor's still burning under the floor!"

And then the light reached Mike and Harmon, drawing them into this place, this strange vision—and with them came the fire.

The room erupted into chaos. The flames moved fast, the paper decorations that filled the room going up and creating embers that floated in the air, still burning and igniting whatever they came to rest on. People were screaming and pressing for the door, but it was blocked now by flames. Anthony couldn't even see his companions over the heads of strangers. For a moment he was certain he would not survive this night.

And then, there she was. The ghost girl, her brow creased in fear, standing directly in front of him. For a moment it seemed she couldn't even see him, as if she were looking through him or past him, at the flames that seemed to be all around now. He grabbed her by the shoulders.

"We've got to get you out of here." He searched the room for an escape, pulling her along through the mass of terrified people to the far wall, away from the flames. He picked up a chair, and when she saw what he was doing, she grabbed another. "On three." She nodded. "One ... two ... three!" They swung their chairs at the windows, breaking the glass. Anthony felt the cold air from outside rush in, and a sudden burst of heat at his back as the hungry flames found the fresh air. Anthony cleared the remaining broken shards from the window frame, and lacing his fingers together, offered the girl a stirrup to lift her up and through the window to safety.

"Get the fire brigade," he told her.

"I will."

He boosted her up, the muscles in his arms and chest straining, and then she found purchase and she pulled herself up onto the window ledge.

"Wait, this is yours," he said, and pulled the pin from his pocket. He held it up for her to see.

Relief was visible on her face as she reached for it—

—and was gone. The pin was in his hand. The wall before him now had no window, just the raw wood of the hotel. He sweated in the stifling heat and watched as the dance hall disappeared, collapsing from the perimeter inward, leaving only the burning hotel, and Mike and Harmon calling to him from where they had broken down the back door. He charged through the flames, the searing heat singing his face and his trousers alighting as he ran out the back and into the stable, where Mike tackled him to the ground and Harmon smothered his burning clothes under a horse blanket.

❋

They sat together at Mike's kitchen table in his tiny house in back of the foundry, the smell of smoke still in the air and on their clothes. Anthony passed a hand over his own face and brushed away the singed remains of his eyebrows. His leg was bandaged; the burn hurt, and he had nothing to ease the pain of it, until Mike produced a bottle and placed it at the center of the table with three glasses.

"We three must agree never to speak of what we saw," Mike said as he poured.

"I'm not even sure what it was I did see," Harmon said. "I know my business is destroyed. I'm not sure that any sideways vision, shared or not, really matters after that." Harmon looked darkly into his glass. "Thank you both for trying. Who knows what would have happened had I been alone."

Anthony lifted his glass to his lips and stopped.

"We all got out. I'm not sure that they all did," he said.

"They weren't real. They can't have been," Harmon said and poured another finger into his glass.

The Many Tortures of Anthony Cardno

"I think they were. I think they're real people, and our fire burned their dance hall down in another place. Or another time."

Mike considered.

"The place did feel familiar. Like someone had taken the hotel and remade it into something else."

"For a different purpose, in a different time," Mike said, sipping his whisky thoughtfully. Anthony put his glass back down, the liquor untouched.

"And if things that happen in our time can jump through to theirs—people may have died tonight."

"You've a peculiar mind, my friend." Mike drained his glass and stood. "The two of you can stay here tonight. I'll show you where to bed down."

"I think I'll stay up a while longer," Anthony said.

"Suit yourself." Mike and Harmon left him alone with his thoughts.

He thought again about the fire, the undecipherable letters "U.S.O.," the eyes of the girl, so like his sister's—no ghost at all, but a living girl. He sincerely hoped that she still lived, wherever—or whenever—she was.

He pulled the pin from his pocket and read the words again: Temperance Society for Historical Preservation. *That's what we need*, he thought. *To protect them from us, and maybe us from them. Preserving the history of every time, without interference from the past, or the future.*

He poured the contents of his glass back in the bottle and stoppered it. The next steamer would have to leave without him. He would stay and see the mayor brought to justice; he would help rebuild the hotel. And he would find a way to keep the tragedy of the night from happening again.

He turned the pin over and noticed for the first time that there was fine engraving on the back, obscured by the hinged fastener. He unhooked the clasp and held it up to the lamp to catch the light.

The words were etched in a tiny, scrolled hand: *Anthony Cardno, Founder.*

I have had the pleasure of knowing Eric S. "Spanky" Bauman for about as long as I can remember; it's a toss-up as to whether I've known him or Michelle Moklebust longer. Eric has always, to my mind, been the better writer out of the two of us, and I hope that this wonderful little horror story (equal parts Lovecraft and King, but at the same time all Bauman) convinces other people to publish him. And let's face it ... who better to torture me than someone who's known me since childhood?

Anthony Takes the Stairs

ERIC S. BAUMAN

Anthony Cardno sat in his cube, typing madly away and trying not to scream. Outlook had recently reminded him that he had a meeting in fifteen minutes and it was no doubt about to ding again to let him know that he only had five minutes to get there now. He was desperately trying to reach a logical stopping point in the documentation he was writing on the new version of the library cataloging software that was due to be released in three months—he hated having to leave off in the middle of a section, because of the difficulty in picking up the thread of his thoughts when he returned.

He didn't even want to go to the meeting. And, to tell the truth, he had no idea why he had to be there anyway. It was a technical meeting with the software developers and the hardware engineers. He knew just enough about computers to get by, but he couldn't tell a hash table from corned beef hash. He had gotten the job because an old friend (one of the software developers, actually) had recommended him based on his writing ability. Three years later, Anthony was still there, plugging away on the keyboard that couldn't seem to remember that he wanted the num lock engaged.

Just as Outlook made it's annoying little sound, he typed the last few words of that section and banged the Enter key. He clicked the save icon in Word,

closed the document. He then (as his friend Eric had shown him) copied the file over to the server so that it would be safe if his hard drive crashed and also so that it would get backed up by the company's archiving software.

He went back and checked the calendar to remind himself where the meeting was and found that it was in the north conference room on seventeen, as he had thought. He locked up the computer and grabbed his pad and pencil (it seemed that everybody else had laptops with wireless connectivity to bring to meetings but for some reason, the company didn't seem to feel that the technical writers needed them—which made little sense since most of the writers he knew could type notes much faster than they could write them out—or more likely, they would claim that his machine was only a year and a half old so it was too soon to replace it.

As Anthony rose to leave, he saw out of the corner of his eye that the "Golf Club" was beginning to gather in the cube across the walkway from him. The cubes on this floor were arranged in pods of six, three on each side of a short walkway. Anthony sat in the front cube on the right side of this pod, furthest from the windows. The three cubicles opposite his were occupied by three members of some team that did something with telecommunications. Usually three or four times a day, these three would gather in one cube or another and talk for up to half an hour about golf, usually rehashing their rounds over the weekend or whatever PGA event was going on. Recently, however, they had been having some serious discussions about the relative merits of various golf balls. Anthony didn't mind them too much because they usually met in the furthest cube from his, back towards the windows. Not this time, though—they were congregating in the cube directly opposite him, so he was glad to be leaving.

And for noise, the "Golf Club" couldn't hold a candle to the group in the next pod over. The "Golf Club," while they met for up to two hours per day, was generally quiet. The next pod over, however, was not; they were a continuous cacophony, especially Robert, the guy who sat in the cubicle right next to Anthony. They seemed to have something to do with monitoring database servers—at least that was what Cardno could glean from what they all shouted back and forth to each other all day.

But Robert was the worst of the bunch to Anthony. Robert had a naturally loud voice—he seemed to have no concept of "inside volume." And he talked ALL...THE...TIME! If he wasn't having a loud conversation with his podmates or on the phone, he was talking to himself, narrating his day. The other annoying habit Robert had was that, even though he had two perfectly functional arms, for some reason he seemed not to be able to hold a phone to his ear, nor did he seem capable of using a headset. As a result of this, Anthony would get to hear *both* sides of all of Robert's many phone calls. Anthony needed to concentrate when he was writing, and that was damned hard once the database server group got going or Robert got a call.

The meeting was nine floors below him, so he decided to take the stairs down. He had been doing this for some time, trying to lose a little weight. And usually, if he only had to go three or four floors, he'd go up the stairs as well. Lately, though, his left knee had begun to pain him some, so on those days, even three floors was too much to try to climb. He thought about stopping in the break area on his way to the stairs to grab a bottle of water, but when he turned the corner, it looked as though somebody was having a birthday party, as there were people spilling out into the aisle. *I'll grab one down on 17*, he thought and walked on by the room, glancing in to see if he knew who the celebrant was.

He got to the door that led to the stairwell and opened it. The sensor beside the door where you would wave your badge for admittance back onto the floor flashed green. He walked to the set of stairs heading down and let the door swing shut behind him. He began his descent.

The stairs were metal and had raised X's running in diagonals along them which were supposed to help with traction, Anthony supposed. They were painted an industrial gray. Occasionally on his walks in the stairwell, he would see dead cockroaches with their legs in the air. *They always seem to die that way, on their back. I wonder why that is.* There were eleven risers in each flight of stairs, and there was a concrete landing at the ends of each flight, one to get to the doors and one between floors.

The walls were a dingy whitish-yellow. There were pipes the same color that ran up the walls near the doors that carried water and steam and who knew what else. There were also blowers which constantly emitted cold air. Above each landing were two long fluorescent light tubes enclosed in wire mesh cages. As he turned the corner between 23 and 24, he saw that one of the tubes was burned out.

As he went, his mind turned—as it often did on these trips—to his writings outside of work. He was currently working on a novella titled *Christmas Ghosts*. He had written the beginning two chapters, and then the last one. He was struggling now to fill in the middle. He knew in broad strokes what needed to happen to whom to get everybody in the right place for the ending. He was having trouble with the emotion, though. He had always had trouble with heavy emotional scenes, and this was probably the most difficult thing he had attempted. Sometimes, he thought that he didn't have the talent to do justice to his story; he could fill the middle, but the reader wouldn't feel what he thought they should—that the reader wouldn't care about what happened.

He hit a landing between floors and came out of his reverie long enough to realize that he had lost track of what floor he was on. As he headed down the next flight, he looked at the ten-foot-tall dark green door below him. Painted in the middle of the door about six feet from the floor was a large white number: "20". He put his head down and began to descend the next flight of stairs, running his hand lightly along the railing. If he started to fall, he would never be able to grab it in time to keep himself from tumbling down the stairs, he knew, and yet having his hand there made him feel a little better. In a hushed tone, he spoke to himself, reinforcing the things he would need to have available quickly for the meeting (or at least what he *thought* he would need to have in the front of his mind) as he made his way down the last six flights.

When he got to the bottom of the sixth flight, he looked down to get his badge. It was on a little metal gadget that hooked to his belt, and it tended to flap around a lot when he walked. His hand closed on the badge and he turned back. Something tickled the back of his mind, a little voice that said *Something's not right.* He ignored this little bit of paranoia and prepared to run his ID card by the sensor.

Except that there was no sensor. Instead there was a metallic numeric keypad with two small lights: red (which was lit up) and green. *What the hell?*

The company that he worked for, Infinity Ltd. Solutions, didn't own the building or even control most of the floors. However, every floor that they *were* on had the electronic sensor beside the door so that only employees could get in through the metal door. And having been to a few meetings on 17 before, he *knew* that that floor had one of those card readers. He looked up at the door and saw the number "19".

That can't be right. I know I counted six flights of stairs from 20. This has to be 17. But the "19" on the door and the keypad beside it said differently.

Anthony waved his badge at the keypad, seemingly unwilling to believe that this was wrong. The red light of the keypad stared at him as if trying to figure out if he were serious or not.

He walked backwards towards the stairs that led up to the next floor, looking back once to make sure he wasn't heading for a fall down the other stairs. He sat down on the second riser and just stared at the door to the nineteenth floor. *I*

The Many Tortures of Anthony Cardno

was on 20, I walked down six flights of stairs, which should have put me on 17. I know that's right. But no matter how hard he tried to convince himself, the door and keypad mocked his surety.

He stood. *Alright, let's see what happens if I go down two more flights.* He walked over to the other set of stairs and firmly grabbed the handrail, as if afraid that he were about to faint or that the stairs below his feet might suddenly disappear.

He stepped onto the concrete landing between floors and took a deep breath to try to clear his head. He was extremely confused. Then he headed down the next flight of stairs. When he was halfway down, he looked from his feet to the door in the wall in front of him, more specifically at the number printed on that door.

"19". And there was a keypad beside the door.

It can't be. He turned and walked back up the stairs to the midway landing. Once there, he turned again and looked down at the floor below. He had to crouch some to see the number on the door, but it still said "19." He shuffled to his right and looked up to the floor above. This door was easier to see, as was the floor number: "19".

The pad and pencil slipped from his hand. He stood still, overwhelmed. *It can't be,* Anthony told himself again. He shuffled back to his left and looked down again. "19."

He sat down on the landing. His hand reached out blindly and pulled the paper and pencil to him, as if seeking comfort from the squiggles on it. The concrete was quite cold and soon his butt began to feel it through the thin slacks material. His brain, however, didn't acknowledge it—it was contending with the paradox before him. *How could there be* two *nineteenth floors?* The simple answer, he knew, was that there couldn't be. There could be a floor missing—like the supposedly unlucky thirteenth floor that appeared in very few tall buildings, but not two floors with the same number. And yet, the evidence was in front of him. This could all be a joke, but it was a pretty elaborate one.

He sat there for about ten minutes, his mind trying to grasp the ungraspable. Then a thought that made a perverse kind of sense floated through his consciousness: *If there can't be two nineteenth floors, then there sure as hell can't be three. And three floors up, if you remember, was the twentieth floor.*

That was true. If his knee would let him go up three flights (which he was sure it could), he could get out of here and take the elevator down to 17. He'd be late for his meeting, and he was sure he'd hear some squawking, but what could he do? He couldn't get to the seventeenth floor from the fire stairs! He knew it sounded crazy and nobody would believe him, but what could he do? It was the truth, no matter how little sense it made.

He stood and brushed some dust from the seat of his pants. He walked up the stairs to the first nineteenth floor then began climbing further. As he rounded the corner on the next between-floors landing, he looked up and felt his stomach sink. "19" was painted on the door above him. He climbed that flight of stairs and, on impulse, ran his fingers along the number to see if maybe it was fresh paint. It wasn't—his finger actually dislodged a small flake of white paint, which fell to the landing. He sighed and headed up the next set of stairs.

The next floor was also the nineteenth floor.

He stood on the landing outside that door and sighed. The next floor was twenty when he came through here going down, and for the sake of his sanity, he hoped it still was. But that little voice of doubt in the back of his head told him that he had to know that it would be different on the way back up. He lifted his left leg and flexed the knee a couple of times, trying to get it to loosen up some and then headed up towards what he hoped was still the twentieth floor.

He made it up the next flight and began to turn the corner. He closed his eyes—he just couldn't bring himself to look at the door before he had made it to the landing there. He shuffled his right foot until it met the riser and he began to climb, counting off the eleven steps silently as he climbed each one. At eleven, he stopped, inhaled deeply, held it for a moment, and then slowly exhaled through his pursed lips. He raised his head and opened his eyes.

He was amazed and not surprised to see that same "19" on the door in front of him. *This was twenty, now it's nineteen. Is everything nineteen?* He didn't see how that could be, but he remembered that five minutes ago, he believed that there couldn't be two nineteenth floors, so why the hell not extend it to a building full of nineteenth floors?

Because that way lies madness, another voice whispered, *and you know it.*

"Maybe I'm already crazy," Anthony said to himself, but there was no conviction to the sentiment. Deep down, he didn't think he was crazy.

But how do you know, the voice answered back. *Do you think insane people know they're insane, or do they think they're sane and everybody else is nuts?*

Anthony had no answer to that. He had no idea if you could pinpoint the boundary between sane and insane in yourself. Perhaps he would read up on it, if he got out of here. He could talk to Claire, his friend who had studied psychology at U.Va. and ask her if...

Sudden inspiration struck. *His cell phone!* He could call somebody on his floor to see if they could come down to nineteen—one of the nineteens, ha!—to let him back in. He excitedly reached for the cell phone clip that was also on his belt. He lifted the leather flap and felt nothing inside. He looked down at his side and saw that, indeed, the holster was empty. He then remembered that he had plugged his phone into the wall of his cube when he first got in because the battery indicator was showing red. And it was still there, probably close to a full charge by now.

Anthony's knees gave out and he sat down hard on the landing, his teeth clacking painfully together. He sat that way for a moment, feeling sort of dazed, and then he rolled over onto his side and rested his head on his arm, looking at the door. He felt as though somebody had changed the rules of the universe and hadn't bothered to tell him. The *Twilight Zone* theme started going through his head, which Anthony dismissed as a cliché. However, when you got down to it, it was an appropriate metaphor. He *had* just crossed over into that land of shadow and substance, of things and ideas, where trains made a stop in Willoughby, where the monsters lived on Maple Street, and where a tall building in the middle of a city consisted entirely of nineteenth floors.

He wasn't sure how long he laid there. A blanket of hopelessness tried to smother him but he fought it off. *I have to do something*, Anthony told himself.

Yes, but what?

He didn't have an answer for that question, not yet. He was sure he could come up with one, given enough time. He wondered if somebody had missed him yet and was maybe looking for him. Some of his colleagues (especially those he was supposed to have met with) were probably thinking about him. They would probably try his cube phone and his cell phone, but they would get voicemail either way. He doubted a search of the stairwell would be mounted any time soon—they probably thought he had just forgotten about the meeting and had gone somewhere or was talking to somebody.

No, if he was going to get out of this anytime soon, he was going to have to take action.

Yes, but what? the voice asked again.

He still didn't know. He laid there and thought for a few minutes. He closed his eyes, even though this might give his body an excuse to fall asleep—if he could. When the idea hit, he snapped his eyes open and sat up.

Maybe I can't get past the keypad, but maybe somebody on the other side could let me in! He stood up and walked over to the door. He grabbed the handle on the door and turned it, not really expecting the door to open, but he felt he had to try anyway. The door did not budge.

He put his ear against the cold door. He could hear almost nothing from the other side of the door. There was a slight susurration which he assumed to be the air system. He could hear no footsteps, though (not that he really expected to—he assumed that the hallway on the other side was carpeted, just like the twenty-sixth floor), nor could he hear any voices. It was quiet. *Too quiet,* his mind threw up at him and he had to stifle a giggle. He bunched up his fist and knocked his knuckles against the door with his ear still to the door.

Nothing.

He knocked again.

Nothing. Or maybe not quite nothing. It almost sounded to him as if the hiss grew slightly louder. *Probably not,* he thought. *Probably just my brain trying to give me hope.*

He turned his fist ninety degrees and banged on the door, shouting "Hey, is somebody over there? I need help!"

Something pounded on the other side of the door. Really hard.

Anthony leapt back from the door and let out a scream. There was another loud smash and Anthony could see the door shake in its frame. Then he heard, over his trip-hammering heart, a sound that froze his blood. It was a throaty growl, animalistic but unlike any animal he had ever heard. He also thought he heard an insistent buzzing sound, although he couldn't tell whether that was also behind the door or his own ear recovering from the punishment of the door and the...well, whatever it was behind it. There was another smash against the door and the growl descended into a low rumble like an idling lawn mower.

His breathing gradually slowed down, as did his heart rate. There was one more small bang on the door, then silence descended again.

Have you found that boundary yet?

He told the voice to shut up and turned around and when he did, another short burst of adrenaline ran through him. When he had jumped back blindly from the door when that *thing* had pounded on it, he had leapt all the way across the concrete landing and had come within three inches of falling off the edge and tumbling ass-over-teakettle down the stairs. His whole body began to shake. He held onto the railing and eased himself into a sitting position on the slab. When he had the shaking under control, he decided that he really didn't want to be near that door, in case whatever it was broke through. He rose slowly and headed down the stairs and crouched in the furthest corner of that landing. He sat and then wrapped his arms around his knees and put his head down. He wanted to hide, he wanted to cry, he wanted to wake up from this nightmare; ultimately, none of these happened—instead, the adrenaline having fully worn off, he closed his eyes and the world dissolved around him.

19

Sometime later, he

(*came to? Woke up?*)

opened his eyes and the world came back into focus. He found that he was lying on his side awkwardly, and as soon as he did move, his lower back let out a yelp of pain and he folded back over, muttering naughty words. Soon, the pain dissipated some and he cautiously sat up again. Once upright, he began to stretch his arms and legs, since he had been curled up tight in a ball. As he did, he looked around. He still couldn't place himself, and the whitish-yellow walls weren't helping. Then he remembered and he looked at the two doors within view. They were both labeled "19."

"I'm still here," he said in a surprisingly gravelly voice. He had been fine when the day started—*assuming this is still the same day,* the traitorous voice said—but now it felt like he had a slight sore throat. *Probably because it's so damn cold in here,* he thought. He cleared his throat and swallowed a large wad of phlegm. He realized that he could have spit it out—it wasn't like anybody was going to complain—but then told himself that worrying about whether to spit or not was one of the stupidest things he could be doing right now.

How long have I been here?

Couldn't tell you, the other voice said. *I left my watch in my other pants.*

He found he was very thirsty and a little hungry, so he had probably been here a few hours. With no windows and no clocks in the stairwell, though, it was impossible to tell.

Maybe you can open the 19 door and ask what's on the other side for the time?

Shut up, Anthony thought and wished that that voice would help him instead of mock him. He remembered that solid *thump!* on the door and decided that he really didn't want to open any of these doors.

Never? What if you need food or water?

He'd cross that bridge when he came to it. *If* he came to it.

19

A while later, he threw his pad and pencil at the lower door and heard it hit on the side with an echoing *thwack!* He had been trying to work on a story to distract himself (and, truth be told, to try to keep the other voice quiet). What little he wrote was horrible and this frustrated him: it was almost as though as soon as he had entered the stairwell, everything had just gone to hell, even things that should not have been affected. His heart accelerated when he thought he heard a skittering on the other side of the door where the paper had ended up. Did he hear it? Did his mind make it up? He didn't know, he couldn't tell, and the uncertainty ate up the little calm that he had. He yelled *"FUCKING DAMMIT!!!"* as loudly as his sore throat would let him (which he instantly regretted).

From the other side of both doors, there came a supernatural chorus of gruff growls and other sounds. In fact, once Anthony thought about it, the noises seemed to be coming not just from the two doors, but from above and below him as well, as if the same cacophony were coming from behind all of the doors on the stairway. They came in waves, each a few milliseconds behind the other, so that he couldn't tell if it was just one thing or twenty or four hundred. And were any of them on the stairs themselves? *Maybe.*

He covered his ears and tears began to stream from the corners of his eyes. He almost yelled at them all to be quiet, but held it in instead; his throat might not have been able to handle it and besides, the yell would probably wake up more of the monsters. So he repeated *"please be quiet"* in his head, like a chant.

After a while, he tentatively uncovered one ear. The noise had greatly diminished. He freed the other ear and used his hands to wipe away the tears and clean up the snot that had run from his nose. He brushed his hands against his slacks. *I'll have to make sure I put these in the wash when I get home.* He laughed bitterly and stood up to go retrieve the pad and pencil.

When he got down to the lower platform, he saw that a memo that he had forgotten about had come out some from the pad. At the top was the company logo (an eight laid on its side with the company name straddling the right-hand edge). He shoved the memo back in...and then stopped cold.

The logo. Something about the logo. He furled the blank and filled pages of the notebook until he found the memo and stared at the logo. *Something about that shape...think, dammit!*

After a moment of struggling, the image came into his mind: a Mobius strip. He had read about it in one of his comic books recently. Although he didn't understand the entire concept, the one thing he did remember was that you could walk along the strip on both of the surfaces and end up exactly where you

The Many Tortures of Anthony Cardno

started without crossing any sort of boundary. You could walk and walk, but you would essentially never go anywhere. *Am I caught in some sort of Mobius strip involving two or three floors' worth of stairs?* The thought opened a drain that sucked down most of his hope. He couldn't be—it wasn't physically possible. At least, he didn't *think* it was physically possible.

Okay, the inner voice said, but the smart-ass tone had vanished. *How do you show yourself whether you are in an infinite loop or not?*

Anthony wasn't sure. He could walk up or down the stairs, but that wouldn't prove anything, since the doors were all labeled the same with no discernable markings to indicate otherwise. Then he looked down at his hands. *But if I leave the pad here on this landing and walk up or down, if I am in an endless loop, I'll come across it again.*

Excellent! Now...which way to go?

He thought about that for a second, then decided down was the way to go. A moment later, he realized that there would be a second landmark of sorts that would tell him whether he was stuck in the same small area or not. The final stairwell, from the second floor down to the first, was about twice as long as the other sets of stairs in the shaft. If he were to hit that longer staircase, he could get to the lobby and then get out!

Anthony felt happier than he had in a while. He placed the pad of paper in the far corner of the landing, right next to one of the thick vertical pipes. He laid the pencil on top of the paper, and with a renewed energy, he began to descend the staircase.

As he went down, it seemed as though the air blowing in through the vents became both colder and heavier somehow. He wasn't laboring to breathe or anything like that—it just felt...*oppressive* was the only word he could come up with, as if, in a way, it were trying to hold him back. The further he descended, the more he began to detect an odor. It smelled of many things, almost none of them pleasant: rotten produce, rancid milk, urine, decay, but also with a tinge of what he swore was lemon, which seemed strange to him. *Well, just add it to the list of strange shit that's been building today,* the inner voice thought. Anthony, for probably the first time today (if it was still the same day as when he entered the stairwell—he still didn't know for sure if that was even true anymore), agreed with the voice.

Each set of stairs had exactly the same number of risers as every other set he had walked down or up so far today. The scenery hadn't changed. Nor had the numbers on the doors—each was labeled "19." The monotony was beginning

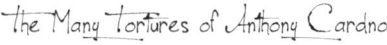

to get to him, and as he walked, his mind began to drift. He wondered just how long he *had* been in this stairwell. He wondered if anybody had missed him, or if maybe somehow he was not only stuck in a physical manifestation of a Mobius strip but also a fourth-dimensional one where time to him went on, but in the outside world, it was as if he had just let the door close behind him to head to his meeting. He wondered if he had perhaps been transported to some alternate universe (a topic which had been done to death in some of his favorite DC comics a few years ago) where all that existed was this vertical shaft of stairs. He wondered what he was going to do if he was indeed trapped in a endless loop with no hope of escape. He wondered if the pad of paper would still be there if he reversed direction and headed up. He wondered...

He heard a *crunch* beneath his foot and stopped moving. He picked up his foot and found a crushed cockroach, its carapace shattered and its body transformed into a sickly goo. Anthony scraped his shoe on the riser, trying to dislodge any bits of insect that might still be there. He placed his foot on the step, but well away from the puddle that had once been Kafka's friend and moved on.

After what felt like another seven minutes or so, something seemed different. The light from the bars on the wall seemed to be slightly brighter and the air didn't feel so heavy. It still felt cold, though, maybe even colder than it had when he started this hike. He turned the corner and stopped, drawing in a quick breath of surprise, followed closely by a lifting of his spirits.

In front of him was a short set of stairs, one with only six steps in it. He knew what this meant: *he was between the first and second floors!* He fairly leaped the six steps and turned another corner. There was a short flat path, and then on the left-hand side at the end of it, there was an opening in the wall. Unless things had changed (and he knew now that he couldn't count out one more sick joke by whichever universe he was in), if he turned at that opening and looked down, he would see a long set of stairs with a tall brown door at the bottom which would let out into the lobby. He headed forward, giving a wide berth to another dead cockroach and stopped at the break in the wall. He took a deep breath (the cold stung his throat), let it out and turned to look to the left.

The long stairway was there. The door at the bottom was there. He couldn't see whether it, too, had the number nineteen on it or not. *There's only one way to find out,* he thought and carefully descended the stairs, dodging two more bugs on the way down.

He soon reached the bottom and faced the door, although for a moment, he couldn't bear to look at it. *What if it says "19" like every other door? I think I would*

go mad. I almost think I would have *to.* He took a deep breath, held it and looked up. He exhaled.

The door said "Lobby".

Anthony smiled. *I may get out of this yet!* He looked at the sign beside the door to make sure what he was staring at was real. It said: "Please open door slowly." That was because this door entered the lobby near a bank of elevators and one could hit a person waiting or exiting an elevator quite easily—he knew this from experience. *I don't think I'll need to worry about hitting anybody out there, not the way this has been going,* he though, but he didn't know that for sure. For all he knew, the Mobius strip he was in—or thought he had been in (*since there was an exit, it couldn't be a Mobius strip, could it?*)—might only exist within the shaft of the stairs: the world might be going on as ever outside of here. He turned the handle and pushed slightly on the door and, to his relief, it did open. He exerted more constant pressure until the door swung wide open.

There were the four elevator doors, two on each side. These elevators took one to the lower floors of the building, only up to the twenty-first floor. Beyond the elevators, he saw the short hallway that lead from the wide lobby to the little shops that shared the floor. The signage for the Quiznos was not on and neither were the lights inside. The light had that gauzy quality to it, as if all of the lights and windows had been covered with a fine silk. He looked up to see what was causing the effect and nearly shrieked in terror.

The ceiling was covered with some kind of webbing, but not like anything that he had ever seen. The strands were as thick as the bungee cords that some people had in their cars for when they were carrying something that was just a little too big for the trunk. Dangling straight down from the webs were three individual strands, and at the end of each was a monstrous horror that Anthony's mind had a hard time grasping. They looked sort of like spiders with ursine heads. The gaping jaws were overflowing with yellowing fangs. And they were *huge!* Two of them weren't moving at all, and the third was moving very slowly, twitching two of its twelve or more legs against the strand that held it. Movement in the webbing caught his eye: a pulsing as of many small creatures trying to get out.

Anthony heard a loud roar and brought his gaze back down. Opposite him, just peeking around the right-hand wall, was a large head. It looked like a bull that a toddler had colored green. The head was massive and the horns on top of it jutted out almost a meter and looked razor sharp. Its mouth, too, was overgrown with fangs. It let loose a bellow and moved further into view.

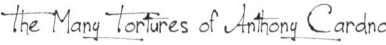

He couldn't stop himself this time: he screamed. The thing was gigantic, easily standing ten feet to the shoulder. And speaking of shoulders, he saw that sticking out of the front shoulders of this thing were two giant pincers. These snapped open and shut a couple of times. Spittle flew from the creature's mouth as it let out another terrifying growl and then it charged.

Anthony screamed again and tried to shut the door as quickly as he could. It probably wouldn't do any good, he knew: those horns would probably smash through the door as easily as nails through balsa wood, but it was instinctual. The problem was, he was fighting the pneumatic hinge at the top of the door which was there to make the door shut slowly. "Dammit, close!" he shouted and pulled all the harder.

He expected to hear the crash of wood over the thing's roar as it smashed through to get him...but he didn't. In fact, the roar sounded like it was getting more distant, and very quickly at that. He wondered what was going on but didn't dare to open the door (even though he knew it didn't really offer any sort of protection). After some time that felt like an eternity but had to be only a minute at the absolute most, he heard a dull faraway thud.

Anthony turned the handle and oh so slowly pushed against the door. It opened. He heard no noise, especially not the breathing of a ten-foot-tall bull-crab monster right outside ready to take a bite out of him. He pushed the door open more, enough so that he could see the elevators to his right. There was nothing there. He pushed the door open all the way and saw nothing.

Well, that wasn't quite true. There was the giant hole in the floor that stretched from where he stood all the way past the furthest elevator door. It was much too big for the bull-thing to have caused. *Huh,* he thought. *I wonder why I didn't see that there before.* He looked down into the maw and saw only blackness. Even so, he still got a case of vertigo and looked up quickly.

You know what this means, right? the snarky inner voice said.

"What do you mean?" Anthony asked out loud. His voice sounded nothing like his usual voice. This was scratchy and barely audible.

The hole giveth and the hole taketh away.

"What the hell are you talking about?"

I mean that while monsters like that one cannot get to you...

"Neither can I get out this way," he said as comprehension dawned.

Exactly, bright boy. There's no way you could jump over that hole from here, even with a running start, which you can't get anyway. And even if you were to somehow get into one of the elevators on the far side, it would still be iffy.

The Many Tortures of Anthony Cardno

Anthony let go of the door and let it close on its own. His snarky inner voice was right. He was still trapped. And as if to underline this realization, the unearthly sounds of whatever was behind all of the nineteenth floor doors rose as if everything had woken up and wanted to say good morning to him.

So there's nothing I can do, he thought and began to climb the long stairs that he had hopefully descended a short time ago. *No matter what, I'm fucked.*

The snarky inner voice stayed mercifully quiet.

He reached the first 19th floor and sat just outside the door, hearing the sounds of sharp things scrabble across the wall on the other side of him. He felt like a deflating balloon. There was no hope. He coughed, a long dry cough that came from down in his chest. He was completely spent, all energy having departed his body. He lay down and silently cried and soon fell asleep.

19

He heard a noise coming from below him. He half-opened his eyes and wondered what it was. He looked up the set of stairs that led to the nineteenth floor and down the other set of stairs that led to the other nineteenth floor. He couldn't see anything that might be making that noise. It almost sounded like a herd of small creatures running across a wooden plank. He shivered with the cold that enveloped him and let out another cough.

The noise began to intensify. He thought about sitting up so that he could see further than just the landing between floors, but he couldn't muster the energy. Instead, he continued to look at the sign beside the door ("SOUTH STAIRS TO LOBBY") below him and the door itself ("19"). He couldn't remember seeing that sign before.

The sound continued to get loud, although not overwhelming by any means. It sounded like a *lot* of little feet now, perhaps hundreds, perhaps thousands. He still couldn't see what might be causing the noise. He let out a deeper cough that make his chest burn.

"SOUTH STAIRS TO LOBBY". What did that mean?

A moment later the source of the sound made itself known, and Anthony's balls crawled up into his stomach. It was a herd—no, an *army*—of cockroaches that came boiling over the top step and straight for him. He swept his arm in front of him and knocked the first rank away, revolted by the feel of them. But no matter how swiftly he swept, they kept coming. They quickly broke through his arm's defense and began to crawl all over him. The sensation of those millions of chitinous legs touching him all over revolted him so much that he felt like throwing up or screaming. But he didn't want to open his mouth. He made himself sit up. Thousands of bugs showered down from his upper body as he did so. They kept coming, though, scrabbling up his stomach and chest. Many had gotten into his pants and were crawling up his naked legs. He felt their legs inside his shirt as well. *Don't scream!*

And for a wonder, he didn't. However, because of the cold that he had developed while here, he couldn't just breathe through his nose—there was too much gunk in there to allow it. He tried to blow his nose to clear it but it didn't help much.

The advancing horde was on his neck and chin now. His lungs were burning. He opened his mouth to take a breath and the wave of roaches poured into his mouth. He felt their disgusting legs walking across his tongue and felt their bodies brushing against the inside of his cheeks. He tried to cough to force them out, but he couldn't.

They swarmed down his throat.

19

He awoke with a strangled gasp. He could still feel and taste them in his mouth. *Except that was a dream,* the inner voice lilted. It didn't matter, he could still...

He felt something touch his uvula and gagged. Then he coughed and spit hard, with a scream following closely behind. The cockroach that had been in his mouth flew over the railing and out of sight down the stairwell. He shuddered. A moment later, something big slammed into the door beside him.

You wanted to bite it, didn't you?

"Shit no!"

Yes you did. Admit the truth and shame the devil. You're so hungry that you would have eaten that roach.

"No." But this was not as defiant as the last denial.

Didn't you?

"Not consciously."

No, not consciously, perhaps. But still...

"Please stop."

Very well. Just one more thing, though.

"Please don't."

"*South Stairs to Exit.*"

The Many Tortures of Anthony Cardno

"What?"

But the voice was gone.

Whatever it was that was trying to beat down the door continued to batter at it for a few moments, then gave up.

The silence crashed in around him again. It was funny, before all this started, he was hoping for some quiet, a respite from the Golf Club and from Robert, he who thought everybody on the floor should hear him. Now that he had that quiet, he longed for the sounds of conversation from anybody except that inner voice that pissed him off so much. Even a noise from the pipes running beside him would have been okay—unless that noise was caused by a large claw, of course. But there was now nothing. Even the air blowers that constantly blew cold air into the stairwells for reasons that he had never understood seemed to be silent.

Thinking of the air blowers made him shiver then a coughing bout began which doubled him up and made him flop over onto his side. An eternity later it stopped and he struggled to breathe through the pain in his chest and midsection.

South Stairs to Exit.

What the hell did that mean? He'd tried the stairs but he wasn't getting out that way, not unless he could fly. He felt on the verge of tears again. And then a bolt of insight hit him right between the eyes: the key word was "South." These stairs let out on the *north* side of the lobby. There was a whole other bank of elevators on the other side of that right-hand wall in the lobby, and these elevators were closer to the revolving door that led out to Eighth Street, and in between those other elevators was another shaft of emergency stairs.

Just one problem: how to get to the south stairs? Going down was out because of that giant hole. And all of the doors above the lobby led to the nineteenth floor and were locked and he wasn't sure if there was access to the south stairway from the nineteenth floor. There probably was (it was no doubt some kind of fire code thing). But if he were able to get out of the stairwell, he wanted to be damn sure that there was another way. For a moment, he thought that maybe, if he could get onto a floor, he could maybe get to the southern bank of elevators and, if they were working, get out that way. But those elevators went from the lobby up to 22 before you could get out.

Except that's not quite true, is it? He and the inner voice asked this at the same time, as if they had simultaneously had the same thought (which would make sense, one would think). The building's cafeteria was on the second floor, and

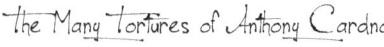

both sets of elevators stopped there to handle the lunchtime crowd, especially the people from other buildings who came to eat there. And in the usual geography of the building, where he was sitting *was* just outside a door to the second floor. And then he remembered something else: *there was no keypad or card sensor needed to get through the second floor door!*

Anthony turned his head so that he was looking up at the door. There was no keypad! The door was still numbered "19," but there was a chance, at least. Now the question was did he want to try going through it? Having heard the banging and growling from behind all the nineteen doors, and after seeing those horrors in the lobby, did he really want to try it?

The voice spoke up, but there was no trace of snark now. *As I see it, you can stay out here and die of starvation or dehydration or the cold. Or you can try to reach the south stairs or the other bank of elevators and get out. Granted, there is still a good chance you're gonna die if you go in there, but do you want to die trying or die cowering out here?*

That was a good question. The cold of the stairway, the coughing, and the lack of food and water had taken a lot out of him. Anthony wasn't sure if he would have the energy to try to evade anything that he might meet beyond the door. But he at least had to try, didn't he?

He closed his eyes for a moment and took some deep breaths. *This is insane.* Yes it was. But when the rubber met the road, he didn't really have a choice. He opened his eyes and forced himself first to a sitting position, then to his feet. One more deep breath to strengthen his resolve. He grasped the knob to the door and turned it, for a moment certain that it wouldn't budge. But it did, and he opened the door slowly and silently, just enough to put his eye to the opening to look in.

Extremely hot, humid air hit his eye, making him blink. It felt like it was about two hundred degrees in there. There was a heavy mist carpeting the hallway. But he didn't see any large creatures. He opened the door a little more, then a little more, until the opening was wide enough for him to sidle in. He took another breath and went in, letting the door begin to shut behind him. He started to briskly walk down the hallway toward where he thought the south stairs were. He turned the corner. Roars began soon after that; at first, Anthony screamed, and then he roared back. Then the nineteen door snicked closed.

Joseph Pittman had a choice: he could make me a townsperson in his family-oriented Linden Corners series, or he could make me an unsavory character in one of his Todd Gleason crime capers. Okay, it wasn't really a choice: as much as I love the idea of spending Christmas in Linden Corners, being conned by Todd Gleason is far more torture. Sweet torture, perhaps, but still. To say more would be to reveal twists better left to the author to reveal.

The Antics of Anton Ardno (A Todd Gleason Crime Story)

JOSEPH PITTMAN

ONE

It wasn't so much that Todd Gleason, the charming, dimpled, self-respecting New Yorker and all around confidence man, didn't appreciate the fabulous figure wafting past him, because normally his dark, curious eyes would have followed her to the ends of the earth and wherever after they led, whether heaven or hell or some special palace of wonders only she knew about, but in truth, the guy seated before him had the better figure.

"I'm sorry," Todd said, "did you say one hundred thousand?"

"For a week of your time. Maybe less, if you're good."

He ignored the back-handed compliment. Instead, Todd thought about that sum of which he'd spoken of for a second, then another, but really the second second was taken up by peering around the end of the long bar to see if the lovely lady whose perfume lingered long after she'd left his presence might still be, well, lingering somewhere in the busy hotel. She didn't appear, and it was almost like she'd never existed. Shame if that were true. Todd's shrug held a hint of regret. One opportunity lost, but another opportunity was gained. His eyes focused back on his guest, large dollars signs in place like a cartoon character.

"I'll do it."

"You don't even know what the deal is."

"As they say in those grand romances, you had me at one hundred thousand."

The man, who was portly and bespeckled and probably thirty-five, maybe forty, but who probably hadn't seen a gym since high school and whose shirt collar barely contained the flesh at his neck, grimaced. He didn't seem to appreciate Todd's sense of humor, but that was often the case, his flippant tongue getting him in as much trouble as his sometimes-foolish initiatives. Which was just a fancy word for a con. So Todd Gleason decided to shut up, and he helped that cause by taking a healthy sip of the vodka martini set before him, his first taste of it since the bartender had served it. His guest was already on his second Scotch, but at least his hand was a little steadier than when Todd had first sat down.

"So, as I was saying, this deal ... it won't be easy."

Nothing about this situation was easy, not how it started, not in planning it, and not in the way in which Todd had arrived here. The job it went down like this: the phlegm-voiced Lucille Lapodowski, who sometimes called Todd for legitimate side jobs, also ran another kind of side business where the illegitimate and illegal came into play, and of course it was the latter category this one fell into. A man of discretion was needed, one able to think fast on his feet, unafraid of being challenged, that's how it been presented to Lucille. Even before he mentioned the hefty payday Lucille stated she knew the perfect man for the job, one blessed with those desired, aforementioned qualities. Todd, of course, was said man. He'd accepted with alacrity and fired off his missive, only to receive a reply within minutes. Which meant someone was anxious.

That knowledge always made Todd happy, to have the upper hand on someone else, even on a situation that still had him in the dark. The proverbial light bulb would go off soon enough, because the email replier suggested a meeting.

"I'll be at the hotel bar, wearing a red tie and a matching kerchief."

Todd replied he'd be there with bells on. He almost added that was just an expression.

So now here he was, in the middle of February, a cold night where a strong wind made for a difficult crossing. See, Todd didn't mind riding in airplanes, and he didn't mind cars or trains either, but boats tended to make him nauseas. The very thought that he had to venture onto a ferry and cross the churning Hudson River, banking on the shore of New Jersey, well, that made his stomach doubly uncertain. Not just mode of transportation, but destination. But a job was a job, made more attractive by that lingering sentiment of "hefty payday."

So, the remuneration established, Todd listened to the man with the red tie and kerchief.

"I need you to sell something for me," the man said.

Color Todd intrigued, but he showed no emotion. He just drank his martini, feeling Bond like.

"You'll need to look the part of a trustworthy businessman, like a man of good tastes," he said. "This ..." he added, waving a finger in Todd's direction, "won't do."

Todd was wearing dark blue jeans, a button-down shirt, and a leather jacket with a cool collar. Very un-Bond like, sure. On his devilishly snarky face was three days of dark scruff that with his dark beard some might have been mistaken for a week's worth. He'd have to shave, he was told, he'd have to get his suit pressed; that is if he was going to impress.

"I can speak business," Todd said. "No problemo."

The man frowned. "You'll be going to Florida."

"There are worse places to go in February. Am I to assume this job needs to be done ..."

"Fast."

"How fast?"

"If you could fly down yesterday, that would work best."

Okay, so not only was the guy anxious, he was also behind schedule. "See, now that's the rub," Todd said, "timing."

"One hundred fifty, for your time and your trouble. Final offer."

Really anxious. Todd detected sweat on the man's brow. He, however, remained cool.

"Plus expenses. Guess I should pack tonight."

The man removed a long envelope from his inside jacket pocket. As he slid it across the bar, that Bond-like sense returned. Todd reached for it and stuffed it into the inner pocket of his leather jacket. He already knew it was an airline ticket and a deposit on his upcoming task.

"The details are also written down inside, as well as an emergency cell phone number. You'll be me, Mr. Anthony Ardno."

"Who would I ... uh, Anthony ..."

"Or Anton, or Tony, or ... well, pick what you're comfortable with."

He was comfortable with Todd. But as distracted as he was by the assumed identity, another word he'd just heard had insinuated itself into his brain and was now pulsing like a headache at his skull. "And, uh, who would I be calling in the case of an emergency?"

"Helen."

"Does Helen have a last name?"

"Not at the moment, no."

"Are you really Anthony Ardno?"

"For now, yes. Except starting now, you are him."

"I'll take that to mean it's an alias."

The man with several names but no proof of identity failed to answer, instead knocking back the final drops of pricey Scotch. He wiped at his pudgy mouth with the bar napkin, keeping the perfectly knotted kerchief pristine. He got up to leave, nearly sliding off the high barstool. Had he a few before Todd arrived?

"Can you tell me anything else of importance?"

"You'll be contacted by a man named Scoville. Fritz Scoville."

"And who is he?"

"He's the man who wants, more than anything, the property you are selling."

Todd had just one more question, perhaps the most important one. "How do I know I can trust you ... to deliver on the cash?"

The man volleyed an equally good question. "How do I know I can trust you at all?"

"You can't, but in this business, that's the chance you take."

"Once I know the transaction had been completed, I'll be in touch."

The men shook hands and exchanged smiles that could only be called conspiratorial.

As the portly man waddled his way away from the bar area of the Weehawken Sheraton, Todd Gleason felt his fingers tingle with excitement. How he loved running scams, living life on the edge, and even more, how he loved trying to find a way to work another person's problems to his financial gain. No pain, just gain. It was enough to make him want another drink to celebrate what was certainly going to be a quick and easy windfall. He would have kept to such a promise, because a successful con can only be executed when the man running it remains totally focused, and if not for the new arrival in the recently vacated seat, he would have qualified.

"I thought that insufferable bore would never leave," the woman said.

Todd smelled the perfume first and then he noticed the willowy figure that he'd only seen from the rear. Now he caught her from the front, she more alluring than he could have imagined. Long, flowing blonde locks, a thin frame that held a bountiful bosom, and, contrasting with her porcelain skin, lips as red as Valentine's Day. Turned out, that's exactly what today was, and she looked like she'd found her sweetheart.

Scraping a red-painted nail across Todd's rough, stubbled chin, she said, "You come here often?"

"Not if I can help it," Todd said, "But I'm certainly glad I made the sacrifice."

TWO

Such a shame he couldn't stay longer, but Todd Gleason had a job to perform. He had to pack and secure a babysitter for Toad, his pet frog, though he supposed it was more frog-sitting than anything else and hopefully Scooter, his reliable associate, wouldn't literally plop down on the aquatic pet. Then he'd need to hail a cab and get his ass to the airport, because his flight was departing in just over four hours and the reality of air travel today meant you practically had to get to the airport before you were born if you were going to get through security and make your flight. Still, all that would have to wait, as first he needed to actually get out of bed.

She still smelled so nice. Like her flowery perfume fed off her natural scent, something their physical exertions had happily produced. Pheromones on high alert. She also tasted nice, especially when he nibbled on her neck in the afterglow, his hand slipping under the cover to tweak a generous nipple.

Her name, she slurred over a couple of drinks at the bar, was Joyce, and she was in New York all week on company business, and no, to allay any fears, she wasn't married in whatever square state she hailed from. She was a single girl who enjoyed a good time on her terms and she wasn't expecting to find one on this trip when her boss informed her, for cost reasons, she had to hole up in Jersey rather than pay Manhattan's hotel prices. She worked for some greeting card company, she said, and as if to prove it she had said to him, as they drained the last of their martinis, "New friends make for special memories."

It was morning now, with last night's meeting with the red kerchief-ed man now a distant memory, special memories indeed having won out. But when the sun cracked through the open curtains and the new day rudely announced itself

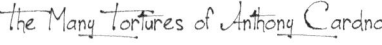

far too early, Todd knew he had to get up, and not in the way he had during the long, lovely night. Trying not to disturb her, Todd made a move to push back the tangled blankets. Joyce's hands suddenly pulled him back to the bed and his head fell back against the pillow. She slid blood-red nails beneath a mat of dark chest hair.

"Hmmm," she said, "I could lie her all day."

Todd wasn't an expert on grammar, but he thought she meant lay. He knew he did.

"Sorry, I've got to run," he said, kissing the top of her head. "I had fun."

"A poet," she said, her laugh throaty.

"That's me, a regular Dr. Seuss."

She wasn't going to let him go that easily, her hands now doing all the talking. What they did next would have made even the most romantic poet blush, and it sure wasn't appropriate to a rhyming tale for kids, and so Todd got a later start on this promising day than he'd wanted. He was already behind schedule and in danger of missing his arranged-for flight. When he dressed and gave the lovely Joyce a fond kiss good-bye, he slipped out of the hotel room and pulled out his cell phone. First things first, he called Scooter and arranged for Toad's care. Next he phoned the airline and ended up changing his flight, not just the time but also the airport.

He was supposed to fly out of JFK on American at 2:30.

What he did was take to the sunny blue skies out of Newark, and why not, he was already in Jersey, and the time of departure was at 11:00 that morning, courtesy of Delta. He was set to make a fortune on this project, what did it matter the cost of an airline ticket and besides, wasn't the portly guy paying all expenses? As to what to do about fresh clothes, Todd stopped at a clothing store on his way to the airport, mostly so he would have luggage with which to board. Last-minute flier, nothing to check, nothing to carry on, you may as well wave a flag at the TSA agents and say, "search me." Not that Todd had anything to hide, at least not on his body.

Unless you counted that little bite mark on his shoulder, courtesy of Joyce.

In any case, he made it to EWR with time to spare, drank down a cup of Dunkin's finest, and then boarded when they called his row. He took his seat by the window, hoping no one took the middle seat, pleased to see a large man with a book that appeared even larger, take the aisle seat. Good, no chance of distractions. Todd didn't like to talk to people on airplanes, they asked too many questions and he never liked answering much. When at last the pilot announced they had been cleared for take-off and the powerful jet rumbled down the runway and shot into the sky, Todd Gleason was already asleep.

He had to keep his wits about him.

Landing fresh and relaxed was his first priority.

His second priority was finding out just what kind of mess he was walking into.

THREE

So, here was the deal, at least according to the sheet of paper provided by Anton-Anthony-Tony. There was this beautiful estate in a coastal village that was for sale, but forsaking the traditional method of using a real estate agent, it was for sale by owner, and he was supposed to sell it to just one man. Todd's role was owner, and he was only to sell it to one Fritz Scoville, who was supposed to contact him just as soon as he arrived, uh, "home."

But first he had to get there.

Florida was one of his least favorite states in the union, mostly because he was actually a enjoyed witnessing the seasons change, but also because he didn't like insects, reptiles, or Walt Disney World, and not necessarily in that order.

He'd flown into West Palm Beach, which at least was smaller and less crazy to navigate than say, Miami or even Fort Lauderdale, the latter of which had been on his original flight plan. Didn't matter, since his destination was the eastern coast town of Delray Beach, and it was there he was headed now behind the wheel of his Chevy Malibu rental. He'd gone for fire-engine red, and it came with a sunroof, because as he'd learned once from a bank robber named Fast Cash, if you wanted to remain anonymous, best you hide right out in the open. Where Todd was going, money talked, and so did style.

That reminded him, he'd have to get himself a makeover.

The lustful Joyce hadn't minded his laid-back appearance, though on second thought maybe she hadn't so much liked his clothes, since she'd removed them quickly enough when they'd retired to her room. But as this Anton-Anthony-Tony guy had said, Todd needed to look the part of a successful businessman. Scoville expected it. So he made several stops along the way, getting a haircut and a shave, and at a men's shop he picked out several suits, dress shirts, and, loathe as he was to tie one on, a few ties. The helpful clerk told him he'd make a killing at whatever business he was conducting here in the Sunshine State, and Todd

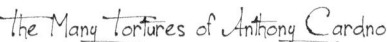

replied, as honestly as he could, "I certainly hope not."

Those were not the kind of complications he needed.

Bodies always left behind such trouble. And the dead never cared.

Delray Beach was a lovely stretch of road that bordered on the Atlantic, rife with beaches and shacks that served all sorts of food, not just seafood but tacos and burgers, and seeing them as he drove by he was reminded that he'd skipped eating today save for a bag of chips on the airplane. Food later. First he had to find the address he'd been given by Anton-Anthony-Tony ... Anton, let's just call him that. Guys with multiple names, he didn't trust them. Look at him.

The address was 19498 Longview Drive, the first part of which sounded more like a zip code, the last part of which seemed as though it would drain his gas tank. Just how far down this winding stretch of road was this house, anyway? But the GPS started yakking at him, telling him his destination was to his left in two hundred feet. He found it, thick walls of green brush lining iron gates, and in the distance stood a mansion with rust-colored rococo slats on the roof, and a white sandstone façade. He could guess at how many rooms it had, deciding it would be more interesting to gain entry and assess that for himself. The code was probably written down on the paper, and so he consulted the paper, just as he had during the flight. There it was, that name again. H E L E N.

Approaching the keypad, feeling like he was being watched, he made quick work of the lock and heard it click open. Stealing a look around the empty road, he still felt like his movements had been observed. He'd have to deal with that later, and instead drove through the open gates and parked in the circular drive before stepping out.

Sunshine beamed down on the estate, as though wanting to welcome Todd with its own special golden hued carpet. The green lawn spread out and around the house, and a cobble stone path led down a steep hill to a huge pool, whose ripples shimmered under the bright sky. Even further, he saw another path wind its way down to a private beach, where he could see waves crashing over a jetty. In the air he could smell the brine of the ocean, and he let out a contented sigh. He might not know what the hell was going on or why, but the setting sure had its perks.

The cold of New York in winter was gone.

So too was the warmth of his and Joyce's entangled bodies.

What he felt now was a wave of chilled uncertainty, because when he looked down at the front steps of the mansion, he was faced with a smear of a familiar red. His mind pictured the tie and kerchief that accessorized Anton's chubby

The Many Tortures of Anthony Cardno

torso, and then he recalled Joyce's crimson nails as they glided teasingly over his body. Neither red could compare to what he saw now.

Yup, you guessed it.

Blood. And fresh blood at that.

"Oh, shit," was how Todd Gleason responded.

FOUR

He approached with trepidation, bending down to examine the shock of blood. It was still wet, and being exposed to the oxygen in the air explained its colorful hue. Facts that supported the theory someone had been here recently, and while the presence of blood could have been explained away as innocently as having scraped a leg against ... what? He saw nothing sharp nearby. Besides, it's not like it was a trail of blood, leading him into the house, his eyes tracking it until he came upon the dead body it belonged to, the rest of its blood having seeped out onto polished hardwood floors.

Talk about depreciation.

Didn't murder houses always scare away potential buyers?

Okay, Todd told himself, enough with the smart remarks, even if they're just inside your head. This calling card could be bad and lead to trouble, and on cases like this he liked to avoid anything resembling trouble. Trouble should be one of those four-letter words, TRBL, like text-speak. You want a vowel, that's $250 per. See, flippancy, it wasn't necessary in this situation but it's where his mind naturally went. He tried to shove all those pesky thoughts off as he stepped toward the front door. Actually, he stepped around the bloodstain, turned the knob and found the door opened easily.

It just creaked, like he was in some old movie.

So long as Norman Bates didn't come at him, he figured he could handle it.

He entered the house, knowing he was an intruder, but thinking he was also being paid to pretend it was his pad, and paid quite well. Thus energized by the final payoff, he made his way through a musty-smelling foyer before stepping into a sunken living room where all the furniture was covered in clingy white sheets. Okay, this was strange, fresh blood on the steps outside, but inside the house was sealed up like a coffin.

Ghosts that bled. Despite the Florida heat, he felt chilled.

He wondered where his next step would take him.

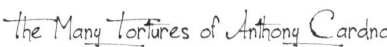

Turned out it was toward the telephone, which just now had begun to ring. Todd didn't jump at the sudden intrusion, the blood had attuned his senses, alerted his mind to surprises. He raised a curious eyebrow at the old-style rotary phone that might have been fashionable during Victorian times. Wait, did they even have phones back then? No matter, he grabbed the receiver on the third ring and spoke simply, Bell to Watson.

"Hello?"

"Mr. Ardno, welcome home."

Play along, instinct told him. "Yes, thank you. I'm surprised you knew of my arrival."

"Don't be coy," said the voice, which clearly had Todd at a disadvantage. "I was told to expect you at FFL. We must have missed each other at the airport, despite my driver waiting in the lobby with a placard."

Ah, FFL, airport-speak for Fort Lauderdale. "Sorry, I got waylaid. Had to take a different flight."

"Regardless of the miscommunication re: your flight, I trust our meeting remains on your calendar?"

"Of course," Todd said, now just flying by the seat of his pants.

"Ellison's Restaurant, be there at eight o'clock sharp. If you don't already know, it's not a shorts and t-shirt type of establishment. You'll know me from my red tie and kerchief and besides, the reservation is under the name Scoville."

Were Scoville and whatever Anton's real name was part of some red-tie fraternity, like those old ladies who liked to wear purple hats and act all loopy? Todd realized the man was waiting for an answer.

"I'll be there with bells on," he managed.

"Excuse me?"

"It's just an expression," Todd said.

"I trust you'll leave the snark at home."

"I even called a babysitter."

A tight silence filled the phone line but Todd thought he could see steam coming from it. Then the man said, "I'll see you at eight. Bring the deed."

Todd said certainly, see you then, of course, and then he hung up.

He realized he had no clue what the man was talking about, but that was just to be added to the mystery of the bloodstain, not just whom it belonged to but where was that person now? He scanned the high, wood-beamed ceilings of the house and realized he had a lot of exploring to do. In truth, he also had the time since his mysterious meeting wasn't until eight o'clock tonight. So he had four hours to maybe find a body, prepare for his dinner meeting, shower, and dress.

He opted for that last option.

Like Anton-Anthony-Tony had said, appearances matter.

Wait, hadn't we decided he'd be just Anton?

This was getting complicated, Todd decided, and real fast.

Too many identities.

Too many names.

Too many questions.

Blood on the steps. No body.

And no answers.

If not for the generous payday he'd been assured by the man with many names, Todd Gleason might still be enjoying the enticing gyrations of a lady named Joyce back in windy New Jersey. Of course, if not for the promised payday, he'd never have been at that hotel bar in New Jersey in the first place, and he'd never have met said Joyce, she of the talented lips and nails and energetic cries. But that's life, twists happen, dalliances are fleeting, and it was how you reacted to them that dictated how well you survived in a world where the truth was as hidden as some people's motives.

FIVE

"How do you find Florida?"

Todd wasn't sure if that was a rhetorical question or not.

"A map helps," he replied, "or you just listen to that nice lady on the GPS. Why does she always sound British? I always feel like I should be on the other side of the road, but that would mean making a left when she says right. Or, I suppose, in the broader scheme of things, you just do what I did, which was rely on the pilot to set his coordinates correctly. He did. I'm here."

"Humor doesn't amuse me," came a stilted, almost strangled answer.

Now that had to be rhetorical; there wasn't possibly any answer to such an oxymoron. Or was what he said a mixed metaphor? Like large shrimp and military intelligence, unfunny humor didn't seem consistent. He let it go because it was already established Todd was no grammarian, and also because he hadn't brought his own laugh track with him, and the guy sitting opposite him was anyway primed for business. His earlier question from when Todd sat down had been one of social nicety. But that was over.

The guy was gruff, with a voice that sounded like nails on a chalkboard and he was reminded of Elaine's father on that episode of "Seinfeld." He was dressed in a pin-striped dark suit and indeed, just as advertised, came with a red tie and kerchief. A thick gold bracelet dangled from a thick wrist coiled with curly dark hair. His face was dominated by jowly cheeks and and his frame a belly that rivaled Texas. But other than the body type and the accessories, there was no resemblance to Anton-Anthony-Tony, yet it was he who became the next subject of business. Todd wondered why the two men just couldn't meet and settled whatever their differences, seal the deal on the sale of the house and be done with it? Why the subterfuge, why the middle man who stood to pocket so much cash you'd need a few of them.

Stop questioning, earn your keep, that's what Todd reminded himself.

So he focused, and the jokes slid away.

"How did you come to buy this house from Mr. Cornue?"

Cornue? That was a new name added to the picture, leaving Todd wondering if it was this Anthony-Anton-Tony guy's last name. It wasn't very alliterative if it was.

"Mutual business associates," Todd said.

"Care to give me specifics?"

Sure, if I knew them. "The previous owner and I met at a golfing charity."

"Casper hates golf."

Casper Cornue, there's even more information, a name for a ghostly presence at dinner. And it was alliterative. Surely, Casper was the portly guy he'd agreed to do this bit of business for. Todd had to agree with himself.

"So do I, it's what we bonded over. But you know, when it's for charity ..."

Scoville looked skeptical. Obviously he knew that the one steak away from a heart attack, large-boned and very out of shape Casper Cornue would not be caught dead teeing off. "Where did this event this take place?"

"Upstate somewhere ... uh, Turning Stone. The Indians own it."

"When?"

"Last September," Todd said, hoping that sounded plausible, knowing he needed more details. "The man invited me back to this house on a lake to discuss investments possibilities. It too had one of the Indian names."

Didn't they all, up there?

"Humph," the man said, and then he took a sip of his drink.

Todd took this chance to assess his surroundings, his first breather since arriving fifteen only minutes ago. The restaurant was upscale even by rich-people standards, with beautifully appointed tables and nice artwork highlighting the luxurious setting. A long, sleek silver bar was hopping with thirty- and fortysomethings who were tanned, stylishly presentable, all looking for the same thing the other denizens of less-reputable bars sought. An escape, a release, perhaps someone to forget their miseries with. Day after Valentine hangovers, or a fresh start on a new relationship, take your pick. Todd and this Fritz Scoville character were seated on a wind-strewn deck outside, on a night lit by the moon, with a soundtrack of ocean waves to enhance the setting. The drink before him was better vodka than he'd had in Jersey, but then again, so was the air.

"Casper was wrong to sell you the house, it belongs to my family."

Todd looked again at that bracelet and wondered what kind of family they were talking.

"You've noticed my prized possession," Scoville said. "A special gift from my daughter, I never take it off."

"Must be water-proofed," Todd remarked.

"My daughter is dead," Scoville said, and that quieted Todd down. He actually felt bad.

"My apologies, sir. So, you were saying, about the house ..."

"I bought it for my daughter as a wedding present," he said, "Fifteen years ago. I put it in her name, told her it came with no strings attached. Helen and I, we were more than father and daughter, we were best friends."

Now why did that name sound familiar?

Helen ... he'd heard it last night, hadn't he? Not his bed partner, she had been Joyce

Helen was his emergency contact person, that's what Anton-Anthony-Tony told him.

Helen was also the code to gain entry to the estate. Curious.

"How did she die?"

"Easy, her husband killed her."

"How ... awful. He's in jail?"

"No, the bastard is selling the damn house is what he's doing."

"I'm sorry, are you saying the man I met ... uh, at the charity golf game, he's a murderer?"

"You ask me, hell yes. You ask the fools who run the courts, no. He was acquitted. And as such, he inherited the house as well as the rest of Helen's sizable estate. Then the insensitive bastard sells the house out from under me, knowing it was my last link to her. He told me he'd never sell it to me, all because I tried to have him framed for her murder. Hell, you can't frame someone who's guilty."

Todd looked around at the busy restaurant, noticing casual diners enjoying themselves, laughing off the day's troubles with an easy sip of a cool drink. Like they could care less that just a few tables away and thankfully out of earshot, two men were discussing topics such as murder, and quite possibly, revenge. Revenge was a dangerous motive.

"Tell me, Mr. Scoville, where did your daughter die?" Todd asked, already suspecting the answer.

"At the house, on the front steps. Blood was ... everywhere, a sight I'll never forget it." He looked into the bottom of his glass, like he'd been there before, and then when he gazed back up with glassy eyes, he said, "I'll pay you anything you want for the house. I just ... I want ... no, I need that house to feel close to my daughter again. No stranger can ever enter through its door."

Scoville lapsed into a moment of mournful silence. Todd took the break in action to assess the situation. His mind flashed the picture of the smear of blood, and he had to wonder if a game was being played out in front of him, a very dangerous one at that. Money was no object to the grief stricken, and Todd had to wonder just how much he could get for the house. Surely above current market price, and certainly more than Anton-Anthony-Tony-Casper was expecting. Could he exploit Scoville's sorrow and score himself an even bigger payoff?

If so, what did that say about his own motives, not just in this scam but in life?

He had no problem with defying the law, it was ethics that sometimes nagged at his sleep.

Scoville cleared his throat, recovering from his momentary bout with loss. He grabbed for the menu not so much to choose an entrée than to hide his tearing eyes. Todd did the same—with his menu, not his eyes—and waited until Scoville spoke.

"I think I'll have the steak," he finally said, summoning over the waiter.

"How would you like it, Mr. Scoville?" the young man asked.

"Rare," he said, "bleeding."

"And you, sir?"

After deciding there was something fishy going on here, Todd ordered the Scampi.

The Many Tortures of Anthony Cardno

SIX

Todd returned to the scene of Helen Scoville's murder just after midnight, his mind reeling from all the stories he'd heard throughout the endless dinner. A father's joy over the birth of his only child, a daughter who he took to dance recitals and Disney World, and how he promised to protect her and spoil her and give her everything she could ever need, and then added to it by providing more than she could ever want. Seemed Helen's mother was no longer in the picture, yet when pushed about the circumstances, Scoville's small eyes darkened, brightening when he resumed speaking of his daughter, and in tones so reverential Todd thought he heard angels singing.

Turned out it was just the wait staff wishing a guest at a nearby table Happy Birthday.

"Helen ran out of birthday's three years ago," was how Scoville ended the night.

Vodka had dulled his brain, and the activity from the day had drained him, so Todd went to sleep in the master bedroom and woke the next morning to find bright sunshine beaming through delicate lace curtains. A lovely Florida day was rising and given his surroundings, there was nothing more enticing than just lazing about without a care in the world. Would that that be true, but it wasn't. Todd had some research to do, and then he had a house sale to finalize. The former he had to leave the estate in order to accomplish, since there was no working computer and no Wi-Fi, and as for the latter, well, let's see what he turned up first.

He found an Internet café along the main drag, where he could get a cup of coffee along with an hour's time on the computer. He fired up a Google search and typed in "Helen Scoville" and watched as the page filled with hyperlinks on his screen. He started clicking away, curious eyes pouring over details, devouring facts and supposition, reading sensational headlines in bold black type about the brutal stabbing of the young woman who "had seemed to have it all, brains, money, status." It didn't escape Todd that they'd left out one notable attribute: beauty. Only when he hit "images" and saw a photograph of Helen Scoville did he see why.

Now, not that he's a shallow guy who's fixated solely on looks, but hey, sometimes the gene pool only dives so deep. Helen's features just didn't ... match. A large nose, a leaning smile that was more Joker than Jester, and a puffy torso that made you look twice—if only to absorb her full size. Yet that hadn't stopped the paparazzi from seeking her out, since Helen's father, Fritz Scoville, was a noted lawyer in South Florida, possibly with ties to the mob if you were to believe some the yellower tabloids. Photos showed Helen accompanying her father to the opera, walking along the beach (a headline about a beached whale as mean as could be), and finally her wedding announcement, and lastly, the formal photograph from the actual ceremony. This was what Todd was most curious about, as he focused more on the guy on her large arm.

It was the guy Scoville called Casper Cornue.

It was also the guy Todd knew as Anton-Anthony-Tony.

He was just as large as his bride, just as wide as he'd been sitting on that poor barstool in Jersey.

Hardly satisfied by this discovery, Todd focused on the murder.

A sun-drenched June day, their second wedding anniversary, Casper Cornue, as he was called, returned home to his gated, exclusive estate, only to find his wife lying dead in a pool of blood on the stone-laid front steps. He called 911 but it was too late, and only after a month of investigation—as well as pressure from the deceased's devastated father—was Casper arrested and tried for the crime. Lack of evidence was cited by the twelve-person jury, and even though the trial took twelve weeks, the deliberation lasted not even twelve hours.

"Not guilty," screamed a newspaper headline.

Which Todd knew was not the same as innocent.

He closed out of the gory details and called up another search. He perused the listings till he found one to his liking and he took out his cell phone and dialed. A pleasant sounding woman on the other end said, "Dubois Realty," and asked how she could be of assistance. When he stated the reasons for his calling, a long pause ensued. It didn't take long after that for a second woman to pick up. Todd had to go through his routine yet again.

"I'd be happy to come to the estate, Mr ... ."

"Ardno," he said, "Anton ... uh, Anthony Ardno."

Todd was getting comfortable in his present role, and with that came confidence regarding what he was plotting. No matter the name we went by, inside he was just Todd, and he had a beautiful house to sell and a deposit to make at the end of it. What he wanted was to know just how much the estate by the water was worth, and not from Casper Cornue and not from Fritz Scoville. But from someone who could tell him the truth.

Truth was the one thing lacking in this entire adventure.

The Many Tortures of Anthony Cardno

SEVEN

As he waited for the eager real estate agent to arrive, Todd Gleason decided to enjoy the benefits that came with living here. He picked up a bottle of bubbly on his way back and let it chill in the freezer while he donned a pair of swim trunks he'd bought and a towel and made his way down to the Olympic-sized pool. Water gleamed blue under the hot sun. He proceeded to dive in and work out some of his frustrations and anxiety by doing laps.

After thirty minutes, he lifted himself out of the pool and, droplets dripping off his body, he ran the towel through his hair and took up residence on the lounge chair. The sun baked his skin, slowly stripping away the layer of winter white with a reddish tint. He didn't want to stay out too long and burn, but his mind took him elsewhere.

He thought about doomed Helen Scoville Cardno.

He thought of Daddy Scoville and his unhealed heart.

He thought of Anton-Anthony-Tony and his manipulation of his former father-in-law.

Clearly, Anton was bilking the man of his fortune, using Todd as the go-between to keep the man in the dark about the true recipient of his millions. He would never pay such a sum to the man he believed murdered his daughter. Todd had to admit that Casper/Anton's scheme was clever, since he knew to play upon the man's sympathies, all while hiding behind not just an alternate identity but another person.

Love was complicated; families even more so.

Were the men women married ever good enough for their fathers?

Were the men they married just substitutes?

Scoville had worn a red tie and kerchief. But Casper/Anton had done so too.

Was he poking fun at Scoville? Had it been a hint for Todd?

And why red?

He thought about the blood stain on the front steps, the one someone had left purposely.

Someone was toying with Todd, and that meant he would toy right back at them.

The blazing sun had begun to sizzle his skin, and thankfully just as he was deciding he'd had enough of the heat he heard the bell chime.

"Company," he announced to himself, bounding up from the chair, feeling a bit woozy from all that sun and all that exposition. Why couldn't he just relax,

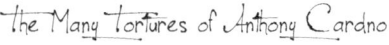

enjoy the quiet? Because he wanted what was coming to him, that promised payday, and he wanted to claim it without further complications. At least, further complications that didn't come from him.

"Mr. Ardno?"

"Yes," Todd said, coming to the gate and pressing the button for entry. He extended his hand and a lovely woman with sweeping brown hair and a deep tan and a blouse of burnt orange smiled at him, showing off teeth that would have made the sun put on protective wear. Speaking of, Todd was clad only in his swim trunks and he apologized for not being more presentable, and the woman laughed it off.

"This is Florida, I've seen worse," she said, Todd feeling her warm gaze on him.

"Uh, thanks, I think."

"Much worse," she amended.

That was better. Todd escorted her down to the pool area, excusing himself by running into the house for a T-shirt and lemonade. It wasn't yet time to crack open the bubbly. When he returned he found his guest typing away on a black iPad, periodically looking up at the house, as though determining the monetary value of every square inch. Todd settled in for a nice chat, and so with fresh drinks in hand and the sun keeping them company, they got down to serious business.

"So, what do you think it's worth, Ms. Dubois?" he asked, jumping into the figurative deep end.

"Call me Debbie," she said, and he took note of another alliterative name. "It's a lovely estate, even without its ... shall we say, checkered history."

"A murder house," Todd said. "Does that send its value down or up?"

Debbie didn't answer him and instead concentrated on her tablet. When her doe-eyes looked back up, she said, "At the time before the murder, this house was valued at eight point three million. After Casper Cornue's acquittal, it dropped to five point one."

"No one wanted to touch it," he said.

"Which is why, I guess, you were able to buy it?"

He nodded, she typed away.

"A shrewd investment," she said, "I think I could sell this place for ten point five."

Todd whistled, the sound catching on the breeze and taking it out to sea. He thought he saw a diving seagull choke on it. Or perhaps that was just a manifes-

The Many Tortures of Anthony Cardno

tation of his own response. His mind was thrumming with schemes and dollars signs, thoughts of off-shore bank accounts. They talked further, and then Todd invited his guest for a tour of the house, and while Ms. Dubois respectfully accepted his offer, she put the brakes on when Todd suggested they venture up to the second floor. She tapped his cheek and smiled up at him and said, "Give me the listing, I'll go to the moon with you."

As appealing as that sounded, as appealing as she was, there was no way he could allow her to sell the house. First of all, the house really wasn't his to sell and to suddenly get a realtor involved would not only go against his instructions, it would draw unneeded attention. The more word spread about the Helen Scoville Cardno murder house being up for sale, the faster it would depreciate in value. He couldn't take that chance, so he bid adieu to Debbie Dubois with thanks, told her he'd be in touch but of course, like any cad out on a date that had not gone as expected, he had no intention of calling again.

"One question," he asked.

"Shoot," she said.

Better than stab, he thought. "What's a realtor's commission?"

When she told him, he smiled. She stuffed her business card into the pocket of his t-shirt and assured him she would pull down the largest sale this side of the Mason-Dixon Line if given the opportunity, and then she pulled out of the driveway in her fiery red Ferrari. Again, the deadly color of red played with Todd's green-colored mind, even as he was busy dialing a phone number he'd been given last on his cell phone.

When the gruff voice answered, Todd said the simplest of phrases.

"I'm ready to sell."

"I'll be there in thirty."

EIGHT

He made it in twenty-five.

"You must have made all the lights," Todd said.

"Or I might have been around the corner and just gave you time to dress."

Todd had indeed changed clothes, not into a suit, he wasn't the one trying to buy respect. But beneath his cargo shorts and loose-fitting chambray shirt his skin turned a shade of red the sun hadn't yet had a chance to. Todd had to remind himself that he was dealing with a man who saw the law as a toy, some-

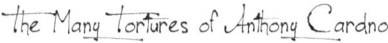

thing to be played with, perhaps manipulated. Lawyers knew all the tricks. Todd could relate, con men had their own slippery sleeves, but still he was dealing with the unknown, and as such he had no idea how this was going to go down.

"Shall we go inside?" Todd said.

Fritz Scoville gazed down at the front steps of the entrance, which glistened bright and clean in the afternoon sun. Todd had swiped away the suggestive blood even before Ms. Bahouth had visited, thinking blood wasn't such a selling point, glad now he'd done so because Scoville needed no reminders of the tragedy which had occurred right before them years ago. The portly man appeared lost in a trance, as though picturing lost moments with his sweet, pudgy daughter, and that gave Todd a moment to question the following: say the husband Casper Cardno, aka Anton-Anthony-Tony didn't actually kill his wife, then that meant the guilty party was someone else.

Was it Todd's job to solve a murder?

Or just make a sale. Get in, get out, deposit, escape.

Todd led Scoville into the kitchen, where he produced the bottle of champagne.

"Don't you think it's a bit too early to celebrate," Scoville said.

"Regarding the sale of the house, I'm sure we'll come to terms. But no, I wanted to raise a glass ... in your daughter's honor. If I may?"

That caught Scoville right in the throat, and so nearly did the cork.

"Sorry."

Glasses poured, a toast presented to the heavens, Todd and Scoville drank.

"Thank you, Todd," he said.

"Mr. Scoville, I am very sympathetic to your loss, of course ... what man wouldn't be. If returning this house to your ownership brings you some kind of peace, I'm happy to relinquish it. But I'm sure you realize that my acquisition of this house was seen as an investment and that I had no intention of settling here. I own real estate properties the world over, so many I've often forgotten. I've actually paid money for a hotel in London when I could have easily stayed in my flat in Marylebone—had I remembered I owned one."

"Your point?" Scoville said, setting down his glass.

"Meaning I hold no emotional attachment to this house. I'd like to hear your best offer."

Scoville didn't hesitate, this was the part he'd prepared for. "Five million."

Todd paused before shaking his head. "I don't think so."

"You're a tough negotiator, Mr. Ardno. Seven million."

Nice jump, he'd just made two million dollars in two seconds. An hourly wage you won't find at McDonald's.

"Earlier today I had the estate appraised …" Todd began, placing special emphasis on that last word so as not to make it seem like some beachcomber's bungalow, "at fifteen point three."

"That's ludicrous," Scoville said.

"Mr. Scoville, I have a buyer lined up, ready to pay sixteen, cash."

"You wouldn't …"

"Why not? It's just business …"

"No, it's personal."

Todd waited, saw defeat claim the man's features. "Twelve point eight, final."

Wait, just wait, his mind told him, reeling from the numbers. He took hold of his glass of champagne, held it in the air to the point that the sun beaming through the window caught its golden glow. "I'm willing to toast thirteen five. Honestly, at the sums being bandied about, Mr. Scoville, what is seven hundred thousand dollars to secure peace of mind? Imagine me selling to a stranger, someone who wouldn't honor the estate's past, the love in which the house was given, and the reverence with which it is remembered. Agree, and I'll take it off the market right now."

Scoville looked like he was ready to cry and Todd wished that wasn't the case.

He'd invoked an innocent woman who was no longer around to defend herself.

This was pure manipulation.

He reminded himself, as Scoville had insisted, this was pure business.

Scoville extended his hand. "Agreed."

They shook hands.

"You have no idea how much you've helped me, Mr. Ardno … Anton … or, do you prefer Anthony … perhaps Tony?"

"Either, neither, pick one. And I'm glad it's all worked out so well."

They raised their glasses again.

"To Helen Scoville," her father said.

"To beauty not even the world can capture," Todd said.

Todd drank down his champagne, feeling the bubbles dance inside his bloodstream.

Either that or it was the knowledge that he'd just doubled the sale price of what Anthony-Anton-Tony had requested of him. What kind of inflated bonus awaited him, he had to wonder, because he sure as hell wasn't settling for a measly one hundred fifty thousand.

NINE

Murders go unsolved all the time, so much so the police refer to them as cold cases.

Helen Scoville fit that description. Her body was long cold, her case frigid.

Todd too would soon return to the cold, too, as he'd just departed Florida airspace, the airplane shooting into the northbound sky. Again, he'd chosen a last minute flight and paid the exorbitant fee, and as they cruised on smooth waves toward JFK, he munching on a bag of Terra Blue potato chips, he tried to sleep but couldn't.

Nice thing about JetBlue, they had satellite television, so he started channel flipping.

It wasn't until they grew closer to New York City that the local NBC affiliate became available. It was just after six in the evening, and even at thirty-two thousand feet in the air the stench of death, murder, and crime was apparent. The evening broadcast had "Breaking News."

"And in a shocking development, police in Weehawken, New Jersey, are investigating the suspicious death of a businessman, found dead inside his hotel room. Mr. Anton Ardno was found unresponsive by a chambermaid and after paramedics were called, he was pronounced dead at the scene."

Not that Todd had gotten used to calling him Anton Ardno, it was still unnerving to hear of his passing. Like being present at his own funeral.

"It appears at first it could have been a heart attack," said the police spokesman, "but we are investigating it thoroughly and at this moment cannot rule out anything, including suicide or homicide."

The man sitting beside him said, "Tragic what happens to some people."

Todd turned off the television and instead stared out the window. The Manhattan skyline was off to his left, and he could see the Hudson River that separated it from the mainland that was the state of New Jersey. He felt he could almost zero in on the Weehawken Sheraton, the swirling lights of sirens and police and an impotent ambulance standing by. But that was his fervent imagination, of course, racing a mile a minute, not quite as fast as the airplane, but good enough to help propel them to the runway. Both landed safely a short while later.

Once Todd deplaned and made his way into the terminal, he withdrew an envelope from his jacket pocket. He found the number, took out his cell phone, and then dialed. Didn't death qualify as an emergency? It was picked up on the first ring.

"Hello, Helen," Todd said.

"We need to meet," she said.

Todd paused before he said, "Same place?"

No answer was necessary.

TEN

See, the thing about figures is this: some stick in your mind for good reasons, some bad. The first one that attracted him when this case began was the one-hundred thousand dollars, a monetary figure. The other that had distracted him came in the pleasant guise of greeting-card saleswoman Joyce, she of the red-lacquered nails and nighttime acrobatics. There were the oversize figures—bodies—of Anton-Anthony-Tony Ardno, nee Casper Cornue, as well as his aged doppelganger Fritz Scoville, and beating them both out on the scale was the very plus-sized Helen Scoville. See, what Todd had discovered was that figures come in all shapes and sizes, but it wasn't the physical definition of the word which was occupying Todd Gleason's mind at present, it was the monetary one of thirteen point five million dollars he'd secured for the sale of the Scoville estate.

The scene was once again the bar at the Weehawken Sheraton. Todd was dressed up in one of his new suits, and just for fun, or perhaps as an honor to this scheme or in some way homage to the dearly departed Antony-Anton-Tony, he'd accessorized with a red tie and equally red kerchief. After all, this was business, and so you had best put your best game face on.

"Well, I would hardly have recognized you," he heard.

He looked up from his drink, smiled. "Joyce," he said. "Or is Helen?"

"It's neither," she said, taking a seat beside him.

"Of course it's not," he said.

Deception aside, Todd was ever the gentleman by pulling the chair out to allow her to slip comfortably onto its soft cushion. He nodded the bartender's way, who was quick with his delivery. A vodka martini, two olives, shaken not stirred, Bond-like. The stemware was cold with condensation. Joyce-Helen lifted the glass without comment and took her first sip.

"You remembered," she said.

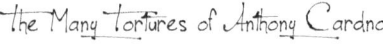

"I'm good at stuff like that."

"You're good at a lot of stuff," she remarked.

"So I'm assuming this was a set-up, though I'm not quite sure why."

She was again wearing a dress that showed off her nice curves, the rise of her breasts, the beat of her heart. Todd peeked, just to make sure she had one. What he didn't fail to notice were those red-lacquered nails, and further up those fingers was an iceberg that, if it didn't quite sink the Titanic, it surely would have left a good hole. The wedding band that came with it kind of sealed the deal.

"It's not how it looks," she said. "You were ... a bonus, at least for me."

"So you and Anton-Anthony-Tony were in cahoots. Married."

"Casper," she said, dryly, and then took a second sip of her martini. "An insufferable and foolish buffoon. But not only did he have money, he was finally going to get an even bigger windfall."

"Let me guess, by selling the house back to the man who had bought it for his daughter."

"Ironic, isn't it?"

"Pretty cruel, considering the guy was charged with murdering the woman."

"Acquitted," she said.

"Indeed, giving him free reign over her sizable estate," Todd said. "Why not just sell it to the highest bidder?"

"Because Fritz Scoville ruined his life. The trial destroyed him."

"It kind of destroyed Helen Scoville, too. Lucky for you, Anton-Anthony-Tony-Casper went first, he could have been a serial wife murderer."

That seemed to quiet her down and again, she sipped at her drink.

"We didn't have that kind of ... relationship."

"You never consummated the marriage?"

She grimaced, as though a rank smell had wafted into the room. "God, he just huffed and he puffed ..."

"But he didn't blow your house down?"

"No, you did that," she said, "You could do it again."

"Let's get back to business, shall we? What was in it for you?"

"The money, of course. Millions."

"Which you stand to inherit, now that Anton-Anthony-Tony-Casper is dead."

"That heart of his never stood a chance," she said, not the least bit wistful about his heart or any other part of his body, all of which now grew cold in some city morgue. Allowing her to sit here, seemingly guilt-free, sipping at her vodka martini.

The Many Tortures of Anthony Cardno

"If he was poisoned, the cops will find out."

"Is that what you came here for, to point a finger? Hell, all I need to do is contact Fritz Scoville and tell him everything I know. Casper Cornue confessed to me after a night of passion that he'd killed his wife, right there on the steps. They were arguing about her father, it was all they argued about, and Casper took a knife and just sliced her."

Todd nodded, the image of the blood on the steps now magnified.

Too much blood, too much red.

"Todd," she said, because she knew his name and why not, she'd called it out often in the darkness of the hotel room, "Why can't we put aside all this awful talk of murder and death and money—for now—and retire upstairs. I know you enjoyed yourself that first night, I did as well.

"Sorry, love, but a previous engagement requires my attention," he stated. "But if you're looking for company, I suggest you look no further than the man sitting directly behind you."

Joyce-Helen or whatever her real name was spun around on a barstool made for that, and she came face to face with another man in a business suit, and he too was wearing a red tie with a matching kerchief.

"Mr. Scoville, sir, allow me to introduce the second Mrs. Cornue," he said. "I'm certain the two of you have much to discuss."

"A pleasure to make your acquaintance," he said, always polite with his words but with an underlying grin that spoke differently. The shiny gold bracelet gleamed under the lights of the bar, like Helen was here to exact her revenge.

The woman with the red-lacquered nails turned back to Todd. "I don't get it."

"Money," Todd said, "isn't that what you were after?"

She was silent, but her gentle nod said it all.

"Then why can't it be my motive, as well? I was hired by your late husband to sell Mr. Scoville back the house he'd given his daughter as a wedding present. Sure, Casper could have just sold the estate to anyone, but to plot against the man who destroyed his life, to bilk him of money by playing on his sympathies and grief, that was genius. He knew Scoville would pay whatever he had to, and quite frankly, he did. And I did as I was hired to do, I sold Mr. Scoville the house. He'll show you the deed. But I also invited him to join us for this meeting of ours, as I knew he would find it revealing. Mr. Scoville, I turn this little tete-a-tete-a-tete over you to and remove one tete from the equation."

"Mr. Gleason, many thanks."

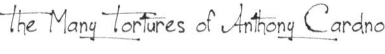

They had talked a lot during the flight to New York.

"No, many many thanks to you, sir, you were more than generous."

"Generous?" Mrs. Cornue said. "How much did he pay you to turn on ... us?"

"Just the going rate for any real estate agent," Todd said. "A very nice figure indeed."

And with that, Todd Gleason made his excuses, drained the last of his martini, and then, for effect, popped the intoxicated olive into his mouth with flair, wondering if Bond would have made such an obvious demonstration. No matter, he wasn't Bond, he was just a guy who liked money and sometimes he used both sides to maximize his profit margin, and while some might question his motives, or his ethics, he knew that on the one hand he'd helped a man deal with his grief, and on the other hand he'd brought down people far worse than himself.

As he made his way out of the hotel bar, intent on catching that last nausea-inducing ferry back to Manhattan, he turned back to see Joyce-Helen/Mrs. Cornue squeezing ever-closer to the portly Mr. Fritz Scoville, the only one of them in this whole scheme who'd never operated under an assumed name.

"My dear, you have brought me peace. Helen can rest now."

"Isn't that why you hired me?" she asked.

"But my dear, the spot of blood on the steps of the estate for Mr. Gleason to find, perhaps overkill?"

"He needed to be kept on his toes, we needed to let him know what was at stake."

Fritz Scoville leaned in and kissed her. "Clever to the end, my sweet Antonia."

If anyone in this collection is suited to write the adventures of an alternate-universe version of me, it's Neal Bailey. Bailey's webcomic Cura Te Ipsum stars Charlie Everett, Charlie Everett, Charlie Everett ... and Charlene Everett, just for good measure. I'm actually surprised Neal didn't make me a woman in this story. He did, however, make me far more patient than I am in real life. That's how you know this is fiction.

I Have a Question

NEAL BAILEY

Anthony Cardno was a rational man. Where normal people complained, he often found himself being patient, the lone holdout in a line of screaming mothers in grocery stores, the quiet one who waited in line humming while other cars honked and jockeyed for position in the wake of some minor fender-bender or another. None of this reddened the color of his cheek or even so much as raised his ire.

One of his favorite anecdotes that he related amongst his friends with pride was the fact that, when he went through the drive-thru, when confronted with an order of salad if he ordered a burger with fries, he'd eat the burger without complaint. After all, food is food. No reason to stress the heart or make an already hectic life harder for himself or the people around him.

This new doctor, then, would prove no real stress for him where it might for others. He had his book and a free afternoon. All the time in the world and Tom Wolfe. The only thing that really concerned him, when it came down to it, was the potentiality of colonoscopy. It had been many years, and he didn't want to have to deal with that nonsense if he could avoid it. If he had to he would, however, and he would do so with patience. Maybe not with a smile, but cheerfulness

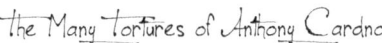
The Many Tortures of Anthony Cardno

is no requisite for good waiting.

"Anthony Cardno," he said, stepping up to the counter. "Here for my one o'clock examination."

The nurse smiled and began to dig in the ditto folder. A pretty girl. Lots of pretty girl receptionists. She handed him some pages. "Here's some paperwork. Just take it over, fill it out, and then bring it back. We'll get you in as soon as we can." The phone began ringing as she finished. Before he could ask for a pen, she picked up the receiver and began yammering away.

That was okay; he had a pen in his pocket. Anthony walked back into the waiting room filled with coughing children, adults on cell phones, and, what, was that? Yes, that was, a smattering of Spanish. He had always regretted never learning Spanish. It would have been useful. His mother had insisted on French. Bleah.

Simple enough forms. Name. Immediate history. Ancient history. He put down the removal of his tonsils, like always. His peanut allergy. His violent reaction to amoxicillin. The broken leg. His kidney stone when he was nineteen. He always enjoyed this part. It was interesting to think of all the things that had happened to him, all the things he had survived unscathed despite a world that seemed to conspire against him with its screaming waiting rooms, captains of industry, and biased, one-sided newsmen who wanted to be president.

When he brought the form back to the young lady, she was still talking on the phone. It sounded like someone had lost an x-ray exposure somewhere along the way. He could hear the man screaming through the phone, and he felt a pang of sympathy, but then a murmur of consternation at the man for losing his cool.

Anthony sat the papers down on the counter and waited. The receptionist kept talking. He waved, trying to let her know he was leaving the papers. She finally saw him, and then started taking them, but he held them, stopping her.

"I have a question," he mouthed, silent as foam under dirt.

The receptionist only pulled harder. He understood. She was trying to divide her attention between two things. He let her yank them out of his hand, even if it seemed a little rude, and stood waiting for her to finish her conversation.

When she did, she slammed the phone down, turned her eyes to him, and said, "Please have a seat, the doctor will be with you shortly."

Anthony opened his mouth to explain that he had a question, but the phone began ringing, and she picked it up and began talking to the person on the other end of the line. It seemed pretty urgent. After a while, she saw he was still standing there. Mid-conversation, she cupped the phone to her hand and said,

"Please, sir, have a seat, the doctor will be with you shortly."

"I have a question."

"Yes, have a seat." She uncupped the phone and began to talk again.

It wasn't much of a question, to be honest, but then, it was a question he had to have the answer to. If he didn't, then he would be faced with the uncomfortable prospect of having to fret and worry. The only thing worse than being angry in his mind was fret and worry, the prospect of sitting up at night with his hands behind his head wondering how he was going to afford his bread at the market in the week ahead. For this he stood his ground, being a man who would often not.

She talked. She talked. She spoke and rendered colloquialisms as if they were cheap or going out of style. Anthony stood and was patient, even smiled when she turned to glare at him for usurping her meager power.

Finally, she hung up the phone with an irate bang and turned her face up to him. "Yes, what?"

"I'm sorry, ma'am. I know you told me to have a seat, but I have a very important question, so I decided it might be best to stand here and patiently—"

"What do you need?"

"The form you gave me had a small block of text that—"

The phone rang again. She picked it up and began talking without so much as an acknowledgment.

That irked him, actually. More than things usually did. Anthony began to feel a little bit of creeping anger, as, without even a glance, she took the paperwork and stuffed it in a file with a few colored tabs before rendering it to its final resting place between Carantan and Cardrick, the phone in the crook of her neck the whole while.

He folded his arms and stood, took deep breaths, and considered.

A larger young man with short black hair came out of the door that led into the offices. He stepped behind the desk and looked at a list on a clipboard.

"Garcia!" he called. He set the clipboard down.

Anthony leaned toward him. "Excuse me, can I borrow you for a second?"

"Sure, buddy, shoot."

"I had a question about the forms, the ones that we fill out when we first get here."

"Yes?"

"There was a block of text at the bottom of the page that indicated that there was a fee involved for the filing of the papers that wasn't covered by most insur-

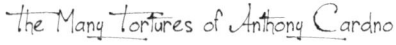

ances."

The Garcia family filed past him, a darling looking little girl, her mother, and a harried looking father who appeared to be on a break that was long over.

The large man waved a hand. "Oh, don't worry about that. It's just a standard thing, no big deal."

"Yes, I understand, but I am on quite a limited income, given the death of my wife and my age, and I need to consider every dollar that—"

"Marsha should be able to help you with that as soon as she gets off the phone. I'm sorry, I have to take care of this." He walked after the family, pulling the door shut behind him before Anthony could protest.

Now Marsha had hung up the phone, and she was holding her forehead in her hand and looking like she needed a drink. Probably did. He felt for her, a bit.

"Can I help you?" She certainly did not want to help him, he realized. In fact, recognition that it was Anthony still standing there brought a tinge of furor into her tone. "Hey, I thought I asked you to go sit down like, three times."

"Yes, ma'am, you did, but as you may recall I had a question about the fee mentioned on the application. I really need to discuss it before I get inside, given that if I can't afford it, I'll have to—"

"It's nothing, really, no big deal. A standard thing they put on those forms. No one ever worries about it."

"All the same, I'd like to know the amount of the fee, if I could, so that I can make the decision myself, if you would kindly oblige me."

She gave him a look. The phone rang. She picked it up without a wave or an indication of care and began talking.

Anthony took a step back and closed his eyes. A baby began screaming in the waiting room. The pain that had been bothering his stomach, the one that had brought him here to begin with, throbbed with new intensity. He doubted that the stress had set it off, but then again, he couldn't be certain it hadn't, either. All he knew for sure was that, patient or not, he was starting to lose his famous cool.

The mother with the baby in tow walked up to the desk and stepped past him. "How much longer is it going to be?" The baby screamed even louder at the jostle.

Marsha cupped the phone. "Ma'am, please have a seat. Sir," She looked at Anthony, "please, have a seat. This is the fourth time I've had to ask."

"How much longer?" The mother shifted the baby to her other hip.

"Minutes."

"How many minutes?"

"I'm sorry, ma'am, the doctor is very busy today. Please have a seat."

The woman gathered her child and walked back. On the way she butted Anthony with her shoulder either purposefully or on accident, but the end result was the same. A throb in his midsection that added fuel to the already growing heat in his face.

Anthony did what he usually did when confronted with a driver that cut across four lanes of traffic to endanger his life. He took a deep breath. He held it. He waited. And like when the truck in the right hand lane rode behind him on his bumper when Anthony was already doing five miles over the speed limit, Anthony held his moral ground, because sometimes, rarely but sometimes, when justified, one had to.

Marsha hung up the phone, in time. It had to have been ten minutes he'd been standing there. This time, the woman didn't even raise her head to look at him.

"Miss."

"Sir, I asked you to sit down. Honestly, I'm not really in the mood right now."

"I have a question that I need answered. It's *important.*"

"The doctor can answer any questions that you have."

"It's a question I need answered before the doctor sees me, you understand, because if I see him, the fee will already have—"

The door flew open. The man from before led the Garcia family in front of Anthony. Anthony stepped aside until they'd passed, then started to step forward again.

"Gary, can you please tell this gentleman to have a seat? I've asked him ten times now, but he won't listen."

"Hey, buddy, if you can't have a seat, you're gonna lose your appointment. It's really crazy in here right now. We don't have time for this."

Anthony's breath caught in his throat. He turned to the man. Maybe Gary would be more reasonable. So far, he was the only one who had listened. "I have a very important question that needs answering before I—"

"The doctor can answer any questions you have, buddy. Have a seat."

"You don't understand. I have to know what the fee is before I can go inside, because I live on a limited income and any processing fee over a certain amount might mean a day I can't eat."

Gary held out his hands like he didn't know what he could do. "I told you,

it's nothing. Really." He'd already reached the door back into the offices and had his hand on the handle.

"Right, but how much is it? Even a little nothing is something to me."

Gary paused. "You know, honestly? I don't know. But I know it's no big deal. It won't stop you from eating unless you're like, totally screwed for cash." He pulled the door shut.

Marsha was already back on the phone.

This time the call was blessedly quick, and when she hung the phone up he walked right up to her. "Ma'am, I need an answer to this question. Right now."

"Have a seat, sir, this is your last warning. I'll take your name off the appointment list."

"You'd what now?"

"If you keep causing a disruption, I'll have to cancel your appointment. There are a bunch of other people waiting here, and you're obstructing the front desk despite my repeated patient attempts to get you to have a seat."

"*Sit down, buddy!*" someone called from the waiting area. "*We all gotta wait, too!*"

Anthony pressed his lips together. "I have a question. I need it answered before I can go in to see the doctor. I'm not doing this to be a nuisance. I'm doing it because I have to know what the fee is or I can't go in. Don't you understand that?"

"Fee?" She frowned. "What fee?"

"The fee on the small print on your application. It states that there's a small administrative fee for processing the application."

"Your application was already processed."

"You took it and put it in the cabinet before I could ask my question. You yanked it out of my hand."

"I did no such thing!"

"Look, would you please just tell me what the fee is? If it's under ten dollars, then it's probably fine, but I just need to know it's not twenty-five, or thirty."

"There is no fee, sir."

"There is none? Then why is it on the paperwork? I recall clearly the paper says that if you sign it, you accept the fee."

"There's no fee on that paperwork, sir, I've seen it a thousand times."

"I know what I saw. Pull the file back out, I'll show you."

"Sir, I'm going to have to cancel your appointment if you don't go sit down right now."

The Many Tortures of Anthony Cardno

Anthony considered. He took a deep breath. He looked into the waiting room, where a bunch of angry people glared back at him.

The fee was probably nothing. Probably fifty cents. Probably a dollar. Maybe it was a glitch in the paperwork they ran off just to have information for their records. Maybe he'd hallucinated it, though he swore he'd seen it there. Maybe a million things this woman was making him doubt within himself. But most likely it was right there, always had been, and she was making him feel like a fool for simply trying to make sure they weren't going to waste each other's time. This made him indignant. It made him righteous in his fervor to find the truth. It made a man resigned turn bold.

So he didn't move an inch.

"Miss, I'd like to speak to your boss, right now."

"*Gary!*" The rest of the patients winced at the scream.

Gary came through the door with a worried look on his face and saw Anthony. "Oh, *you.*"

"He refuses to sit down."

"Cancel his appointment."

"I just did."

Gary turned to Anthony. "Buddy, you're going to have to leave now."

"I want to speak to your manager."

"The doctor is my manager, and he's busy with about ten patients right now."

"I had a question, that's all. A simple question."

"Leave now, or we're going to call security." Gary held up his hands, as if to apologize. "Not my call any more. You had your shot."

Anthony frowned. He put his hands on his hips. "Fine. I'll go. But I need my application back."

"Your what?"

"The piece of paper with my name and information on it. I don't want it processed. I won't pay a fee to this office." Anthony held out a hand. "Give it to me and I'm out of your life. I'll go away. I'll find another doctor and be grateful for it, because frankly, you people are rude."

Marsha rolled her eyes at him. The phone started ringing. She spoke over it. "I can't give you a file that's already been processed. That's part of the deal. That's why you sign at the bottom before you hand it over."

Gary stood beside him, inside the comfort bubble they'd spoken about at the office on retreats. That place you're supposed to stay out of.

Anthony pointed to Marsha. "She yanked the paperwork out of my hand. I didn't want to give it to her. It was non-consensual, and I want it back. I *won't* be charged a fee for this."

Gary put a hand on Anthony's arm, in the back, and held almost too tight for comfort. "You're disturbing people. It's time to go."

Anthony ripped his arm back. *"You get your damned hand off me."*

The waiting room sighed, a disapproving crowd. They chided him:

"Watch the language, pal!"

"Get out of here!"

Gary turned to Marsha. "Call security. I'll watch him."

"Please hold." Marsha hit a button on the phone, switching lines and started calling for hired muscle.

Anthony gritted his teeth and stood his ground.

Gary squared off in front of him, lifting fists. "You don't want to do this, man."

"I haven't done anything!"

"Just go!"

"I will *not* let you charge me for this! I want that piece of paper!" Anthony pointed to where she had put his file.

"It's not happening."

Marsha cupped the phone. "They're coming, asshole. You'd better get the hell out of here. They'll thump your skull for you."

Anthony, a man who had once politely apologized to the man who rammed his vehicle from behind, lost his patience. He walked past Gary. Gary put a hand on his chest. Anthony brushed it aside, leaned behind the desk, and reached. Gary grabbed him about the time he got his hands on the file.

"Let go of me."

"Get away from her."

"Let go of me! Now!"

Gary's grip tightened. It began to hurt more than it had before. Anthony's stomach flared. He took his free hand, his right hand, and swung it around in a full arc, more a reflex than an intent to harm. The fist took Gary square on the jaw and connected well, throwing him to the wall. Gary slumped, moaning.

Marsha screamed. The waiting room began to murmur louder. One of the men stood. A large man.

Anthony held the file up at the man. "They took this from me without my permission. There's a fee, and they won't tell me what it is. I've been accused of things I haven't done! This isn't what it seems!"

The man from the waiting room got between Anthony and the door. Anthony walked up to him. "Let me go. I'm leaving."

"You're not going anywhere, pal."

"Get out of here!" Marsha screamed.

The door opened. A large security guard stepped through next to the man from the waiting room and looked around. "Who?"

Everyone pointed to Anthony.

The security guard stepped toward him. "All right. Time to go."

"He stole a file." Marsha pointed to the file in Anthony's hand.

The security guard held out a hand.

Anthony held it away. "This is mine. Its has my name on it. You're not taking it. I'll leave, but this goes with me."

"Hand it over. Now. The police are on their way." The security guard stepped forward.

Anthony stepped back, five steps. "You're not getting it."

"Hand it over, pal. Don't make me come over there."

"This is mine. You're not taking it. I'm not moving. The police can come and talk to me about this. I'll have all your jobs. I'll talk to your manager's manager. This is awful. You are awful people. You're all terrible. This is a horrible place."

"When will we see the doctor?" The mother from before asked.

Anthony turned to face her with an incredulous look on his face. That's when the guard charged him. Anthony got a lucky turn on the charge. The guard slipped past him on the linoleum into Gary, who had stood to brace Anthony on the other side. Anthony whirled to flee, amazed to still be standing, only to find the man from the waiting room still standing in front of the door.

The man punched Anthony in the stomach, and something inside his belly went. Something he'd held onto for so long, so long. It had been tightened and bunched up on his insides, burning and burning. He went to these people for help, and instead they'd unleashed the very worst bile that had churned in his insides as he walked down the street every day watching children bully other children, men screaming in laundromats, drunks stumbling from bars. He'd bottled it all up, and here it had been unleashed. The green poison worked its way around his insides, spoiling his body. The pain grew sharp, and he realized, without having to be told by a man in a suit, that he was dying.

When he next realized anything, he was slumped against the desk at the front. Marsha was talking on the phone. Gary was escorting the angry mother

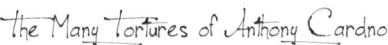
The Many Tortures of Anthony Cardno

in even though she'd arrived long after he had. The security guard stood with the police over him as they waited for the ambulance, but Anthony knew he wouldn't make it that long. He felt death coming, like a wash, like a cheetah closing on the herd, afraid like a man in a waiting room.

"What's your problem, pal?" The cop asked, bending in. "What's your stupid problem?"

Anthony smiled. He tried to talk. Then couldn't. Then could.

"I have a question."

Maybe he said it. Maybe he didn't. If he had, they might not even have heard him to begin with. It didn't matter. Anthony was dead.

The Many Tortures of Anthony Cardno

"Magical realism" is a term that gets tossed around with a bit too much ease when it comes to describing the work of authors from Latin America or of Latin American descent. Sabrina Vourvoulias' work is not always heavy on the magic, but even when it is her characters are about as real as you can get. By the end of this story, "I'm" a bit farther along in age than I am in real life ... which is both a blessing and a curse, as you'll see.

The Bar at the End of the World

SABRINA VOURVOULIAS

For a moment Anthony Cardno can't remember what country he's in.

It isn't his fault. Most of the countries in the Human Rights Watch unit he reports on are in upheaval, and nations in upheaval look alike. More, they feel alike.

The paper flags strung across the bar's ceiling rustle in a stray gust of wind. Bars in the tropics and semitropics are often like this—half outdoors even when you're sitting inside. The breeze kicks dust off the floor and catches it in the condensation on the bottle in front of him.

The foil label on the beer is how he remembers. Central America. The bigger of the two countries he's special rapporteur to. The one he loves, despite his better judgment.

Anthony doesn't always concur with stateside political prognostication, but there is no denying that most of the countries he frequents are balanced on the thinnest of edges. And edges are where atrocity lives.

This morning he had met with a woman he'd heard about back when he was last in the country, some two weeks ago. She was young, second year at the university, pretty in an indistinct way. Except for her skin. Torture with electrodes

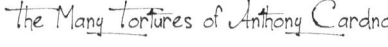

leaves keloids on certain skin types.

She hadn't been able to tell him much more than how and when she was grabbed and taken. Her mind had walled off the rest. A kindness really. Anthony can easily guess what has been done to her in the name of security, in the name of information gathering. He has dossiers full of different names, all subjected to the same ugly techniques. Some things transcend years, regimes and borders.

He sighs, looks around the humble bar with the strange name. Its cheap alcohol, generous baskets of plantain chips and the breathtakingly hot sauce to dip them in makes it the favorite of all his hangouts while he's in-country. Because it's damnably hard to find, the joint has mostly homegrown patrons with only a few astute expatriates sprinkled in. John Herit—the Associated Press stringer—is at the bar.

"Join you?" he says when he catches Anthony's eye.

Anthony nods, shoves the remains from the meal Corazón has deigned to make for him to the far side of the small table.

"Why aren't you out chasing the story?" he asks as the reporter sits in the chair opposite him.

"Everyone's clammed up since last night's press conference about the accident," John says, motioning to the bar for two more beers. "Have you heard anything new?"

"Nothing real," Anthony says. "We've been given a copy of the police report and requested copies of the autopsies, but you know we won't get those for another six months at least."

"You can autopsy burnt bodies?"

"They're not so burnt they couldn't i.d. them as Aura López and her kid," Anthony says significantly.

"That poor family," John says.

"Watch it, you'll be pegged as a sympathizer," Anthony says. He makes it sound like a joke. "Anyway, it's possible we'll be given the kid's autopsy, but we're not getting hers. They never give us anything official when it's an activist's body."

John shakes his head. "Crazy country."

"I've got some audio I can share with you, if you want," Anthony says. "Statements from a couple of years ago, after her husband disappeared."

"That's not going to get me a front page."

Anthony grins at him. He likes the reporter. Always has. Since their first meeting on the airport tarmac.

The Many Tortures of Anthony Cardno

Corazón walks over with two Gallos running with melting ice chips from the cooler chest. She's short and solid, dressed in a smock with a colorful print Anthony has only ever seen on vinyl tablecloths.

"Señor Antonio ¿está investigando lo de Aura?" she says as she hands the beers to them. She always overestimates Anthony's ease in switching back and forth between languages, and it takes a few moments for him to answer her question.

"Yes, I'm investigating the accident," he says. *Along with about 10,000 other equally suspicious incidents,* he thinks. But Corazón knows that part already and he doesn't need to say it.

"Yo lo llevo con quien le puede decir lo que pasó," she says, laying a hand briefly on his shoulder before going back behind the bar.

"What did she say?" John asks, irritation and curiosity battling for primacy on his face.

"She said, she'll take me to someone who can tell me what happened."

"You mean, she'll take *us,* tell *us,*" John says, with a cocky little smirk on his face

"It's useless for you to go," Anthony says. "I refuse to get bogged down in translating."

They argue it a bit, then settle into their beers. *Despite the language handicap, John's not a bad reporter,* Anthony thinks, *just out of his league.* The European news agencies rely on local stringers, and the big U.S. papers have veterans from foreign bureaus shuttling between the countries in play.

"How'd you get this gig anyway, Herit? I thought the AP had their Mexico City guy covering Central America."

John looks away, mumbles something.

"What? Speak up, man."

"I have a certain talent," he says more audibly, but still not loud.

"Like?"

"Like I *know* your friend there is going to lead you to something real," he says finally.

Anthony brings the beer bottle up to his mouth, studies John over its lip. Embarrassment has tattooed the reporter's cheeks with splotches of bright red.

"Well, okay," Anthony says, setting the now-empty beer bottle on the table.

"Okay, what?" John looks at him, eyes narrowed.

"I've got a talent too. And so does Corazón. Maybe between the three of us we can get somewhere on this. Come on, then." He shoves his chair back.

Without his having noticed her, the barkeep is already at his elbow, a garish plastic tote nested in the crook of her arm and a dark, woolen shawl wrapped around her head and shoulders.

John gapes. "She doesn't need that wrap in this heat," he says.

"Yes, she does." Anthony throws the words over his shoulder as he strides away. He keeps his eyes fixed ahead of him, but hears Corazón's footfall a few steps behind him, and then John's scramble out of the chair to catch up.

"Ya la," Anthony hears Corazón say half under her breath.

As in: "Now you've done it."

It makes Anthony smile. She's melodramatic. And fond of current lingo. Not what you'd expect from a legend, but both attributes help her pretense. And from what Anthony understands, she's never broken cover.

Not once in the hundreds of years she's lived under it.

❋

The person Corazón takes them to for help is dead.

Anthony sees John step back as the woman shoves aside a spiny shrub midway down the gulch they've been slipping and sliding through. The body is on its stomach, with arms grotesquely outstretched where they're caught on the inch-long thorns on the shrubby lower branches. The distance from the road is longer than what is to be believed from the specifics in the accident report, and for a moment Anthony wonders if the body was planted where they found it. But then, why hide it?

It's a man, thirty at most, and even before he's fully disentangled, Anthony knows who it is. This is his talent.

The man stands upright before him, hauntingly whole and mute next to the mangled corpse

"Jesus," John says, as he works his way closer and barges unseeingly through the vaporous apparition. "Did that happen in the crash or did some animals already get to it?"

The corpse has no face, just a mass of red, dripping shreds of tissue where his features once were.

Corazón, whose hands are still under the man's shoulders after turning him over, shoots the reporter a disgusted look.

"I'm betting he already looked like that when they put him in the car with Aura," Anthony says, "It would have had more impact that way."

The Many Tortures of Anthony Cardno

"It's her husband," he adds.

"Can't be," John says automatically. "He's been presumed dead for almost two years."

"Trust me on this, Herit."

The reporter stares at him, then looks away.

"There's no way you can prove it to anyone," John says after a moment. "He's unrecognizable. There are no full teeth left to be matched with dental records, and if you ask the government to DNA test anything, you know the results will come back identifying some poor Juan Doe caught in a drug deal gone bad. Or something equally unimaginative. Face it, nothing you give them is going to compel the truth."

"I don't plan on giving them anything," Anthony says.

"Ya, Señor Antonio," Corazón says. "Se hace tarde."

"It's getting late," Anthony translates, then turns to the woman.

Corazón takes her shawl off and then kneels on it beside the body. She sets the plastic tote down and rummages inside. After a minute she brings out a banana leaf, about three-feet long and eight-inches at its widest point. An old knife so often resharpened its blade is half the size it should be. A sack full of freshly mixed masa like she uses to make tortillas. A battered tin of lighter fluid. She gives this last to Anthony and motions for him to get going.

"Come," he says to John. "We need to gather some deadfall."

"What are we doing?" John says, stumbling after him. "I don't understand."

"You will."

When they've gathered several armfuls of wood, Anthony leads them back.

John starts over to Corazón, but Anthony motions him back. "We need to clear space for the fire. It's got to be decent size, and we're going to need to keep it going for a couple of hours at least."

"Jesus, if I didn't know better I'd say you were planning to cook him."

When Anthony doesn't answer, John drops his armful of logs. "I'm not doing this."

"We're not going to eat him, Herit."

Anthony can see the confusion in John's eyes. If the reporter really does have a talent hinged to the unseen, he's got to be feeling the weight of it folding in on him about now.

"Okay, but I'm not doing anything illegal," John says finally.

"Everything we're doing here is illegal," Anthony answers, "but that doesn't mean it's wrong."

The country is in its dry season, which means they won't need the lighter fluid to get the kindling-size pieces going. But they soak the larger pieces of wood in it, then clear a good three feet around the large mound they've stacked. They walk away without lighting it and rejoin Corazón.

"¿Listos?" she asks them.

Anthony nods. "Ready," he says for John's benefit.

Corazón puts her hands to the remaining tissue where the man's cheeks should be. She starts humming tunelessly. At first it grates the ear, but the longer you listen the more melodious it becomes.

It's a complicated piece of music. The tones coming from Corazón have the sound of a marimba—the plunking of wood slats and the breathiness that follows as the sound resonates and gets caught in empty gourds strung beneath—along with a wailing, reedy top note that raises hair on the back of Anthony's neck.

Brown-black things about the size and shape of cockroaches surface from inside the corpse and crawl onto Corazón hands. They don't stop there. They scuttle up her forearms and then her upper arms; up her neck to swarm on the skin of her face. Forehead, cheeks, chin—every part of the broad face—vibrates in time to Corazón's humming.

Then the humming shifts down a half-octave as she moves her hands to the corpse's shoulders. The dark things that emerge travel up her arms, under her smock and become visible again as they march down the exposed skin of her legs. She continues like this, humming at different pitches and placing her hands for a time on each part of the corpse, until every visible surface of her body is settled by the migrating, muddy shapes.

When she draws her hands back entirely, the humming turns to bass. She shifts off her knees, unsnaps the smock and drops it to the ground.

Every inch of her is covered by the small, dark vibrating marks. She moves to stand with arms extended, legs apart, a book laid open before them.

"Quick," Anthony says to John. "You have to read la Sin Nombre's tattoos like rebuses, like a story that can't be fully understood until you're done."

He steps up to Corazón, and after a few minutes is so deeply sunk in the narrative that he is only vaguely aware of John behind him, clicking, as if he were a giant beetle moving its mandibles and whirring its chitinous wings between the snaps.

Anthony reads the details none but the dead would know. The ways and hows and wheres of the years of detention and torture. The names and loose words heard on the last night, as they brought him out of captivity.

The Many Tortures of Anthony Cardno

How they took his eyes and peeled back his skin in front of his wife and child in the moments when the family was finally together again.

How they staged the crash. How all trace of him, of them, of every and all possible evidence against the powers that be, were incinerated in the accident.

Then, as in all printed matter, a correction. In Spanish it is called fe de errata—literally, faith in mistakes—and its the only kind of faith la Sin Nombre offers.

The final rebus Anthony reads has the dead man's body flying through crushed metal and breaking glass to find a resting place hidden from the eyes of his tormentors instead of burning in front of them.

"You changed the end of his story," Anthony says to Corazón. When she doesn't answer, he turns away from his reading and comes face to face with the apparition he had seen before.

"Alfonso," Anthony says.

That was the man's name, a name surely none had called him during the two years of torture and detention, because to use a name is an admission of shared humanity.

A small smile plays on the hazy face. There is a slight nod, an instant of motion really, and the spectral seeming is gone.

The clicking behind him stops. The humming stops. The silence is oppressive, overwhelming.

"Now what?" John's voice is strained to breaking when he finally speaks.

"Now, this," Anthony says.

Corazón walks over to the pile of things she's left by the body. She grabs the knife and quickly slices the banana leaf into squares. Then she pokes around whatever is still in her tote and comes up with a book of matches. She tosses it at Anthony.

He walks over to the stacked wood, strikes a match, lets it fall. The kindling catches immediately and the combustible-soaked wood beneath it not long after.

She brings the squares of banana leaf to the fire and holds them one by one over the flames so the oil comes to the surface and turns them pliable. The orange flames play on her skin, making her look as if she were made of lava and the tattoos bits of stone and earth caught in the flow.

When she's done, she returns to the corpse. She squats to cut a small piece of scalp with some few hairs and a bit of tissue still on it. Then she reaches into the sack of prepared masa and pats a handful to an oblong that enfolds the piece of human meat within. She wraps one of the banana leaf squares around it and

The Many Tortures of Anthony Cardno

secures it with a strip she tears off the end. Then she places the neat packet on the ground, and moves on.

She cuts away a piece of jaw with a broken sliver of tooth still attached—her old knife slicing through it as if it were no more resistant than butter—and repeats the process with the masa and wrapper. Next, a portion of skin with keloid scarring. Then a piece of bone with bits of marrow still clinging to it, and like that until there are some ten packets stacked at her feet.

They look like gifts wrapped in, with and around the things native to the land under their feet. The sight of them fills Anthony with a dreadful tenderness.

Corazón ducks to retrieve her smock and starts snapping it back on.

"Our turn," Anthony says, prodding John.

The reporter turns a dazed, uncomprehending gaze on him, but follows as Anthony approaches the body. Anthony empties the lighter fluid tin on it, then they carry the corpse to the fire and toss it on the flames. The smoke billows, dark and oily.

"Why not bury him?" John says. "He deserves something, I don't know ... caring, decent?"

"When Rights Watch publishes my report, the military will come back to their 'accident' scene to figure out how I know what I know," Anthony says. "I don't want to leave any material with which they might concoct a plausible alternate story."

"I get the DNA tested stateside," Anthony continues, "I use one of the fresh food shipping outfits to send the evidence through. A lot of immigrants up there ask their families to ship tamales to them, so customs sees a lot of them. They don't unwrap any, just put them through the x-ray machine. That's why Corazón cuts the flesh so small and adds the masa to it, so it looks right."

"Jesus," John says. "What a grisly piece of business."

"One piece of many," Anthony says.

"Vengan," Corazón motions for them to come to her. She's wrapped in her shawl again, and in the gloaming the half-hidden tattoos look like varicosities, or birthmarks, or the scars of some especially virulent torture enacted decades ago. When she sees them noticing, she gives them a wide smile. For a moment her teeth seem long and needle sharp, then as she turns her face, the firelight makes them normal again.

"Aquí tiene sus tamales de actualidad, Señor Antonio, y usted su artículo, Canche. Con eso basta por ahora," she says. She turns her back and walks away from them, back up the gulch.

 The Many Tortures of Anthony Cardno

"Are you going to translate for me?" John says after she's disappeared from their sight. "Or explain, even?"

"She said, 'Here you have your fact-filled tamales, Mister Anthony, and you your article, Blondie.' More or less." Anthony says as he starts up the hill.

John hurries to keep pace. "Those marks on her skin, they aren't permanent, are they?"

"Not even a creature from legend can bear that kind of story forever."

"What is she?" John says after a moment.

"A bar owner. A middle-aged woman with a hellacious recipe for salsa," Anthony says. "La Sin Nombre—the Nameless One."

"I thought Corazón was her name," John says.

"She's earned as many aliases as there are years. It's that way with monsters, Herit. You think you know them, but you don't."

"A monster who fights monsters," John says so quiet it's clear he doesn't want Anthony to hear, but he does.

"A monster who understands all about the kill but can't abide the twist they've given to what comes before," Anthony says. "Or—who knows?—maybe monsters have the same hope of redemption as humans do."

"You want to believe that," John says, quiet.

"Yes." The smile he gives the reporter is sad. "She's a loyal ally. The only one I have."

"Maybe not the only one," John says after a moment.

When they get to the road and start back toward the city, Anthony says, "By the way, those photos you took aren't going to come out."

"You heard the camera?" John gives him a sheepish grin.

"Yeah, Herit. I did."

"You know, the story's not going to do me much good without proof," the reporter says then.

Anthony laughs. "Look around you, man. Monsters. Ghosts of the disappeared. A government killing its own people. We're surrounded by stories without proof. If you stay, get used to it. Or even if you don't stay. Every country I've ever spent time in has a hidden history."

❂

Another cadaver of the disappeared shows up, and when Corazón's ghastly cook-out takes place, John is by Anthony's side again. Four times they throw the tortured remains in fire together; four times they read the language of oppression side by side. Anthony wonders how he ever bore the burden of the gruesome process alone.

And yet, if he looks into John's eyes—eyes that were once uncomplicated—Anthony sees the cost of constancy.

Walking home after dealing with the latest corpse, Anthony allows his arm to fall across John's shoulder.

The reporter turns to meet his eyes. "Do you know, that's the first time you've ever touched me?" he says. Seconds later, John's hand creeps up to where Anthony's rests. He covers Anthony's hand, makes sure it stays where it is.

The warmth works its way through to Anthony's shoulder. "You have no idea how unwise this is, Herit," he says, very quietly.

"I can guess," John says.

A few minutes later Anthony slips his hand from beneath John's. "I'm leaving."

They stop where they are, in the middle of the street.

"What?"

"I come and go," Anthony says. "You know that."

"But you're going for good this time, not just for a few weeks," John says.

"I didn't say that."

"I have a talent for knowing, remember?" John says.

Anthony doesn't answer, then starts walking again. When he doesn't hear the reporter matching his steps, he turns back to look, John is in the same spot. Frozen. Like an animal blinded by the light of what will eventually smear its guts on the asphalt.

❖

The streets outside are so choked with people, Anthony has a tough time finding his way to the bar. Then he's got to throw a few elbows to get in.

The counter is packed with reporters wearing credentials from the big name papers and a few from newspapers that have never before bothered to send anyone to this small neck of land. The end of decades of repressive military dictatorship is big news.

He finds an open seat at a table full of people he doesn't know, which isn't strange given the years he's been away. They're mostly expats, but a few are citizens back from exile in Europe or the United States, and he sees hope written on their faces as clear as if they were each la Sin Nombre.

She—Corazón—must be here somewhere, but Anthony doesn't see her. He feels a bit guilty at the relief that surges through him.

A cold bottle of Gallo beer is plunked down on the table before him.

"Jesus, you've gone totally white," John says, grinning at him. "Good thing the rest of you is fine."

"At least I've still got my hair," Anthony says.

John runs a hand over his shiny scalp. "Yeah, well, I'm not bald. I shave it."

"Sure, that's what everyone says."

John disappears for a moment, comes back with a chair. He turns it so the back faces front, then straddles it to sit.

"I was wondering if you'd come back for the inauguration," he says to Anthony.

"You never fully recover from your most destructive loves."

John shakes his head. "Kind of wish you were referring to me, not the country."

Anthony raises his eyebrows. John laughs.

One of the unfamiliar faces around the table interrupts them. "I'm sorry to eavesdrop on you, but it sounds like you both have spent some years here," she says. She's young, dark-haired, well-dressed and well-spoken.

John nods.

"What about you?" Anthony asks.

"I grew up here but left ten years ago," she says. "This is the first time I've been back. It's not as I remember it, though. At least, I don't ever remember this number of people out on the street, hanging out as if it was safe."

"It is safe," John says. "For now. Nobody knows what it means to have a civilian president. Or what he'll do. I think this is that moment when all of our collective breaths are drawn."

She turns to Anthony. "Do you think it'll hold?"

John laughs. "He's the wrong one to ask. You see that head of thick, perfectly white hair? This place gave it to him. And he loves it anyway. You can't trust the guy's judgment."

The girl smiles.

"Hey, if you really want to see something you never thought you'd see here, come with me," John says, extending his hand to her as he gets up.

She hesitates a moment, then puts her hand in his. "If this were back when I lived here, I wouldn't trust you," she says.

The Many Tortures of Anthony Cardno

"If this were back when you lived here, I wouldn't be offering," he says, grinning.

Anthony feels a pang of jealousy as he watches them wind their way through the bar and out the door. He wants a new, fresh memory of this place, too.

A hand falls on his shoulder. He looks up at Corazón's well-remembered features.

"Seems a whole lot of people have finally found your bar at the end of the world," he says in Spanish. He's kept up with the language though he speaks French a lot more frequently these days.

She smiles. "Señor Antonio, it doesn't do to underestimate how fickle people are. Last night they were all drinking at the bar at the Camino Real, and tomorrow it'll be the Omni."

"And what about the rest? The changes? Are those fickle too?" he asks.

"There will always be monsters, you know that."

Anthony looks down, takes a swig from his forgotten beer. "Almost every beer I drink is better quality than this one, and yet this is the one I think of when I think of beer."

She drops her hand on the one Anthony has on the bottle. "Señor Antonio, this place isn't safe for you anymore."

It startles him into a laugh. "Herit seems to think it's okay."

"He wants you to stay; he'll say anything," she says, then fits her hand to his and yanks him to standing. "Follow me."

She takes the same route out of the bar as John and the girl took. She pulls him straight through the crowded streets until he isn't surrounded by bodies, and then she lets go of him.

He's in the plaza in front of the National Palace. The broadcast vans are parked at the edges, amid a swarming throng of news cameras and onlookers. But the plaza is still. Row after row of people stand, mute, facing the grand colonial structure. They hold placards with photos and the words "Alive they were taken, alive we want them returned." But Anthony can see that every one of them has a ghostly version of their disappeared standing alongside them.

"Stay, and your heart breaks," Corazón's words brush against his ear. "You understood that once."

"Go, and my heart dies," he answers. "Which do you think is preferable?"

She steps back, shakes her head. "I've lived more years than I remember, but I haven't had many friends. Don't make me regret that you've been one of them."

The Many Tortures of Anthony Cardno

She walks away and disappears into the crowd. He's tempted to follow her back to the bar—that familiar, never-changing place—but he doesn't. Instead he walks streets that are the same as he remembers only so different he can't recognize them.

He gets lost twice, then ends up at the bar at the Camino Real, which is as empty as Corazón's bar was full.

"Have you ever heard of la Sin Nombre?" he asks the bartender who sets a bottle of Harp before him. Gallo's too plebeian for this establishment.

The man's face scrunches, then he gives a nod.

"What do you think she does to her victims?" Anthony asks.

"All of those legends of monsters, they've got more terrible choices and regrets than blood in them, don't they?" the bartender says after a moment.

"You ever heard of any of the monsters having friends?"

The man shakes his head, moves quickly away as a new customer steps up.

Hours later, John shows up. "Jesus, you're trashed," he says instead of hello.

"I'm not. And anyway, it wouldn't matter if I were," Anthony says. "This is the hotel I'm staying at."

"Well, come on then. Let's get you to your room," John says, guiding him off the bar stool.

"I'm not done here," Anthony says.

"Oh, you are *so* done here."

Anthony stops, squints suspiciously at John. "Did Corazón send you with that message?"

"Nah, man, the old bat's got so many people at the bar she doesn't have time to spare you a thought," John says, propelling Anthony down the hall toward the elevators. "Not that I pay attention to what she says, even when she does have time."

"You should," Anthony says. "Monsters know things."

John laughs. "God, you're in worse shape than I thought."

When they get to the hotel room, Anthony leans his forehead against the doorjamb as John fiddles with the key card.

"Don't you remember any of it, Herit?" Anthony says. He hears John swear, then the sound of him trying the key card again.

"No, of course not," Anthony says. "That's how you've stayed sane. You only ever saw it that handful of times. I went through it—how many times?— triple digits for sure, maybe even quadruple."

"Aha! Got it," John says as he opens the door. "All right then, in you go."

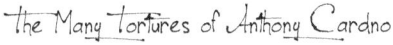

The Many Tortures of Anthony Cardno

Anthony follows him inside, then he goes to the window and pulls the curtain open. "This place isn't very pretty, seen from here," he says. "Ugly, really. Still, I've loved it. What a waste."

"I'll say," John says.

Anthony turns around. "Where'd you leave the girl?"

John shrugs the mention away. "Partying with her friends. Seeing all of this through rose- and nostalgia-tinted glasses."

"And you? What glasses are you seeing it through?"

"Yours, it seems," John answers.

Anthony drops his eyes. "Corazón tells me I'm no longer safe here."

"And you believe her."

"Do you *really* not remember what she is?" Anthony says.

"Of course I do," John says. "But as I recall, the marks on her skin are all about the past, not the future."

"That's the thing, Herit. When you get old enough you realize the past *is* the future."

"Jesus, cut the horseshit, would you?" John says. Then, only marginally less annoyed, "Do you think sometime before I die you might call me by something other than my surname?"

"I didn't realize it bothered you," Anthony says after a moment.

"Yeah, well, you don't realize a lot of things," John says. He turns around, stalks toward the door. "So, in this mood you're in, can I trust you not to do something stupid after I leave?"

"John," Anthony says. "Wait ...."

John turns around. Two spots of color flame on his cheeks. "Fifty-seven," he says. "I've read fifty-seven tales of horror off la Sin Nombre's skin. My bureau chief thinks I'm a fucking investigative genius."

Three steps. Anthony can't remember if he takes them or John does, but then they're in each other's arms and kissing and it is as if it is the only real thing they've ever known.

●

The taxi driver has never heard of the bar and Anthony has to dig deep to remember how to get there. He wonders what that means. Like maybe the years have started taking his best memories.

When he walks in it's empty, no one on either side of the counter. He sits at a table and hooks his cane on the back of one of the spare chairs. He doesn't keep track of hours, but he knows it's a long time before a girl comes out from the back room and sees him sitting there.

She ties on a half apron and grabs a pen and order pad as she comes over.

She's got a long, horsey face which is made even more equine by the large, silver hoops jutting out of the piercings at the corners of her mouth. As if she were actually wearing a bit. Her hair—a glorious ripe chestnut color and very long—keeps sliding over her face. She looks to be about 18.

"You want something?" she asks. In English. *So the clientele of the bar must have changed*, Anthony thinks.

"I do want something," Anthony answers, "but it looks like I won't find it here anymore."

She studies his face, then her eyes dart to the cane and back again.

She shoves the pen behind her ear and sticks out her hand. "I'm Sig," she says. "The owner of the bar. Sorry about before, I didn't recognize you."

Anthony shakes her hand. "I'm Anthony, and I'm quite sure you don't know me."

Even her laugh is horsey. "Okay. If you say so."

"I was hoping to see Corazón," he says. "She hasn't ... umm ... died, has she?"

She gives him a startled look. "No. Of course not. She's around. Probably at one of her bonfires. I'm thinking you probably know where to find her."

He inclines his head at his cane. "These days I'd have a hard time reaching her. You wouldn't have a way to get a message to her, would you?"

"Are you kidding me?" she asks. She sounds outraged, but then something softens in her face. "Oh man. You're not faking, are you? Okay, I'll send someone to fetch her. Meantime, why don't you let me get you something to drink?"

"Whatever you have," he says, a bit disconcerted by her strange attitude.

She comes back a few minutes later with a Gallo in one hand and balancing a basket of chips and a bowl with bright yellow salsa in the other. It's a different color than Corazón's salsa had been, so Anthony doesn't expect it to taste the same. But the first bite floods him with memories.

"Tastes exactly as I remember," he says to the girl's retreating back.

"Sure," she answers without turning around. "We all put the same spice in it."

"What's that?"

"Regret," she says, then disappears to the back and he doesn't see her again.

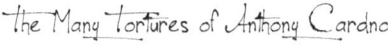

The Many Tortures of Anthony Cardno

93

He's two-thirds through the beer when Corazón appears. She looks exactly the same, down to the vibrant print smock.

"Qué bueno verlo," she says.

It sounds genuine to Anthony, this expression of how good it is to see him, and it makes him feel guilty at his purpose in seeking her out. A quick flash of John's face sets him back on course.

"I need your help," he says, motioning for her to sit.

"Help? That's not what I'm known for, Señor Antonio," she says as she sits.

"Nevertheless, that's what you did, all those long years ago."

She turns away from him, sweeps her eyes over the empty bar. "I liked the bar. The constant influx of new people. The regulars you got to know, sometimes better than they knew themselves."

When she looks back at him, her eyes are very dark and her expression keen. "Why haven't you brought el Canche with you, Señor Antonio?"

"John died," Anthony says. The words stick in his throat, as they always do.

"Here?" she asks.

He nods. "This is where he wanted to be. In the end I think he loved this land as I do."

"Silly," she says. "So human."

"The thing is, he didn't have anyone but me," Anthony finds he has to clear his throat before going on. "And I don't have anyone either. When I'm gone it'll all disappear. As if it didn't happen. But you could wear it on your skin. The whole of our story."

She looks as if she's weighing what he's said. "The stories I tell are about violent deaths. No one's going to lift a hand against you. The human monsters who stalk the street these days kill mostly women and girls."

"What about the inhuman monsters?"

"You are my friend, Señor Antonio," she says automatically.

"That's why I'm asking you to do it."

"All right," she says at long last.

"And you'll bear the tattoos on your skin long enough so another can read the story?"

She nods.

"When?" he asks.

She grabs his wrist in a vise grip before he even sees her arm leave the table. "You don't get to know that, Señor Antonio," she says. "You see how it is? Not time, not place, not which kind of death will come for you—like any human

The Many Tortures of Anthony Cardno

being. You see what you've asked of me?" When she lets go the indentations from her fingers stay on his skin for a long time.

"This has gone on long enough," she says after while, as if she's speaking to herself.

"What do you mean?"

She gives him a sidelong look. "What do you think of the new bar owner?"

"Weird. Like most of her generation. I've never understood what compels them to put so many holes in their faces."

"She probably won't be here long," Corazón says. "Many are crossing the border these days. Matter of fact, I'm thinking of going myself. None of us gets listed on the customs declarations or packed in the luggage, of course, but we go anyway. Wherever a person steps, a monster follows. And some of the people we follow ... well, we can't do without them, no matter how hard we try."

She leans over, covers his hand with hers. "We live for that moment when both we and they realize it, you remember? The look of recognition followed by utter fear and utter love?"

When she notices the expression on Anthony's face, she laughs. "Oh, Señor Antonio, don't look so stunned. You have crossed borders more times than any of us, but it is only this one that ever mattered—isn't that so?"

"What are you saying?" he says.

"I'm saying Herit understood."

"John's and mine is a story about love and shared life purpose." He's agitated now, close to hyperventilating. "And the shuttling back and forth of two very human lives woven together. Your tattoos cannot say elsewise, you understand?"

She doesn't answer.

Anthony doesn't know what pity looks like on her face, but he think that's what is on it when she leaves.

❋

Is it faith that announces itself with sound? Or is it our mistakes, resonating without cease?

He hears something when he leaves the bar: wood torn by flame and the hiss that escapes a body as it catches fire. But maybe it's memory he's hearing.

Headed back on the empty familiar street, cold fingers of air reach to caress him. The wind hums. He stops where he is, in middle of the roadway. The gust rushes past him, then it stops. He can feel its regard while he stands still, as if he had been pinned to the road by a vehicle.

It takes him forever to get back. Around him, he hears the noise of revelry and late night celebration. But these aren't the noises he's listening for. He's listening for what hunts him. For the footfall of the one he's always known would be his demise. For his friend.

In his hotel room at last, his heart beats wild with the exertion. And, yes, there is some panic in the breaths that reverberate in the big, empty room. He sinks to the edge of the bed.

"Are you here?" he says.

The silence stretches on.

"I'm ready," he says to the emptiness. "Truly I am."

Then he adds, "I don't ask for pity, and I don't regret the bargain made. But if I can ask a favor, let me see your face before it is done."

There is an indrawn breath, not his.

He feels his knees turn to water, but struggles to his feet anyway. He takes a step toward the sound. Then another. And another.

The light leaking through the window's open curtains outlines the familiar profile. He reaches, lets his finger touch the mouth. He remembers exactly what hides behind those lips.

Love and terror, both utterly without temper of reason, flood him.

"I've read the end written on skin so many times I've forgotten the count," he says to the figure poised before him. "And it is always the same."

He makes no other sound.

Not when the teeth punch through his skin and claws pin him. Not when the blood flows red and so very human. Not when he draws his last, sobbing breath.

❋

Fe de errata, faith in mistakes:

"I've read it on skin so many times I've forgotten the count," he says to the figure poised before him. "And yet I've never gotten to the end."

He doesn't know what to call the sound he makes as Anthony takes a step out of shadow to move toward him. A whimper maybe. Or something else that includes welcome.

"John," Anthony says as he runs a monstrously clawed hand tenderly down

The Many Tortures of Anthony Cardno

Herit's cheek. "Love of my life."

John makes no other sound.

Not when Anthony's lips are on his and desire pins him. Not when the memories flow, shared and so much more than human. Not when one sobbing breath leads to another and takes them where they both want to go.

Michelle Moklebust, another childhood friend, has been obsessed with vampires and Atlantis for as long as I can remember. Even our Arthurian fan-fic concept tied to Atlantis and featured vampires. Atlantis doesn't make an explicit appearance in this story, the third in her self-published short story series "The Chosen," but vampires certainly do, along with her most recent obsession: zombies. As with Eric Bauman's story, Michelle proves that old friends really do know how to nail you: no one else in this collection has made a character point of my horrible posture. Michelle's keeping it real ... or as real as she can in a world post-supernatural-apocalypse.

With a Flick of the Wrist

MICHELLE MOKLEBUST

HOPE

Zombies swarm through the bunker we all moved into nearly two years ago to avoid the walking dead, filling it with their stench and inhuman groans. We fight back, but there's so many of them. D, Dimitri, our undead unofficial leader, didn't want me to use my gun, but it's the quickest and the most direct way to make sure the revenants stay dead.

I remember a time when my stake was the only weapon I needed, but now's not the time to get all nostalgic.

Focus, I remind myself as I squeeze off another shot.

Despite all the discoveries they made, all the funky potions the scientists whipped up, no one has invented time travel yet. If they had, things sure as hell would have been easier these past few years. Instead the scientists focused on things like enhancing the already enhanced-by-birthright Chosen, the ones born to fight all the scary things that come out at night. They're responsible for the mess we're in. They brought Armageddon down on Southern California by way of Barrel Springs, a small town northeast of L.A. on the edge of the Mojave

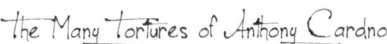
The Many Tortures of Anthony Cardno

Desert. Some nutjob scientist got a bug up his ass and vaporized the potion they used to reanimate Chosen like me. But he never got the containment system right. Unfortunately, the stuff used to bring us back from the dead turned the general public into mindless, brain-eating, shuffling, groaning monsters. And now we have to clean up the mess.

Trapped in the middle of a ring of six of them, I swing the sword in wide arcs and kick when that doesn't work, trying to take their heads off but succeeding only in knocking them back. I raise my sidearm and fire, throw an elbow when I have to. The muzzle of my gun smokes, and all around me, heads bounce off the floor when Bas, also Chosen but not reanimated—nothing's managed to kill him—or someone else decapitates one of them.

The room is filled with battling bodies and swirling dust. The report of gunfire is deafening and their odor stings my eyes, makes me tear up. Mariah's little cry is abruptly cut off. She used to fight right alongside us, but since she lost her marbles, it's all about protecting our best scientific mind with the hope that one day she'll stop playing dollies long enough to reverse the effects the vaporized formula had on the general population. In my peripheral vision, I glimpse Peter scooping Mariah into his arms. He and Davis, our wandering seer, run for the tunnels that lead away from here. Hopefully, there will be some kind of barrier— maybe a blast door, wishful thinking—we can lower to trap the walking dead inside. Most likely, once we take off, they'll decide to go back to the surface. None of them can stand being in confined places for too long; neither can I.

I slice one that's reaching for me across his neck. His two body parts separate and fall to the floor with dull thuds. I don't think this one will manage to reattach its head, so I don't bother with any fancy brain stabbing since I really need to get gone. My arms feel like they're going to fall off, and I'd rather not leave that delectable snack behind, so I shove the sword into its scabbard and jam the gun into my waistband, freeing up my hands in case a little hand-to-hand becomes necessary. I remind myself there's nothing wrong with running when things go badly. It gives us a chance to regroup and come back stronger. I slip through the doorway, leaving the moans, groans, and stink behind.

This tunnel is darker than the one we used earlier, if that's possible. I'm wound tight, ready to strike at anything that gets in my way, doesn't matter if it's friend or foe. When my muscles feel like they're going to snap like a rubber band that's been stretched too far, anything becomes a trigger. And very little calms me down or expends the energy. Except a fight. Or a tumble, but none of the guys are candidates for that. I don't mix business and pleasure.

My feet carry me deeper into the passageway until I am alone. We didn't exactly have time to discuss where to meet up, but I assume it's the safe house on the edge of town, closer to the Air Force base. Allegedly, there are tunnels that run from the base to Nevada, maybe Area 51. That's where the few remaining government officials have gathered to ride out the end of the nation. I don't know how they will react to D and Peter—the feds and soldiers are twitchy when it comes to vamps—but I'm hopeful they won't kill Bas and me on sight. After all, we're still quasi-active duty. If they don't, since we're a package deal, they'll have to accept our fanged friends. Of course, all this depends on the mythical tunnels actually existing and hinges on whether, if they do, they're passable. With our luck, we'll have to hotwire a car and drive. But it would be so worth it. At this point, any place free of zombies sounds good to me. To live above ground, be able to shower, maybe meet some new hot dude who feels the same about commitment as I do ...

Suddenly, my thoughts are too loud and the underground labyrinth too silent. Slowing to a walk, I keep my eyes and ears—and that sixth sense I have for the monsters—wide open. I'm not dumb enough to think that no one else has ever hidden out down here beneath the streets. Vigilance is my middle name.

Some far-away door slams behind me, and I stop moving. Stop breathing. Stop thinking. The place where I stand is so narrow, I don't think Bas and his wide shoulders could fit through here. Have I taken a wrong turn? Is this corridor going to shrink the further into its belly I tread and eat me? Or maybe I've stumbled down the rabbit hole.

Get a grip, I tell myself. *Keep moving. One foot in front of the other.* I repeat the phrase like a mantra.

DIMITRI

Peter, Davis, and Mariah arrive at the safe house before us. They barricade themselves in after busting a few zombies wide open en route. Most of the walking dead were concentrating on the bunker; the two men eliminated the ones that attacked quickly. It's good to have Peter back in fighting form, no matter the how. I'll contemplate the repercussions later. I step over a zombie sprawled in the dirt, its brains leaking out of the hole in its skull.

I glance between Bas, sand and grime settling in his hair and coating his face, and the former church. It used to be that vampires couldn't set foot in a

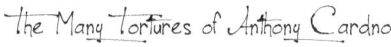

House of God, but that changed when the people fled. With the structure abandoned, and no one to fill the many pews on Sunday—no fervent faith re-energizing the sanctity on a regular basis—the energy of the place has changed. I remember sitting outside, listening to the hymns and music wafting on the evening air in the summer. I've always loved church music. Too bad, now that I can enter, no one can play the pipe organ.

We sprint toward the carved oaken doors. Either side of the entrance is decorated with stained glass scenes of saints and angels. The heavy wood flies open, and a human shape moves swiftly across the dormant lawn to meet us, stake in hand. The door slams behind him and I hear it being secured, the snick of the lock cutting through the silence like a gunshot. The lithe figure moves too smoothly to be a zombie: it's got to be Peter. He's been denied the ability to fight for so long, and he's eager for it. He runs at Bas first. The soldier turns and captures the wrist holding the stake. The momentum of Peter's attack carries the vampire forward a few inches and the sharp wooden point grazes Bas' cheek, carving a vertical line in his otherwise unmarred face.

I smell the blood the minute it starts rising in the furrow and my instinct is to seize the boy and partake of the sanguine elixir my body craves. We're all hungry; living blood, at this point, is a delicacy, but none of our companions with heartbeats is an appropriate donor. My fangs drop. Bas shoves Peter back and whirls to face me, longstaff raised to strike if necessary. A solid shove sends me sprawling in the dirt. Laying on my back, I watch as the sharpened tip of the weapon hovers above my heart. "Don't even think about it, Nightcrawler. I will take you out so fast ... And you know you'll let me." I nod in understanding, transmitting that I'm okay now, that it was just a momentary lapse. Scrutinizing my face, he considers this then offers me a hand up. He turns back to the vampire sprawled in the dirt. "You okay Petey?"

"I'm fine. I've got more self-control in my pinkie than that dolt has in his entire body." He gestures in my direction as he pauses. "Years of practice." He sounds slightly resentful of his former situation, although I daresay it just saved Bas' life.

"Hope here yet?" Bas asks.

Peter shakes his head. "What do you say we move this inside? No telling who will show up out here. Don't fancy being here when they do."

An hour and several blood bags later, Bas and I go back out to patrol and hunt for Hope. She isn't prone to getting lost, and I know she knew where to meet if we got separated. Bas and I are performing a sweep when a demon pops

The Many Tortures of Anthony Cardno

up. Of course, Bas senses it right before it rushes from the cover of a pile of rubble that used to be the bank. The demon is humanoid but its skin looks like the Minotaur and a hippo had a baby. I don't bother to identify the misshapen creatures by name anymore, except to review what will kill them.

Bas is fast to react. He grabs one of his many modified weapons and aims. The creature pounces, knocking the gun from the soldier's grasp and sucker punching him simultaneously. Bas falls into me, and we collapse to the cracked and rust-stained pavement. The weight of Bas disappears. Shaking my head, I bounce to my feet. Someone is here, waiting to move in. I can sense them, which means that it must be some kind of vampire.

"Hold!" a man's voice calls. The creature, which has hoisted Bas overhead, sets him down and steps back.

"Stupid move," Bas says, pulling the silver sword from the sheath on his back.

I lay a restraining hand on his arm, and he glares. He doesn't like being interrupted when he's working. He shrugs my fingers from his limb and adjusts his grip on the leather-wrapped hilt. I may have been his Handler once upon a time, but that was many years ago and he has long since stopped needing my guidance.

A woman with flowing blond hair follows the man from their hiding spot. "You are the ones who still call this little slice of Hell home, non?"

I recover from the shock of her appearance first. "Who wants to know?" From the corner of my eye, I see Bas straighten, tipping the sword point down.

"Marie. And you are?" Light colored eyes watch me expectantly.

When I don't offer a response, her thick-skinned pet advances on Bas, seizing him in a blur. The boy's breathing falters as the beast tightens its grasp, crushing his throat. With unexpected speed, Bas whips the sword point up, severing the creature's arm somewhere below the elbow, releasing its hold on his neck. The demon howls and clutches at the stump. Its blood sizzles against the barren earth.

An impeccably dressed male advances, leaning heavily on the cane I suspect is as much a weapon as decorative, trying to fool us into believing he is a vampire although it is clear from the pink undertones of his cheeks that he is most likely not. I suppose he could be the woman's personal drinking fountain. "Please, we wish no one any harm. Anthony and I have come here seeking asylum," the woman says in a lilting French accent. "The zombies have broken through the Los Angeles defenses and destroyed our settlement. We learned of your exis-

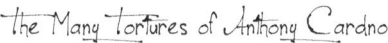

tence from one called Davis and have come to negotiate with the master of this region." It sounds plausible, but I shoot Bas a look telling him to keep his guard up. And if Davis wasn't in thrall when he gave us up, I will kill him.

I step forward, arresting their focus from Bas, and neatly avoid being smacked in the chin with the sword's grip in the process. "I am Dimitri, the de facto master of this valley." I can feel Bas behind me rolling his eyes. "Sadly, we cannot help." *As if I would,* I add silently, hiding my thoughts behind a friendly smile. "We have barely enough to sustain ourselves. The zombies have overrun this place, and it is not safe to venture into the residential areas any time of day."

Marie locks eyes with me, and I feel the power swirling from her, looking for a target, trying to burrow its way into my skull. The shuffling sound of shoes being dragged on concrete reaches my ears. Bas whips his head in the appropriate direction; his enhanced senses probably sift through a million things at once as he tries to identify the source of the sound. "Sounds like Lefty," he tells me, completely ignoring the others.

Hope appears at the edge of the gutted building behind him, her face drawn and pale. She is gulping air like she's just resurfaced after being stuck under water for hours. One moment she's bent over, huffing and puffing, the next she is straightening, her eyes wary, hands held loosely at her sides in case she has to fight. No matter how tired Hope is, the girl is first and foremost a hunter and her training—second nature after all this time—always kicks in. "Who are they?" She gestures at the newcomers with her chin, keeping the rest of her exterior cool.

The man steps forward first. It's no accident that he maneuvers his bulk so that Marie is completely shielded from Hope's dark eyes. The man is in his fifties at the least, as the graying hair at his temples attests. His shoulders are slightly stooped, but that could be an affectation designed to make him look harmless. He reaches out, engulfing Hope's hands with his. "Anthony Cardno."

Her eyes widen at the contact but she quickly arranges her features into the calm mask she habitually wears. I doubt the pair noticed. "Yeah. Nice to meet you." Hope snatches her hands back and rubs them on her jeans as if she's trying to clean them. "What do you want?"

Marie steps forward, smiling broadly. "You are a hunter." Her crystal gaze skips over to Bas. "As are you." She sounds almost gleeful. Obviously delighted by her discovery, she clasps Anthony's hand. "You see? I told you there were people here who could help us."

Hope rests her hand on the blunt end of one of the stakes jammed into the

The Many Tortures of Anthony Cardno

bandolier. "You're kidding me, right?" She gives a dubious laugh. "Us, help you? No frickin' way."

Marie appears genuinely confused. "Why not? You live with these two. You help them."

"Yeah, well, that's different." She turns those dark orbs on me. "Can I kill her now?"

Anthony steps forward, his hand raised before him. An evening when the breeze doesn't blow through Barrel Springs is a rare event, but now the wind kicks up, picking up and swirling the dirt and detritus that haven't yet been blown away. Once more, Hope freezes. Her voice fades. Eyes bugging out of her face, she throws me a panicked look. My eyes dart between them, assessing the situation. Hope's eyes don't pop out of her head under any circumstances. Power weaves around my frame, seeking entry. Marie's companion is more than he seems. Peter appears in the doorway.

The demon shrinks back, away from the dirt devil. A Russian thistle skitters down the sidewalk, its bare limbs scratching the gray cement like rat's claws.

Bas positions himself next to Hope, seemingly unaffected by the man's display. Peter positions himself behind him in a show of solidarity. We share a look, and I think that perhaps it would be prudent to befriend these two, at least long enough to learn what they know as well as discover the man's capabilities and their limits. Then, after we've moved beyond the getting-to-know-you phase, we can bury the man and scatter her dust.

Marie looks over at Anthony. "Enough, Anton. We mustn't offend our hosts."

Hope falls forward on her hands. Recovering quickly, she paws at her neck while kneeling and clears her throat several times in succession. "Dude! What the hell!? You Darth Vader or something?"

"Or something," Anthony says smugly before turning his adoring gaze on his mistress.

Groans and moans arise behind us as the undead army resumes its monotonous cadence as they approach our position. Hope's panicked glance sets my senses on high alert. "You know, it's been lovely," she wrinkles her nose as she addresses Marie. "Really. But right now, we got to go." Without seeking confirmation from me, she turns on her heels and heads inside. Davis greets Hope at the door, a loaded bow raised and trained on Marie. He ducks inside to let Hope pass.

"You understand why we can't invite you in," Peter offers before disappearing in a burst of vamp speed.

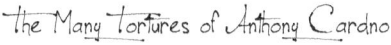

The pair looks forlorn, like we've abandoned them. Of course, with a demon bodyguard and a human who can subvert a hunter's will, they really have nothing to fear from the shuffling masses heading our way. Still, something inside me tells me it would be unwise to alienate them. Especially before we discover what's landed on our doorstep. I move toward the pair with caution, feeling Bas' rising tension as he gauges the magnitude of the impending zombie influx. "I can't stress how much we don't have time for this," he tells me as I cross before him. His gun sits in his waistband, and he's raised his wrist-mounted crossbow, sighting down his arm.

Ignoring him, I set myself before Marie. "It gets bad here at night. I have no idea how your," I inspect the leathery demon's hide, "pet will fare against the walking dead." The towering, misshapen figure remains motionless. "But you and your companion are welcome to wait them out over there." I indicate a small house at the rear of the church property. I think the pastor once lived there with his family, but don't mention it. If the dwelling is still consecrated, I don't know. Nor do I care.

I can tell by the sparkle in her azure eyes that she knows the church building no longer presents a threat to our kind. Her delicate mouth turns down briefly when she considers my offer. "Might we share a meal first? The boy there smells divine."

Cued by her words, a bolt flies by her head, grazing her curls. "I'm not on the menu," Bas informs her tersely. The demon bellows and strides toward him.

A gesture from Anthony halts the beast in its tracks. "So I see." Marie offers a polite smile. "My apologies." She closes her eyes and inhales, stretching the tight bodice of her dress to its limit. "Ah, there is another. Not the dark-haired shrew. Someone else." Her eyes pop open and she gazes at the doorway beyond our shoulders. "Come here my dear."

"That's it." Bas charges the demon first, his sword out and ready. The dumb creature doesn't seem to think for itself as it makes no move to protect its neck from Bas' blade. The metal slices into the thick skin effortlessly. Bas has to use two hands to continue through the thing's spinal cord, but the monster's head bounces on the ground once before erupting in flames. The headless body falls and ignites. Marie and Anthony jump back, no longer playing at being civilized beings. Marie charges Bas, who sidesteps her attack easily. The she-vamp spits and hisses like a mountain cat. She's sloppy for a vampire of such advanced age. Anthony moves in their direction, but I intercept him. Whatever magic this man is capable of is not welcome here.

The Many Tortures of Anthony Cardno

Leveling my gaze, I look into his faded blue eyes. "Walk away. Leave my town." Exerting my will, I await confirmation that he will comply, which comes in the form of a nod. "Good." A whisper of answering power dances over my skin. He doesn't need to be enslaved to a creature like her. He has power all his own, although it only seems to affect Hope and possibly the demon the pair travels with. I'm not certain letting him go is the most advisable course, but we can barely feed the mouths we have.

The pair behind me continues trading blows. Spinning, still grasping the woman by a shoulder, Bas delivers a vicious punch to her upper torso. Limbs flail, feet fly, and fists collide with flesh. Bas has abandoned his weapons and is beating on her with raw knuckles. Blood streams from near his ear, where her dagger-like nails tore his skin. Her eyes are swelling and it occurs to me that she has never had to fight for a scrap in her life, never mind having actually ever faced one of the Chosen who is protecting the person he cherishes most. A turning roundhouse doubles the vampiress over, and a back kick finishes her off.

Marie falls, tearing the skirt of her dress. *Why would anyone travel in something so impractical?* I wonder. Shaking my head, I clear the errant thought. Near the edge of the cemetery adjacent to the church, a lone zombie appears. I whip Anthony around to face the creature. "You see that? That's a scout. The rest of the horde will descend upon us momentarily, so I suggest you and your girlfriend get moving." He nods in understanding.

Bas lifts his eyes from the unconscious punching bag at his feet. "You coming?" he calls. Kicking the downed vampire in the ribs one more time, he turns and runs for the church. I can't blame him. We're all tired. Hungry. Certainly not in any condition to take on a zombie army for the second time in twenty-four hours.

Without the slightest regret, I release Anthony and sprint to join my family. Let the newcomers fare however they will.

HOPE

The two morons stand there, gaping at the zombies. Like they've never seen one before. And maybe they haven't, but I'm not buying. No one makes it out of L.A. without either some serious help or fighting their way through a swarm of the gray beings at every turn, or both. Not lately.

My insides hum, and my muscles twitch. The thought of putting those

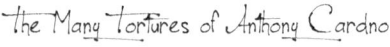

things out of commission has me nearly salivating. Scrubbing my itching palms down my thighs, I try to rub away the impulse—need—to go out there and bash some skulls.

D hovers behind me, totally in tune with my thoughts. He knows me too well. He accused me of being suicidal once, after a lapse in judgment on the battlefield nearly killed us all. Since then, if we're together when the brain eaters come out, he plays babysitter. I wish he'd just let me go out there and do what I'm meant to, and to hell with the consequences. I've had a good run. If I die and take a few of these things with me, then it's a good day.

But he doesn't see it that way. "I'll take that," he says, gesturing to my bandolier of stakes. "And that." He wiggles his fingers, indicating the weapons belt in which my gun and all the extra monster-killing ammo resides. "You can keep the sword." Big of him.

"I'll take first watch," I offer, not taking my eyes from the creatures gathering in our front yard.

"Yeah. I don't think so. You need sleep." He climbs the narrow stairs leading to the belfry, where he can watch the action unfold unobserved.

I fall into step alongside him. It's a tight fit, so we brush shoulders. He arches a dark eyebrow, glancing at me from the corner or his eye. "Come on. You know I'm too wired to sleep." He nods. "I promise to be a good girl, okay?" A thought occurs to me, and I lightly lay my fingertips on his thick forearm. "Can I bring the bow up?"

He gives me that placating expression I remember my dad shooting my way whenever I got all determined and obstinate when I was a kid. Now it rolls off my back, and I run downstairs to gather my second favorite long-distance weapon, the first being pretty much any gun.

By the time I charge upstairs and settle in to my post, there's an army of at least a hundred of them out there surrounding the strange pair. What strikes me, though, is how silent it is. Those things never stand still like that. The walking dead are always on the move, shuffling and shambling through the deserted streets. And they never stop that incessant moaning and groaning. Zombies don't roll like that. Which is why their inaction makes no sense whatsoever.

Squinting through the darkness, I watch the vampire priss and her whatever-he-is face the horde. They seem to be at a standoff, like each is waiting for the other to make the first offensive strike.

Anthony steps away from the she-vamp, moving to the middle of the street. The revenants remain frozen in place. He stands alone, moonlight glinting off the pendant at his throat, his arms upraised. I wish I could see better; his features are difficult to discern. Dimitri sits on the edge of the wooden beam he's perched upon, his attention glued to the scene unfolding outside.

"What's going on?" I ask, knowing D's night vision will reveal things mine misses.

"His lips are moving, but he's muttering. Can't hear a thing."

"Why the hell are the zombies just standing there? If that were one of us, they'd attack like a pack of rabid werewolves." He shrugs. We watch in silence for a few more minutes. "I'm going downstairs." His hand flies out and closes around my upper arm. I glance down at the fingers lightly pressing into my skin. I roll my eyes. "Fine. I'll stay by the door." He gives me a doting look, like a father would a pouting child, and dismisses me with a lift of his chin.

The air down here feels thicker than upstairs. BS isn't a humid place, especially not in winter. I waver on my feet briefly before grabbing the smooth wall for support. An icon of the Holy Mother and Child gazes at me lovingly. Inhaling, I shake my head, trying to disperse the fog enveloping my brain.

Stumbling to the door, I set my feet and yank the knob, which slips out of my grip. My insides are so tightly wound I feel like they're going to explode and spray my innards all over the pristine white paint of the vestibule. The door finally swings inward on the third attempt, but I fall. I try to climb to my feet, but my body feels heavy, weighed down by some invisible force that has invaded this once-sacred space.

Rhythmic footfalls alert me to someone's approach from within the church. Cool hands clutch my shoulders. "Easy, there." The voice sounds like it's coming from down some miles-long tunnel. "What's wrong with you?"

I wave off his concern because I can't get my voice to work. If I could speak, I'd tell him to back the hell off. But I'm in no state to pull an attitude with Peter. He holds me by the shoulders, peering into my eyes with beautiful gray-blue orbs. I smile, and a part of me rises and floats away. If he hadn't been supporting me, I'm sure I would have slid to the golden oak planks beneath our feet as if I didn't have any bones. I don't understand what's happening. I feel drunk.

Peter drapes me across one of the pews. This church must have been nice back in the day. The cushion isn't the softest, but it's a step up; the church I got dragged to when I was a kid only had wooden benches. My eyes flutter then drift shut, but I don't sleep. I listen to the retreating scrape of his motorcycle boots against the wooden floor. Davis mumbles something unintelligible. "Easy, lad," Peter tells him in a hushed tone. Silence envelops the former worship space.

The Many Tortures of Anthony Cardno

I wish I could sleep, but my insides won't let me. I feel like my nerves have tangled themselves into a giant ball and the knot tightens with every flick of a finger or toe. Finally, after I don't know how long, the vampire goes death-still. Sitting up, I swing my feet to the floor. Dancing dots flood my field of vision and my head pounds. Outside. I need to get outside.

Moving furtively, I cast a wary glance toward Peter and Davis. They're both asleep, as are Mariah and Bas. I don't know about Dimitri, but I'm not going to go looking for trouble. He'll have me hog tied and stuffed in some closet that locks from the outside in an instant if he knew what I was planning. Removing my boots, I offer up a quick prayer that the floorboards won't creak, and set off for the entrance, sword strapped to my back and a pair of stakes stuffed in my pockets.

Holding my breath, I creep to the door. I know the snick of the lock sliding from the strike plate will alert D to my plan, but I'm going for it. *Slow or fast like a Band Aid,* I wonder. Heavy footfalls in the rafters make my decision for me. I yank the door open and plunge into the darkness, running as fast as possible so I can find a place to hide from the vampire.

Chest heaving, I flatten myself against a boulder that occupies the planter in the middle of the church property. The sound of the door closing reaches my ears through the darkness, and I know D isn't coming after me.

Exhaling in relief, I straighten. The zombies are gone. No corpses lie rotting in the middle of the abandoned street. Marie and Anthony are gone, too. Unsheathing the sword, I straighten, turning in a circle to confirm that I am actually alone. The breeze ruffles my hair. The area is completely deserted. Setting off in the direction of the house Dimitri said they could stay in, I realize that it sits empty, a desolate place harboring nothing. I don't know how I know, I just do.

Cross the street, a voice in my head urges.

Keeping my head down, I follow the voice. I stalk the cracked ribbons of asphalt and tromp through overgrown yards, avoiding the sticking Russian thistles and on the watch for coyotes. Those mangy mutts' population has grown considerably since the zombie infestation, no longer having any reason to hide out and their food supply as disrupted as ours. They roam the streets at night, their yellow eyes warily watching the walking dead and following their hunting parties, ready to fall on whatever few scraps might be left. If any. The last coyote I saw was so malnourished that it was little more than skin stretched over bones.

Tonight, the scavengers watch me from the shadows. I can feel those glowing orbs on me, but can't see them. Winding through BS, I pass old self-serve stations and hollow buildings, their windows staring through the night with blind eyes. I walk from one side of town to the other, finding no one, foolishly following the voice, taking every turn it says and then doubling back when I reach a dead end. Finally, it leads me to one of the several abandoned elementary schools.

The windows are dark and there's no way to know if anyone lurks inside, but the front door is propped open. "What, no welcome wagon?" I mutter. Withdrawing my favorite stake, the one I always pull from the body immediately after I plunge the point into some vamp's heart, I cling to the shadows created by the overhang that blocks the moonlight. The immediate area is absolutely silent, not even the crickets sing. Makes me wonder if an earthquake is on the way, but I shake my head dismissing that notion. The earth can shake, rattle, and roll all it wants, so long as no demons slip through the cracks.

The school is very different from the ones I attended back east as a kid. There we had multiple hallways. Here, in the Southern California desert, only the building housing the principal's office branches off into actual corridors and most of those lead outside. There might be a few rooms connected to the office hub, but most of the classrooms are portables. Makes my job easier. Without hallways, I don't have to worry about hiding places. Not that I'm worried. Actually, I feel really, really calm. Which should raise a ton of red flags all on its own.

A nearly imperceptible noise, like the scuffing of a shoe against tile, reaches my ears through the door marked "Cafeteria." Grasping the handle, I hold my breath and close my eyes. Don't want to end up the main course at some zombie banquet laid out on folding tables.

Satisfied no revenants lie in wait on the other side, I press the slim silver handle down and push the door in. The expansive room smells like stale food. It's hard to believe no students have attended a single day of school here in years.

"Welcome," a masculine voice that sounds startlingly similar to the one that coaxed me from the church says from the darkness. Pale moonlight filters into a glass-walled atrium, providing enough illumination for me to make out the shapes of folded tables lined up along the walls and plastic chairs stacked in the corner, as if the kids are only gone for the night. Eerie.

My vamp sonar pings, and I whirl to face the stage at the front of the room. Two figures shrouded in shadow stand at stage right, their bodies pressed together tightly, as if they share a supportive embrace. The rustle of a skirt gives their identities away: Marie and Anthony. "What the hell are you doing here?" I take a few steps toward the stage. She's ripe for killing and then that poor sap

The Many Tortures of Anthony Cardno

111

will be free of her compulsion. I tighten my fingers around the stake.

Anthony raises his hand. Now that my eyes have adjusted to the dim room, I see that his palm is facing toward me. "Desino."

I freeze in place, my feet unwilling to take another step and my thoughts unable to command them. The fog from earlier drifts across my mind. Something is in my head again, and I can't for the life of me figure out what's happening. I imagine diaphanous fingers invading every nook and cranny within my skull, and I can't block their explorations.

"Good," he says as he moves down the few stairs leading to the floor. "Drop your weapon."

My fingers open, and my favorite stake rolls toward the tips, dropping to the floor with a clatter that echoes off the walls. Why the hell did I just do that? Once more I try to reclaim control of my limbs. The urge to kill him nearly overwhelms me, but I can't move. Too many thoughts swirl around my head, looking for an outlet, seeking to be expressed, but they are as trapped as my body. With a flick of his wrist. What did he do to me? What the hell is he?

Anthony steps into my personal space. I want to step away, but am unable to. "Right now, you feel frustration that your will has been suspended."

I'm gonna kill you, you bastard, I think. I blew by frustrated the minute I couldn't command my body.

Anthony steps forward, a self-satisfied smile stretching his thin lips. "I want you to meet some new friends." He looks across the multi-purpose room, at an alcove I guess leads to another outside exit. A half dozen zombies step into the waning moonlight. They don't shuffle when they move, nor do they moan and groan; they walk. Like regular people.

"What is this?" I manage to push out. The victory of reclaiming control is short-lived. He flexes his power, crushing my will like a cigarette underfoot.

"Tell her," Anthony directs one of the figures clad in jeans, a suit jacket, and loosely knotted tie.

"We are his sword. He is our light. We serve him faithfully." Intelligible words, not a hint of the normal guttural utterances.

If it could have, my jaw would have unhinged and dropped to my toes. Zombies don't speak. They sure as hell can't think, unless they're fresh from the grave.

Panic seizes my middle, knotting my nerves and twisting my stomach on itself painfully. "Not sure what you're seeing? I can rectify that." He gestures at another one of the creatures. "Go to her. Kiss her cheek but don't eat her."

The thing walks toward me silently, his eyes fixated on my cheek. Cold, dead lips press a peck to my cheek and I gag despite Anthony's hold over me. The creature's mouth opens a little wider, like he's going to take a chunk of flesh out of my face. Anthony makes a small gesture with his hand and the zombie pulls away without so much as a nibble. "You see, I control them. They do my will, as will you."

I want to make some kind of grand defiant gesture, say something caustic at the very least, but I can't find the words. "How?" I breathe out with an effort that leaves my forehead clammy and my insides shaking. A wave of nausea sweeps up from my stomach and then back down to settle in the roiling acid filling my middle.

"It won't do to fight. I'll just tighten my hold."

Deep down I know he will. And there is nothing I seem to be able to do to resist him. I'm fucked. My insides scream with this knowledge. It's painful. Outwardly, I'm as still as a statue, soaking up his words and feeling the black stain of his power creeping over my soul.

ANTHONY

"Here's how this is going to go," I tell her, pushing the peppermint in my mouth against my cheek. "You're going to return to your ragtag band of freedom fighters. You will not tell them anything about this interaction. You will act as is typical for you. Except you will stop killing my people. You will accompany your bloodsucking friends on their journey east. But you will answer my call. Anytime. Anywhere. Do you understand?" I pause to let that sink in. "Blink once for yes."

Her eyelids snap down and up one time.

"Good girl. Oh, and you will not come after either myself or Marie. You are mine." I turn my back on her. Predictably, she strains forward, nearly toppling over in her attempt to reach me. Her hands remain down at her sides. I planted the suggestion that they moved. I shake my head in amusement. Too easy. "Don't worry. You'll be able to move shortly. Marie?"

Marie's skirt rustles when she steps toward the hunter, smirking. Marie loves to taunt. "Poor little Chosen. Can't kill the evil vampire." Her musical tone further irritates the girl, I can see it in her eyes. "You will not remember any of this conversation."

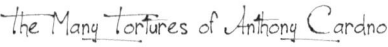

Asserting the power I have over the revenants, and now this one, to ensure it overtakes the Chosen's, I watch the internal struggle evident in her eyes. Normally, mind-control doesn't work on the legacies, but something has changed this one, made her ripe for the picking.

"Of course," she says.

Once more, I raise my hand and lay the palm over her forehead. I see her mentally recoil from my touch even as her body refuses to obey her thoughts. I look at the zombies awaiting my command. "Go. This one is off limits." The mindless dullards shuffle like they should. The outer door shuts behind them with a soft click. I return my attention to the girl and smile. "You're going to take a nap now. See you soon, sweetheart," I wink.

Her head falls forward. Marie maneuvers her to the floor gently, as expected. Marie always does as I expect. That's why I let her remain by my side.

HOPE

I wake up alone in the abandoned school cafeteria. My tongue feels thick, and my head pounds as if I had one too many last night. Pushing up off the floor with effort thanks to muscles that weigh a thousand pounds, I stagger a step or two before finding my way to the exit.

We're supposed to head out for the base in the morning. Time to go. I have places to go and people to see. Monsters to kill. Just an ordinary day.

The second issue of Fireside *Magazine saw me Tuckerized into a story by Damien Angelica Walters, who afterwards became a great friend (as did Christie Yant). In Damien's story I am not the lead character, but my presence motivates the female lead. And in this story, I'm Straight. And Married. Damien really nailed my worst nightmare, didn't she?*

carred

DAMIEN ANGELICA WALTERS

Violet carved her hate into her flesh one name at a time.

Her skin was riddled with scars, some barely visible, others dark and ruddy. The oldest, the first name, was on her right ankle, above the knobby bone. It revealed a halting progress, with many gaps in between the lines and curves.

He suffered for a long time.

❁

Anthony looked up from his dinner plate and smiled. "This is really good, babe."

"Thank you. I wanted to make something special for tonight."

The cooking classes were her idea. Anthony had been worried about the knives, of course, although he hadn't said anything with his mouth. Only with his eyes. The first time his hand had touched one of her scars, he'd paused, his eyes curious. Concerned.

She'd looked down at her hands. "I had a ... problem when I was younger, but I'm better now."

"What do they mean?"

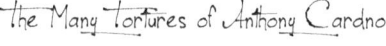

"Nothing," she'd said. "Nothing at all."

A breeze blew in through the open windows, fluttering the curtains, and the late spring air was heavy with the scent of flowers. Children's voices called out and their neighbor's dog barked several times, a deep, growling sort of bark. She and Anthony grimaced at the same time, caught each other, and smiled.

"Happy anniversary, babe," he said.

"Happy anniversary."

She smiled and twisted the ring on her finger. The year had passed so quickly, yet seemed a lifetime. Anthony had asked her to marry him on their sixth date. Crazy, perhaps, because they'd barely known each other, but she'd said yes without a second thought. Three weeks later, they were standing hand in hand in the courthouse promising forever, a promise she intended to keep.

Mrs. Anthony Cardno was a good person.

But Violet isn't and you know it.

That wasn't true. She *was* a good person. Sometimes she got ... lost. That was all. But it was all in the past. She was better now. So much better.

●

With Anthony softly snoring in the bed beside her, Violet clasped her hands together on her chest and recited the names. Too many names.

"Please forgive me," she whispered when she was finished.

She rolled onto her side and touched Anthony's cheek, his skin soft, yet rough at the same time, beneath her fingertips. The sleeve of her pajama top slipped up to her elbow, revealing the edge of a name: *Sabrina.* Her best friend in grade school. Violet closed her eyes.

It wasn't her fault. She hadn't meant to hurt anyone. She hadn't known.

Liar.

●

She woke before Anthony and padded down to the kitchen to make coffee. From the kitchen window, she saw the next-door neighbor's children, already up and about, kicking around a red rubber ball. She smiled and touched her belly. Two months ago, she'd thrown out her birth control pills. Nothing had happened yet, but they were both young. There was plenty of time. Anthony would be a wonderful father. And she would be a good mother even if the baby didn't sleep

The Many Tortures of Anthony Cardno

well or cried all the time.

"You were always crying when you were a baby," her mother had said time and again. "Drove me crazy. You'd cry if you were hungry or full, wet or dry, it didn't matter. It was like you came out hating the world and wanted everyone to know it." Her mother would tap her cigarette into her overflowing ashtray, pat Violet on the bum, and smile. "Grab me another beer, okay?"

When her mother had married her stepfather, Violet had hoped that everything would be okay. Now she had a real family. Her mother would be happy, wouldn't drink so much, and wouldn't forget to go food shopping or pay the electric bill. But her stepfather had only made things worse. So much worse.

But we took care of him, didn't we?

No, no matter what he'd done, he didn't deserve what happened. No one did.

✦

Long after the sun had faded from the sky, she and Anthony took a walk through the neighborhood. The children and dogs had been collected for the night, and lights behind windows winked out one by one. His hand gave hers a quick squeeze.

"Next year we'll go away someplace for our anniversary, how does that sound? Somewhere with a beach and blue water."

"And fruity drinks with paper umbrellas?"

"Absolutely."

He pulled her into his arms and kissed her softly beneath the glow of a streetlamp. Then they heard the shout. She jumped, pulled away, and scanned the street. No one else was outside. The shout came again, more muffled this time, from a small green house with a swing on the front porch.

Anthony took a step toward the house. Violet shook her head.

"Don't."

"But if someone is hurt ..."

A voice snapped in anger, followed by a whip-quick sound that Violet knew all too well—a slap.

"Let's go back home."

Anthony gave the house a long look. Violet tugged his hand.

"Come on. It's not our business."

✦

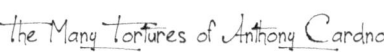

Violet was collecting her mail from the mailbox at the end of the yard when a dark-haired woman and a little girl of perhaps four or five in a yellow dress and white ruffled socks walked past. She looked up just in time to see the bruise darkening the skin of the woman's cheek. Violet's hands clenched into fists. The little girl pulled her thumb out of her mouth and offered up a wide, innocent smile.

You can make things better.

No, it wasn't her fight. She didn't know them at all. She watched them turn onto the sidewalk leading up to the green house.

But you could if you really wanted to. Just one more time. Help them, then I'll go away.

The voice whispered so sweetly, but it lied. Oh, how it lied.

●

Violet pulled out a knife to slice tomatoes for a salad and paused. The overhead light glinted in the metal. She closed her eyes and saw the little girl's face, the woman's bruise.

You can fix it.

"Leave me alone," she whispered.

Two years after her mother had married her stepfather, the voice spoke to her for the first time. Eight-year-old Violet had been sitting in the corner of her bedroom with the door locked, wiping tears away, with a fresh set of bruises on her upper arms.

"I hate you," she whispered. Over and over again.

I can help you, a voice said.

She'd jumped up, stifling a shout, looked under the bed, checked inside the closet and out the window. The voice had laughed softly.

I won't hurt you.

She'd covered her ears. Buried her face in the pillow.

Trust me. It will be easy. So easy.

It had whispered and whispered, and eventually her hands had dropped from her ears. It had told her what to do, and when the house had fallen silent, Violet had tiptoed to the kitchen and pulled out a small knife.

Good girl. That's a very good girl.

She'd closed her eyes when she had touched the blade to her ankle, and the pain had not been nearly as bad as she'd imagined it would be. Beneath the copper bright tang of blood, she'd smelled something dark and terrible like the sweet stink of roadkill or the scummy water left in a vase filled with dead flowers. She'd felt something light brush against her skin, opened her eyes, and saw a shadow flickering across the floor. One quick flicker and then it was gone.

She didn't know then what it would do.

A few days later, her stepfather had collapsed in the back yard. The doctors had called it a rare, aggressive cancer, but Violet had known they were wrong. The malignant cells hadn't eaten him away from the inside. Her hate had.

Let me out.

She dropped the knife back into the drawer and slammed it shut. It bounced back open with a little jingle, offering her a hint of the silverware within.

"No!"

She took several long deep breaths. She would not do it. Not now. Not ever. She recited the names. Once. Twice.

"I am sorry, I am so sorry."

Words. Useless words. Her stepfather had said them so many times.

He wasn't really sorry. You weren't either.

❋

Standing in front of the green house, Violet noticed the white letter sticking out of the mailbox. She stepped closer, casting quick glances over both shoulders. The letter was out far enough for her to make out a name: *Kevin Turner.*

With her mouth set into a thin line, she turned and walked back to her own house, the name a heavy weight inside. She couldn't hate him. She didn't even know him.

You could if you wanted to. He's just like your stepfather.

She didn't know that. The woman could have fallen down. How many times had she done something stupid, something that—

Excuses, excuses. You know you want to. That's why you looked at the letter.

No, it wasn't that way at all. She wouldn't do anything. She'd promised to leave it all behind. For Anthony's sake. For her own sake.

❋

Sabrina Ogden had been her best friend all through grade school. In their first year of middle school, Violet had spoken of what her stepfather had done. Sabri-

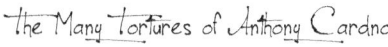

na had told another friend who told another and on and on. The whispers had followed Violet through the hallways. The shame had burned like a brand.

When the dark voice had whispered, Violet had tried to hold it in, but she hadn't been strong enough.

The doctors hadn't been able to cure Sabrina either.

Tears burned in Violet's eyes.

If she'd been your friend, she wouldn't have told anyone. If she hadn't—

"Violet?"

She jumped and the paring knife in her hands clattered into the kitchen sink. She stared at the blade for several long moments, her mouth dry. She didn't remember opening the silverware drawer. Did she?

You know you want to. I've been waiting for so long.

She slipped on a smile and turned around.

"You looked like you were a million miles away," Anthony said.

"Sorry, I was woolgathering."

She went to him and rested her head on his chest.

❋

In the dark, she stared up at the ceiling. Recited the names.

Joey, who'd tried to take advantage of her at a party in high school. Sarah, that same year, who'd blackened her eye and fractured her wrist for telling the principal about the smoking in the bathroom. Christopher. Laura. Matt. Jake, who'd broken her heart. Peter, who'd shattered it. Ryan, who'd promised to love her forever. He hadn't deserved to die such a terrible death.

And so many more. She wanted to forget them all, but she held tight, fearing she would.

My fault, my fault. All of them, she thought.

Every time she'd carved a name, the darkness reappeared, a slithering shadow she could only see as a human-shaped haze in the air. Did they see it come for them? Did they taste its fate in their breath?

And did they know she'd sent it?

❋

Just one more time. Please.

"Stop it, stop it, stop it."

She didn't want to hurt anyone. She was a good person now. She *was.*

●

Violet saw the little girl again, playing in the front yard of the green house. She was digging in the dirt with a stick, singing softly to herself. When she heard Violet's footsteps, she looked up and Violet saw bruises on her forearm, four finger-shaped marks. Violet's hands curled into fists. Her heart beat heavy in her chest.

We can help her.

No, it was not her problem. But her steps were heavy on her walk back home.

●

An image of the girl's bruises floated in Violet's mind, and her fingers tightened on her open book.

One more time. I promise I'll go away.

Why wouldn't it just leave her alone?

You know you want to help her.

But not in that way. She would call Child Protective Services in the morning. They could help the little girl.

What if they don't?

The words on the page swam into a blur. She recited the names. Ran the tip of her finger over the edge of a scar. Recited the names again.

Her cup of guilt was deep, the brew within thick and bitter. No matter how many swallows, she could never drink it all down. Not in one lifetime or ten.

"Honey, are you okay?"

Violet looked up from her book. "Yes, why?"

"You had the strangest expression on your face."

"I was just focused on the story, I guess."

He touched the back of her hand.

"If something is bothering you, you can tell me. You know that, right?"

"Of course I do."

She put her hand atop his. The words gathered in her throat, but she swal-

lowed them down. Anthony was the first, the only, good thing in her life. If he knew the truth, the things she'd done, he'd run as far away as possible.

❋

Violet put the phone down, her mouth set in a thin line.

They won't help her and you know it.

But they would. The woman on the phone said they would send someone out. A snippet of memory crept in. A woman from CPS came to her house once. In spite of the bruises on Violet, she hadn't done anything except write a report, but things were different now. They took bruises more seriously. The little girl would be okay.

But you can make sure of it.

Violet sagged against the counter and groaned into her hands.

"Leave me alone, please, just leave me alone."

Never.

But she already knew that. It would never go away. Never give her peace. She was broken. Wrong. She yanked the silverware drawer open and grabbed a knife.

"Is this what you want?"

Yes. You know you want it, too.

No. She wanted to be well, to be happy.

She made a tiny cut.

Yesss ...

"No! I will not do this. I will *not*."

She threw the knife down, sank down with her back against a cabinet, and put her head in her hands. Recited the names. A harsh sob bubbled up from deep inside her chest. The names. The deaths. All her fault. She was a monster. With a grimace, she scrambled for the knife.

You want this. You know you do.

She slashed at her skin, her grimace turning into a smile at the sharp, beautiful sting of the knife. Even that was wrong. It never hurt enough. She cut again and again, the letters distorted. Wet, red mouths dripping crimson pearls. When she finished, she threw the knife down.

"Are you happy now?"

And there, on the delicate skin of her wrist: *Violet.*

One last name, one last death, to pay for them all.

What did you do? You stupid, stupid woman.

 The Many Tortures of Anthony Cardno

Tears blurred her vision as the blood dripped to the floor.

"Please forgive me, Anthony," she whispered, her voice small and insignificant in the quiet. "It's so much better this way. You deserve someone so much better."

No, no, no! You can't do this. You cannot!

She had to. It was the only way. Her limbs filled with lassitude, her mouth dropped open, and her breath came long and slow.

A shadow emerged from the wound like a ribbon, taking shape as it grew. It slipped free slowly, ponderously, its weight feather-light, its stench thick and heavy. It caressed her cheek in a hideous lover's pantomime. She took a deep breath, steeled herself against the pain to come, yet the shadow slithered across the tile, moving away from her without a sound.

"No, no, no."

She reached out, but her fingers passed through the darkness. She grabbed again and again, caught nothing but a kiss of air against her skin. Then the shadow slipped beneath the door, and she sobbed into her hands. She didn't understand. She'd carved her name. Why didn't it take her? She rocked back and forth, her arms wrapped around her knees. No voice whispered in her mind. Only a strange, calm silence. Could it have been that easy all along? But all those deaths ...

No. It had to come back for her. It *had* to make her pay.

❋

Ambulance lights cut the night with slashes of red and blue, and Anthony's hand gripped Violet's tight, his skin warm against hers. The neighbors watched from their porches, their eyes filled with curious alarm, as the paramedics wheeled a stretcher out of the green house.

"I wonder what happened," Anthony whispered.

Violet rubbed her finger along the cut on her wrist, still in the pink of healing. A few moments later, the dark-haired woman stepped out of the house, her face expressionless, the little girl by her side. And on the girl's ankle, not quite covered by a white ruffled sock, Violet saw the name carved into her flesh: *Daddy.*

No, oh, no. A chill raced down Violet's spine. Her mouth went dry.

Anthony tugged her hand.

"Come on, let's go back home."

Violet heard his voice as if from far away. She couldn't move, couldn't take her eyes away from the little girl.

"Violet, honey, what's wrong?"

The little girl met Violet's gaze, her lips curved into a dark, familiar smile. A smile laced with hate.

The Many Tortures of Anthony Cardno

Bryan Thomas Schmidt has published two of my short stories in his anthologies. He didn't have time to write something all-new for this anthology, but he did offer to change the name of the freighter captain in this story from "Buj" to "Cardno," and I took him up on it. (This is not the first, or last, time I've been Tuckerized into Bryan's Davi Rhii universe.) Let's go beyond the sun and into the future for a rollicking good space battle.

The Hand of God
(A Davi Rhii Story)

BRYAN THOMAS SCHMIDT

Cordelia shivered, her hull groaning as Cardno pushed her engines to full and spun her into a sharp, diving turn with the hopes of evading further blasts from the pirate ship's cannons. His hand slipped on the stick, wet from the sweat which now covered him. He took a deep breath and relaxed his grip. "Come on, baby. Hold together now."

He glanced down at the scanner to see the pirate ship echoing his dive and spin, falling back only slightly as it stayed on his tail. He cursed, then adjusted his rear shields to seventy percent. Might as well protect what needed protecting. It was supposed to be a simple honey run—basic supplies for the colony on Kempol I—nothing of interest for anyone. Except a pirate. They always needed basic stuff to survive. Still, he had to try.

Flipping the comm to an open channel, he keyed the transmit button. "Freighter *Cordelia* to raider ship, I have nothing of value on-board."

His answer was another volley of laser cannons, the blasts rocking his ship as they exploded against his rear deflectors.

"Basic supplies for Kempol I." A scratchy male voice came back over the comm: "Your ship has no markings. That's illegal in this system. Stop engines and let us board."

Cardno's mind raced for an excuse to stall. The ship attacking him had no markings either. They couldn't be Alliance official then. Who was this guy?

"Your ship has no markings either. What right have *you* to stop me?"

"Citizen's Patrol. Keeping the shipping lanes safe for honest pilots."

"What makes you think I'm not honest?"

A blip lit up his screen and he quickly pulled back on the stick just in time for the torpedoes to fly past his left wing, a near-miss.

"Last chance to avoid disintegration."

Cardno's hands moved like lightning on the controls as he pulled up quadrant scans, one after another. His eyes searched the screen for something—anything—a suitable place to hide. Then he saw them: the dwarf twins, Romulus and Remus, named after an Old Earth legend. The only dwarf planets in the system, out in nowhere land between Kronis and Plutonis. Kronis was his destination but the chase had forced him off course, and the two dwarfs were now his closest option.

Explosions rocked his ship as the pirate's lasers raked his shields again. He pushed the joystick forward into a twisting dive as he turned and headed toward the dwarf twins.

Shutting off the comm, he dropped two mines in his wake right in the path of the raider, but the pilot was skilled and deftly slid his ship between them, fly-ing the large freighter almost like a fighter. *He definitely flies like a military pilot.*

He increased *Cordelia's* speed and shifted horizontally and vertically in a zig-zagging pattern, trying to stay out of range of the freighter's weapons. The pirate stayed with him, hit-and-miss explosions rocking his ship as they exploded on or near his shields.

I'm not going to make it!

Then Cardno recognized the ship and he knew for sure he was in trouble. At that moment, the pirate's laughter echoed over the comm.

✸

Major Farien Noa was leading his squadron on a deep space probe when the alarm sounded. One of his pilots defined it for him, even as he checked his computer.

"Explosions and laser blasts—some kind of battle," Lieutenant Solanus Rhii said, sounding much like his father twenty years before.

The Many Tortures of Anthony Cardno

"Anything on how many ships are involved?"

"Negative," Rhii replied. "We're a quadrant over."

"Well, let's change that. Accelerate in formation, shields up, weapons armed." Farien complied with the commands even as he issued them, then laid in a course and accelerated his fighter, leading the squadron toward the targets.

"There's two of them," a young voice said—Farien's son, Yao, named after an old friend of Farien and Solanus' father.

Farien nodded as he checked his computer. "One of them's a freighter." The scan was fuzzy on the other. Farien typed commands into the computer, even as he completed his arc and straightened his VS37 for a direct approach from above toward the fighting ships.

"I've seen that signature before," Rhii said, his tone evidencing the search running in his mind. "On reports ..."

"It's an odd construction," Yao said.

Farien smiled. Still so much to teach him. "It's probably employing sensor blockers as well as been custom modified to confuse them."

"Got it!" Rhii called. *The Hand Of God.*"

"*The Hand Of God?*" Yao's concerned voice echoed.

The Hand Of God was the name of a ship belonging to a pirate who'd been terrorizing smugglers and other commercial pilots throughout the area for six months. What was he doing out here alone? Supposedly he had great numbers? Had he stumbled onto the freighter by accident?

"He rarely works alone," Farien answered. "Where's his gang?"

"I only read two ships," Rhii said.

"An ambush?" Yao asked.

The two battling ships came into view through Farien's blast shield as he keyed the comm. The Hand's ship was tight on the tail of the freighter, explosions rocking it as it struggled desperately to continue evading. Clearly the freighter pilot had some real skill. "This is Major Farien Noa of the Borali Alliance," Farien said into the comm.

"Kill your engines and come to a full stop so we can inspect you."

The only answer was laughter over the comm. Farien shuddered. Why did he recognize that laugh?

"The freighter's barely hanging on," Rhii said. "My weapons are locked."

"Fire warning shots," Farien said. "Don't damage them. Just scare them."

His squadron slipped into attack formation around him, all seven VS37s sliding into a V-pattern, their weapons locked. Farien held back as the others

 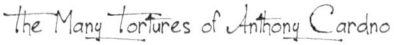

fired at both ships. Explosions rocked the pirate ship with a couple other blasts singing the freighter.

"I say again," Farien repeated into the comm, "kill your engines and prepare to be inspected."

"You already shot at me!" the pirate's rasp snapped back over the channel. "Why would I trust you?"

"Trust me if you want to live."

The pirate's only response was laughter. The *Hand* fired two more blasts at the freighter, then swerved off in an erratic pattern, clearly designed to prevent further damage from the squadron's cannons.

"Stay on him!" Farien ordered. "Yao, you and Lake check that freighter."

Yao's voice was full of disappointment. "Yes, sir." The two fighters served off, leaving the formation and heading toward the freighter as the rest formed up on Farien and increased speed, chasing the pirate.

●

Cardno listened to the chatter on the radio as his ship rocked with more explosions. Then the fighters fired too, barely missing his wings. Had they missed on purpose? Farien Noa? Where did he know that name?

He heard explosions from behind him but his ship didn't shudder. He checked the display and saw five ships closing fast on the pirate. Two more had turned off and were closing on him as the pirate led the others off in an attempt to evade. Cardno didn't want Boralians aboard either, but they'd probably saved his life, and he couldn't outrun them.

He killed his engines, allowing *Cordelia* to drift as the VS37s closed in.

"This is Lieutenant Yao Noa of the Boralian Alliance," a young voice said over the comm. "Please identify yourself."

Another Noa? Were they related? "This is Cardno of the freighter *Cordelia*," he responded.

"You're flying without markings," another voice said. "That's illegal in this system."

"I just had my ship refit. The markings will be added once I arrive at my destination."

"What is your destination?" The first voice, Yao, if Cardno recalled correctly, asked.

"Kempol I," Cardno answered. "I have supplies for the outpost there."

 The Many Tortures of Anthony Cardno

The VS37's matched *Cordelia's* velocity and settled in along either side.

"Leaving port without markings is asking for trouble," the second voice said. "And it looks like you found it."

Cardno sighed. "He came out of nowhere. I don't know how he found me."

"You're lucky we came along when we did."

Cardno chuckled. "That's for sure. Thanks for the assist." The comm went silent for a moment. Cardno assumed the two pilots were talking with each other. *Please don't let them board me.* He was already delayed because of the encounter with the pilot and the supplies were on rush. If he got them there on time, he'd gain a large bonus. He really needed the money.

"I'm afraid we're going to have to escort you to the nearest port for an inspection," the pilot Yao said.

Cardno groaned, cursing to himself, then keyed the comm. "I'm kind of in a hurry. I could lose a major bonus. I really need the money. Can't you cut me some slack? You know he was preying on me."

"Sorry," said the other pilot. "Major gave us strict orders."

Switching his engines on auxiliary, he slowly accelerated, matching his speed and course with the escorting fighters. *There goes my bonus.*

◆

Adrenaline raced through Farien's veins as his squadron gave chase. It had been a while since they'd seen any real action. Their deep probes generally involved encounters with merchant ships and passenger vessels either in trouble or committing minor violations. Usually they issued warnings for the violations and sent them on their way, stopping only to assist the vessels with trouble. But in this case, a mini war had been waged. He had a responsibility to find out what was going on, especially if the pirate was indeed *The Hand Of God.*

The pirate's ship rocked as blasts exploded just off his engines but he continued evading their shots like an expert.

Who is this guy? Farien knew a lot of people who'd love an answer. "Pree and Ami, cut him off. Rigel, stay with me. The other two hit him from the sides. We need to shut him down."

As the squadron broke apart, Farien fired another burst at the pirate's engines, striking the heat shield and rocking it again as the silver hull turned black from the flames.

"You want him alive, right?" Pree answered, a chuckle in his voice. The

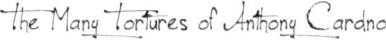

chubby veteran was one of Farien's best pilots and had a reputation as a prankster, but he was always on top of his game when he needed to be.

"The pirate, yes—his ship, no," Farien replied.

Pree laughed as Ami's high pitched giggle filled the comm. "Let's leave enough of her to see what she's made of."

"You can indulge your fascination with starcraft on your own time, Ami," Pree teased. "We're on official business here."

Farien could almost hear the female captain rolling her eyes as she responded to her wingman. "You're the wingman, remember? Just follow my lead."

Farien watched as she accelerated rapidly then arced sharply and spun around to face the oncoming pirate, firing head on. Pree slid in beside her and did the same, forcing the pirate to dive and roll to avoid their blasts.

The dive was so steep the fighters had to abruptly change course to keep him in their sights and maintain their positions. Farien noticed the pirate was leading them toward an outer moon of a nearby planet.

"His course is taking us toward that moon." Even as he commented he launched his computer into a long range scan. "He could have a base there."

"Or be hiding his fleet," Pree added.

"My sensors pick up nothing," said Lieutenant Hest. The youngest Squadron member and Farien's wingman sounded nervous.

"The moon could be hiding them," Ami said.

"Or the planet," Farien said. "Let's keep our eyes open and get ready for evasion if we need to."

Farien accelerated, Hest staying right with him. The pirate ship disappeared around the arc of the moon as Farien glanced around and spotted the black, sleek bodied snub nose craft of his squadron closing in. Suddenly, the pirate ship spun into a sharp arc, curving back around right side up and firing its cannons straight at Farien and Hest.

"Hest! Evasive now!"

Farien scrambled with his own controls, hoping his young wingman was doing the same. His ship rocked from explosions as a blast singed his right wing, leaving streaks on the dark painted hull. As he slowed back to turn toward the pirate he caught a glimpse of Hest's limping fighter nearby. A blast had knocked out one of the engines and torn a jagged cut into the hull plating just behind the cockpit.

"You okay, Hest?"

The young wingman sounded surprisingly calm. "Fine, sir. A little shaken but I'll be okay."

The pirate ship arced back around toward the moon, following the curve of its atmosphere. It was moving so fast it would soon be out of sight. Accelerating, Farien's teeth clenched as he checked his targeting and fired blasts at the pirate ship's disappearing engines. Pree and Ami fired from above as well, then his computer beeped. The blip that was the pirate ship disappeared.

"He's gone?!" Ami's voice was almost a squeal.

Farien typed frantically into his computer. "He can't be."

"He is," Pree said softly. Farien could sense his disgust.

"What the hell—?" Ami yelled over the comm as Farien heard the pounding of her fist on her cockpit wall. Ami always pounded when she was irritated.

"We don't have time to argue. Circle the moon and do another scan. Spread out." Farien turned, with Hest on his tail and arced around the moon as he ran through more scans on his computer. There was no sign of the pirate ship and he knew none of the others would find any either.

In moments, they'd confirmed it. The *Hand Of God* was gone.

Farien sighed and keyed the comm. "Let's get back to the others."

❀

The moment his scanner beeped, Cardno knew they were all in trouble. In moments, his screen filled with blips and ships began popping out of lightspeed all around them—ships of the menacing kind. The *Hand's* pirate compatriots had found them.

His escort's voices revealed their panic. "Who are they?"

"Stay calm, Lake," he heard Lieutenant Noa answer.

"There's a lot of them!" The other pilot's voice cracked as it rose in pitch.

"Radio the major for help," Noa instructed. "Mr. Cardno, we have visitors. We're increasing speed, please stay with us and activate your shields."

Cardno didn't even bother to respond. His shields had been on since he'd identified the blips as hostile. He increased speed to stay with the VS37 fighters and wondered how they'd survive an attack of seven ships to three.

The VS37s began to dive and Cardno followed into a steep trajectory angling them away from the newly arrived ships. But then the stars ahead fizzled a bit and more ships began to materialize right in their path. Now it was twelve to three. *We're dead!*

"We're in trouble," Lake said, his voice almost a whine. "I can't raise the

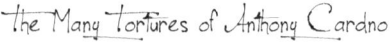

major on the comm!"

"Our best option is to put as much space between us and them as we can," Noa answered, leading the squadron into a turn that would arc them around the newly-arrived ships.

"There's so many of them!"

"Stay calm, Lieutenant."

Not waiting for further instructions, Cardno typed a code into his computer, modifying his arc a bit so his tail angled back at the new arrivals. As the squadron soared past, mines dispatched from their special compartment in *Cordelia's* hull, leaving a nice string where the ships couldn't pursue without passing them.

"Are those mines?" Noa asked.

A little extra insurance policy," Cardno answered.

"You may have just destroyed any chance they're friendly."

Cardno rolled his eyes. "These are pirates, Lieutenant. They're not friendly."

As if in confirmation, the ships' cannons began firing in unison, sending scattered bolts and torpedoes into the space surrounding *Cordelia* and the fighters. Explosions rocked *Cordelia*, shaking the cockpit but there were no direct hits so far. Cardno had no doubt that wouldn't last long.

Noa steadily dispatched orders. "Increase power to rear shields! Evasives. Engines full! Keep heading away from them." Cardno was impressed by Noa's calm in the face of attack.

Cardno's computer beeped and he saw the pirate ships closing in. He punched a code into the computer to activate the mine's tracking systems. Moments later, he saw explosions on his combat screen as the mines zeroed in on the nearest targets and did their jobs.

"That ought to piss them off," Cardno muttered.

Then a final ship appeared close on their tails and the comm beeped, indicating an open channel. Cardno recognized the new ship as The Hand. He'd escaped and come back? Where were the major and the rest of his squadron? The comm beeped again and he flipped a switch.

"Attention freighter *Cordelia* and fighter escorts, you have twenty seconds to stop engines, lower shields, and prepare for boarding or we will destroy you." The Hand sounded almost amused this time. He had the upper hand and clearly knew it.

Cardno cursed himself for taking the common shipping route at the last moment. It was faster, which is why he'd made the switch, putting aside his reservations about just the kind of trouble he was having now.

The Many Tortures of Anthony Cardno

Yao Noa's voice was confident as he replied. "I'm sorry, we can't do that. We're on an official mission for the Boralian Alliance. It is you who must stop all aggression now to avoid arrest."

The Hand laughed heartily and his crew began firing again. The Hand's own missle rocked *Cordelia*, and the warning alert sounded as the shield strength lights flashed. Shields were down twenty percent.

Cardno flipped the comm to the VS37's private channel. "We can't win."

"We just have to hold out until help arrives," Noa replied.

"I thought you couldn't reach them?" Now the boy's confidence was starting to get annoying.

"If the Hand is here, they'll be right behind."

Cardno had never met a pilot who wasn't prone to overconfidence, but he found himself questioning the Academy's teaching methods. Realism was also a necessity for survival.

Cordelia rocked again, shields dropping another five percent. He saw explosions rocking the VS37s too. They were done for. His heart pounded the walls of his chest like a prisoner attempting to bust out of a cell. This wasn't the way he'd wanted to go out. He had no control. His mind raced considering things he might have done differently.

The combat system beeped as Cardno adjusted the controls, strengthening the rear shields. More blips suddenly appeared and he saw behind them.

"This is Major Farien Noa of the Boralian Alliance, you're all under arrest by authority of the High Lord Councilor." The voice was commanding and firm as it came over the open channel on the comm.

Cardno closed his eyes and sighed a moment. At least the squadron could help them escape. They couldn't possibly win against so many bigger ships but their arrival at least meant Cardno might have a chance to survive.

✺

As soon as he came out of hyperspace, Farien's ship rocked with explosions and he had to gather himself as he sorted out what was going on. He sensed his squadron appearing around him and sliding quickly into formation. Farien's eyes were too busy searching for the VS47s and freighter he'd left behind. There they were—in the middle of a fleet of attackers of all shapes and sizes, evading as best they could an onslaught of laser blasts and torpedoes. Every few minutes, they'd surge toward an opening in an attempt to break free, but then a pirate

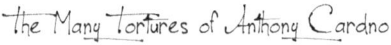

would cut them off while his teammates deluged them with fire. Farien was amazed they'd held out at all.

"This is Major Farien Noa of the Boralian Alliance, you're all under arrest by authority of the High Lord Councilor," he announced over the open channel on the comm.

He switched the squadron channel and keyed the comm again. "Squadron commander, shields on full, weapons ready. Fire at will." As his Squadron split off to obey the orders, Farien sped toward his endangered pilots. "Lake, Yao, you okay?"

Yao sounded amazingly calm. "Yes, sir. Just wondering what took you so long."

Yellow and orange flashes lit his cockpit from behind as his fighter rocked from an explosion. Farien immediately began turning the VS37 as he searched the scanner.

The Hand's scratchy voice came over the comm. "Weapons and shields off. Engines full stop. And tell the freighter to prepare for boarding." The pirate sounded amused as he added: "Trust me, if you want to live."

"Not gonna happen," Farien replied, noting that the pirate's ship had closed up fast to ride tight on his and Hest's tails.

"I was hoping you'd say that!"

Farien's ship rocked again as the pirate fired torpedoes, narrowly missing his engines. He saw Hest peel off to his right in an attempt to evade, but the torpedoes stayed locked and exploded against his right wing. Hest's ship wobbled as the young pilot struggled to regain control.

"You okay, Hest?" Farien called.

"I think so, sir." Hest's voice was shaky. "She's a little hard to control."

"Fall back and assess the damages," Farien said. "I'll deal with our friend."

Matching his arc to Hest's as the wingman turned back, Farien pulled up, spinning his fighter and coming down straight at the pirate's ship from above, lasers blazing. Farien cackled as explosions rocked the pirate's ship as he spun to evade and dove up to meet Farien. *How'd you like that one, pirate?*

Then the Hand suddenly changed course and raced to follow Hest's crippled ship, firing lasers and torpedoes simultaneously.

Farien screamed inside his cockpit as he arced around onto the pirate's tail, but he could already see he was too late. His fist clenched around the joystick as he silently urged the engines to somehow defy physics and fly beyond their capabilities.

The Many Tortures of Anthony Cardno

Hest's ship exploded into thousands of particles of light.

Farien cursed as he let go at the pirate with every weapon he had. His breath froze in his throat, so intense was his focus. But then he had to breathe and he saw that the Hand was already diving again and slipping out of range.

Flashes on his combat scanner and through the edges of his blast shield confirmed that the rest of the squadron was also engaged. But they couldn't last long against these ships. Farien typed into the computer, sending a distress call to the Boralian fleet. He only hoped a military ship was near enough to arrive in time to help.

"We're way outnumbered, Major," Solanus said urgently over the comm. It was the first time Farien had heard the young officer lose his cool in combat. "We need to get out of here!"

"Leave these pirates to keep terrorizing everyone?" Pree sounded disgusted.

"We can't take them on alone," Ami replied.

"We already lost Hest," Solanus added.

"I sent an alert to the fleet," Farien replied, swallowing the rage within. He cleared his throat, bile sliding back down his throat with the anger. He glanced out the blastshield to see Yao and Lake with the freighter, turning back from another attempt to break free of the surrounding pirates. Each time they tried, a ship moved in to block while the others opened fire. They'd all three taken significant hits but somehow avoided major damage. Farien knew that couldn't last. "I'm going to get the others to safety and then we can go FTL again and head for home."

Breaking off from the Hand, he spun again, racing back toward the freighter and VS37s at the center of the attack. He pushed his engines as fast as they could, firing at any enemy target that came into range.

The fighters had formed a circle with the freighter, facing outward and were somehow managing to return fire and operate thrusters simultaneously, spinning themselves in a circle, each wobbling in and out of place to evade as necessary. Farien was amazed.

"Lieutenants, break off engagement and form up on freighter *Cordelia*. The three of you follow me!"

"I alerted the fleet, but it appears no one heard," Lake said. "You didn't respond either."

"I never got a message," Farien answered, instinctually checking his communications settings. Sweat dripped off his brow onto his flightsuit. His body felt slick inside the plastifiber material. He reached over to adjust his cockpit

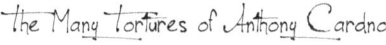

environmental controls.

Thoughts raced through his mind of all the men he'd lost under his command. Each one was personal, like a jagged edge ripping through his gut. He'd never forget the faces, never forget the names. Now, there was another. For a moment, he wanted to abandon everything and go after the Hand. But then he shook it off. He had other pilots to protect.

When the fighters were in formation around the freighter, they began a barrage of lasers, designed to clear a path through the ships. Explosions rocked some of the smaller pirate vessels, but instead of moving clear, they seemed to be closing in.

"Is it me or is this not working?" Solanus said over the radio.

"Push your speed. We have to get clear or they'll tear us apart," Pree said.

"We'll never make it," the freighter pilot commented.

"We have to try," Yao said.

Farien held back on commenting. He had to sound confident, but at the moment, he was more rattled than he'd been in ages. They were right. It was a long shot. And while the fighters could outmaneuver the pirate craft, they were severely outgunned. It would take hours to disable or destroy them all and, given the numbers, the odds were in the pirates' favor.

Explosions rocked the fighters as several of them took direct hits from pirate guns.

"To hell with this!" Pree suddenly peeled off and headed straight for a small pirate ship lying directly in their path.

"Pree! Come back! That's an order!"

But Pree ignored him. Farien tensed as he watched. Pree was a veteran, but he couldn't take on the whole armada alone.

"What are you doing, Pree?" Ami asked, almost pleading over the comm.

"Giving us a chance," her partner replied.

"You should have taken my offer while you stood a chance," the Hand's raspy voice said over the general channel.

"What do you want from me?" Cardno roared. "I just have basic supplies for an outpost!"

"We need them more than those people," the Hand replied.

Pree began zipping in and out around the small pirate ship, targeting the engines, then the cockpit, trying to break through the shields. The pirate craft shifted, in an attempt to aim her guns and fire back, but Pree was too fast for her.

"I hope he knows what he's doing," Farien muttered over the comm.

"He's the best, sir," Ami replied. "Let me help him."

Farien sighed. "Go. Breaking through may be our only chance." As Ami's fighter spun off to join her wingman, Farien hoped he hadn't just sent another pilot off to die. They were his two best people, but still, it was a suicide run. Once the other pirates came to their fellow's aide, it could be over quickly, but then again, Farien and the others might be able to use the distraction.

As Ami and Pree worked together to attack the small pirate ship, it shifted course, moving toward two larger compatriots, obviously hoping to lead the fighters into range of their more powerful guns. In the process, Farien saw an opening was being created which the rest of them could use to clear the center of the pirate armada.

"Center your fire to keep the path clear," Farien instructed. One fighter alone wouldn't scare most of these ships, but concentrated fire from a squadron could do real damage.

✸

Cardno was fed up. The Boralians might be skilled pilots but they were clearly used to formations and planned attacks, not the improvisation required for the situation they all found themselves in. The major's decision to bring his entire squadron inside the armada to help "rescue" Cardno and the others was the last straw. Of *course* the pirates let them in, but getting back out would be the trick. Cardno and the two fighter pilots had been pinned down for over thirty minutes now. More than likely, the major had just signed everyone's death warrants with his commands.

So enough waiting around, Cardno would show these military jocks what improvisation meant. He'd been running schematics and estimates through his computer for the past five minutes and he believed the scenario he had in mind might make a difference. The decision by two of the jocks to distract nearby pirates just aided him.

He had to figure out how to get away from his escort and lay the mines. He'd already programmed his computer to load the mines into the torpedo bays. The mechbots had followed the order without questions an advantage of the old fashioned kind he employed over the newfangled Artificial Intelligence models they'd come out with over the past decade. Bots that think and reason? How could anyone have considered that a good idea.

He double-checked that the mines were ready then punched in the code

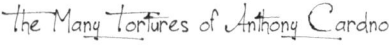

to activate the sequence he'd programmed. He enaged his breaks and fired his thrusters, sliding straight down between his escort and shot out around them to clear space where he could execute his plan.

As soon as the targeting computer said he was clear, he launched the sequence and the mines began firing from the torpedo tubes, homing devices activated. In their present mode, the mines would seek the largest heat signature they could find and latch onto it, waiting for his signal to explode. If it worked right, the pirates would be so surprised and distracted by the hull explosions and he and the fighters could escape. But all that wouldn't occur until Cardno finished planting the mines.

He swung out further to avoid one of the mines homing in on a fighter or two. Now, if those two jockeys playing games distracting the pirates would just stay clear, he'd be okay. Either way, as long as he escaped, he'd be okay with the losses. Pilots die in combat—it was unavoidable.

His radio beeped as fighters adjusted, racing to form around him again.

"Captain, what are you doing?" Major Farien demanded over the comm.

"Stay put, Major. I'm doing what I can to give us a chance. Trust me."

"You're firing devices at the pirates and making yourself a sitting duck in the process," the major answered.

"He's launching mines," Yao corrected.

"Mines?"

Cardno smiled. "Yes, Major. And if the plan works, it might just give us the opening we need. Stay clear of their heat seeking tech until I have them all place, okay? Just a few more minutes."

Farien gave the order. "Lay down cover fire and keep them distracted," he said.

The fighters began firing haphazardly at the various pirate ships, clearly a tactic designed less for damage and more for distraction, but, Cardno hoped as he continued deploying his mines, it just might work.

"You are aware, Mr. Cardno, that heat-seeking tech is illegal outside military channels," said Lake, the other pilot who'd escorted Cardno.

"Now's not the time," Yao scolded. Cardno could almost hear him rolling his eyes. Every squadron had its rookies.

In a few moments, Cardno finished deploying the last batch of mines. According to his computer, one or two had latched onto each of the pirate ships, except the original one. The Hand had flown erratically, zipping in and out and, so far, managed to avoid any of the mines.

The Many Tortures of Anthony Cardno

It would have to do.

"Okay, boys and girls, get back in formation and be ready to move," Cardno said into the comm. He navigated back toward the fighters as they formed up around him again.

The pirate's raspy voice came over the general channel. "We've tired of your games. Enjoy the last moments of your lives, pilots."

With that, the pirates began a barrage of fire unlike what they'd subjected them to before. It was as if even the freighter's survival had been taken off the table. Cardno entered the command and let the mines go as he and the pilots zagged evasively, trying to keep from being hit.

Explosions rocked the pirate ships and the barrage suddenly stopped. Several of them shifted position, as if trying to preemptively evade, not realizing where the attack came from. He saw the two attacking VS37s firing at the damaged pirate ships, working to weaken them in already damaged areas. In the process, as the pirates tried in vain to evade the new threat, a large gap opened up. Cardno and the fighters seized the opening and shot through.

❖

Farien was amazed that the freighter pilot's crazy plan worked. Despite the use of illegal weaponry, it had saved them all. Farien decided perhaps some details could be left out of his report. As he curved back to view the pirates and account for his men, he saw an explosion rock the two VS37s which had lagged behind— Pree and Ami.

"I'm hit," Pree called.

"I've got you, Pree," Ami answered.

"Too late, get clear." Pree's voice trailed off as his ship wobbled then seemed to teeter and point straight down toward a pirate freighter.

"Pull up!" Ami screamed, but moments later, the fighter exploded against the freighter's engines, stopping the pirate cold and ending Pree's life.

Farien cursed at yet another loss as he heard Ami's scream over the radio. Then Ami began firing maniacally at anything in sight.

"Ami! Get back here! Now!" Farien forced out the words. He knew how she must feel but they'd never survive once the pirates regrouped and came after them. Explosions rocked his cockpit. He glanced at his scanner to find the Hand's ship on him again.

"Transmitting coordinates for rendezvous," Farien said into the comm as he

did his best to evade. "Get there and wait for me. Captain Cardno, that means you, too."

"Let us help you, sir," Solanus urged.

"No, I can handle it. Get to safety!" Farien spun his ship into a loop and dove upward, curving so his cockpit was upside down from his earlier position as he looked down on the Hand from above.

"We won't leave you, Major," Yao said.

"We have a civilian to protect," Farien said. As he arced back, he saw Ami's fighter break away from the pirates and rejoin the others. The pirates themselves were regrouping, leaving their disabled comrade to drift as they did. Then he saw the Hand's ship adjusting course to intercept him head on.

"Don't sacrifice yourself, sir!" Solanus pleaded.

"I'll just distract them 'til you're clear," Farien said. "Go! Now!" He had no idea if he could get away or not, but it didn't matter. He'd lost enough men. If anyone else had to die, it would be him.

Then Lake's fighter and the freighter leapt into FTL, smearing across the stars and disappearing into space.

Farien breathed deeply with relief, then saw the remaining three turn back toward him.

"We can't leave you, sir," Ami said.

The pirate ships were racing toward them again.

"I'll be right behind you! Go before they trap us again!" His ship rocked as he and the Hand exchanged fire head-on, then dodged last minute to avoid colliding. *So that's how you want to play it, is it?*

The other fighters fired at the Hand's ship as he circled around, but he evaded their shots again, heading back toward Farien.

Farien forgot his companions and put all his focus on the Hand. *Two of my pilots are dead because of you. It's time you paid for your sins.* The Hand fired, but Farien waited, targeting, hoping for just the right moment.

Then his scanners beeped. Blips began materializing around them. Farien looked up to see the pirate armada, changing course. They were arcing back to flee. Still, the Hand kept coming. Farien fired, lasers strutting across the enemy's upper hull, then the enemy was past him and Farien began to turn.

"Someone call for help?" A familiar voice said over the comm.

"Commander! Are we glad to see you!" Solanus called out.

Farien recognized the markings on the new arrivals—the Boralian fleet had come to their rescue. But he didn't have time to chat. He had to get the Hand.

 The Many Tortures of Anthony Cardno

He lost sight of the pirate as he arced around, but when he came back straight onto the position where the pirate had last been, once again, the enemy had disappeared.

"Where'd he go? Do anyone of you have a fix on him?" Farien cursed to himself. Sounding panicked in front of his men wasn't going to earn him any marks for leadership.

"He's gone, Sir," Yao replied.

Farien's fingers danced on the keys, sending a code through the scanner and it searched again. The wait time seemed interminable but lasted only a few seconds. Farien cursed. What kind of technology did this guy have to disappear so fast?

The commander's voice came through the comm sounding almost amused. "Is this how you greet a Senior Officer, Major?"

Farien sighed as he keyed on the mic. "Hello, Commander. Welcome to our party."

"My men will round up these pirates. Your ship appears damaged. Are you okay?"

Farien sighed. For a moment, he considered mentioning Hest and Pree. Of all people, his old friend Davi Rhii would understand. But he shook it off. Time to lead again. "I'm fine, Commander Rhii. And so's your son. He distinguished himself today."

"Well, come aboard so we can thank you properly."

Farien sighed and turned as the other fighters formed up on him. He heard Ami sending a radio call to Lake and the freighter, asking them to return. Explosions flashed outside his blast shield as six Boralian destroyers finished mopping up the much smaller pirate armada as they fled in desperation.

Some day, Hand. Some day.

With that, he led his squadron back toward the command ship of his oldest friend.

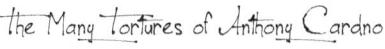

Readercon. Oh, Readercon. Where I first met in person several of the authors I'd made friends with on Twitter, including Damien Walters and Sabrina Vourvoulias. And Bear Weiter, whom I met thanks to Damien. I was excited when Bear asked if he could get in on this project—I mean, why would someone I'd only just met want to torture me in print if I hadn't offended him in some way at the convention? Turns out, no, I hadn't, but he had a story idea ready to go and thought this was a worthwhile project. Parke Godwin said "who you are may depend on whose telling your story." Weiter's tale implies it might also depend on what you're wearing.

The Old Suit

BEAR WEITER

Anthony pulled the suit on, adjusting how it sagged on the hips and shifting it around the shoulders until it fit. It took several minutes to get it right, and even then it felt thin, papery, nearly worn through.

He smoothed the front down, checking himself in the mirror. "It'll have to do," he said out loud.

Afterward he dressed, slipping into tan slacks and a striped button-up shirt—casual, unassuming, even boring. *Perfect.* He wished it meant few would notice him, but that ship had sailed—many called him friend, and he rarely encountered a day without at least one person talking to him. It was part of his job, after all.

He scarfed down a quick breakfast, packed up his computer bag, and headed out for the day.

The sign of a bad day started right away.

His neighbor, Nora, stood at the end of her driveway. She waved as soon as she saw him.

"Anthony!"

He walked to her, a warm smile across his face. He knew it was warm be-

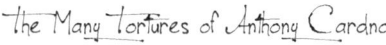

cause he had practiced it often and used it daily to great success.

She returned the smile. "I was going to complain about the trash pickup, but you always seem to make the day brighter."

"I don't believe in negativity," he said. Standing next to her he realized how much he loomed over her small frame. He could keep her from talking with one hand, and permanently shut her up with only a bit more effort.

Instead, he let her ramble.

She started in on the trash service after all, how it had changed days again. She followed this with her frustration regarding the neighbor cats and what they had done to her gardenias, pointing out the damage in detail. He nodded solemnly, and offered encouraging words when it seemed appropriate. Before excusing himself he helped her bring in the still-full garbage cans.

"You're the best, Anthony!" she squeezed his arm with affection. Her face dropped a second later, switching to a look of concern as she eyed the place she had touched.

He withdrew a couple of steps, flashing his warm smile. "Have a nice day, Nora." He hurried on.

Stay out of range with anyone else today, he told himself. That proved easier said than done.

The bus driver greeted him by name, as did a couple of the passengers. After taking his seat, Old Man Rory came to sit next to him. Rory enjoyed talking quietly, conspiratorially—regarding politics, corporations, and the Illuminati—which included a lot of touching of Anthony's back, and a heavy dose of foul breath.

Where Rory's hand rubbed, something felt odd.

Still, Anthony agreed with Rory's sentiments with his own hushed words, helping the conversation forward. He even suggested a connection in Rory's thoughts that Rory had failed to see. It wasn't true—nothing Rory said was even close to the truth, Anthony knew this quite well—but it kept Rory talking.

"Right you are, my friend. Right you are." Rory stood as the bus approached a stop. He glanced at Anthony's shoulder, but met his gaze once again and winked. "We'll talk more soon."

Rory got off the bus, leaving Anthony alone for several minutes.

He took advantage of the free moment by pulling out a pen and pad of paper. He made notes of the interactions so far—words said, people waving, all of it. This was his job, and he did it well. He did not care for it—had come to loathe it, actually—but that did not affect his performance.

He got people talking—from the mundane to the exciting, their day-to-day activities as well as adventures in times past. People opened up to him, and he sucked it all in. Those he interacted with the most thought him to be a writer, which proved to be a perfect cover for his note taking and report making. That, though, was merely a facade, a character.

Anthony Cardno did not exist.

Not all of his kind had such roles. When he had first begun, he thought his was the dream job. Certainly it took little effort, and had less risk than others. But there were the hidden dangers only revealed through years of work. Speech, once new, now scraped past his ears like sandpaper. The lightness of smiling now stabbed pain behind his eyes. And the freshness of human ideas now stank with the staleness of compost.

Even his suit had started to show its age.

It could always be worse, he told himself—a strange thought, an *Anthony* thought. This scared him. *I'm even starting to think like them!*

He got off the bus at the mall stop. He passed through every week or so, to watch, to talk, and to record. The density of people and experiences beat nearly all other locations. It was ideal.

And it started right away.

"Hi Anthony!"

"Anthony!"

"Hey, Anthony!"

People called him over, came up to him, waved from a distance. There were hand shakes, back patting, and even the occasional hug. They asked about his writing, told him their own stories. He knew the names of their children, their pets, their lovers. He gave them just enough of his own made-up stories to satisfy them, and expertly turned the conversation back to everyone's favorite topic—themselves.

A few gave curious glances after the physical contact—he could tell something did not feel right to them. Until he could get his suit issue addressed he'd have to reduce the touching.

In between the encounters he would sit on a bench, or in the food court, and write it all down. Even there people would interrupt, starting new discussions on inane topics. He greeted each one with his warm, perfected smile.

It exhausted him.

A couple of hours after noon, he exited the mall and walked across the street. Unlike the mall, the Chinese buffet would be nearly empty this time of the day, and that was just what he needed.

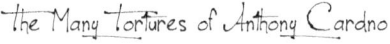

Plus, he did quite enjoy the worminess of Lo Mein, the sliminess of Moo Shu anything, and the satisfying meatiness of their General Tso's chicken.

Mr. Chen, the long-time owner of the restaurant, personally sat him at what he said was Anthony's favorite table, in the back. Anthony had no favorites—being away from people right now was the key. With only a few other tables occupied, it was an easily satisfied goal.

Anthony prepared two plates of food, heaped high. Back at the table, he consumed all of one plate and part of another within minutes, before pulling out his machine. He transcribed his notes between forks of food.

"Is that one of those new laptops?" Mr. Chen asked.

He had appeared silently, almost causing Anthony to drop food on the input surface.

Anthony glanced down. He had used the thing for so long he had stopped thinking about it, but it did look quite a bit like a sleek, high-end laptop. "Yeah," he said. "Work only gets me the best."

He had just entered the first of his daily notes. *Suit's getting thin, may fail soon. Requesting acquisition of another. Prefer change of persona, something less people oriented.*

"So it's fast?" Mr. Chen stood parallel to the screen, but leaned over as if wanting to see.

Anthony turned it away. "Oh it's fast alright. But it's work stuff." He offered Mr. Chen a shoulder shrug. "I'm not allowed to show anyone." *The things I could show you,* he thought. *Horrible, nasty things. Gloriously violent things.* He showed his warm smile instead.

Mr. Chen bowed and stepped back. "I understand." He smiled. "Have a nice day, Anthony!"

Anthony offered a wave and a smile of his own. He deleted the last few words of his notes and wrote: *Prefer change of persona, something that allows for violence. Soldier, hitman, serial killer.*

He finished his notes, along with three more plates of food. Mr. Chen came to talk to him twice more during his walks through the buffet line.

Some afternoons he volunteered time at a retirement community, and he headed there next. Most of the people didn't talk as often, and he appreciated that. Plus, when they did say something it was usually less guarded, even on a first meeting. He didn't know if their looseness had to do with the frequent mixup between him and a loved one, or if they just didn't care what they said, so close to death. Either way, it worked to his benefit.

He didn't get that far today.

At the entrance, a new nurse sat behind the desk. Her name tag said Theresa. He fired up his warm smile as soon as he saw her, and introduced himself. "Ha, muh num ith ..."

She stood, a quizzical look across her face.

"Uh ..." he said. It sounded wet and floppy.

"Are you okay?" she asked.

Anthony put his hand to his face. The left corner of his mouth had sagged, slipping from its connection points. He worked the loose flesh with the tips of his fingers.

"Are you having a stroke?"

Anthony extended a finger—*one second* it said. He moved his jaw around, testing everything. "No," he said. It sounded normal. "I'm good. This just happens sometimes." He pulled a big smile to prove it was all fine.

"Why don't you sit. We have a doctor in today—"

He interrupted her. "No, that won't be necessary. I ... uh ... was just leaving anyway."

He backed away. He strengthened the smile, turning it up even further. This only increased her look of concern.

He ran out.

Good move. Make them notice you for all the wrong reasons.

He slowed his pace, walking at a normal gait the rest of the way to the bus stop. He realized he may need to volunteer at a new retirement home, but if that was the worst of this slight misadventure, so be it.

As the bus pulled up, he recognized the driver—Gary, who worked the afternoon shift on Anthony's usual route. The driver waved even before pulling to a stop.

"Hey Anthony!" he said as he opened the doors.

Anthony bounded up the steps. As he reached the top, and just as Gary was asking how he was doing, a loud rip resounded from behind. In the stunned moment of silence, a distinctive smell wafted up around them.

They looked at each other with the faces of two men in an elevator, where one had just farted—Gary tried to hold back a growing look of disgust, while Anthony's face fell in embarrassment.

He knew immediately what had happened. His suit had given out, ripping in such a way as to sound like flatulence. In doing so, his own body's secretions were exposed to the air, carrying his natural scent out into the bus.

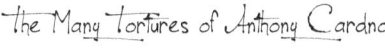
The Many Tortures of Anthony Cardno

It was not a bad smell—in fact, he secretly enjoyed his own heady aroma. But it was plain to see Gary did not. The man gagged, covering his face with both hands.

Anthony did the only thing he could. "Excuse me," he said quietly, grabbing his backside in one hand and squeezing it closed. He walked backwards into the bus, heading all the way to the rear.

The two other passengers got off before the bus could pull away, and Gary mercifully drove without stopping until Anthony's. No words were exchanged along the way, nor looks in the mirror. The bus quickly drove on as soon as Anthony stepped off the bus.

He walked that way back home, with one hand holding the suit closed and the other carrying his computer bag. Nora was sitting on her front porch as he neared. She called his name and waved as walked by.

He ignored her.

Once inside, he opened his machine, ready to put in an emergency request. Instead, the receipt icon blinked green repeatedly—the higher-ups had replied to one of his messages. He tapped it and read.

Request denied. Must deal with suit for the time being. Your assignment as Anthony Cardno continues for the foreseeable future.

He wanted to rip the suit off of him, to shred the skin with his claws, to gnash it to bits with his second set of teeth. He wanted no part of this assignment, or having to deal with these foul humans and their trifling existence. He would show them real fear. Let them talk about the thing that came tearing out of the flesh of some guy.

Carefully, tenderly, he removed the suit and hung it on its support frame. And he did the only thing he could—what Anthony would do—he spent the rest of the evening rebuilding his Anthony Cardno suit.

Tomorrow's a new day, he thought, and hated every bit of thinking it.

Thanks to Australians Kaaron Warren and Frank Dixon, "torturing Anthony Cardno" is now an international endeavor. Kaaron has written some of the most wonderfully creepy stories I've ever read, and in fact has helped make one of my own stories even creepier. This story takes one of my personality traits—that I do in fact hope for the best in all things—and turns it in a sinister direction.

The Optimist

KAARON WARREN

This is not my body. Dry skin, bones protruding. Limbs all over scabby, flies like black paste licking at the blood there, the pus.

This is surely not my body. I am a big man, muscles strong enough to crack a windpipe, teeth good enough to open a bottle of beer or a vein. Stomach round, full of good food.

This stomach is round, but swollen, hollow. I feel gassy, like a balloon, a bony balloon.

My eyes are caked with pus. I can see through slits; people, tents, flat land stretching out.

My stomach holds a dull pain, same as the time I swallowed too much ice cream, a tub of it, I remember, slid straight down to rest in my belly, slowly melted. My stomach chilled on the inside.

I lift one bony arm, rub my stomach. My fingers are sharp as sticks. My arms are sticks.

I shift in my mother's arms.

I know she's my mother. I recognise the smell of her milk. My tongue creeps out, I can see her nipple and perhaps a drop of milk there.

I stretch up to grasp her nipple in my mouth, but I can't reach.

Sighing, she lifts me higher. "Nothing there, baby, nothing." Tears splash onto my cheek.

"Don't waste water," I say, raising my arm to pat her.

"Baby's talking," she says. "Such a clever baby."

I remember those words; they're good words in any language. In my previous body, "Such a clever baby," when I learnt the potty method, when I learned to read, when I finished high school.

That was the last time anyone called me clever.

Flies crawl into my mouth. I snap it shut. They taste chemical, they're slightly crunchy. A wing flitters down my throat and I cough.

Why won't my mother give me water?

"Water," I say, squeezing her breasts to get attention. "I'm thirsty, Mommy." I remember what to say to make them move.

She shakes her head, squeezes me, puts me on the ground.

"No water," she says. "There is no water."

She walks away, abandons me, and I cry for a few moments, while my energy lasts.

Then I lie back in the dirt, let it slowly cover me.

I can mostly see feet from here. Brown feet.

I've been abandoned before. Do they think I care? That's not something that matters to me. I've been abandoned half my life but I'm not bitter. I'm the stronger for it.

I wonder who won the lottery for my lovely other body. Those muscles, strong legs, that appetite.

I'm hungry. I'm hungry. I'M HUNGRY.

Someone just dropped a grain of rice in my mouth. Uncooked. For me to suck on.

They made a lot of money off me, the government. All the lottery money is meant to help the family of victims, or, if there were no survivors, other unfortunates.

I don't see a cent of it.

No reward for keeping my body strong and healthy.

They wouldn't reward someone like me. I'm to be punished, just to show me who's boss (and someone squeezes a drop of water into my mouth. From a rag. The water tastes like blood). They steal my body and punish me.

They can give me a body not my own but they can't save the world from

The Many Tortures of Anthony Cardno

starvation.

And they call me the criminal.

I remember how to roll onto my stomach and I do it. Someone would coo, if they were watching. No one is; all eyes are on the sky, because a distant hum, a purr, means the helicopters are coming.

I know where they'll land. I begin to crawl.

They're very pleased with themselves, in the courts. "Anthony Cardno, we sentence you to death," they said, and you could see them all jumping out of their skins at their own cleverness. And on the steps, on the News, like some ancient TV show, "We have the technology." Typically with these things, it's all about the idea, nothing about the follow up. Because they don't realise what happens; I've retained my brain, my soul. No one's bothered to tell them.

I won't either. Why spoil it for those who'll follow?

I had choices. The old trick. "Do you choose to die by noose, gas or knife?"

"I choose not to die," I said. They laughed.

"That's not an option. The death penalty is incommutable."

I laughed, then. I couldn't move, they had me strapped so tight. My pulse was slow through my veins, blocked, sluggish.

My choices were displayed before me, vivid pictures.

I could have chosen to become a child about to be shaken to death by her step-father, a gay man bashed in an alley way (I could see his brains on the pavement. It had been raining. Brains and pavement glistened). I could have drowned at sea after eighteen hours balancing on an upturned boat. I could have had my heart ripped out by a mass-murderer (and didn't they chuckle over the irony of that?). I could have smothered to death in a pile of tar, a foolish accident, all my own fault. I could have had my head kicked in, died in a swimming pool, a fire, with friends, alone.

I could have picked any body close to death. I chose this one, tiny and starving.

A woman picks me up. Not my mother. Her eyes look into the distance, at her destination.

She's taking me to the far field, where bodies lie lined up.

She thinks I'm dead.

"No," I cry, using all my strength. "Waah," is what I say, but it's enough to make her look down, see my eyes flutter.

"Not dead yet?" she says.

I hear irritation in her voice; she can't understand why I'm hanging on.

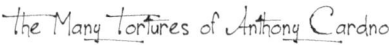

Because I've lived a life already, I think.

I lie in the dirt. I see the sparkle of something and I know sparkle pays. I stretch my fingers out to reach it and a man treads right on my palm.

Crushes my fingers like pretzels.

My mouth is full of salt, like a zombie.

My stomach is a balloon.

The sparkle is a bug, a shiny bug. Saliva fills my mouth now.

Children whimper all around me. The only ones who scream are the new-comers, those who don't know what starvation is yet.

They look so healthy. Flesh on their bones.

If I was bigger I would eat them.

If I had my old body back.

I ate a lot in my old body. I liked to eat. Feasts of fifteen courses. I spent enough on one meal to feed this whole camp for a day.

I loved anything roasted, and those you could keep alive till the last minute, then kill. I ate my cat the day the fancy took me. Roasted him all brown and tasty.

The bug crawls towards me. I watch it, try to hypnotise it. *Come to me, come to me.* The problem is you need strength to feed yourself, and I have none. I only want to close my eyes and sleep, but I need to keep blinking or I'll be lined up in a paddock and I'll never crawl back from there.

The bug is sleepy too. I catch it, roll onto my arm, lay my cheek on my hand, eat him up.

I see a child with a gash on her arm. There are many injured here. The sight of her blood, and I can crawl, now, over and into her lap, the adults think it's cute, they coo and laugh.

The girl closes her arms around me and I lick at her blood, lick lick till she pushes my head away.

"Here, baby," she says, and offers me her teat.

Four years old, she offers me milk.

I suck and chew and bite her nipple off.

She screams, throws me to the ground. People ignore her. Screams mean nothing.

I crawl away.

No one cares about anyone, and that's the truth. I'm stuck with this punishment for something they all want to do. How many have dreamed of doing what I did? I'm punished for my courage, for doing what they want to do.

I rest in the shade of a man who stands leaning on a long stick. He's slumped forward and I think, it won't be long. He'll tip over soon then I'll see what he has in his pockets. I have to shift though, when he pisses down on me. Piss splashes, burning the skin of my legs. I crawl quickly, before the shit falls.

I see a man, dead, because I've seen dead men before. In his hand a crust - how is it no-one has taken it away?

His lips foam slightly. I'm not afraid of disease. Better to die sick later than starving now.

I should have chosen death of a rock-climber. At least I'd smell good air at the end.

I could have died right away, last words then evaporation. I considered it for a while, just to piss them off. They don't really like evaporation. They like to keep the bodies for the lottery, to pay for new roads nobody can use.

Evaporation feels like being eaten by black ants. Tiny ones, who take cell-size bites.

"We'll make it last a long time," they said. All they could threaten me with was pain. I had no family, no friends. Women cried at my trial, but not for me. They cried at the uselessness of life, that this is what it comes down to, one man against the world, standing up for what he believes in.

"Murderer," they shouted, as if that was an insult. I could tell them why but they didn't care.

It was for the sake of the children. Why would they want to grow old in this terrible world?

So they call me a murderer.

There is a little girl nearby holding a piece of bread. I can smell the starch, the goodness.

She was given it. I have to take it. That's the way.

I crawl over and she stares at me with those blank eyes. She isn't even human any more.

There is food to be had, and water, if you don't mind snatching it from the mouths of babies.

I intend to grow up again.

I choose not to die.

I crawl over. The little girl lies on her back. I wriggle until my stomach is over her face, covering it.

I can feel her sucking in my flesh, hoping for air. As she struggles, I lean back and take her bread. By the time I finish eating it she is no longer breathing.

They made a mistake sending me here.

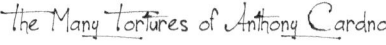

They thought I had just hours to live.

But I don't die that easily.

The helicopter lands. I have judged it well, worked hard. I have made the word "HELP" in stones and I sit beside it, keeping my eyes wide, intelligent. People kick my stones; I am patient. I put them back in place.

My eyes wide open.

A soldier approaches. I wish I could sing. I move my arms, semaphore, and I catch his eye. A white-skinned muscleman with red hair.

He comes, stands over me. Reads my stones.

"Help," he says.

He stares at me, confused.

"Who did that?" he says.

I place my hand on my chest.

"My God," he says.

He picks me up and sets me in his knapsack. He gives me fruit.

"Come on, little bubba. You stay with me," he says.

I nod.

Sure I'll stay.

Until I grow up again.

Dennis Miller's "One Woman's Vengeance" is a brutal western with a strong female lead; when I asked Dennis if he'd like to participate in this project, I hoped I'd get a chance to interact with Nora Hawks (even if it meant being killed by her). I didn't tell Dennis about that hope, though, so instead I got a truly great story about the power of stories to teach and to change us. The fact that I'm not the storyteller, but the little boy to whom the stories are told (and younger than Dennis' son Nathan was when we first met) only adds to the punch of the story. I can't go back in time, but reading this I feel like I have.

The Story Teller

DENNIS R. MILLER

"I'd like a story about, mmm, about a man who is scared, uh, and then gets brave ... and chases all the giants out of the land forever!"

It was the first time the timid little boy had spoken and his friends looked at him in surprise before nodding in agreement.

Uncle Jesso, as the children called their new friend, smiled so that his graying brown mustache bent upward like the wings of an old gliding gull. His uneven teeth, slightly stained with the ghosts of uncounted cigarettes, were still white enough to be friendly.

"Ok, Anthony." The man's gentle voice had a faint hoarseness, as if he'd been talking to a large crowd for hours. He cleared his throat. "Once upon a time there was a little boy. His name was—" Uncle Jesso stopped and squeezed his watery brown eyes shut in exaggerated intense thought. "What was his name?"

The children studied Jesso, as if to extract the name from the depths of the storyteller's mind. "Call him Anthony!" A girl said with sudden excitement. "It's Anthony's story." This made perfect sense to everyone, even though many had silently hoped the story hero would bear their name.

Uncle Jesso opened his eyes and nodded in a solemn but satisfied way, as

if together they had solved an intricate but important problem. "His name was Anthony." Jesso looked at the boy who sat on his knees, head bent shyly to his chest with this unexpected burst of attention. "Anthony was a little smaller than our Anthony, and he was usually a shy guy, and when the wicked giant Odo stomped into the land, roaring and stinking from no bath and eating all the cows, Anthony ran and hid ..."

The children sat at attention on this still summer day, absorbing Jesso's words in the vast vats of their young minds where Odo's image was as real as their parents.

Uncle Jesso was a gift to the children. No one knew where he came from. He had appeared in town and he was theirs and that was that. Uncle Jesso created personal stories for each child, a gem to be shared by all, but valued most highly by the individual requestor. Each child had a turn every Saturday on the Franklin Town Green where they gathered with the old man.

The children's parents were not quite so ready to accept without question this soft-spoken mystery man. As Betty Wylie told it, the fellow simply appeared on her doorstep one Sunday and asked if he could rent a room upstairs where she rented three rooms by the month.

"He had very nice manners which you don't see much of anymore," she told Alice Wygant. Mrs. Wylie nudged the graying bun at the back of her head as if to make sure it hadn't changed its position of 35 years. "His clothes are old but you can see he keeps them neat, just like his room. I gave him the room that Arthur used as a den before he died, you know. Keeps to himself except for meals, and he don't eat nothin' to speak of." She nodded. "Takes his walk just after supper," she added thoughtfully.

The neighbor nodded. New people in town were commonplace after the rush in the early 70s of Philadelphia and New Jersey residents to buy homes in quiet Pennsylvania towns like Franklin. There was a several-year shake-up as the flatlanders bought property that had been in the same family for generations. But finally in the '80s the life of the small town settled back into the floorboards of its 19th-century structure. Folks still clipped coupons for their Saturday ventures to the Acme or Super Duper. They made quick stops at Jim's General Store at the south end of town for a carton of milk or a pack of cigarettes. The businessmen continued their 10 a.m. coffee in Bonos. Franklin had incorporated its emigrants, but as open as the people might be, when a single man with a grayish face, no past and a distinct aversion for small talk appears, it is noted. Quiet though he was, Jesso stood out like a Brooklyn accent. Some parents were concerned about his weekend activities with the children.

"Well, I say it's better they listen to stories out in the air than sittin' glued to that TV set all morning," one woman told another as they sat like two rumpled astronauts beneath hair dryers in Tina's Salon on High Street.

The other woman sniffed. "Maybe, but at least I know what Mindy's getting when she watches cartoons—mild trash. I have no idea what that man is putting in Mindy's—or your Jennifer's—head."

Anthony's father, Jack Cardno, was a quick-tempered mechanic at the Ford garage. He took a less speculative attitude on the matter. He said he didn't like the creepy little city shit guy and didn't trust him. Anthony, who a few weeks before would have hung his head and said nothing, defended Uncle Jesso, but Jack Cardno finally cut him short and sent the boy to his room. Anthony closed his door and opened a book of fairy tales Uncle Jesso had helped him find in the Franklin Library.

Sandy Kovich, a Trenton, N.J. native, wondered out loud if Jesso might be a pedophile, using stories to make the children trust him. It was this rumor, which attracted embellishments and conviction as it made the rounds, that sent one of the fathers to ask Police Chief Steve Jones why this Jesso character hadn't been checked out.

"I have," Jones said reassuringly. "He has no record of any kind." Jones didn't say that the man seemed to have very little background at all.

Steve Jones was a slow moving, handsome man whose outward nonchalance belied the sharp, nonconformist mind. Most people in town knew he had an English degree with a minor in philosophy. But few yet knew he spent his free nights reading Carl Jung, Otto Rank, mythology, and Henry Miller, the latter of whom would have caused Franklin residents of all religions to have grave suspicions about the popular officer. No one knew he wrote short stories at night based on his experiences with the Franklin folks.

Jones' saddle bit briar was rarely out of his mouth, though council members had asked him on the side to remove it so he would look more aggressive. It wasn't that they minded him smoking it. It was just that, damn it, he didn't look like a cop was supposed to, smoking his pipe and tipping his hat to women.

But Jones kept his pipe and with apparent effortlessness kept the Franklin daily machinery oiled and purring. No one could accuse him of not keeping order. In fact, folks often talked about the time Jones shot Shorty Mackenwraith, one of the rowdy Mackenwairth family members who lived in shacks in the Appalachian mountains outside town.

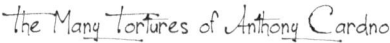

Shorty got drunk one afternoon and robbed Daisy's Boutique on the corner of Main and Troy Streets. Steve Jones chased the burly logger for five blocks until they were outside town where Shorty, winded, mad and in need of a drink, turned and fired at Jones. The bullet ripped the ground in front of the officer.

The young chief shook his head as if disappointed, and shot Shortly cleanly through the right thigh. He then walked over, took the whining man's gun, lit a cigarette for him and radioed the ambulance. Then he lit his pipe and sat down beside Shorty and talked until the volunteer crew arrived. Shorty and the whole Mackenwraith family became Jones' defenders and Shorty told the story with pride that he had been shot by Chief Jones. "He stared me down so I couldn'a hit a barn door if I'd been inside it. Then he shot me clean. He coulda killed me if he wanted." He shook his head in admiration. "He's some sonofabitch."

There were several such stories about the young chief.

One evening Jones bumped into Jesso on Main Street during the man's regular walk. "Police chiefs are usually quicker to greet me," Jesso said, smiling politely up the six-inch distance between his head and Jones'.

The young officer pushed his hat back over his dark hair. "You travel a lot, Mr. Jesso." He made a motion with his hand and they started down the walk together. There was little traffic and few people about. The town was quiet.

Jesso nodded, stroking one side of his mustache with his finger. "You're quiet and efficient."

"You're welcome to stay as long as you like."

Jesso nodded appreciatively. "I like to be around as long as possible."

"Coffee?"

Jesso smiled and said sure. They crossed the street to Bono's. Inside, Walt Bono, a gray-haired bear of a man whose long love affair with cheap whiskey had eaten deep creases into his round face, ambled to the booth with two coffee in chipped cups. "Keepin' law 'n order?" Walt stuck his tongue between his rotted teeth and his face wrinkled into a large, grinning walnut.

Walt had been off the bottle a full year. Before that, Jones had locked up Walt several times. Walt turned from Jones to the older man. "Hey, Jesso, got a story for an old man with acid indigestion and a bad back?"

Jesso chuckled. "The only thing that can help you is to drink somebody else's coffee."

Walt let out a raspy, appreciative laugh. "Ain't *that* the truth!"

He lumbered off toward a new customer. Jones smiled and leaned back in the booth. "The parents are concerned about you. It's not everyday that a man shows up and keeps to himself except to play Homer to the munchkins."

Jesso coughed and nodded, smiling. His intelligent eyes, the color of Walt's muddy coffee, studied Jones. The stare was direct, unselfconscious, and weary. He has nothing to hide but his illness, Jones thought. "I like children. Children like stories," Jesso said.

Jones tapped his pipe out against his palm, pulled his tobacco pouch out, and reloaded the crusty bowl layer by layer. Men in a hurry or with something to hide became very nervous during this ritual. Jesso watched, interested, and pulled out a cigarette. Jones lit his pipe, and smiled through a blue cloud. "You were an ad man for, what, 20 years?"

"A copywriter."

"You left the job and sold your home."

"Medical bills. The high cost of being sick in America." The man had been interviewed often, Jones thought.

"You've been traveling since then."

Jesso nodded. "About five years ... telling stories."

"Why?" Jones asked with open curiosity.

Jesso coughed, stared at his cigarette and took a sip of coffee. "I do it because not enough time is given to children."

"Shouldn't their parents worry about that?"

Jesso shrugged. "I never had any kids of my own." Jones waited patiently. The man was road weary, ill and, what? Jones couldn't tell. Frightened, maybe.

Jesso sat back in the booth and studied his cup. "Kids sit in rows in school. They're trained in groups, fed processed information by a tired teacher and then more processed information on television."

Jones puffed his pipe and studied the tired man before him. "So you give the kids stories."

"A personal story. They tell me the subject, which revolves around their personal lives, and if I can figure out the problem, or come close, I give them a story that might help." He paused. "Adults have tobacco, alcohol, religion, sex, and, sometimes, an occupation they like. A kid has himself and a budding soul. I keep them acquainted with the power of the spoken word and imagination— positive addictions, as I see it."

Jones nodded, hypnotized by the man's smooth speaking voice and the power of his belief.

Jesso toyed with the ashtray that read First National Bank of Franklin. "Children are unspoiled little gods. All I want to do is give them something to have

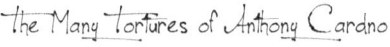

when they're on their own." He seemed to read the chief's minded and smiled. "Yes, if they remember me and my stories, it's a small immortality. It worked for our Homer, didn't it?" Jones nodded. "But more importantly, if one of them understands and learns and later tells his own stories to others, isn't that ... something?" He looked into Steve Jones' eyes. "Isn't that maybe all we have?"

Jones nodded again and laid pipe carefully in the ashtray. He thought before he spoke. "You're dying, aren't you?" His voice was quiet and gentle.

Jesso smiled sadly and rubbed the side of his mustache. "You're a smart young man," Jesso said. "The town is lucky to have you." He smiled. His eyes were tired. He leaned back in the booth. "You know the answer. The real answer."

The answer, Jones knew, was this: We're all dying. Some of us who are dying faster than others single out a purpose and pursue it to the exclusion of all else. The young cop looked at the man whose peaceful expression was of one who has fully realized and accepted his mortality. He now focused his limited time on the next generation of adults. His personal stories gave them a torch to carry into the dark labyrinths of adulthood.

●

Saturday. The children sat in a circle around Uncle Jesso. After two stories he asked casually where Anthony was. A girl volunteered that his dad wouldn't let him come anymore.

"Sometimes Anthony's bad and gets punished," another added.

"Yeah, once he got his finger broke cause he made his dad real mad. He had to wear a big bandage." The little narrator held out his hands to represent the exaggerated cast. The others nodded.

"Anthony's dad says you're bad," another said. "But you're not, are you, Uncle Jesso?"

Jesso smiled sadly. "No." Encouraged by the sudden openness, another girl said her mother told her to sit at least six feet from Jesso and asked him how far six feet was.

"Right about where you are," Jesso said. "Not very far."

They sat in confused silence as slow traffic chugged by, stopping at regular intervals at the Main Street traffic light. Jesso broke the tension by looking around theatrically. "Do you know how this town started? Anybody? No? Franklin began in 1844 when some brave people settled here and cut down the trees and made farms and this town. And they named it after a great American, Ben

The Many Tortures of Anthony Cardno

Franklin. And you know what? I've walked all over America and this is one of the most beautiful towns anywhere."

The children nodded, struggling to comprehend the magnitude of Uncle Jesso's pronouncement. To some, the town that had been their world suddenly expanded and became an important place in the huge world that Uncle Jesso had seen. Jesso turned to a brunette. "Now, Sandy, a story for you ..."

❋

At the council meeting, Steve Jones listened to the members voice their concerns about Jesso. Bill Ralph, a middle-aged man who moved here from New York, told Jones to "keep a close eye on this character" and made sure it was reflected in the minutes. Jones answered what questions he could and repeated that the man was doing nothing wrong.

The concern, and the conflict, was shared by the parents. They didn't trust Jesso, but parents who had taken turns watching the storyteller from a distance, agreed that he did nothing but talk. They were not proud of their suspicions, but in a world of serial killers and child pornography, they weren't ashamed either.

The next Saturday, despite a cold drizzle, the children gathered around Jesso under the town gazebo. "Uncle Jesso, is there a heaven?" It was Sara, a girl with bright red hair and large round green eyes.

Jesso studied her and finally nodded. "Heaven is as real as anything else."

"But after you die, and all of you is gone, is there heaven?"

He wished he could light a cigarette. "Part of you is never gone. That's why heaven never ends." He motioned to her and she came to him. "Someone you love is gone."

She stared at his knee. "My mommy."

He held out his hand. She took it. After a moment he pulled her to him and hugged her gently. "There's a heaven, Sara."

In a car down the block, a man watched. He saw that it was a comforting hug and that the girl was Sara, whose mother was killed in a car accident last year. The girl was having a hard time adjusting. So was her father, Frank Muller, who'd started drinking heavily. The man was torn between jealousy of a stranger who could comfort a girl, and some strange sort of hope that if anything ever happened to him, someone like this man would be here to help. Not understanding his feelings, nor wishing to think about them, the man drove away.

Just as Jesso was about to ask Sara if she wanted a story, a little blond head

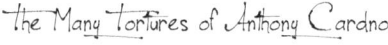

popped up between the balusters. "Anthony!" Jesso was too surprised to hide his pleasure or his concern. "I thought you weren't allowed to come here."

"Dad had to work today and I got brave!"

They stared at each other. Jesso surveyed the children. No one smiled or tried to mask their uneasiness. "Maybe you should go back home, Anthony," Jesso said gently.

The boy looked confused, hurt, then defiant. "I want another story. A quick one. Please?"

Jesso closed his eyes and imagined pleasant things to hide his anger and the pain in his body. "Yes, I'll tell you the story of Broton—"

"Can't his name be Anthony?" Sara squeezed Jesso's thumb.

The man shook his head. "No. Not this time. It must be Broton because Broton is from a race of people who live to be one thousand years old.

"And though Broton is very big and strong and wants to fight the three-eyed Trokodites, he can't until he's at least five hundred years old. Broton is only two hundred, so he must be patient and learn things and feel the world around him. You know one of the things he liked to do best?" He looked around to each of them. Their eyes were wide and they shook their heads slowly. "He loved to read flowers."

"Read flowers!" A boy to Jesso's right yelled. "Are there words on flowers?" Everyone laughed loudly.

Jesso held up his hand for silence. "There are whole books in flowers." He told them, paying particular attention to Anthony, how to begin reading flowers. "And after Broton spent three hundred years reading flowers and trees and grass and clouds, you know what he did?" They shook their heads again, wondering what Broton did.

"He learned to read people," Jesso said. They nodded. "And after two hundred years of reading people, he didn't want to fight. He knew that reading people is better than hurting them. He spent the rest of his life teaching the three-eyed Trokodites to be nicer."

✸

As happens, word spread around town, and as it was spread, distorted. The combination of Jesso holding Sara and Anthony defying his father was too much. The next Saturday Uncle Jesso sat alone in the gazebo.

A few nights later Steve Jones stood on the corner of North and Main blow-

The Many Tortures of Anthony Cardno

ing tobacco juice from his pipe stem as Jesso rounded the corner. Jesso smiled. "You work long hours, chief."

Jones worked the stem back into the shank and smiled. "I like street corners. Once in awhile I meet an interesting character." They walked. "You were deserted last Saturday."

Jesso nodded slowly. "It happens." He went into a coughing fit and they had to stop. When he finished, he looked like he could barely stand. "The damp weather we've been having," he said quietly.

They had come to the end of the block and Jones stared up the street that led out of town and became Route 6 which wound like a long humped gray snake through the Appalachians, blue-tinged in the distance. "Where will you go now, Jesso?"

The small man looked into the same distance, then at Steve Jones. "Nowhere."

The bitterness of the cold tobacco juice bit Jones' tongue. "Take another chance on Walt's coffee?"

Jesso looked up at him, smiled, tired. "You're buying?" Jones nodded.

❖

When the ambulance picks up someone in Franklin—except Mrs. Constance who is a regular with her fainting spells and Ash Buckley when his emphysema flares up—the word spreads quickly. So when the Franklin Volunteer Ambulance stopped at Mrs. Wylie's apartment house and returned to the Franklin Community Hospital, everyone knew it was Jesso.

Steve Jones, who had been giving testimony at the county courthouse 19 miles away, walked over to the hospital when he returned, but the ailing man was asleep. Doc Tillinghast, who ran the little hospital and had delivered nearly every male and female of the last two generations, including Jones, was in the emergency room dispatching a girl with a newly bandaged hand. Steve waited until the girl was gone. "How is he?"

Tillinghast turned from the sink and dried his hands. "Bad."

Doc Tillinghast was a round-faced man mildly wrinkled from 32 years of helping people enter the world, repairing and maintaining them, and easing, when he could, their departures. He tossed his towel on the bed. "He has a day or two, depending on his will. But I don't think he has much of that." He turned his gaze from the towel to the police chief. "He's weak, tired of life, and alone."

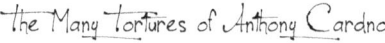

He stared at Jones to let it sink in.

The young chief's eyes swept across the bottles of antibiotics, sterilized needles and cotton swabs. Medicine now enables man to die germless and almost painless, he thought, but no lab has developed a loneliness suppressant. He'd only known Jesso a few weeks, but he felt as he did when Jimmy Kringer, his best friend since high school, blew the top of his head off after his wife Cathy left him four years ago. "People shouldn't have to die alone," he said.

Tillinghast shook his head. "No. They shouldn't." Despite three decades of daily intimacy with life and death, the doctor's green eyes still sparkled. "You're more than just a police chief, Steve. You're creative."

Jones looked at the old doctor, puzzled. Tillinghast continued. "You uphold rules made by men. A dying man doesn't give a damn for those rules." He picked up the towel again and wiped his hands thoughtfully. "When you're attending to the soul, man's laws don't count."

The young chief thanked the doctor and left, at first feeling inspired, then, later in his office, anger and frustration. Jesso had obeyed all the rules. But he enchanted the children and with a unique gift, attending to each one's need with a story and thereby helping all of them. He frightened the parents who now blocked them from Jesso. Christ, they were probably relieved the man was in the hospital.

Doc Tillinghast would let the children in, he implied, but how would Jones convince the parents to let the children come? In his office, he chewed his pipe stem so hard it cracked.

The next day, angrier still and ready to take on the whole town even if it meant his job, Steve Jones drove off for the parents' homes. He was going to tell them what he thought of them and their hypocrisy, their warped values, their fright. Anyone who would deny a dying man some comfort. ... An hour later, he began wondering if there was a big auction somewhere. Seven houses. No one was at home.

He stopped at Jack Cardno's, took a deep breath and knocked. Jack, two years older than Steve, taller and heavier, answered the door. "Jack, I know how you feel about Jesso, but the man is—"

"Ferget it." The large man cut him off.

Steve fought to keep his anger in check. He hadn't slept all night. "Jack, damn it, I'm—"

"Steve, *ferget it!*" Morgan shoved his hands in his pockets. "Anthony's already gone. I let him go 'bout a half hour ago. He came up to me big as hell this

The Many Tortures of Anthony Cardno

morning and demanded to go to the hospital. Said he didn't care if I called you to arrest him."

They studied each other a moment. "I figured if that Jesso could put that kinda piss 'n vinegar in Anthony ..." He shrugged, then swallowed. "Word is the guy's dyin' ..."

❋

Jones pulled into the parking lot and found it half full. The Buick belonged to Frank Daniels; the Taurus to Red Mailer; the Lincoln belonged to attorney Farrel. There were more.

Inside, the waiting room was crowded with quiet, anxious parents. Jones couldn't make any sense of it. Why were the parents here and the children missing? John Farrel, who joined his father's law practice years ago, strode over. "Steve, why didn't you tell us?"

"Tell you what?"

"That this Jesso fellow is dying."

Jones studied Farrel, who defended, by men's rules, the people Jones arrested under another set of rules. "Why does it make a difference, John? What he gave, he gave because he was alive."

Farrel looked at the floor and nodded. "I know," he said quietly. "That's why we brought the kids in." He shrugged with a hint of embarrassment, "Actually, the kids organized and ... well ... we brought them over."

Jones nodded and rushed out of the room, fighting back tears of relief and joy. Beside the door of Jesso's room was a scribbled note: "You may go in, whatever your age. Stay as long as you want. Dr. Tillinghast."

Forming a ring around the bed, the children stood quietly looking up at the pale, motionless man. "... and we brought you flowers to read," said Sara, pointing to the bureau laden with daisies, roses and daffodils that Jones recognized as former residents of the gazebo flower bed.

Jesso's mustache raised slightly in a weak smile. "Thank you." The gentle story-telling voice was now a whisper.

Anthony, at the head of the bed, softly touched the man's shoulder. "Uncle Jesso? Can you tell us a story? One for all of us?"

There was a long silence as the sick man opened his eyes stared at the gray ceiling. "I can't tell ... anymore stories, Anthony." He coughed weakly. "I'm ... sorry." His body relaxed after the effort to speak.

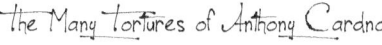
The Many Tortures of Anthony Cardno

There was a long silence. The children stood motionless stared helplessly at the edge of the bed.

Finally Anthony looked at his friends who returned his silent request for help with confused, frightened stares. The little boy looked up at Steve Jones who nodded to him. Anthony looked back at Uncle Jesso and leaned to the man's ear. "Then we'll tell you a story, Uncle Jesso. Ok?"

Jones swallowed and blinked several times. He looked away and then back at Anthony. The boy was suddenly pale, realizing the magnitude of his offer. He looked lost and scared. "What do you want a story about?"

Jesso closed his eyes and sighed. A foot shuffled. Someone sniffed. Jesso was motionless and Steve wondered with sudden panic if he was dead. Then he whispered: "Is anyone afraid of the dark?"

The children looked back and forth at each other and a few reached out to hold hands. One of them said no. Another said, "Sometimes." The others nodded.

Jesso wet his lips. "So am I ... sometimes." He swallowed painfully. "I'd like a story ..." He swallowed again. "About the dark." Jones knew that Jesso was giving the children one last lesson, helping them crack another barrier of fear. Yet beyond this, beyond words and physical age, deep in the body-bound soul, Jesso needed a story of his own. The young chief studied the little faces that showed innocence and understanding in the awesome presence of a dying man, the determination of wanting so badly to help their friend that they didn't know what to do, and despite that, nothing would stop them.

Time seemed to stop. The silence was heavy as the children stood motionless.

Jones rubbed the sweat from his forehead and realized his hand was shaking.

Then, quietly, like a lovely spring breeze, a musical voice began. "Once upon a time a nice man traveled all over the land." The child paused, then added, "And everyone loved him because he was good and kind." The child stopped, not knowing where to go.

A moment later another continued, haltingly, as a bird first learning to sing. "But then a big night came and the man was in it. At first he was very scared." Someone sniffed and started to cry, then gulped it away. "Because he couldn't see the world anymore."

Jesso's eyes were closed, his face peaceful. "It's lovely," he whispered. "Keep going. Please." The children looked at each other, and one-by-one they took each other's hands. They waited now for someone who might have the next line.

Steve Jones stepped out of the world that belonged to the group as Anthony, who had been reading Jesso's face, took the man's pale hand. Though his large blue eyes were bright with tears, the boy's voice was quiet and steady. "Then he saw that the night was full of stories ... and in the stories were friends who would always be with him ... so he would never be afraid ... ."

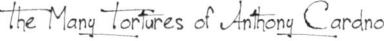

When I was a kid, I was not the most adventurous eater. When I started branching out from the meat-and-potatoes and Italian dishes that were our standard fare at home (Dad's parents were native Scots, so his taste was bland; Mom was Italian and Polish but mostly cooked Italian food my father wouldn't eat), my father famously declared that I must have been adopted. I'm still not the most adventurous eater in the world (I have a very strict "no fish, no fungus" rule), and it seems somehow Mary Robinette Kowal picked this fact out of the ether to inform her (rather egotistical, demanding, and outright jerky) version of me in this story.

The White Phoenix Feather:
a tale of cuisine and ninjas

MARY ROBINETTE KOWAL

Viola leaned across the white tablecloth of Luigi's Interstellar Cafe and Pub. "When I said the ninjas were no match for us, I meant it. Joe will have the White Phoenix Feather by dessert." She checked the edge of her fish knife. She hated clients like this. "Quit gaping and finish your soup."

Anthony Cardno stirred his habanero spinach bisque, mixing the crème fraîche into the soup in marbled swirls. "I don't doubt your skills."

A dark shape scuttled past the wall of tinted glass, silhouetted by the lights illuminating the ships waiting at New Rushmore's spaceport. Crap. She hadn't expected any ninjas until later. "May I have your soup?"

"My soup?"

Without explaining, she hailed a passing waiter. "Two brandies. Neat."

The native species of New Rushmore were more akin to spiders than humans and had acquired their nickname from their middle arms, which ended in a long curved spine as though they were holding a katana.

They were a real pain in the ass.

A ninja dropped from the ceiling, bladed arms extended. Viola hurled Cardno's habanero spinach bisque, splashing it in the ninja's face. He screamed as

The Many Tortures of Anthony Cardno

169

the fiery soup spattered his eyes. Viola punctured his airway with her fish knife and stepped back as he sagged to the carpet.

The diner closest to them slid her chair back to avoid the pool of ichor, but otherwise ignored them. Everyone else continued with their meals and studiously ignored the fight, only a raised eyebrow or curled lip expressing their opinion.

A new ninja leaped down, blades at ready. Viola groaned and looked for the waiter. Ninjas always traveled in pairs.

With the prompt service she'd come to expect at Luigi's, the waiter appeared with the brandy she'd ordered. She tossed it and the table's candle at the new ninja.

He flambéed.

This caused some consternation among the other diners as the ninja staggered away from her table and into their zones. Yanking the tablecloth off the table, without disturbing the stemware, Viola tossed it over the flaming ninja and knocked him to the ground. She rolled him over and trussed the creature securely as smoke trickled out from the edges of the tablecloth. It would be unfortunate if the smell lingered.

Straightening, she tossed her hair back and raised a single finger to summon her waiter. He appeared like a wraith at her side. "Madam?"

Viola held up her fish knife. "I'm so sorry, but I'm afraid I need a new knife."

With a bow, he took the ichor-glazed blade in an immaculate white napkin and almost smiled. "Of course."

She seated herself at the table where Cardno gaped blatantly at her. Around them, the busboys of Luigi's moved in a silent frenzy of activity, trundling off the ninja corpses and resetting their table with a new cloth in the quiet efficiency that made this her favorite spot to escort their gastronomy clients. As the snowy white cloth draped across her legs, her waiter laid a new fish knife at her place.

"Thank you. I think we're ready for the salad course." Viola paused to check with Cardno. "Unless you wanted some more soup?"

He sputtered something in the negative and shook his head. Amateur. A true gastronome would have wanted to sample the chef's offering despite the interruption in service. With a bow, the waiter vanished into the hush of the dining room. Viola took a sip of her 2148 Frameworks Viognier, savoring the touches of slate and pear on her palate. She swallowed, enjoying the lingering anise on the finish, and eyed Cardno who picked up his own glass—Cabernet, 2152 Coastal Highlands—and buried his nose in the glass rather than meet her gaze.

"There is something you have not told me."

 The Many Tortures of Anthony Cardno

He lowered his glass and tried a smile. In another place, she might have found the thirty-year old actor charming, with his dimpled cheeks and tousled brown hair cut in a retro-Regency style, but his pretensions at being a gastronome disgusted her. Gastronomy might be fashionable, but it was clear that, no matter how successful the star might be, he did not understand food. "I should have thanked you, straightaway. That was nicely done."

Viola set her glass carefully on the table and swirled the straw pale liquid around the glass. "I meant, that you have an opportunity to explain why ninjas are attacking you now."

"Because of the White Phoenix Feather—"

"Spare me. It's not here yet and they stand to gain nothing by attacking you rather than trying to stop Joe." She leaned back in her chair as their waiter appeared with the salad course. "So, what I want to know is why?"

Viola picked up her salad fork and lifted a slice of the roasted persimmon, without releasing Cardno from her gaze. Licking his lips, he moved the escarole and sea beans around on his plate, destroying the chef's composition. She waited, savoring the fruit as she did. In her opinion, the balsamic vinegar played nicely with the caramelized natural sugars on the fruit and the goat cheese gave a tart complement to the subtle flavors, but she expected nothing less at Luigi's. At last, after her second bite, Cardno put down his fork without tasting the salad. "All right. I have been holding out on you."

Viola raised an eyebrow, waiting for him to tell her something that she did not know.

"I might have ... It is possible that I mentioned something about the White Phoenix Feather to my girlfriend." He wet his lips. "She's very discreet."

Picking up her salad knife, Viola tilted the blade to flash light in Cardno's eyes as she cut a slice off the persimmon. The knife was too dull to do any serious damage, without being inventive, but she was still satisfied when he flinched. "I see. So ... at this point, the ninjas clearly know that the White Phoenix Feather is being sought, which compromises Joe's mission. Was our contract not perfectly clear?"

"I'm sorry. I should have told you."

"You apologize for the wrong thing." Viola took a bite of her persimmon. "You should not have told your girlfriend. Then you would have had nothing to tell me."

He shriveled. "But she wouldn't have told anyone."

"Of course not." Viola said, though she believed no such thing. She signaled

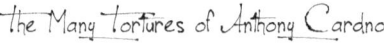

the waiter. "But you must understand that ninjas are everywhere on this planet. Simply because you do not see one is no indication that it is not present."

He scoffed openly. "Even if they overheard, they're harmless."

Viola raised her eyebrow and indicated the scorched spot on the floor. To be sure, ninjas normally ignored humans and were even sometimes useful, but the White Phoenix Feather changed everything. She turned to the waiter. "Might I have some fresh ground pepper?"

As if he had anticipated her request, which at Luigi's was a certainty, the waiter offered her tall wooden grinder, a new immaculate napkin over his arm. "Certainly, madam."

"Thank you." She nodded, not taking her gaze away from Cardno, who flushed red. "Ninjas are everywhere." Viola took the pepper-grinder from the waiter and stood on her chair. Sweeping the wooden grinder over her head, she twisted the top, flinging ground pepper in an arc. A muffled sneeze came from behind the ceiling tile. She leaped toward the sound, thrusting the grinder upward like a club and dented the tiles. From behind the tile, came a squawk and a moment later, a ninja dropped into the dining room.

Sighing, Viola clubbed it with the grinder and the ninja toppled over. She handed the grinder back to the waiter and seated herself again. "As I said, ninjas are everywhere but do not usually pay attention to us unless something prompts their attention, such as an attempt upon the White Phoenix Feather."

"But you talk about it freely here—" Cardno sputtered.

"Because the meal has begun. As our contract states, bragging rights prior to the meal add an additional hazard fee, however, we can discuss that later." She swept her napkin back into her lap. "Meanwhile, it is clear that we must anticipate a visit from a samurai."

His face paled. The ninjas were the male of the species. The much larger and more colorful females had acquired the nickname of samurai. They were less common and significantly smarter than the males of their species. Each samurai kept a stable of males, collecting them from other females and trading them with their favorites in the way a human might show dogs. Simple-minded and loyal, the ninjas could be set to tasks for which they would be rewarded with an opportunity to breed with the samurai. Viola prided herself on helping with their natural selection by removing so many ninjas from the breeding pool.

Wiping his face with his napkin, Cardno asked, "Why do you think a samurai will come?"

"Because ninjas always travel in pairs. There was only one in the ceiling."

She laid her fork and knife at precise angles across her salad plate, signaling that her waiter could take them. She really must leave him a good tip. His service was excellent thus far and she had told the maitre d' that this dinner would only cause a minimal intrusion. "How is your salad?"

Cardno shook his head and pushed the plate away from him, without trying it at all. Viola clenched her jaw in an effort to control her urge to reprimand him. She was perfectly willing to accept their money with certain *very* strict contractual guidelines and speaking of the White Phoenix Feather was strictly forbidden before dining for very good reasons.

As the ninjas were not ninjas, the White Phoenix Feather was not truly a feather. It was a frond-like growth which samurai only sprouted during mating season. The pheromones from it gave ninjas the urge to prove themselves in battle in order to earn the right to mate with the samurai. In humans ... in humans eating it produced a euphoria and a temporary reversal of aging. Much like fugu fish on Earth, the danger involved in eating White Phoenix Feather was part of the allure, albeit from ninjas rather than toxins. There were levels of danger and one's enjoyment and subsequent bragging rights were dependent on those. Viola's company specialized in Extreme Dining. Her job was to sit at a table and look decorative, while protecting the clients. In order to maintain the illusion of risk, she brought no weapons to the table.

But the presence of a samurai would change everything. Their arrangement with the samurai from whom Joe harvested the White Phoenix Feather was profitable and normally left Viola with only ninjas to deal with during dining. While the smartest ninjas were no more intelligent than a well-trained dog, the samurai were fully sentient. The samurai they dealt with used these dinner engagements as a way to clear her stables of lesser ninjas.

But Cardno's indiscretion meant that *another* samurai would attempt to get the Feather. With it, she would potentially be able to steal the entire stable of ninjas that would be drawn to it. While ninjas were plentiful, a samurai without a stable had no resources. Viola could not jeopardize their business partner in this way.

She considered her options as the table was cleared for the entree. She had ordered salmon roasted on a Lekejera-wood plank with sea urchin ceviche, wasabi risotto and sauteed radishes. If a samurai were about to join them, she needed to add another item to her order. Raising her finger, she hailed a waiter.

"May I add the fondue to my order?"

The waiter bowed, "Of course, madam. Would you like that with your entree

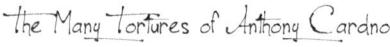

The Many Tortures of Anthony Cardno

or before?"

"Before, but don't hold the entrees. Bring them out when they are ready. Also a baguette, if you don't mind. Unsliced."

"Seeded or plain?"

She settled back in her chair and considered. "Seeded, please." It should provide a better grip.

Cardno continued to gawk at her. Viola favored him with a smile and sipped her wine. "Since you are already paying for it, you might as well let your fans know that you are Dining on White Phoenix Feather this evening."

"Now, wait a minute. I didn't say anything about being willing to pay extra. I told one person—maybe."

Viola set her glass down. "Oh? Then shall I let you handle the samurai by yourself?"

"If it comes." He scowled like a petulant child. "How do I know that you don't set all this up to scam people?"

Always ... always when they made a mistake, the wealthy tried to blame it on someone else. "I assume you checked our references before hiring us."

"Yeah. They said you have an arrangement with a samurai. That's how come you can always get the White Phoenix Feather."

Smoothing the tablecloth, Viola took a moment to calm herself before she answered him. "This is true. However, this will not be that samurai. This will be one of her rivals and she will not be friendly." A flash of yellow and red at the door caught Viola's attention. "Ah. There she is."

"She?" Cardno turned his seat to see what had attracted Viola.

"The samurai. They are always female." Without standing, Viola turned toward the kitchen entrance, looking for the waiter. She might have to stall until her order arrived. The samurai stalked through the dining room, too large to fit through the ceiling tiles the way a ninja would. Perhaps Viola should not have sent her salad away, so she had an extra knife. "Are you still going to contest the charges?"

"This is extortion."

"We did sign a contract, which listed these charges, however, I am perfectly happy to restrict myself to the activities we originally discussed. I will note, however, that the samurai will attempt to kill you in order to claim the right to the White Phoenix Feather." She slid her fish knife across the table. "You may want this."

The samurai choose that moment to charge, unlimbering her bladed arms as she did. She let out a high-pitched shriek as she bounded through the dinner tables. Cardno flinched, almost knocking his aluminum chair over. From the acrid stench that rose, he had just wet himself. Viola took that as permission to engage the samurai. Snatching the fish knife off the table, she stood. She lifted her chair and thrust the back between the samurai and Cardno. The blade came down on the chair, skidding along the metal. Viola thrust the fish knife into the samurai's wrist, twisting as she did.

The creature yanked back, howling with rage. The knife wrenched out of Viola's grasp, but the samurai's wrist hung limp. Viola kept her grip on the chair and snatched up a fork. This would be an excellent time for the waiter to arrive with her fondue. Luigi's normally had such prompt service. Without the fondue, she was forced to make do with the fork.

Viola spun swiftly and attempted to bury the fork in the samurai's neck, while she was distracted by the knife in her wrist. The creature used her other blade and blocked the fork with ease. Viola slid under her guard and aimed a kick at the samurai's leg. The samurai swept the blade down and Viola barely got the chair between her and the samurai. She dodged to the side in time, losing the fork.

Cardno had ordered squid-ink pasta with fresh peas so he did not have anything sharper than a butter knife. Snatching it, Viola faced the samurai again. With the chair held as a shield, she flipped the knife, aiming for the samurai's eyes.

As the blade left her open hand, the waiter appeared and placed the fondue and baguette on the table. Without waiting to see if she had hit the samurai, Viola snatched the baguette and thrust it into the fondue's spirit lamp, lighting it. She lunged at the samurai with the flaming loaf. Briefly distracted, the samurai blocked with her sword, slicing through the bread. In that moment of distraction, Viola dropped the chair and flung the fondue on the samurai. Molten cheese coated the creature's face and upper torso in a blinding mass. Viola snatched one of the long fondue forks from the table as she ducked behind the samurai. Pinning the creature's sword arm, Viola shoved the fondue fork against the samurai's chin.

In their hissing language, she said, "Do you yield?"

The creature stood for a moment, utterly still, and then spat an assent.

Viola stepped back. She disliked killing samurai but had found it necessary twice, both times with young ones who would not yield. The samurai stalked out of the dining room, cradling her injured wrist.

Shaking more than she would like to admit, Viola turned to the waiter. "Thank you. The fondue was exactly as I had wished."

He bowed. "I'll clear your settings then for the entree, if you are ready."

"That would be lovely." She glanced at Cardno who sat, shell-shocked, in his seat. Standing as she was, the stain on his trousers was obvious. "Perhaps you might show my companion where the restrooms are?"

Only raising an eyebrow, the waiter nodded. "Of course."

As he led Cardno to the facilities, Viola righted her chair and sat. By the time the staff and busboys had repaired the damage and removed the samurai, the waiter returned with Cardno, who had been given an clean set of trousers. Thank heavens. The stench would seriously interfere with the aromatics of her salmon.

She smiled as he sat, but chose not to say anything. He picked up his wine glass and drank the entire contents without pausing to savor the bouquet. He asked for a bottle of Cabernet, without specifying which one, without noting that a Cab of any providence would overwhelm his entree. When the wine arrived, Cardno downed his first glass as though it were a mass-produced soda. They proceeded through the entree with Cardno chattering in increasingly animated tones to which Viola said nothing.

The salmon was exquisitely succulent and had picked up deep resinous notes from the plank on which it had been fired. Pity she hadn't had it when the samurai had been here. The wood made an effective shield. To her relief, no more ninjas appeared. The rest would arrive with dessert.

Cardno continued to ramble about the film he was involved in and the starlet who shared his scenes as he finished the bottle of house wine by himself. As the waitstaff cleared the entrees, the diners at the other tables all turned, subtly, to watch them. No doubt they understood what was coming next. Viola settled back in her chair with the cognac she had ordered and swirled the glass, enjoying the caramel and apple notes. Cardno fidgeted with his napkin.

"Well?" He tossed the napkin down. "Where is it?"

"Joe will be here."

As she lifted her glass to hide her scowl, the waiter stepped out of the kitchen. She stiffened at the sight of what he carried. Joe normally presented the White Phoenix Feather himself, resplendent in a white silk dinner jacket. If he sent the waiter in, instead, something had gone horribly wrong.

The waiter carried a plate sealed with a clear glass dome. Inside was a bowl of sweet cream gelato, adorned with the White Phoenix Feather. The frond trem-

The Many Tortures of Anthony Cardno

bled with every step. Pure white at the tip, it shaded to a deep vermillion red at the base, tinged with yellows as though lit from within.

The waiter bowed as he presented the dish, setting it in front of Cardno with a flourish.

He leaned over and whispered in Viola's ear. "Pardon, Madam. Your partner wished me to let you know that he was in good health but not presentable for dinner." It was not the first time, by far, that Joe had been injured while delivering the White Phoenix Feather, but this contract had been for a minimal risk dinner. That's why the dessert was in the hermetically sealed tray until the last possible moment. In normal events, if Joe kept it sealed until serving, the diner could usually finish it before ninjas arrived. Of course, that reduced the risk, so most true gastronomes had it served without the covering.

Cardno was no gastronome. He did not even wait for the waiter to step fully back, before yanking the cover off the White Phoenix Feather. Aromas of coriander, honey, and autumn leaves rolled out, underlaid by the subtle musky fragrance of the samurai's signature. Viola inhaled slowly, savoring the fragrance.

"Huh." Cardno stared at it. "How am I supposed to eat this?"

"With the chopsticks." Viola nodded to the ebony ones under the dome, carefully chosen to serve as a contrast to the White Phoenix Feather.

Cardno picked them up and struggled with his grip. Viola had to bite the inside of her cheek to keep from stabbing him with her fork. He didn't even know how to hold a pair of chopsticks?

"Is it okay if I just pick it up with my fingers?" His cheeks were quite flushed, more from the wine, than from embarrassment, she suspected.

"You may do whatever you see fit, of course."

He reached for the White Phoenix feather and stopped. "Oh, I should totally get a pic of this." Patting his pockets he fished out his handy and started to pass it to Viola. "No, wait. That's a terrible idea."

Then—in Luigi's Interstellar Cafe and Pub—he addressed the table next to them. "Would you mind taking a pic of us together?" Bad enough that he was ignoring the food, but he couldn't even ask a waiter? He had to disturb someone who was *enjoying their meal?* Viola shook with rage. Had he no respect for the sanctity of Dining?

No. No of course, he didn't. "If you don't eat that soon, more ninjas will arrive."

He flashed her a sloppy smile. "You just defeated a samurai with a breadstick. I'm not worried about a couple of ninjas."

The Many Tortures of Anthony Cardno

Thankfully, the waiter intercepted the camera and took their photo so that she did not have to be part of any further intrusions into the other diners' meals. When she saw Joe again, she was going to insist that they institute a better screening process. If she had to—

Two ninjas dropped from the ceiling. She grabbed the chopsticks and slammed them into each ninja's throat as they straightened from their landing. "Will you eat."

Cardno settled back in his chair and took her picture. "Hey ... I'm paying you to protect me while I dine. I want to get all the buzz I can out of this."

Viola was going to kill him.

He nodded over her shoulder. "Behind you."

Viola spun, raising her arm to sling the cognac at the ninja—but it wasn't a ninja. It was her waiter. She managed to not hit him in the face and instead splashed the drink over the front of his spotless white shirt. Flushing, Viola stepped back in unholy shock. "I'm—I'm so sorry."

"It is quite all right, madam." He held out a short glass of whiskey, a single malt from Islay, judging from the aromas of butterscotch and cherry. "With the compliments of Luigi."

With reverence, Viola took the glass and lifted it to her nose, savoring its complex peatiness. Luigi had graced her with, not just an Islay, but a Glenmorangie aged in honey willow casks imported from Beta Five. "Thank you. You anticipate my needs as always."

As she placed the scotch on the table in front of her, Cardno frowned at the glass. "What's that for?"

"For me." She rose as a ninja dropped from the ceiling. "It's going to be a long evening."

Viola hefted her chair and reflected that she would have to leave the waiter a very good tip. He was a true artist who understood what his patrons needed at any given moment.

She might lack the will to shield Cardno any longer, but a good single malt was worth protecting.

This song was written by Barry Mangione and his online audience during the live web show Barry On The Spot. *Each week the artist and the audience collaborate on a different topic to write a song in 30 minutes. For this show, the inspiration was "Six Degrees of Anthony Cardno." Lyrical inspiration for this song was provided by Anthony Cardno, Elsalee Jay Flynn, Scott Witt, Hunter Martin, Katherine Sauchelli & John Sauchelli, Melissa Boyer, Sarah, Jamie, Brent Lechner, Matt Colson, Jonathan Cornue, Deven Owen, Melanie and Abby. I really did try to get them to write a song about how much they hated me, but they insisted on singing my praises. I still blush.*

The Ballad of Anthony Cardno

BARRY MANGIONE AND THE MUSICAL GENIUSES

He's got a Stephen King beginning
But everyone wants to know
Where's the Hollywood Ending
For Anthony Cardno?

Some folks call him Anthony
Some folks call him Talekyn
Call him whatever you want
I'll just call him my friend

He's a writer, an actor and a playwright too
"Sneakers in the Sand" was about a bloody shoe
He's a role-playing gamer extraordinaire
And on top of all that, he's got a great head of hair

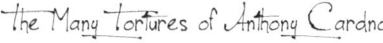
The Many Tortures of Anthony Cardno

He's the best man that I've ever known
If Anthony's your friend, then you're never alone
He's the best man that I've ever known
If Anthony's your friend, then you're never alone

He seems to have found the fountain of youth
He looks just like he did in 1982
He travels for his job, and that's just great
'Cause he's got friends in all 50 states

He's the best man that I've ever known
If Anthony's your friend, then you're never alone
He's the best man that I've ever known
If Anthony's your friend, then you're never alone

I got my copy of *The Firflake*
Signed by Anthony, the man
When it comes to the music of The Dalliance
He's their number one fan

He's the best man that I've ever known
If Anthony's your friend, then you're never alone
He's the best man that I've ever known
If Anthony's your friend, then you're never alone
He's the best man that I've ever known
If Anthony's your friend, then you're never alone
He's the best man that I've ever known
If Anthony's your friend, then you're never alone

I've had the pleasure, thanks to Twitter and the interviewing I've done for my website, to get to know a number of young singer-songwriters. Frank Dixon is already winning songwriting awards in his native Australia, and collaborating with Kelebek, who has appeared on Australia's version of X Factor. He posted this original song to his YouTube channel in 2012, and I immediately joked that he'd used my name on purpose. His mother Christine tells me she was surprised to hear the name, because I'm the only Anthony Frank knows. Frank himself is still keeping quiet about the inspiration.

Why, Anthony, Why

FRANK DIXON

Time stands still
and now they're eye to eye
Anger took hold
and now there's blood all over this brand new floor
Pressure builds up
and the top just finally blew

Oh why why oh Anthony why?

Red and blue and high pitch sounds
Surround the grounds
Windows are smashed
and doors are broken in half.
Hands tied behind his back
and he's driven far far away

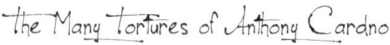

Oh Why why oh Anthony why?

And now he sits here
in his solitary home
Behind the nine-inch-thick iron bars of his soul
If only he said "hey I'm mistaken - oh and let's let's make it ok ..."
There might be someone here today

Oh why oh Anthony why?

The media takes the police's place on the case
Everybody knows his face
and they know his fate ...
You get the trigger-happy, couldn't-care-less, congregation dancing in the streets
all night long

Oh why why oh Anthony why why why ...?

And now he sits here
in his solitary home
Behind the nine-inch-thick iron bars of his soul
If only he said "hey I'm mistaken - oh and let's let's make it ok ..."
There might be someone here today

Oh why oh Anthony why?
Why oh Anthony why?

Saturday afternoon and he's walking down the green line
The wood slams down
and justice has been served
Sunday afternoon and he's watching his last sunset ....

Oh why, why oh Anthony why ...?

Day Al-Mohamed is another author I've gotten to know very well thanks to a brief-lived online writers' group and the glory that is Twitter and whom I have yet to meet in person. Day provides us with the first piece of flash fiction in this anthology, which also happens to feature the most Tuckerizations of people other than me. See if you can pick out all of the other authors mentioned. As Colin Hay sang: "Sometimes the sun shines / well, here comes the flood..."

When the Waters Recede...

DAY AL-MOHAMED

So this is what Noah felt like. Yeah, that Noah, from the Bible. The stories I heard growing up always focused on the animals, two-by-two, marching into the ark. And the forty days and forty nights of rain. I never really thought about what it meant to stand on the deck as the world drowned. Forty seconds, forty minutes, forty days...

Scowling, I hit play on the screen in front of me as I float in the space station's exercise area.

"Hi Dad! Play this video on Day Twenty-Seven. Hopefully, you haven't peeked ahead. If so, shame on you."

I can't suppress a grin. Brian always makes me laugh.

"Are you ready? Chapter 17." Brian's voice is still preadolescent high, though likely not for much longer. I open the book and try to focus. Even in the largest room, it's difficult to ignore the other astronauts. They have congregated at the other end, by the exercise bikes, and are in a heated discussion.

"How can he do that?"

"Doesn't he understand that we're going to die?"

"Maybe everyone else is already dead! Hell, even his kid!"

The Many Tortures of Anthony Cardno

My gaze snaps to them for a moment before returning to the page, trying to keep my attention on the book and my son's voice, as we read together. Tears gather at the back of my throat. I reach behind my glasses and give my eyes a preemptive wipe. Am I just deluding myself, hanging on to a memory?

Noah had his family. I have four other astronauts: Christie, Neal, Mary Robinette, and, no doubt, the instigator of the current angry exchange, Frank. The average shuttle mission is seven or eight days, which makes me the long-timer having been up here a full twenty-eight days. Papa Bear with four cubs.

Six days ago, Damien and Barry had used the shuttle to head back to Cape Canaveral despite the storms and flooding. They didn't want to stay. My raven and my dove, they promised to send word. So far, nothing. And so we wait.

Is this all that's left of humanity? Five of us on a station, floating in the sea of space? To the left is a porthole where I can see the bright blue of earth. All blue. Did Noah feel fear? Did he worry what would happen if the water never went down? Did he truly believe and hold to his conviction every single moment of the journey?

"We can't just wait here!"

I'd been doing my best to ignore Frank, but it isn't working. I lean my head against the wall. It isn't teak or gopher wood, but smooth, sterile plastic. This is my Ark and I am her Captain. I push off and rocket to the forward part of the exercise area.

"All right, Frankie. You have my attention. What do you want me to do?"

Frank winces. He hates being called Frankie. Says it makes him feel like he's twelve years old. The other three make a point of looking everywhere but at me and quickly scoot off to other parts of the station. There aren't even enough of us to march away two-by-two.

"I don't know. Something. Anything!" Frank's anger has a ring of desperation.

I raise an eyebrow.

He sputters and fumes, running out of words, his hands moving agitatedly. "Anthony—"

I reach out and touch him gently on the arm, "We're all scared. We're all worried about our families, but we need to hang tight. Make sure we know the full story." I can't tell him that I already know the story. Eight years of catechism classes burned it into my mind. Did Noah have to reassure his family? Did he speak words of comfort wondering if all he did was offer false hope? Or worse, lies?

The Many Tortures of Anthony Cardno

Frank nods, accepting my reassurance.

"It'll be okay. I know it." I smiled a smile I didn't really feel. "How old is your daughter now, six?"

"Eight." He said. I could hear the pride in his voice.

"Already?" I didn't have to feign surprise. I tipped my head back towards the video, "Brian will turn thirteen in a week." My words are slow and calm. I speak as if the future is assured. Of course Brian would turn thirteen, and there'd be cake, and his other father would sing *Happy Birthday*, loud and off-key. I swallow hard, thinking of Joe. We'd been together only three years before we adopted Brian.

The last week of computer readings told us about storms and deluges and the flooding of the earth. Now we watch and scan the great blue planet below, seeking our Mount Ararat; hoping to find a metaphorical olive branch that heralds land. This is my Ark with the remains of the whole world encased within. I didn't build it. I didn't call forth the animals. I cannot be Noah. Noah wouldn't have taken people like me, would he? I refuse.

Heading towards one of the treadmills, I proceed to strap myself down, ignoring how my hands shake. We'll need every ounce of muscle if we return - when we return - I correct. "Tell me about her, Frank."

And Frank talks, and I listen. I've never been much of a believer. You'd think an astronaut would believe in God. And Noah. And that the waters will go down. But I guess you just need to believe in it for one second. This second. And then the next. And the next. Forty seconds, forty minutes, forty days...

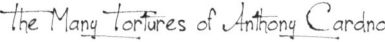

I'm not much of an athlete. I'm a strong bowler, pretty decent at archery, and once upon a time I could play darts reasonably well. Shin splints got me to stop jogging before I'd even really started, and I've never gone back. So it's interesting that Jennifer Ryan, this volume's sole Canadian author, sent me the only sports-related story ... and also the only story in which I'm gender-swapped.

The Chase

JEN RYAN

Toni Cardno does not quit. Toni Cardno does not quit.

"On your marks,"

Toni Cardno does not quit. Toni Cardno does not...

"Get set,"

quit!

Bang!

And we're out of the gate. I start off in sixth place, maybe seventh. We've got four laps to go, though, so I'm not worried. Not about that part, anyway. I maintain a decent pace, keeping myself in the middle of the pack. Some of the racers, they panic. It happens every time, you'll get one or two that start off at a sprint; they just can't keep their fear in check. Naturally, they burn out after a couple of laps—right when it's important to pick up speed. The chasers are released as soon as the last-place racer finishes their second lap.

Bang!

There it is, the second shot. We all know they're coming now, but no one dares look back to see how close they are. The over-eager racers that started off in first and second place are starting to slow now, while the rest of us speed up.

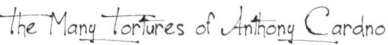

187

Each of us is running for our life. The chasers are *usually* put down before they catch up to a racer, but there are no guarantees. Sometimes the racer needs to be put down, too, which is unfortunate since we're such a precious entertainment commodity these days.

Shit. I can sense a chaser closing in on me. I don't know how he got past the half dozen racers behind me; I'm not sure I want to know. I lengthen my strides, find speed I didn't know I had left in me, but I can't seem to widen the gap enough. I sense him coming up on my heels.

Then I hear a third gunshot, just in time.

I round the final corner. I allow myself one quick glance over my right shoulder. I seem to be in first place now. I usually finish in the top three, but the track is no place to take anything for granted. I'm sprinting like hell but, as per usual, time seems to slow down while I'm in the home stretch. And as per usual, I remember…

●

I was seventeen and ready to quit. I was so tired of running. There had to be more to life. I told my mom that I was going to withdraw from the track program, that I wanted to get into the trades instead. Maybe I could be in construction or policing. Mom wouldn't hear of it. She said that the best chance we had for a future was my running. I was talented, I could make some good money in racing. We could afford a nice, reinforced house where we'd be safe for a while.

She started right in on me: Now that my dad was gone, it was up to me to help keep us afloat. I didn't understand. I was just a kid, why was this my responsibility? We'd made it this long, I'm sure I'd be just as helpful as a reinforcement engineer. But Mom was stuck on this idea that there was a lot more security in racing. Kept talking about stadiums and guns. I was so tired of hearing this stuff, I walked out of the apartment to get some air. Mom refused to let me off the hook. She just followed me out and continued the lecture.

"You never quit, baby. Toni Cardno does not quit!"

Those were her last words, before that zombie bastard got a hold of her. I survived. I ran, and I haven't stopped running. They call me a racer, but really I'm a nothing but a coward.

●

The Many Tortures of Anthony Cardno

Finally, we're at the finish line. I fell to second place, but that's alright. The company will keep me around for a while longer; I'm a fan favourite. The crowd is on its feet in a round of morbid applause. The girls in last place are likely to be out of job now. They'll have to go back to the outside world, where the wild chasers are—the zombies that aren't under stadium security's watchful eye.

Today's chasers have been eliminated. The racers made it. The stadium is safe; we live to see another day.

Yeah, right. Some living.

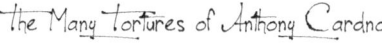

The Many Tortures of Anthony Cardno

189

Steve Berman and I connected on Livejournal long before he started paying me to write book reviews for the now-defunct (and sorely missed) Icarus magazine. We have, as I think Steve would agree, entirely too much in common and are bad influences on each other on a regular basis. This story is about a smoky room and a ghostly boy. I have experiences with the latter, but the only time I've ever smoked was for a stage production of "A Shot In The Dark" at Elmira College in the summer of 1989, and that only because the plot hinged on the cigarette burning after my character left the stage. Antony seems far more adept with a cig than Anthony ever could be.

Three On a Match

STEVE BERMAN

A tattered boy named Antony sat on the unmade dorm room bed rolling a cigarette. His nicotine-stained fingertips maneuvered loose tobacco through the channel made by the curling paper thin as onionskin. The effort left him squinting behind round wire-framed glasses.

The room reeked of tobacco smoke. The ceiling might once have been white, but it and the upper reaches of every wall were tinted a bluish gray. The naked lamp bulbs accentuated the evidence that a thousand thousand cigarettes had been smoked there.

A wise boy named Ewan leaned against the far wall, close to the door, and watched. His narrow arms were folded, with hands tucked into the warm pockets of his pale blue hoodie. "Anything in that?"

Antony's tongue darted fast to lick the exposed edge of the paper. "Are you worried?"

"I just don't want to be smoking embalming fluid."

"They do that?" Antony finished and then leaned on one elbow while he made the crafted cigarette dance along the tarsals of his hand, like a magician's coin.

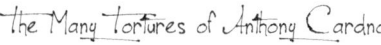

"Call 'em 'wets.' Really moronic ... and it's all because some idiot confused a nickname for PCP with actual embalming fluid—"

"Where does a guy get his hands on that shit?"

Ewan shrugged. "Formaldehyde's easy to find. Every high school bio lab has jars of the stuff."

"You're really smart, aren't you?" The cigarette stopped moving, pinched tight between Antony's thumb and forefinger.

"Are you flirting?"

"Are you here to get laid?"

"Yes."

Antony's laugh was brief. "Well, that wasn't really flirting. Maybe you're not so smart after all." He reached for the worn leather jacket he had flung on to the bed once they arrived in the bedroom and he retrieved from one pocket a Zippo, its metal skin scratched from many accidents, many falls.

With a practiced ease, Antony flicked the lighter open and thumbed the black wheel. A steady flame grew. "Don't worry. No embalming fluid. No marijuana. Just tobacco supposedly from Turkey, but I suspect really Iowa."

"Didn't think that was a cash crop there." Ewan began to wander the fringes of the dorm room. On top of the dresser, he saw ashtrays brimming with the powdered remains. On top of the desk, amid the papers and closed textbooks, ashes and butts obscured much of Western Civilization.

"Well, that's where the website I bought this stuff is."

"A website isn't anywhere." He lifted one butt, pinched at the end. Let it drop back into the old coffee mug, its home.

"Sure it is."

"No, it doesn't take up physical space. It's in the ..." Ewan gestured. His fingernails were scored, bitten down to the quick, stained brown from dried blood, not yellow like the other boy's.

"Æther?"

"Yeah, guess you could call it that. What you mean is the company is based in Iowa. Or maybe the servers."

Antony lit one end of the cigarette, and then motioned with that hand. "Come here."

"My breath probably smells like beer." Ewan covered his mouth with his fingertips a moment. Ran his tongue along his front teeth.

"This will cure that."

Ewan walked across the room, avoiding the piles of discarded clothes and crumb-covered plates. He sat down at the foot of the bed. He curled an arm around the nearest of the wooden knobs of the footboard.

Antony put the cigarette to his mouth and inhaled. The lit end blossomed in oranges dying to black and gray that fell like snow onto his worn Red Caps concert T-shirt. The ash drifted across the faded lettering.

"I know a trick," Antony whispered.

Ewan leaned in closer. "A magic trick?"

"There's no other worth knowing." He handed the cigarette over. "Do you want to see it?"

"I thought we were going to …"

"Fuck?"

Ewan winced at the word but nodded. He inhaled deeply the smoke a moment, then let it stream through his nostrils as if he were an irate cartoon bull. Or some ancient idol found in a fiery cave.

"If that word scares you … this trick would make you lose your shit. Maybe you should run back to high school."

Ewan dropped his cigarette. Both boys scrambled through the loose and dirty sheets to retrieve it before scorching the bedding. Their hands mingled and slapped and stroked one another in the process.

Antony recovered the cigarette and handed it back. "Newb."

He started rolling another cigarette. "The more smoke, the better my trick. Sometimes I just buy packs 'cause it's easier, faster. Has to be Lucky Strikes though. No other brand works. But I can leave them burning in an ashtray and … well, you'll see."

Ewan adjusted the front of his jeans as he watched the other boy.

Once their mouths were occupied by purported Turkish tobacco and releasing streams of blue-gray vapor, Antony began rubbing Ewan's knee through the faded denim.

"I'm addicted."

"To these?"

Antony shook his head. "No, to a ghost. Or maybe he's made of æther. You'll see." He let his hands roam higher until they slid across the soft material of the hoodie, and then he began pushing against the other boy's chest. Gently to start, then more firmly.

Ewan slid back but Antony kept forcing him further until he had met the edge of the bed.

"The floor?"

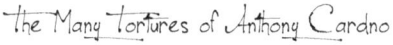

"Trust me." Antony smirked. "Isn't it so late that you're too tired to do anything else but trust me?"

Arms lifted like ballet dancers to keep their smokes safe, they tumbled to the cheap, industrial carpet. A glimpse under the bed revealed even more full ashtrays, the discarded cellophane from countless Lucky Strikes packs. Dead matches, resembling the burnt limbs of spiders.

"Ever been in love?" Antony asked.

"Once. Or I thought I was."

Antony blew a series of smoke rings that mimicked his rounded lips. But the rings soon bloated and warped as if under a breeze that stole its way into the college dorm room, stole its way without ever being felt. They drifted one after another to the air above the bed. Ewan moved, leaning up on his elbows, to watch his own tobacco breath stream after the misshapen rings, even when he tried to blow smoke off to his left, to his right, down into his palm.

"Me too." Antony frowned. "Even if I'm with other boys, I need him to be there. I don't hook up unless I bring them back here." He gestured at the cloud of smoke somewhat visible from where both boys lay. Floating inches above the mattress an unfashioned figure was being born.

"I've wondered if maybe he's a boy that once went to school here. Not like I'm a detective, not like there's anyone to ask. And I'm not even sure I really want to know who he was. That would destroy the mystery. You need mystery to make a magic trick work."

Ewan almost stumbled as he stood. "Have you named him?" Another deep inhalation, release, and he watched as the smoke drifted down, layering onto the floating mass. Features developed but the whole remained a crude sculpture of redolent fumes with a suggestion of youth despite the square jaw. No fingers, no lines of clothing, no shoes or toes.

Antony stood beside Ewan. Rubbed his back, let his hand slide down and grabbed hold of his ass. "I call him Beauty." His voice sounded raspy, as if those thousand thousand cigarettes had, at last, eaten away the soft, warm lining of the boy's throat. "I never want to leave him."

"Has he ever spoken?"

"No."

"Woken?"

Antony sighed. "Maybe he isn't sleeping."

Ewan walked to and fro beside the bed. Like a skeptical member of a magician's audience he passed first a hand and then a pillow between the sleeping beauty and the mattress.

"We should smoke more. I want to see him whole," he said.

Antony went for the Lucky Strikes, though their odor was comparable to coffee left on the burner rather than the scent conjured by the loose tobacco.

"When you bring back boys, do you make them kiss him too?"

Antony hesitated as he lit the first three cigarettes on the same flame. "Bad luck three on a match I heard, but don't know why. But yeah ..."

"Why? And how many are cool with that?"

"I thought maybe he'd wake up. I've given up my lungs to make him appear. What more can I do? Maybe I'm not a Prince, not Charming enough. Or whatever works with magic these days. Probably needs someone pure or sweet."

"And I seem like either?" Ewan offered a slight smile but stepped close to accept a Lucky Strike.

"Most guys balk at even the talk of magic tricks. They think it's slang for meth bumps up the ass or something."

Ewan looked back at floating Beauty. Wavy locks of hair had developed. A slender nose. Closed eyelids. Ewan leaned in close and exhaled over where the mouth should be and waited as thin lips, parted ever so slightly, coalesced.

"Any guy stay?"

"Once. I think he was on E. His teeth chattered as we messed around and I found him in the morning down the hall in the bathroom drinking out of the sink like a weird pet."

"So not the sort of ménage à trois you wanted."

"No. Beauty didn't stir." Antony stepped behind Ewan, their torsos touching, older boy's chin resting on the younger's shoulder. He slid a hand down the front of Ewan's jeans, between denim and cotton underwear. Fingers curled.

A hitch in Ewan's breathing. "There's another boy at school that everyone knows is gay. My dad's a teacher, so they leave me alone, but this boy ... they pounce on his every move. He can't go anywhere without hearing the word 'faggot.' If he fights back, he earns a black eye. Or a suspension.

"One day he texts me—took me a while to figure out it was him, as I didn't have his number on my phone, that shows you how close we were—and tells me he's going to kill himself."

Antony's hand stopped moving. He whispered in Ewan's ear, "Damn."

"Yeah. I didn't know what to do. Do I call nine-one-one? I didn't even know where he lived. I try to talk him out of it, then go through the loops—friends of friends of friends, which takes forever, to find his address. The way only seven-

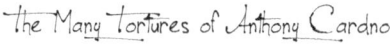
The Many Tortures of Anthony Cardno

teen minutes can feel like forever.

"I drive there. The house is dark. No car in the driveway, but I can hear the engine's heartbeat behind the garage door. He left the front door open. He wanted to be found."

"What did you do?"

"I went inside. Found the door to the garage. I know you can't smell carbon monoxide. Can't see it, yet I was disappointed as I opened that door. I expected to see ..." Ewan gestured around himself with his hands, one trailing a stream of smoke from cigarette to Beauty, like an umbilical cord.

"And?" Antony squeezed the hardness beneath his hand. Ewan gasped.

"And the boy who planned to die is lying on the hood of his beat-up car. As if he were out in the woods and stargazing. He turned to me and nodded as if I weren't interrupting anything special.

"Which is why ... which is why I didn't even cough—there was as much carbon monoxide in the garage as there is here, from our cigs—and I scooched over onto the hood beside him.

"When I turn to talk to him, he brings a hand over my mouth—"

"Like this?" Antony brought up his other hand, the one with a lit cigarette, and held it close to Ewan's lips. As Ewan inhaled from the older boy's cigarette, he thrust an eager crotch against a wanting hand.

"And ... and ... then he leans over and kisses me. First time I ever kissed a boy."

"And neither of you died?" asked Antony, who continued stroking.

"No, my kiss was magic ... the magic trick. We both lived. Lived to see the paramedics arrive."

Warmth spilled over Antony's fingers and soaked the cotton. Ewan stumbled forward.

Antony maintained his hold for a bit longer, then slid his hand from the younger boy's pants. He dropped his lit cigarette into the nearest ashtray and wiped his hand dry on his shirt.

"Will you kiss him? Kiss Beauty? Maybe you can bring him back—"

Ewan curled his lips. "You haven't even kissed me yet."

"Not yet." Antony took the inches of cigarette from him and pressed chapped lips against chapped lips. Teeth tapped and sour tongues explored.

Arms lifted, hands tugged at clothes. Shirts lifted, layers peeled away, denim dragged down and off stick legs.

The carpet chafed exposed skin.

 The Many Tortures of Anthony Cardno

Antony cried out, "Please."

Ewan did not release his hold until the other boy pleaded, ordered, begged. Stroking became fumbling as they stripped each other bare of the many layers of clothing. Faces roamed over bodies. Saliva and sweat mixed and the taste in both their mouths was flavored by old spilled ashes.

When naked Antony rolled off bared Ewan, the latter said, "He's gone," and pointed one scrawny arm towards the mattress. With its mess of stained sheets, it looked like so many other boys' beds.

"He was never here. Remember? A trick. To get laid. Smoke and mirrors."

"I think you're lying."

Antony shrugged.

"No Beauty?"

Antony stared at Ewan. "Maybe some." He stroked a cheek, ran his fingers down the curve of neck.

Ewan closed his eyes. "My trick's no better than yours. Actually mine is far, far worse."

Antony pressed a thumb against the corner of Ewan's mouth and made the lips pout.

"When I opened the door to the garage, I choked on the fumes. Had to turn my head. I was only smart enough to flick every switch, so the garage door went up but the lights came on and I saw him there, saw him lying on the roof of his car but his eyes stared up at nothing.

"I tried to wake him. Slapped his face. Even kissed him like they do in movies and television, but nothing happened. He didn't wake."

Antony edged closer so there was no distance between their limbs, their feverish skin. "So we're both liars."

"Smoke and mirrors." Ewan ran a hand through Antony's hair. "At least tell me your name."

 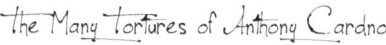

My most recent Tuckerization into the pages of Fireside *magazine was through the words of Adam P. Knave. Adam actually asked me on Twitter what kind of story I'd like to be Tuckerized into, and I asked for a Western (since I didn't get a Western from Dennis R. Miller). Adam obliged, and I do think this is about as straight-forward an Old West tale as one could hope for. Yee-Haw, y'all.*

The Brutal and the Simple

ADAM P. KNAVE

I rode like hell down the shit and dirt we called a road. Head down, I pushed on, spurring the horse under me to just keep going. I'd wear the horse out, I knew, but being smart and careful wasn't in the cards. Not now. Now was a time for running. My Pa'd chide me for cowardice, but let him come up out of the grave and face down this level of bullshit and then he could give me more endless sermons.

Doc Kemper used to tell me the secret of humanity was that we are both brutal and simple. Now, I always did disagree with the good Doctor, mostly because of the fact that none of my friends'd ever shown themselves either brutal or simple. The Doc'd be laughing right now, next to my Pa.

"Anthony," he'd tell me, "trust in the Lord. Believe in your fellow man but understand they're fallible." He laugh and nod before tossing in his closer. "Always carry spare ammunition, is what I'm saying." And we'd have another drink and ease the night to bed. Still. I didn't believe him. I didn't want to. And now, my face pressed against this sweaty horse neck as dust kicked up and wind tore at my clothes, I realized he'd been right all along.

A sharp crack sounded by my head and I jumped in my seat, startled. The

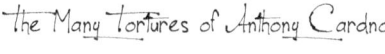

horse startled too, and took it as a chance to throw me and take off at right angles to where I landed, hard, on the ground. Traitor.

A second crack, followed by the whine of a ricochet, exploded the dirt near my hips. I grabbed the bag, oh that bag clutched tightly in my fist, and fumbled until I stood. Running, could you call it running? I hobbled into some scrub brush as best I could. It wouldn't give me cover, not really, but it might hide me a while. Night was falling, regardless.

I stayed there and remembered when my life had turned to crap.

✳

It was a Thursday. The explosion rattled my ears. Standing too close to the blast again, like a fool. I choked on and was blinded by dust. Grit scraped across my eyes as I squeezed them shut and rubbed them.

"What?" Bertrand shouted at me, following up by thumping his fist into my shoulder.

"Just coughing up half this mine," I said.

Gabby laughed at that. She would. The woman never seemed to have problems in the mines no matter what happened. Light went out and she'd learn to see in the dark. Air got thin she'd just stop breathing. Seemed like much of nothing could make Gabby flinch.

I admit, in those days my estimations may have been a bit higher than reality when it came to Gabby, as I was decidedly sweet on her. Not that she knew. No, if she'd known she would have mercilessly teased me about it and made it a point of humor for the whole crew. So I kept my peace.

We were a small crew of four, if you counted Kyle. Kyle did the lifting mostly. We didn't place much stock in his thinking and, though we all stood close in each others estimations, I'd have to admit that more than once we each considered Kyle a piece of equipment more than a man on the team. Kyle'd been the only one not in the mine when we blasted, seeing as how he'd been lugging a load of rubble up topside.

Something glinted ahead in the lamplight. The dust tried to settle and I swiped at it with my hand, hurrying it along as I moved forward. Gold. It had to be gold. That sort of glitter wasn't no shanty rock or normal quarry stone, it could only be gold. I hacked around it with a chisel and pried it free. This was a coal mine, or was gonna be when we got deep enough. Gold wasn't on the menu. The vein popped free and fell to the ground with a solid thump. Yup, if it weighed that much it'd be gold.

I showed it to Bert and Gabby both, and Kyle when he came back and we discussed our fortune. "Folk," I told them, "this is it. This here lump funds the rest of the mine with no worries. Why, we could hire others to do the rest of the work for us and just kick back and laugh."

"Or we could split it and just abandon the mine," Bertrand said.

Gabby cut in, "It ain't gonna last a lifetime, split four ways. Now if only one of us—"

"It's all our find, together," I said. Now truth the mine was mostly mine, Cardno Mine, the deed said, but these were my partners. Fair only counts when it it's easier not to be.

"Yeah, ours. Together." Gabby said. A look in her eye and I saw a hardness I'd never noticed before. I brushed it off. I shoulda paid better attention.

❋

A rattlesnake made itself known near the scrub I hunkered behind. Forget Thursday. Thursday laid dead to me. I dropped the bag on the snake, cruelly, letting the weight of the gold inside crush it quick. Best thing that gold had done for me so far.

The worst part about that Thursday, the sun setting as we left the mine with the gold bundled up in secret, had to be that it was now, as I laid waiting to be shot, only Friday night. One day is all it took. I grabbed the rattler, with its crushed skull, and looked around. Horse long gone, edge of the desert, no supplies — this would be where I died if I wasn't smart. And by smart I mean stupidly lucky.

A third shot called out, lifting a clump of dirt near the bushes. "Anthony," Kyle shouted from the darkened distance, "Just come out and I won't have to shoot you."

"You tried shooting me well before I was hid," I yelled back. He knew where I was, anyway, didn't matter none telling him. Only Kyle would claim this was hid.

I took a chance. I stood up, rattlesnake in one hand and the incredibly heavy bag in the other. "Fine, Kyle," I said, spotting him just standing there with his rifle aimed at me, "here I am, then. No shooting, right?"

"No shooting, Anthony," he said. "Just toss over the bag."

I wound my arm back, to toss over the gold, but threw the dead snake at his

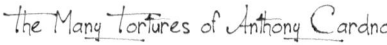

head, instead. He threw his arms up, dropping the rifle, as it sailed through the air toward him. We would've laughed about his fear of a snake he didn't know was already dead, in the old days.

These days, instead, I rushed him, knocking him over and kicking the rifle away. He flailed more as we tangled and the gold bag swung down accidently, catching him in the head. We lay there and I realized Kyle wasn't moving no more. The bag, stained red, sat too deeply in his skull to mean anything other than stupidly lucky won the day. I hated myself for feeling grateful.

But I pushed the hate down and took his gun and his horse and made for town again. If I could get back to town and the Sheriff I could maybe survive this night. So I started to ride again, just as hard as I'd ridden while running from Kyle. I knew that Bert and Gabby were out there, hunting me, but I also still wanted to believe they'd come to their sense before anyone else had to be hurt.

Town lay a good twenty miles away and the darkness ate all land navigation. I used the stars best I could, wishing I could be up there and not stuck down here with this shit-eating life. Kyle's horse didn't like it, being pushed to ride again after such a short rest. I didn't like it either, would've loved a nap, or maybe something to eat beside my own fear in the last twelve hours or so, but we had to do what we could to survive. The night grew cold, out there, and I leaned down on the horse to share some of his warmth. We made it back to town somewhere approaching midnight, and I let the horse go free. He just stood there, on the verge of collapse. I felt the same and sighed, leading him to the nearest trough to drink his fill.

Hefting the bag once more, I walked to the Sheriff's office, seeing a light still on. The door opened with a kick, and I dropped the bag on a nearby desk. Stood near it, too, of course, while Sheriff Danes came by to look me over. He didn't look surprised. That put the fear back into me, my bowels feeling weak.

"Tony," Danes said, tipping his hat back slowly, "you come to turn yourself in?"

"Wait, am I here to what?" My hand reached out for the bag again. I stopped, my fingers just touching it, when the Sheriff laid hand on his gun. He could draw quick, I knew, and Kyle's rifle ... crap, I left it on the horse. Shooting a Sheriff wasn't on my big list of things to get done, anyhow.

"Now, Tony, Bert already told me you stole from your crew. Said you'd try and hide here if possible, and spin some tale. Let's just have that bag there and round everyone up to settle this." Danes started walking toward me slowly, hand still on the butt of his gun.

I held out the bag and let Danes get closer. He could get the drop on me, fast draw that he was. Still, something people who aren't miners never seem to wrap their heads around: gold's damn heavy. Heavy as a man, a bag of it this size. It don't take much. Now when you spend your days hauling rock you get used to it. We were all of us built for it and used to reinforced bags for lugging stuff around. But a sheriff, no, he'd give it no mind at all.

He got close and I held the bag out to him and then made it look like my hand slipped, dropping the bag. Pretty sure I could hear every bone in his foot shatter like kindling. That was before he screamed up a storm, of course. I grabbed his gun from the hostler, quick as I could, and pistol-whipped him to sweet unconsciousness. I gotta say it was a kindness I did to him then, not having to feel that foot.

Danes got dragged into the nearest cell, no easier or harder to move than a sack of gold, say, and locked the door. He'd keep for a little bit at least. The bag I grabbed on my way out, and Danes' gun slipped easily into my belt.

The street stood empty, which suited me fine. Dark and silent.

"Anthony," Bert's voice rang out, making a liar of me.

"Bertrand," I replied, rolling my eyes. There comes a point when the pressure just stops mattering. A respite from the hell that your life might become. That shining moment when you simply no longer care. I'd slid into that state of mind and only noticed when I checked and didn't feel any sort of remorse over the fact another loyal friend stood down there wanting to kill me. "Bert, look, just walk away," I said.

"Can't do that, Anthony. Can't," he said, "leave you to take our money."

"Our money, Bert! But y'all refuse to split it and are willing to kill for it all. You want me to just... oh forget," I said and tossed the bag high as I could. Got a good wind up, though my shoulder almost separated doing it.

The bag arced, and for a second we both watched it. But only for a second. We both drew down and fired, the flash of the muzzles blinding me. I heard Bertrand hit the dirt and knew there would be no getting back up for him.

I didn't enjoy it, myself, but he'd given me no choice. I walked over and reached down to grab the bag, but my arm hurt. A splatter of blood rolling off my finger to hit the ground let me know he'd got my arm. The shock numbed me, and I took the lack of pain as a blessing. Shoving the gun back into my belt, I grabbed the bag with my other arm and started off toward the mine.

I stopped at the entrance, setting the bag down for a minute while I thought and prepared a few ideas. Then I kept walking deeper. I could hear someone

moving. The trolley rolling makes the sort of noise you don't forget easy. Had to be Gabby.

Whatever emotional numbness'd come over me while dealing with Bert washed away. I liked Gabby, was sweet on her, didn't want to kill her. "Gabby?" I asked the semi-darkness.

"Unless you come to give me that bag, you oughta not be talking, Anthony," she said. I could see her, just a bit, crouched behind the trolley cart. Steel cart like that would stop a bullet easy.

"I've had to kill Bert and Kyle already today," I said, "I don't want to have to kill you, too."

"Then you got a simple option," she said, "in just handing me that bag and walking out of here. I won't harm you none. You got my word, Tony." I believed her. But where would that leave me? I'd still have to leave town, Danes would want to lock me up and might even be so mad at losing what he thought would be a share of gold that he'd try to kill me.

So leave town, be broke, friendless, and have no job at all. No money, nothing but the clothes on my back and maybe, at best, Kyle's horse and Danes' gun. She'd walk out of here rich, having had to do nothing except wait.

Or I could stay here and have a shoot-out with a woman I had feelings for. Even if I won I'd still have to leave town, but I'd be rich. Rich can cure a lot of ills. The thing was, I realized, the ill it couldn't cure was the hurt of my friends going bad on me. The gold brought me nothing good so far, so I had to think that moving on with it wouldn't exactly improve my life.

Still, didn't seem right that she benefitted from that. "I tell you what," I said, "I'll give you one more chance here."

She laughed, thumping the side of the cart and making it ring loudly in the rock-sided mine. "You'll give me... oh Tony. Sure then, what's this chance?"

"We split the gold and leave here in peace."

"Or I could kill you," she said.

"If you could've," I said, "you would've. You ain't one to sit and wait. No you got caught unprepared, didn't you?"

"Damn you, Anthony, I did," she said. That's when I knew she was buying time. Her lies always came too quick. I had minutes, probably, before whatever plan she cooked up went off. She'd been here possibly all day, waiting for the last of us to come looking for her. But she wasn't ready yet, and that's what mattered.

"So, what do you say, then?" I asked. Her answer didn't matter. Either way she would kick off her little plan and kill me. It wasn't me, personally, mind.

The Many Tortures of Anthony Cardno

No, I knew that. Death sat planned for whoever tripped up by showing their face here. She just didn't have to know that her words were ash in the wind to me.

"I say give me the gold and go on your way and no one else has to get hurt."

I nodded. "You're right," I said, lobbing the bag of gold in her general direction. "You have a good life, Gabby," I said as I turned my back on her and started for the entrance.

"That's it?" she asked. "After all this you're really gonna—"

"Gabby, I'm doin' like you asked." I stopped near the entrance of the mine and looked back at her. "I'm moving on and leaving you the gold. Hell, I'm leaving you the whole mine. I'm out of this town."

On my way out, I lit the fuse I'd set up at the mouth of the mine. The explosion rattled my bones, just like it always did, and sealed up the mine tight. We hadn't gotten deep enough to find bigger passages, and one person wouldn't be able to clear enough of that rubble before they ran out of air, food, or water. Whichever came first didn't matter much to me.

Let her have the gold. They'd each already had my trust and killed it. Money didn't matter after that.

❀

I unhitched Kyle's horse and rode out of town. Didn't know what direction to head, so I let the horse choose. My Pa'd chide me for cowardice, and Doc Kemper would say I shoulda been colder, but they could both go hang. I'd find a little town far enough away that no one would ever hear of this and I'd... who cared? I found I didn't.

I just rode.

There's steampunk, cyberpunk, dieselpunk, gaspunk and now, thanks to David Lee Summers ... Zombie-punk? Between Michelle Moklebust and Summers, I appear to have great potential as a mad scientist. I have to thank David for allowing me to bring the snark.

The Zombie Shortage

DAVID LEE SUMMERS

Professor Cardno gritted his teeth as he tapped an indicator mounted to a pipe that ran alongside a huge vat. The pressure was nowhere near as high as he'd like. The lights were dim—not just in the ancient brewery he had converted into a makeshift power plant, but all across the city. A menacing growl sounded from within the container. The professor pounded the vat's side, then moved on to a vast electrical panel. He checked gauges as he walked by on his way to a bank of switches, each as long as a man's forearm. Lightning arced outside the brewery's high windows and the lights went out.

Swearing to himself, the professor lowered a pair of goggles onto his eyes and searched the panel before him in the wan light that filtered in from above.

A banging sounded at the door.

The professor ignored it as he threw first one large switch, then another. Sparks flew from the electrical panel and the lights returned, weaker than before.

The banging resumed.

"Schmidt! Get the door," bellowed the doctor as he checked yet more gauges.

The professor's assistant emerged from the shadows, wearing a leather gas mask across his mouth. He shuffled across the dusty concrete floor and opened

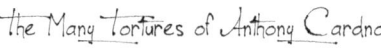

the door.

A man wearing a top hat and cape stepped in from the deluge. He removed his hat and shook off the water, then did the same with his cape. He handed them to Schmidt. The assistant looked at them, shrugged and tossed them over a pipe that ran along the wall.

"Cardno! I've come to have a word with you about the lights," called the well-dressed man.

Professor Anthony Cardno spun around and looked at him. He recognized the Honorable Mister Harris from the town council. "Mr. Harris, I really have my hands quite full right now, trying to keep everything functional during the storm. We can speak again when it abates."

"I will have a word with you now." Harris stepped over to the professor. "The people of this city expect the lights to stay on. Mr. Buckholtz complains that he can't keep the conveyor belts running in his factory."

Professor Cardno took a deep breath and let it out slowly. "As I recall, wasn't it Mr. Buckholtz's factory where the problem first appeared?"

"I don't understand." The councilman's eyes narrowed.

"Twenty-five years ago. It was Buckholtz's factory where the living dead first appeared—people with an insatiable hunger for human tissue—for brains—the flesh rotting from their very bones. Poor buggers. I suspected toxic waste from the machines."

"That was never proven." The councilman's tone was firm—a decision more than a statement of fact.

"Whatever." The professor shook his head, turned, and climbed a ladder to a catwalk that ran between several of the brewery's vats. The councilman looked at the dirty, rusted metal, then crinkled his nose and followed the doctor.

"Twenty-five years ago, the living dead overran the city, then the state, then the world," said the professor, as the councilman reached the top of the ladder. "It was apocalypse."

"I remember all too well," said the councilman. "Many of us lived in caves. It seemed civilization was over."

"I took refuge in this old brewery. And that's when I had my revelation." The professor pointed down into a glass-topped vat. Within, zombies shambled about, mindlessly. Two of them bumped into each other. In a corner, half a dozen of them huddled near a cow's carcass. They had torn into the skull, and were ingesting the cow's brains.

"Yes, we thought you were crazy when you started luring the zombies in

The Many Tortures of Anthony Cardno

here." The councilman smirked at the memory.

"The revelation," continued the professor, impatiently, "was that the zombies produced methane as they rotted. I could convert that methane into power. I could rid the city of zombies and I could restore civilization in one fell swoop. Twenty-five years after the zombie apocalypse, you live rather comfortably, don't you, Mr. Harris? All because of crazy Professor Cardno who took refuge in the old brewery."

"And we will be eternally grateful," said the councilman. "But today—what about the problem with the lights? What about now?"

"Don't you see," said the professor through gritted teeth. "That's the problem. We are running out of zombies."

"Running out?" The councilman blinked. "How can that be? The whole country was overrun. Can't you get more?"

"The zombies eventually rot into little stinking puddles of flesh and bone. The only way to get more is to have a human being infected by the zombie virus." The professor took off his glasses and cleaned them with the tail of his lab coat. "What's more, plants like this have sprung up all over the country. Businessmen like Mr. Buckholtz have become reliant on them and haven't come up with an alternative." He returned the glasses to his face, as though punctuating the statement.

The councilman opened his mouth to speak, but turned when Schmidt appeared behind him on the catwalk. Harris put his hand on his chest. "I wish you wouldn't sneak up on me like that. And must you wear that mask?"

"I'm afraid he must," said the professor, who had donned his own mask. "It's not prudent to breathe the air from the vats."

"Breathe the air? I don't understand."

As soon as Professor Cardno saw that Schmidt had opened the vat, he dashed forward and gave the councilman a shove. The politician dropped through the hatch to the floor, two stories below. Seeing the hatch opened, the zombies turned. Some tried to climb the smooth walls of the vat toward the professor and his assistant. Schmidt closed the hatch on the screams of Mr. Harris.

The professor and his assistant turned to inspect the other vats. Once they reached the third one, the lights brightened. "Ah, Mr. Harris must have taken his place among the chosen." Cardno turned and held up his finger. "You see, Schmidt, that's the real brilliance of this power supply. The zombies may rot to nothingness, but there's no end to the supply of idiots to replace them." He took out his pocket watch and examined it. "When are we expecting Mr. Buckholtz?"

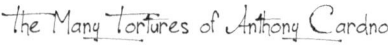

The Many Tortures of Anthony Cardno

If Christopher Paul Carey's name is familiar, it's because he's one of the authors hand-chosen by Philip José Farmer to tell new stories of Farmer's seminal creations, including the characters Kwasin and Hadon of Ancient Opar. This tale is set in a world of Chris' own creation, an alternate history in which Anthony Cardno is Anthony Cardinaux, but you can feel the pulp and Farmerian influences all throughout, albeit with a literary flavor. I look forward to further Fly-Leaves stories, with or without my namesake.

With Dust Their Glittering Towers: A Fly-Leaves Story

CHRISTOPHER PAUL CAREY

"The end of our foundation is the knowledge of causes, and secret motions of things; and the enlarging of the bounds of human empire, to the effecting of all things possible."

—*New Atlantis*

The note arrives during midmorning tea. After tipping the young courier boy, Alicia returns to the sitting room and sets the small slip of paper on the table beside the latest number of the Bacon Society journal, which she has been poring over in preparation for her afternoon outing. She reads:

My dear Miss Leith,

A trust case I had thought long buried again rears its many ugly heads, and I fear I can't dig myself out of the Brobdingnagian stack of papers weighing down my desk in time to accompany you and Mrs. Bunten to Highgate this afternoon as we had planned. I have informed Mrs. Bunten, who suggests we might try again next month, if I am so lucky as to extricate myself from this mess by then.

The Many Tortures of Anthony Cardno

Sincerest apologies,

P. W.

Alicia feels she might be mean-spirited for thinking it, but she is little surprised by Parker's bowing out of their little adventure to poke about the ruins of old Arundel House. A man of the heart, Parker is prone to overcommitment, something Helen never fails to remind her each time his name comes up. Alicia can hardly blame her sister, knowing the man well enough to suspect he was well aware of the labyrinthine trust case that lay before him even when, in the drawing room of the esteemed Mrs. Henry Pott, they hatched their plans for the trip to Highgate. Alicia also knows how infectious Mrs. Pott's little speeches can be. When the matron of their cause speaks so compellingly of the mysteries surrounding the supposed death of their dear Francis St. Alban at Arundel House, who can fault one for dismissing his prior obligations in the heat of the moment?

Certainly, Alicia cannot. Nor can she, despite having received Parker's disappointing note, bear the thought of letting down Mrs. Pott, the very founder of the Bacon Society of London. Twenty years Alicia's senior, the freethinking matriarch has become something of a role model for the younger woman. Mrs. Pott has recently suffered a relapse of that nervous illness which beset her just over a year ago, right at that crucial time when their case for Bacon's authorship of the so-called Shakespeare plays was about to take the world stage. Though she recovered in time to make good use of the furor caused by the Hon. Ignatius Donnelly's visit to London to promote his *Great Cryptogram*, Mrs. Pott is once again homebound and unable to pursue her researches in the field.

Alicia picks up Parker's note and runs its coarse grain across her lips. Then, with a curse she knows would astonish the high-minded literati of her social circles, she crumples the letter into a little wad and throws it against the window pane before her. Her missile hits the glass like a swallow hell-bent on suicide and drops onto the tabletop, coming to rest almost exactly where she picked up the note in the first place. With an angry swipe of a hand, she whisks the crumpled paper from the table, storms from the room, and readies herself to leave the house unchaperoned. *Social circles be damned.*

❂

The steep cobbled way of The Bank stretches before and below Alicia as she

The Many Tortures of Anthony Cardno

makes her way on foot from Highgate Station. Though the high heels of her boots have already nearly toppled her onto the slick, icy stones a half-dozen times, she counts herself lucky; were the station located to the south of Arundel House, she would have to climb up The Bank's precipitous rise, not shuffle ever so carefully down it.

A little thrill runs through her at a simple thought: Francis Bacon himself doubtless walked this very street some two and a half centuries ago! Would that Mrs. Pott have been able to accompany her on the day's journey. The woman has an uncanny way of conjuring up the past when she speaks of Francis St. Alban, as though she can open up a portal and transport her listeners straightaway to another world, like Alice stepping through her looking-glass.

All the same, Alicia feels she has already stepped through the mirror. Something in the crisp winter air seems indefinably *different* from the atmosphere of London. She inhales deeply the winter's cold. Beneath the acrid smell of coal smoke drifting from the train station lies a trace of some faint scent she can only describe as *healthful*. Perhaps this is the same "sweet salutarie air" she read about in Norden's 1596 survey of Highgate. Those of wealth and high birth unable to be cured by physic were often known to bequeath themselves to the hospitality of Lord Arundel and repair their ailing health at his great mansion by taking in the provincial restorative air. Is this not why many say Bacon himself took up residence at Arundel House, only to catch pneumonia in a damp bed and meet his death but a few days later? Supposed death, she corrects herself, for Mrs. Pott has every reason to believe Bacon's reputed demise to be nothing more than an artful deceit.

A cluster of holly trees appears on Alicia's left, their crimson fruits and dark green leaves adding color to the otherwise bleak winter scape. She considers that Mrs. Pott's arrival on the scene amid Bacon's dry critics makes for an equal contrast between vibrancy and desolation. Indeed, Alicia would not even be here had Mrs. Pott not pointed out that the very reason alleged for Bacon's presence in Highgate just prior to his averred passing stinks of premeditated misdirection. That Francis St. Alban caught a chill while stuffing a hen full of snow following an argument over the preservability of flesh can only be a ludicrous allegory at best. The tale's sheer audaciousness, Mrs. Pott insists, seems calculated to distract inquisitive minds from the well-documented history of Arundel House as an escape route out of England. Why, Arabella Stuart herself is said to have fled through the tunnels beneath Lord Arundel's manor before ultimately being apprehended aboard a French vessel bound for Calais.

The Many Tortures of Anthony Cardno

Alicia crosses Cholmeley Park, the great brown brick face of Channing House looming before her. A sign beside the street entrance reads in bold letters: High School for Girls.

Rider Haggard, whose African adventure story Alicia recently published in her literary journal, told her over tea only yesterday afternoon that the Misses Sharpe who ran the school were the daughters of the late Samuel Sharpe, the renowned Egyptologist. Below Channing House, Mr. Haggard said, Alicia would find "the sorry modern excuse for a dwelling" that now bore the name of Arundel House. The original structure, it seemed, was torn down some years ago. Who owned the property today he did now know, though town lore had it that the building on the south side of the latter-day Arundel House served as the basis for Mrs. Steerforth's house in Dickens's *David Copperfield*.

True to Mr. Haggard's word, down the hill a small white house hides behind a gated wall of plaster and black iron grille work. Alicia stops before the gate and waves to anyone inside the house who might see her. After waiting long enough to feel foolish, she follows the wall along the house's southern side, measuring her stride so that she might search for remnants of the original property.

Near the back of the house she comes to the wall's end, which opens onto a den of bare-limbed oaks and hornbeams. She smiles, rewarded by the sight of a low stone hedge crumbling amid a field of patchwork snow. Abandoning caution, she crosses onto the property and strides across the den, her boots crunching the frozen ground.

"Have you had your swearin' on the Horns, dearie?"

Alicia stops before the hedge and whirls about. A man wearing a moth-eaten wool coat over dirty work clothes hunches over a gnarled oaken walking stick. Mounted on top of the wooden shaft, a horn-headed visage confronts her: a bull's skull grinning like a prop from some unholy ritual. She gasps, then clears her throat in a pitiful attempt to conceal her fright.

"Oh, don't worry, m'lady!" The man bobs the bull's skull in a hand as if playing with a puppet, his beady, bloodshot eyes narrowing in what she takes for sadistic mirth. "It's just the way we Highgaters greet traveling folk that pass through town." The man's face is red from the cold and his thinning hair wisps in the wintry breeze. He snickers and spits a stream of tobacco juice through a gap in his teeth, then bows deeply and pulls himself upright with a groan and the help of his hideous staff. Yellow teeth grinning, he swirls a grease-stained hand in a second, shallower bow.

"Cardinal Antonius at your service, m'lady!" He guffaws long and loud be-

The Many Tortures of Anthony Cardno

fore a hoarse belly-cough cuts off the seizure of frightful jollity. "That's what my master calls me, anyway, though my mother christened me Anthony Cardinaux, bless her Hell-bound Gallic soul. Whom do I have the pleasure, dear lady?"

"Miss Leith," Alicia replies, not comfortable revealing her given name to the odd fellow. "Are you employed here, Mr. Cardinaux? I wonder, might I have word with the property owners? I'm conducting historical research into the estate and—"

"Never mind the owners, Miss Leith, they ain't got hide nor hair! I'm the groundsman here an' can tell you what God an' the Devil's left to know about the place. Me an' no one else. But first you got to swear on the Horns. Arundel's secrets ain't for outsiders, dearie." Again, the yellow teeth glisten and the bull's head bobs.

Alicia summons a childhood memory of her father, recalling how, in a moment of playful teasing, he once asked her to "swear on the Horns of Highgate." When she asked him what he meant, he laughed and said it was but a foolish pub oath and nothing more.

Now, staring at the devilish bull's skull wagging before her, a verse from Lord Byron comes suddenly to her:

Many to the steep of Highgate hie.
Ask ye, Bœotian shades! the reason why?
'Tis to the worship of the solemn Horn,
Grasp'd in the holy hand of Mystery,
In whose dread name both men and maids are sworn,
And consecrate the oath with draught, and dance till morn.

The man standing before Alicia nods and grins as though he has peered into her thoughts and found them worthy.

Finally, she shrugs and returns his smile. Has she not indeed hied to the steep of Highgate? Why not grasp the holy hand of Mystery and see if this groundskeeper might not know of any unusual features on the property that could have facilitated Bacon's concealed flight from Arundel House upon the ruse of his death? In any case, the fellow seems harmless enough, if a bit cracked, and the oath nothing but a silly pub joke.

Cardinaux lifts his staff and shuffles forward, jabbing the stick forcefully into the half-frozen ground at Alicia's feet. "Upstanding an' uncovered!" He motions for his initiate to remove her hat, which she does with aplomb now that she

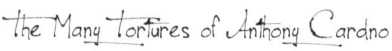

has gone all in to play the man's little game.

"Upstanding an' uncovered! Silence! Take notice of what I say to unto you, for *that* is the first word of your oath! Mind *that!*"

The bull's skull now looms before her at eye level, the man crouching behind the bovine head like some demented ventriloquist with his ghastly dummy.

"You must acknowledge me as your father, an' I must acknowledge you as my daughter. If you find yourself again in this village of Highgate an' you have no money in your purse, call for a bottle of wine at any house an' book it to your father's score. If it be found that you have money in your purse, you must forfeit a bottle of wine for trying to cozen an' cheat your poor old an' decrepit but most kind an' generous father." The stick bearing the bull's head tilts forward. "Now, my daughter, kiss the Horns—or a pretty man if you see one here, whichever you like best—an' so be one with Highgate fair!"

Alicia shudders, but can see no other way for it. She leans in and kisses the air before the hideous skull, hoping the man cannot see her lips have not truly touched the filthy old horns.

Wanting to be done with the abominable rite, Alicia points to the ruins of the crumbling wall. "Does this stonework date from the time of the old mansion? And that area where the ground has sunken in before it ... I've heard of a maze of tunnels said to run at length beneath the old house. Might not this depression be evidence of such a labyrinth?"

The man's eyes do not leave her. Instead, they narrow until she can no longer see the thin red tentacles writhing in the sea of white around the coal-black centers.

"My master warned me there'd be folk like you come asking after the property. Ain't no one showed in all these years. You're the first, O daughter of the Horns." The man steps uncomfortably close to her, his breath stinking of stale wine and something rotten.

"You kneel down there by that basin, daughter, an' I'll show you your old tunnels." He prods her forth by sweeping the end of his stick low to the ground like a broom. Alicia suddenly notices it comes to a point like a stake.

She moves sidewise toward the wall, unwilling to turn her back to the man and let him out of her vision.

A cry comes from the house and the groundskeeper starts. A woman's shadowy silhouette appears against the darker shadows arcing behind the house. Again, the cry, this time louder.

The man looks back at the advancing form, his features creased with worry.

"My cue, miss. Now don't go pokin' around that old wall." He shakes his bull's head staff with menace. "You're father's a-watchin'!" Then the man is scurrying off beneath the bare-limbed trees. By the time the woman arrives, he is gone.

❋

Over tea and biscuits in Mrs. Shaw's parlor room, Alicia learns little about the latter-day Arundel House other than that the residence has had no proper groundsman for nigh fifteen years; Mr. Shaw, who's business has taken him into the city through next week, is still spry enough to manage the estate, thank you very much. The hefty middle-aged woman goes on to chide Alicia for not knowing any better than to travel about the country alone, what with the Whitechapel murders still fresh on everyone's minds and the killer still at large. Mrs. Shaw is adamant that she knows of no one in town named Cardinaux, nor has she ever seen the man with whom Alicia spoke out behind the house.

Here she lowers her voice to a bare whisper to tell her guest that she's heard tell of strange goings-on in the dead of night at the nearby Highgate Ponds. Although Alicia waits for Mrs. Shaw to elaborate, the woman says no more. When pressed further for information about the residence, Mrs. Shaw tells Alicia that if anyone in Highgate knows anything about the history of old Arundel House, it will be Reverend Trinder of the parish church. But Miss Leith will have to come back another day, she says, as the vicar is currently away on church business in Twickenham.

The late-afternoon light now slants through the parlor's windows. The thin golden beams burnish dust motes hanging listlessly in the air, transforming them into a microcosm of tiny suns.

Alicia dismisses herself from Mrs. Shaw, her mood gloomy. The early winter evening comes and she must now make all haste to the train station before nightfall. Alas, she has utterly failed in her mission in Highgate, but perhaps once Parker has freed himself of his litigation she will be able to coax him to return with her and Mrs. Bunten to question the vicar. Persistence, as Mrs. Pott is ever fond of saying, is the only way the Baconians will be able to dig through the strata of the ages that now buries truth of Francis St. Alban's concealed life.

Making her way from the residence, Alicia sees what looks like a large pheasant scurrying in the arcing shadows along the south gate. Still under the spell of her mentor's aphorism, she feels a sudden compulsion to take one last

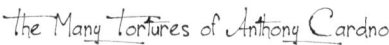

look at the old wall before ascending The Bank to Highgate Station. Perhaps Dr. Garnett of the British Museum might be able to make something of it if she can provide him with a more thorough description of the architecture.

Alicia follows in the fowl's wake along the house's southward side. The bird—if that is indeed what the animal is, for now she thinks it could in fact be a medium-sized dog—veers into the shaded den behind the house, its dark form skirting the crumbling wall. When she arrives at the ruin, the creature has vanished.

She recalls the sunken hollow at the wall's base, wondering whether the pheasant might roost in the depression on the cold winter nights. She crosses to the other side, suddenly worried the strange man might return to harass her with his horns. But she can be on her way in an instant, once she has had her look. And once she is on The Bank, in the full view of the many residents of Highgate Hill, the man will surely not dare to hassle her.

A great black hole yawns at the foot of the crumbling stone where she is sure was only a shallow declivity before. Or is the hole but an illusion of the failing light?

She pulls up her dress's hem and creeps to the edge of the blackness. A ripple of faint greenish light phosphoresces around the crater's rim, startling her. Then she is falling, sliding, rolling rough and tumble into the dank earth.

❁

Her aching frame heaps upon cold, flat stone. A weak diffusion of light comes from the shaft down which she has fallen. The damp air carries both the oppressive rankness of a chicken coop and the bitter stench of stagnant water. She pushes herself up from the floor and staggers to her feet, wincing as pain enflames her right ankle.

A narrow cellar fades into the gloom before her. She reaches out to either side, runs her hands over rough stonework. Despite the pain stabbing at her ankle, she surges with joy at her discovery: a tunnel running beneath old Arundel House, just as Mrs. Pott claimed!

Buoyed by the knowledge that her mission has been fruitful after all, she hobbles forward, wincing each time she places weight on her right foot. From somewhere ahead, how far she cannot discern, comes a faint but flickering glow. Perhaps the tunnel runs beneath Mrs. Shaw's property and beyond it, where it ascends and opens onto the surface at an adjoining estate. The inconstancy of the illumination might be caused by foliage rustling in the wind above the twilit opening.

She sloshes thorough a pool of foul-smelling water where the stone floor dips several inches. A faint pressure against her feet and the creep of dampness through her leather boots tells her the rank stuff now crests her ankles. She curses, realizing she has thoroughly drenched her dress's hems.

Though the daylight wanes and she risks missing the last train out of High-gate, the promise of the light ahead pulls her on. She can always hire a coach, after all. Her sisters will doubtless balk at the flagrant squandering of their inheritance, but the magnitude of the discovery dwarfs such petty concerns.

The floor rises slightly. She continues forward, taking a sharp breath with every other step. The fetid air is cool but does not carry winter's bite. For this she is thankful, though she knows it to be but a temporary respite before she must return to the surface in her wet clothing and footwear.

She nearly pitches to the floor when her outstretched hands fall away from the stonework walls into empty air. She stops and regains balance on her good foot, then hops forward with her hands still extended to her sides. The touch of what feels like cold, abrasive brick and seams of chalky mortar rewards her effort, informing her that she has in all likelihood just passed a cross-tunnel.

Slowly, she progresses down the corridor in her awkward, hopping gait. The rank odor only worsens as she advances. She wonders what has died down in these tunnels, then shudders to think of what might live here still.

The tunnel turns sharply. Dim light, greenish and spectral, phosphoresces out of a rectangular frame of darkness.

The glow from the room ahead spangles over the rough stone walls that cloister her. She imagines her passage down the tunnel as the final stage in a journey out of the shadow of ignorance into the light of truth. Did not the initiates of the Eleusinian mystery cults once creep along murky caverns such as this one, until at last they emerged from their ritual Hades into a chamber of brightness where the secrets of life and death would be revealed?

If only for a brief moment, her ridiculous metaphor distracts her from her fear. Now, nearing the light, a shiver tremors through Alicia's frame, and she fights to keep from fleeing back down the tunnel. She tries to slow her breath, but fails. She curses again, this time at her own inability to control her emotions. Would Bacon, that great rationalist of his age, act so if confronted by the unknown? Anger surmounts her fear and she forces herself to move toward the strange emanation.

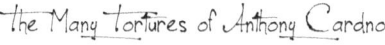
The Many Tortures of Anthony Cardno

The light grows with each step she takes, until it looms large and swollen like a sickly moon. Covering her nose at the pervasive bird stench, she passes through the frame of darkness into a chamber of indeterminable size. Directly before her, a two-foot-diameter orb hangs in the air with no visible support, its unearthly green light radiating but a couple of yards before dampening to utter blackness. The orb transfixes her. Astonishment saps the thoughts from her mind before they can blossom into words. At sporadic intervals, tiny tendrils of yellowish-green electricity crackle over the globe's surface. She has never seen its like.

Alicia reaches out toward the apparition. A tendril of electricity arcs jaggedly from the luminous ball, branching into five wavering arms of yellow-green flame that absorb without accompanying sensation into her fingers. She pulls back her hand and laughs in wonder, and for a moment again forgets her fear. She feels renewed, as if the sphere's unearthly energy has passed within her and revitalized her waning strength. Even the sharp ache in her ankle has numbed.

She forces herself to turn away from the strange apparatus and explore the room, passing through the oddly distinct border between light and dark. In the face of unqualified blindness, she stops and extends her hand back into the light. Though she can still see the orb as plainly as before, a shroud falls over her eyes when she looks into the darkness. She stops and extends a hand back into the light. Her forearm and hand appear disembodied, a sharp line on her coat sleeve demarcating where the orb's ghastly light ceases abruptly and unnaturally, as if the darkness of the room beyond has physical substance.

Alicia withdraws and turns back into the palpable shadow, shuffling forward blindly, a hand probing before her. After passing what she judges to be fifteen feet beyond the luminosity's border, her hand meets cold stone. She runs her palm along the chamber's curving wall as she orbits the room with cautious steps. Again she is forced to limp as her ankle's pain returns as suddenly as it vanished when she touched the orb. Despite the discomfort, she continues her exploration of the wall.

Opposite the room's entryway, an angular obtrusion juts from the smooth and closely mortared stonework. The rotten egg smell of sulfur combined with the acrid stench of bird droppings reeks from a great rectangular opening in the wall. Alicia explores the structure with her hands, finally deciding she has found large chimney or brick stove, its sulfurous emissions perhaps indicating its original purpose was alchemical in nature.

As she feels about the masonry, her fingers fall upon an ancient inscription carved deeply into what feels like smooth marble above the hearth. In the darkness, her fingertips trace the fine Latin letters:

VERULAM

Just as the import of her find crests her stultified wonder, Alicia hears a heavy rustling deep within the ancient firebox. Slowly, she backs away from the great stove, until at last she crosses the stark barrier between the enshrouded chamber and the globe's radiance.

The rustling ceases. She stops, her skin creeping with coldness.

Glistering with the same unnatural yellow-green as the orb, two tiny pinpoints of light glare at her out of the chamber's dark.

The sight propels Alicia toward the doorway that leads from the chamber. In the haste of her flight, she missteps. Pain flares through her injured ankle and she cries out as she crumples to the cold damp floor.

Behind her comes a bloodcurdling screech. A chaos of feathered wings thrashes and beats toward her.

Alicia scrambles onto her hands and knees. Her ankle throbs with such pain she feels faint, but terror pushes her toward the tunnel. Her dress tangles her legs, slowing her. When she passes over the chamber's threshold, she presses out with both hands against the narrow tunnel walls and pulls herself up to her feet.

The thing thrashes only a few yards behind her, but Alicia is too frightened to look back. She presses her hands against the walls for support, then crutches herself forward with precipitous abandon, crying out each time her right foot alights on the stone floor.

She emerges from the tunnel, her throat now raw from her repeated yawps of pain. The narrow cellar where she plummeted from the surface encloses her. Dim twilight rays slant down from a hole some fifteen feet above, falling on piles of broken boards moldering in a low dirt mound where the chamber's side has caved in. The wood pile, she knows instinctively, was in some past age a stairway to the surface. Now that it has collapsed, she has no way out of the cellar.

She bends low, balancing on her good foot, and picks up a beam from the pile. She lets out a sob as timber crumbles to dust and soft pieces in her hands. The thrashing grows louder through the tunnel opening. Along the floor she spies a roughly circular patch of blacker shadow in a corner of the cellar. She hobbles over to it and again gets down on her hands and knees, this time bunch-

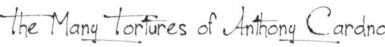

ing up her dress and skirts over her hips to unencumber her movement.

Another shriek fills the chamber.

"'Cowards die many times before their deaths,'" she mutters, and crawls through the small dark hole.

* * *

Alicia stumbles along the pitch-black tunnel until she believes she might go mad. Time must have some connection with light, she thinks, for she can no longer even guess how long it has been since she tumbled below the earth.

At occasional and irregular intervals, a light breeze touches her cheek, wafting fresh air over the omnipresent fetor of bird droppings; then the cold air stills.

When she judges she has hobbled down the low, narrow tunnel for the good portion of an hour, she stops and collapses exhausted on the stone floor. Though she sits on layers of bird filth, she is too weary care.

She strives recall her life before the dark labyrinth consumed her: The joy at seeing her first book come back from the printer and cracking open its pages to smell the freshly pressed ink. Spending long afternoons with Mrs. Smith poring over submissions for *Atalanta*. Picnicking with Parker on the little green at Cornwall Gardens after convening an informal meeting of Baconians at Mrs. Pott's residence.

The latter memory brings her full circle. How can she reconcile what she has seen—the extraordinary apparatus burning with unholy light in the workshop beneath Arundel House, and the frightful thing that roosts in the chamber's ancient alchemical stove—with her quest at Highgate?

Her imagination races. She knows Bacon spent much time on the property at the hospitality of its owner. Had Lord Arundel constructed the subterranean maze as a laboratory for Bacon's scientific experiments? And if that were the case, has she just witnessed one of those experiments, still phosphorescing with some unknown energy over two and a half centuries after Bacon set the apparatus running?

She knows there can be no other explanation. The inscription in the marble above the stove makes it certain: VERULAM—the very title bestowed upon Francis St. Alban in 1618 by King James I.

And what of the thing that chases her? Is it merely an ordinary bird—a pheasant or some other large fowl—that has come down through the hole, intent on roosting in the tunnels for the winter? The air here is warmer and more

The Many Tortures of Anthony Cardno

regular than on the surface. What better conditions are there for an avian retreat?

But she cannot keep from her mind the story she has long believed a myth: that Bacon's final experiment before his alleged passing centered on preserving the flesh of a slaughtered hen. She has long considered the incident to be nothing more than a fable covering for Lord Verulam's feigned convalescence at Arundel House. But might not there be an element of truth in the lie? Had Bacon—author of the *Historia Vitae et Mortis*, a learned tome on the science of life extension said to be two hundred years ahead of its time—somehow discovered the very secrets of life and death, and turned his great learning upon the subject in his secret chambers beneath Highgate Hill? Could the thing that pursued her have been a part of the great experiment, perhaps the slaughtered hen itself re-animated like Mary Shelley's monster and kept alive throughout all these years by the vital energy of the labyrinth's unearthly orb?

Just when she thinks her imagination has gotten the better of her, the words of Mr. Cardinaux, the false groundskeeper, come back to her.

"My master warned me there'd be folk like you come asking after the property. Ain't no one showed in all these years. You're the first, O daughter of the Horns."

Alicia shudders, remembering now the peculiar man's parting admonishment to stay clear of the old wall.

"'My master ...'" she whispers, and tears well in her blind eyes.

She cries aloud in anguish, knowing she must cast off such thoughts or indeed plunge into madness. Her predilection for losing herself in bookish speculations, no matter how creative or insightful, will do nothing to help her escape the tunnels.

Hope rises from despair as cold, fresh air again caresses her cheeks. This time the faint breeze carries with it the sweet-and-stale smell of dead grass.

Grasping the rough edges of stone that line the confining tunnel, she pulls herself to her feet and resumes her journey through darkness.

The tangible evidence of a world apart from this underground hell—the surface world she can now barely remember—spurs her forward with an upwelling of renewed vigor. She increases the pace of her hobbling progress. When her high heels threaten to tumble her, she stops to hurriedly doff her boots. She continues on barefoot, the thick layer of bird droppings that cover the floor caking between her toes.

Though the sense of time has abandoned her, Alicia's growling stomach tells her a great span must have elapsed since she took tea and biscuits in Mrs. Shaw's parlor. She thinks of Helen and Emily, and how her sisters must be sick

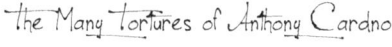

with worry over her failure to return home. Would they organize the search for her straightaway, or rather wait up all night sleepless, hoping she would walk in the door and dismiss their apprehensions with nothing but a laugh and an adventurous smile?

The low, narrow tunnel closes further about her, and now she must stoop in order to proceed forward. The pungent dankness returns, but she allows herself to hope. If the air ahead stirs, then an opening to the surface must lie somewhere before her.

She stops as the hope of but a moment ago sinks into a sea of despair.

Above the sound of Alicia's panting breaths comes a hollow rustling from behind. A moment later, a rhythmic, grating clatter resonates from back down the tunnel.

Clackity-scrape-clack. Clackity-scrape-clack.

It can only be horny avian claws scurrying over stone. The thing has found her again.

She wants to cry out in frustration, but she gnashes her teeth to combat the pain in her ankle and starts forward at a hobbling run.

The rough stonework juts unevenly from the tunnel's sides and scrapes Alicia's shoulders, tearing at the fabric of her ruined dress. A low hang in the ceiling smacks her right temple, and warm wetness spreads over her high cheek. The blow releases tears too long repressed, and she sobs without restraint as pained steps carry her along her way in utter blindness.

The tunnel curves to the left and the pitch-black that surrounds her lightens ahead to a dark grayish-blue. The intensity of the glow increases as she moves forward. The rank air freshens.

Suddenly she is emerging from the side of a low hill tangled with overgrowth. Before her a plain of ice stretches into the distance, awash in the slate-blue moonlight. Some distance to her left, at the foot of a low hill, sits an old but apparently still-serviceable wagon, its sole horse tied to a bare-branched hornbeam.

Alicia starts when she sees Cardinaux, the counterfeit groundsman, stroking the mane of the old roan. He seems unaware of her presence. What has brought the strange man here? Had he seen her fall into the labyrinth and, knowing where the tunnels would lead, come here in search of her?

A hellish screech erupts from the tunnel entrance. Alicia turns as if a spell commands her.

In the pale light, a demon struts before her, the bullet head atop its gross

The Many Tortures of Anthony Cardno

and deformed avian body reaching nearly as high as her shoulder. Luminous yellow-green eyes burn with malevolence. The thing is partially denuded of feathers, though tufts of dirty plumage and bare quills cover its sagging, pockmarked skin in random patches. A rippling phosphorescent seam surrounds the demon, outlining the opening in the hill just behind it. The unearthly aura, identical to the one that flickered around the hole down which she fell, frightens Alicia almost as much as the creature that confronts her.

Then the demon-thing is upon her, scraping and slashing at her dress's fabric with its razor-sharp claws, its monstrous chicken beak thrusting over and over into her upraised forearms as it tries to peck out her eyes. Alicia screams, kicks, hurls herself to the ground. She rolls violently from side to side, beating her assailant with her fists, but the thing attacks unrelenting.

Something clamps viselike on her upper arm, flings her roughly across the snow-covered ground. For a moment she lies there, too stunned to understand her whereabouts or situation. She shakes her head and lifts herself up on an elbow, horror surging over her as she sees Cardinaux striving alone and barehanded to beat back the demonic bird. He has torn her from the creature's talons and thrown himself upon her attacker with no thought for his own safety.

The thing's wattles dangle like dark masses of tumorous flesh, enveloping the man's hands as he tries to throttle his opponent. The bird viciously bites and hammers with its beak. A darkness that can only be blood stains the man's once-white shirt where it frills from his coat.

The realization that Cardinaux has been trying to help her all along jolts through Alicia. When he had fled Mrs. Shaw, the man had warned Alicia to stay away from the opening to the tunnels. Now he would sacrifice his life for hers. She thinks of the oath she swore on the old horns. Had the ritual somehow indebted Cardinaux to her?

She shakes the thought from her mind. It does not matter. Already the monstrosity has laid the bloodied Cardinaux prone and straddled itself on top of him.

The man reaches out to one side, grasping for something just beyond his reach. It takes a moment for Alicia to understand what it is.

She pushes herself up from the ground with all her remaining strength. Then she is running barefoot over the frozen earth, heedless of the pain that stabs through her ankle, until she stops before the object of the man's vain flailing: Cardinaux's bull-headed staff.

The man's blood-streaked form, torn and battered, lies still beneath the great avian, which continues to rake and peck at its victim in unbound fury.

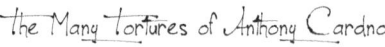

The Many Tortures of Anthony Cardno

Alicia grabs up the staff and, swinging the sharpened end of the stick before her, charges. The stake drives deep into a bare patch of skin on the creature's breast, the wet splintering sound of rent flesh and fractured bone drowned out by the thing's furious screeching. The force of the impact rears up the great bird on its spindly legs, causing it to scamper wildly backward. Alicia does not stop her charge but rather continues to push with all her weight against her makeshift spear. The bird lunges its beak at her, then teeters off balance. The shaft, still embedded in bird, tears itself from Alicia's grasp as the creature falls backward into the tunnel's black maw.

Alicia's ears ring with a dissonant keening that terminates in a sharp electric snap. She looks up from where she has fallen. The phosphorescent seam about the tunnel entrance has winked out.

❂

Alicia makes her way to Cardinaux's side. The man's wounds are grave. His coat and shirt have been torn from him by the monster, and his chest has been flayed to bloody ribbons.

Carindaux coughs and sputters, clearing blood and phlegm from his throat. "I should have slaughtered an' roasted that bird for dinner years ago." He smiles wanly. "But I been on my own with nary a word of guidance from my master in ... well, long since before you were born, miss. I worry, oh, how I worry about my master. But soon no more, no more—" Again, a coughing fit seizes the man.

Alicia picks up Cardinaux's shredded and bloodied hand, holds it to her ruined dress. The man quiets, then looks up and fastens Alicia with an unyielding gaze.

"You tell that Pott woman to mind her business, now. I've had my eye on her."

Alicia's blood runs cold. She has told Cardinaux nothing of Mrs. Pott and her interests in Highgate's mysteries.

Cardinaux's face brightens with Alicia's increasing distress. He raises his free hand, a stump of bloody bone that was once an index finger pointing unerringly at her. "It's you, O Daughter. Somehow, I knew it ... yes, knew it all along. The new Keeper of the Horns." His lungs whistle with fluid, but by some means he finds the inner strength to go on. "Ain't had time to train you none, no, but that don't hardly matter: my master's spirit is in you. I can *see* it."

Briefly, Alicia thinks she can see a faint radiance glimmer in the man's eyes.

The Many Tortures of Anthony Cardno

It is same luminous gaze as that of the dead creature beside them. Fear shivers through her. Then the trace of light is gone.

"Mr. Cardinaux!" She lifts his hand to her face and mixes tears with blood.

He smiles again, this time weaker. When he speaks, his voice is a bare whisper.

"Do you recall the first word of your oath, daughter?"

At first she is at a loss. The world seems to reel topsy-turvy and for an instant she cannot place her surroundings. Then her vision settles and all that has led her to this moment returns to her.

"'*That*,'" she whispers. "'*That*' is the first word of my oath."

The man's face grins back at her, but his eyes are now still with death. Gently, Alicia lowers his hand and places it upon his ruined chest.

She does not move from his side until the bells of St. Michael's toll softly over the countryside and the eastern sky brightens over the frozen pond.

✸

A red-breasted robin alights on the windowsill outside the spacious and elegantly furnished drawing room at 8— Cornwall Gardens, its cheerful song echoing the mirthful chatter of the little group of Baconians who have gathered at the Pott residence following the Society's latest meeting. Alicia sits in a deeply upholstered chair, awash in the warm glow of midafternoon sunlight that beams through the tall windows. She nods and smiles as the lively conversation dances from speaker to speaker, finding little need to add commentary of her own other than the occasional murmur of support for a speaker's thesis. The weeks-old scars from her ordeal at Highgate have now faded, and joy washes over Alicia with the realization that a sense of normalcy has at last returned to her life.

She is happy as well that the nervous illness that so recently incapacitated Mrs. Pott seems to have vanished as quickly as it had beset the woman. The matron of their cause has resumed her station at the hub of the Society's activities, and even that doubting Thomas of a secretary, Mr. Theobald, has deigned to partake of the afternoon's reception. Alicia suspects he recognizes that holding court with Mrs. Pott will go a long way toward securing his popularity among members in the upcoming election, especially the way he is chatting merrily away with Mrs. Bunten, whom he has long been at odds with over certain particulars of the authorship question. All the same, it is heartening to see the founder of the Society once again assuming her proper role.

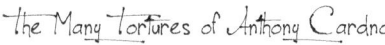

All too soon, members of the little party begin to dismiss themselves, bidding a happy Sunday afternoon to Mr. and Mrs. Pott. Alicia remains nested in her chair's deep cushions as Helen catches her eye to signal that they too must be on their way if they are to arrive at Albert Hall in time for the early recital of Handel's "The Triumph of Truth and Time." Meanwhile, Emily chatters on with Parker, clearly so mesmerized by his wit and charm that she is oblivious to the late hour.

At last, Mr. Theobald rises to thank his host and hostess for their hospitality, and with him departs the remainder of the guests but for Parker and the Leith sisters. Alicia waits for Helen to practically drag Emily from her conversation with Parker so they might bid the Potts a good day. Then Alicia herself rises to join them.

Mr. Pott stands quiet and cheerful as his wife showers praises on Parker and the three sisters for their enchanting and much welcome conversation. When the party makes ready to leave, Mrs. Pott turns to Alicia and asks if she might have a brief word with her on Society business, telling the others she will not hold them up for but a few minutes.

Helen takes Emily by an arm and leads her down the little flight of stairs to the first floor, the quiet and patrician Mr. Pott making his way slowly behind them.

Parker remains to cast a somewhat anxious look at Alicia, as if she is yet too feeble from recent events to be on her own in the world. Alicia smiles, genuinely touched at his concern, but nods him on. Her sisters' laughter titters up from the room below as Parker turns to follow the creak of Mr. Potts' footsteps down the winding stairway.

Mrs. Pott stands tall and regal before the entrance to the adjoining hall, her royal blue dress matching the lace cap ribboned into her long and still-dark hair. The woman's secretive smile reminds Alicia of Da Vinci's *La Gioconda*.

"Let us repair to the study, shall we?"

Alicia follows the woman down the short hallway into a small room in the back of the house. The dark floral curtains are only partially drawn, leaving the room's far corners in deep shadow. Bookcases set into the walls sag beneath the great weight of rows upon rows of tomes. Heaps of pamphlets and books rise from the polished oaken surface of the study's desk like sedimentary stacks emerging from a placid sea. On a low table beside a reading chair upholstered in burgundy velvet, a well-read copy of Bacon's *Promus of Formularies and Elegancies* lies open with numerous papers jutting out from the sheaves, the revealed

The Many Tortures of Anthony Cardno

portions of the notes scrawled over in Mrs. Pott's distinctive violet-colored ink. The smell of paper hangs thickly in the air, easing Alicia's nerves and reminding her of the study in own her home. Mrs. Pott takes up a position behind the desk, her hands clasped behind her back like a school teacher mindful of her student's overdue report.

Before Alicia knows what she is doing, the floodgates open and she begins to pour out her confession of the strange happenings of six weeks past. She has told the full details of her story to no one, not even Helen, and the deluge of words, though furious, is a welcome one.

Mrs. Pott, however, does not permit Alicia to indulge in her catharsis for long. With a wave her hand, the woman draws closed the floodgates and the torrent of Alicia's testimony sputters to an exasperated halt.

"All in good time." Mrs. Pott turns from Alicia and peers outside through the opening between the drapes.

Alicia stifles a sob. It is almost too much to hold back the outpouring of repressed emotions now that she has unplugged the spigot. She waits, her hands trembling, for some clue, some direction from her mentor as to how to proceed. Finally, the older woman speaks, although her back remains turned to Alicia.

"The secrets of a lifetime must be revealed incrementally for them to be properly understood. That much I have learned in my study of Lord Bacon." The woman swishes back the drapes, flooding the room in a glare of sunlight, then turns from the window and smiles warmly at Alicia. "Though I myself have pulled back truth's impenetrable curtain and seen a great deal of its hidden glory, there is much more that I do not know or, having glimpsed it, cannot claim to comprehend. One day, however, we *will* know and understand the mysteries we plumb. I shall see to it, rest assured. Be that as it may, few are equipped to accept truth undefiled without preparation. Without, one might say, having been put to the test."

As I have, Alicia almost dares to say. But without knowing the depth of Mrs. Pott's understanding of matters, she says nothing. Still, the woman must know much. Otherwise, why would she cut off Alicia's recounting of the dark secrets at work beneath Arundel House—of the very mysteries they have both sought for so long to unravel?

Mrs. Pott leans forward, her hands pressed against the edge of the oaken desktop as if her majestic frame is a medieval cathedral and her strong arms its buttresses.

"You know as well as I that certain viewpoints are deemed unacceptable

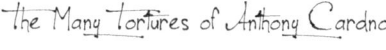

within the bounds of the Society." The buttresses slide forward and the woman lowers herself into the chair behind the desk. "Thus, I have decided to take action. Already have I created a wheel within a wheel, a secret body of likeminded souls who seek to polish the rusted links of history's unbroken chain and reveal the luminous truth hidden underneath. Membership, however, is to be restricted only to women, who cannot be bound by the oaths, and equally tremendous penalties, of the secret brotherhoods whom I believe to be behind the obfuscation of Bacon's past. Further, members must be those who have been tested and found capable of accepting the truth."

Alicia tries to rouse her courage to speak but again she falters.

The woman smiles and continues. "I have christened the new guild the Fly-Leaves, after the pages that have been so mysteriously torn out of such a great number of the original printings of Bacon's works. It is our aim to recover such stolen knowledge and, if we judge it proper, expose the thieves. What you have uncovered in Highgate is only the beginning of our quest."

Alicia's mind whirls. She recalls Mr. Cardinaux's warning, that she must implore Mrs. Pott to mind her business, that he has had his eye on her.

But the woman already seems to know *so much*. So much that Alicia herself burns to know and to understand.

She teeters on the brink of refusal, of telling Mrs. Pott that her search for the truth will only lead her to the same fate as the odd man with his staff of horns. Then, at the thought of the old horns, of her oath upon them, Alicia knows she cannot turn back from the truth. Not after all she has seen. Horns, after all, were meant to be seized.

Alicia buttresses her own hands against the desk's edge and leans forward to fix her enigmatic elder with a fearless gaze.

"If I may ask, just how many members abide within your secret wheel?"

Again, Mrs. Pott smiles like Da Vinci's *La Gioconda*.

"So far, only two."

The Many Tortures of Anthony Cardno

Of course, I couldn't resist the chance to torture myself in print. I grew up in Mahopac, New York (specifically the community of Lake Secor). We were all obsessed with the caves/mines on "the big island." How much of the following really happened, I'll leave up to my readers to decide. Some names have been changed to protect ... someone.

Canopus

ANTHONY R. CARDNO

We were all obsessed with the cave/mines on "the big island" in Lake Mahopac.

We didn't live on the big lake back then, in 1980, and we didn't own any kind of speedboat or pontoon boat at any of the marinas. And if you didn't own property around or berth a boat on the big lake, opportunities to explore the three islands were scarce.

I've never been on Petra Island. It's always been privately owned. These days, it has a home based on Frank Lloyd Wright designs sitting on the edge of it, perched out over the water, quite the sight as you circle past it in a boat. Back then, it had a small stone bungalow, but you still couldn't get near it. If you tried to walk to it during the winter or if you boated too close during the rest of the year, two growling, drooling Dobermans and an equally mean German Shepherd would bound out of the tree line to the shore; they'd even run out on the ice or swim after boats. The owner came close to getting sued once or twice, until one of the dogs drowned during a spring storm and he started keeping them in the house. But that was years later.

I've been on Farie Island once. The parents of a summer camp friend of a friend of mine had a home on Farie, and we were invited for a party one week-

end. All of the houses on Farie belonged to people with a fair amount of money, New York City lawyers and doctors and at least one big-time book editor. Adam's house was rich without being ostentatious. We got there early, my friend and I, and Adam showed off his weight bench and speedbag for me, while our mutual friend helped Adam's mother set out soda and chips. I think that's when I developed my fatal weakness for redheads. But that too was years later, spring of my senior year of high school, and another story completely.

Canopus Island was the largest of the islands and still uninhabited despite being privately owned. The caves on the island had a mythology that we kids just couldn't resist: Once colonial settlements started showing up around the lake, there were occasional disagreements with the natives. The constabulary tried their best to mediate but one fine spring night some of the farmers and townsfolk coerced a group of natives out to Canopus and down into the tightest, darkest, dampest parts of the caves. Then they built a roaring fire in the cave entrance that sucked all of the oxygen out. A few natives tried a run through the flames but didn't make it; the stories vary as to whether shots were fired to help the flames do their work. There were no survivors. No living survivors, at least.

I was fourteen when I set foot on Canopus.

It was Demarco's idea.

If not for boy scouts, I don't think Demarco and I would ever have been friends. We went to different elementary schools, were in different Cub Scout packs. We met when we were Webelos and despite having lots of different interests (he was into hunting and stock car racing; I was more interested in bowling and television), we found some things to bond over: bike riding and comic books, for instance, and the fact that neither of us was any good at basketball. Not many of my old Cub Scout den made it past the first full year of Scouts. I certainly didn't. Demarco stuck with it, made Eagle, and became a scoutmaster for a short time.

It was during Webelos and middle school that our den started to drift apart. Except for Demarco, we were all still neighbors and mostly rode the same school bus, but our interests were changing. Being somewhat less than athletic and a fair-to-middling academic student, I started to become the odd man out. I wasn't good enough for the track team like Charlie or Eddie, and I wasn't enough of a bad-ass to hang out with Howie in the smoking area.

Demarco and I started spending more time together, since he was already outside the group anyway. We started hanging out more in school, having some of the same classes and a lunch period together. We slept over each other's hous-

The Many Tortures of Anthony Cardno

es a few times.

It was one of those times when Demarco decided we needed to explore Canopus.

"Come on, you know all of the stories about the caves. Don't you want to see them?" He was sitting on the edge of his bed, hands gripping the bed sheets; it was the closest he ever came to really bouncing up and down with excitement. He was right: I did know all the stories. Even then, I collected stories like other people collected baseball cards.

I was sitting on the floor, lightly tossing a baseball up and down. It might have been a vague attempt at juggling, but I wasn't convincing either of us that I was coordinated enough to move on to two balls yet. We'd eaten a late dinner, and all I really wanted to do was sit in his room and listen to him tell hunting stories while STYX played on the stereo. Instead, I shrugged, tossed the ball again, and said, "Well, yeah, I mean, who in our troop doesn't want to see them?" The ball came back down and I managed to bobble it. It hit his hardwood floor and bounced a couple of times before rolling into the hall. If you really used your imagination, it sounded like a drumbeat.

"Klutz." Demarco smiled and ruffled my hair as he walked past to get the ball.

"Everything alright?" I heard his Mom call from the living room.

"Yeah," he answered. "We're a bit beat, gonna shut the light and just tell scary stories til we fall asleep, okay?"

"All right. Good night, boys. Love you."

"Love you too, Ma."

He came back in the room with the ball, shutting the door and rolling his eyes. It was part of our ritual; he pretended to be embarrassed whenever he told his mother he loved her, and I pretended to believe him.

"Okay, check the desk drawer. I have extra D-cell batteries in there, and another flashlight." He started pulling his hunting rucksack down from his closet shelf.

"Whu—?" I stammered for a second, then realized what the plan was. He'd decided we were sneaking out and going to Canopus.

It was early February, so getting to the island wouldn't be difficult. The winter had been a bitter cold one, and the big lake had enough ice on it to support a fire truck. There was a little sliver of a moon, just enough to see by without being so bright that people from shore would be able to see us. Demarco at that time lived about a ten-minute walk from the big lake, at the top of a hill my mother

absolutely hated driving up. Our only problem would be getting on the ice, if there were still ice fishermen at either of the marinas.

We dressed in layers, as we'd been taught, but nothing too bulky. I left my heavy coat in his room, tucked into the sleeping bag on the floor in case his mom checked in on us. We figured the walking would keep us warm on the way, and once we were there the temperature in the caves would be warmer than the winter air. We snuck out his bedroom window and practically tip-toed down the driveway. Once we made the road, we walked normally and talked a little bit. I warmed to the idea of doing something a little dangerous; a definite change in character for me in those days.

We tried the little marina first, and sure enough, the last of the cars in the lot was pulling out and going down the road away from us. If he'd seen us walking down the shoulder of the road, he'd still have had no idea we were going to cut into the marina.

Cut into the marina we did. We stayed as far away from the office as we could—which was not very far when you consider it was maybe 50 feet from the guardrail by the road to the shore of the lake. Of course there were no boats tied to the wooden docks. Demarco tested the ice around the docks by sitting on the edge of the wood and pushing down with his legs. The ice was thin where it touched the shore, but even the ice around the dock pylons was thick.

"You remember what to do if the ice starts to crack?" He glanced back at me.

"Watch you sink and then run like hell for help?" I offered.

"Dork." He slid his ass off the edge of the dock and put his full weight on the ice. No sound. He jumped up and down a few times, and we could hear "whale song" burble under the ice across the lake but no cracking. "C'mon. We don't have all night."

I followed him onto the ice in the same fashion, and we started toward the dark shape of the island. We stayed a good five or six feet apart, so that if one of us hit a thin spot (spring-fed lakes being prone to them; we'd heard all the horror stories) the other would have time to go flat and toss him the end of a length of rope we were each carrying (scouts are always prepared). I kept sucking on the water bottle I'd brought, and I could see Demarco in front of me doing the same (Scouts also know to stay hydrated). I almost lost my balance a few times. We kept our flashlights off to avoid attracting attention from any of the still-lit houses on the shore. The crossing seemed to take forever in the dark. But we finally made the shore of Canopus.

None of these islands were exactly huge. We called it the Big Lake because

The Many Tortures of Anthony Cardno

at a couple of miles in each direction, it was the biggest in our sprawling hamlet. The lake I lived on, by comparison, was barely a mile long and a quarter-mile wide at the widest. Still, the big lake was big enough to support motor boats and such. Canopus just looked that much bigger rearing up slightly off-center. And of course, the legends made it seem even bigger.

That there were caves on Canopus there was no doubt. They were on the surveyors' maps, and there was a ferry (decades ago, before it sank) that took hotel patrons (decades ago, before they went out of business) to the island for a look at the caves. But no one in our age range had gone into the caves themselves. Every grade in our school had a handful of students who somehow made it onto the island to party, and that always generated a few stories, but when pressed for details the storytellers would usually admit they'd been too drunk or stoned to bother with the caves.

I've tried looking for corroboration of the Bonfire legend in the various histories written of our county, but haven't ever found anything. Perhaps they're just small-town legend; perhaps there is some lost truth. Demarco loved to tell the stories on scout camp outs and sleep overs. I loved to listen to them. A scary story still has power over me all these years later, and there's no better way to spend a chilled autumn evening or a hot summer night. But that night, stepping onto Canopus and trying to get our bearings as to where one of the cave entrances might be, I for one did not want to hear the Bonfire legend ever again.

"This way." Demarco motioned inland and to our right. I followed him silently; I was pretty sure he was wrong and figured questioning him would make him change direction and accidentally stumble on a cave entrance. We left the shore and stepped into snow up to our knees. I was hoping after a few minutes of stumbling up the slight incline in the deeper snow, he'd give up and we'd head back to the shore.

"What's that?" He stopped and pointed to our left, farther inland. There was a bit of rockface showing between the trees. It didn't look too far away, and it appeared a little too flat and perfect from this distance to actually be a cave entrance. So to make it seem like I was enjoying this trip, I suggested checking it out.

It wasn't quite as flat and perfect as it seemed. The slope got steeper, leading up to what was in fact a bare spot on the hillside about ten feet wide and seven feet tall. It was the kind of thing you see where a mudslide has taken the soil layer off the underlying rock. We had to get within a foot or two of it to realize that the center of it, a space about 6 feet wide and 6 feet tall roughly speaking,

was actually a small cave. Demarco gave out a silent "whoop" and walked up to it to make sure we weren't seeing things. I held back just slightly. He checked it out for a moment, then clumped back through the snow to me.

"Come on, it goes in a little ways at least. Can't see how far without the flash-lights. We'll turn them on when we get in there."

I just looked at him, not sure what to say. Whatever bravado I'd been feeling had fallen away now that we'd stumbled on an entrance and Demarco wanted to continue. He put his arm around my shoulder and gave a squeeze that sent a shiver through me.

"Look, there's nothing in there to hurt us ... they're just stories. We won't even go in that far. Just far enough to say that we were actually in there."

And with that, we were moving towards the cave entrance.

"Wait." We were right up to it, about to step in.

"What?" I was hoping he'd changed his mind.

"I've gotta piss. Let's mark our territory." His free hand was already tugging down his zipper. "You've gotta be full, too ... you drank as much as I did on the walk over."

"Fine." I used my free hand to pull my zipper down as well, and we went about our business.

"Watch out for splash-back!" He grinned and aimed his stream to cross mine, aiming for my boots.

"You're nuts." I laughed as we zipped back up. For a few moments, I'd for-gotten to be uncomfortable. He had that effect on me.

"Well, here goes nothing." He took a first step into the cave, and I followed. "First guys of the class of '84 into the Canopus caves." He might have pumped his fist in triumph—I couldn't see it but heard the rustle of his jacket. Then his flashlight went on, aimed at the floor in front of us. I turned mine on too.

The cave floor was hardened mud. The cold winter air went still around us but it didn't seem any warmer. The floor sloped slightly down in front of us.

We didn't get very far, maybe fifty feet, when we pretty much hit a dead end. The wall in front of us was rock, solid to the touch, and we couldn't feel any air moving. I silently mouthed *"thank you"* as I raised my eyes upward. Demarco played his flashlight across the cave wall.

"There." He pointed to a fissure running from ceiling to floor, about a foot-and-a-half wide. Definitely tall and wide enough for us to continue. *"... for noth-ing,"* I silently added, rolling my eyes upward again.

Demarco squeezed into the fissure sideways, which seemed to give some extra room. I mimicked him and tried not to think about how much rock and earth were on top of and around us. It felt to me like the fissure was narrowing as we moved forward, but Demarco kept going. When I felt rock scrape the top of my head, I knew it was getting shorter at least. After a few minutes, Demarco stopped.

"Cool," he muttered.

"What now? Another dead end? Ancient runes?"

"Just follow me." He squatted down and duck-walked sideways. I played my light where his head had been a second before, and saw tan wavy rock that looked a little wet. I angled the light down and saw an opening and Demarco's hand motioning for me. I squatted, grabbed his hand for balance (or at least, that would be my excuse if he asked), and duck-walked sideways after him.

We came into a larger room. The ceiling was probably ten or twelve feet high, and our flashlights couldn't hit the far wall of the room. There was water dripping. Demarco took a step forward, and I went to follow him.

I hit a slick spot on the floor, my feet went forward and my torso back. I landed hard and the air went out of me in a rush. Somehow, I didn't hit my head, but my shoulder started throbbing. My flashlight rapped against the rock and sputtered down to a weak thin glow that barely reached my feet. I could feel the wetness of the cave floor seeping through my jeans even though they were winter-lined, and the sting of dirty water into the cuts on my hands from hitting the hard rock.

"You alright?" Demarco squatted next to me.

"Yeah. Think so. I should just sit here a minute. I broke the flashlight."

"Yeah, catch your breath and stay right here, so we don't forget where that little door is." He stood up. "I just wanna see how far the room goes."

"Demarco ..." My voice cracked, and I blushed in the dark.

"Two minutes, I promise. You'll be able to see my light, and I won't go any farther than where I can see yours."

"Alright."

He started slowly walking away, being careful of slick spots that might land him on his ass like me. After about thirty seconds I let my eyes wander away from him. With his light blocked by his body and moving away, my eyes started to adjust to the darkness of the cave. I tried not to imagine being in here without any light at all. I was definitely starting to feel a little claustrophobic.

I thought I could feel air moving around my face.

I thought the air was so still you could choke on it.

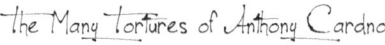

There was no rational way both could be true.

It was deathly silent, save for that water dripping somewhere nearby. The sound was mesmerizing.

In the dim glow from my broken flashlight, I could sort of make out the wall closest to me. Something seemed off about it. A slight indent, a different coloration.

I blinked a few times, to try and reset my eyes.

The wall still looked odd.

I wondered if I had actually hit my head and had a concussion. I'd never had one before, but I was pretty sure they made you see and hear things.

Things like something a different color from the rest of the wall.

Things like a drumbeat low and far away.

The thing that was a different color suddenly looked like a body. If I squinted, I could make out a head, wrinkled skin, capped with long white hair. A wiry bare torso, one arm visible directly alongside it.

I blinked, squinted again, thought I could make out hips, leg, feet.

The drumbeat seemed a little closer, and quicker by just a touch.

I put the palms of my hands over my ears, pushed to create pressure, and pulled them loose.

The drumbeat didn't change.

I tried the old trick of moving your eyes left or right without moving your head, to focus someplace else and see if the image changes, like you do when you're staring at stars in the night sky and they seem to disappear.

The image changed alright.

The head turned to look at me, eyes open and staring.

I dropped my flashlight and it went out, rolling with the tink of metal on rock to a point between me and the body in the wall.

In the black, I could still see the face, the whites of the eyes.

"Fuck." I whispered.

Or tried. Nothing came out when I opened my mouth. I tried to call for Demarco, but couldn't get my vocal cords to work.

I was glad Demarco had made me pee outside.

I started to slide back on my ass towards where I knew that little opening was. The eyes followed me; as I moved backwards they came forward, maintaining the same distance they'd had when my flashlight was still on.

Or had they gotten closer?

I tried to keep my eyes wide; blinking even for a part of a second felt like a very bad idea.

Light flared in front of me and my vision swam, eyes tearing. A hand grabbed my shirt at the shoulder and started to haul me backwards.

"Come on, let's get out of here."

Demarco's voice, urgent, but I couldn't see him. His flashlight was in my face. "Turn around and go through the hole."

"I can't ... The flashlight ..."

"Just fucking turn around and start moving. Forget the other flashlight."

I turned, felt with my hands, found the hole and duck-crawled through. Demarco's hand stayed on my shoulder the whole time, lightly pushing me forward. I got through the hole and felt the narrow walls to stand up. Too quick, I cracked my head on the low ceiling and felt the sting of clay or dirt getting into a cut. Demarco's hand had slid down to my leg as I stood up, and the pressure he was putting on me to move was more than just a suggestion. I reached down and grabbed his shoulder as he came through and was glad to feel his coat and not bare skin. My head still stung, and I reached up to feel the cut.

"Move," he hissed in my ear. So I did. The narrow walls scratched at my hands as I felt along. He dropped his flashlight and put both hands on my shoulders to push me forward.

The cave entrance came up quick. Outside, he didn't say anything. His hands were still on my shoulders, and he steered me towards the nearest shore. I couldn't see his face, but I was sure he kept glancing back at the cave entrance. I didn't need to look back myself. I was sure the face I'd seen would be there if I looked back.

The closer we got to the shore, the easier it was to see. Stepping onto the ice was almost a relief. Demarco didn't let me catch my breath—he broke into the closest thing to a jog we could manage on the ice, keeping his hands on me to keep me steady and ignoring the little noises I was making as my back and shoulders throbbed in protest.

We made it back to his house and back through the bedroom window. He latched it shut and clicked on one small desk lamp. I collapsed onto his bed, shaking.

"You're a mess," he said, reaching for the first-aid kit on his bookshelf. I thought to say the same about him: his face was pale and his eyes still looked startled and unsure of the shadows of his own room.

We thought about concocting a story that would explain how I got bruised and cut up in his bedroom, but realized nothing would make sense. We'd just

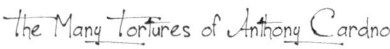

have to fess up that we'd snuck out and were messing around down the road when I got hurt. No need to mention Canopus.

He sat next to me on the bed and gently cleaned out the cuts on my scalp. When he was done, he put his arm around my shoulder. I shivered again.

Neither of us mentioned the cave. Not for the rest of that night, and not to anyone else afterwards.

I somehow fell asleep with my head on his shoulder. I'm sure he didn't sleep at all.

Demarco and I stayed close until I quit Scouts a year later when our assistant scoutmaster died. Most of my old Cub Scout den quit at the same time.

After I quit Scouts and joined the drama club, Demarco and I drifted a little bit. He had hunting buddies and a job; I had theater after school and Rocky Horror on the weekends. We both graduated and finally lost touch.

I never found out what he saw in the cave, and I never told him what I saw.

He died in our mid-twenties, while I was living at the other end of the state; accidentally shot himself. I found out weeks later, didn't make it to the funeral.

I regret that, but in a way I'm also relieved. Some parts of the past are better left where they came to rest.

We end this volume with a story by Jay Lake. Jay has been an inspiration to me, as a writer and as a person, for years now, and I'm flattered that even in the midst of chemotherapy last year, he took the time to write such a beautiful story for this project. This may be one of the last Jay Lake stories to ever see print. Even with participation in medical trials at the National Institutes of Health, Jay lost his battle with colon cancer on June 1, 2014, just five days before his 50th birthday. We love you, Jay, and we miss you. A bright light of the universe has gone out. (On a happier note: Jay, trickster that he was, managed to work almost every one of my nicknames into this story as a character or place. See if you can identify them all.)

 Cold Statues

JAY LAKE

The *Anthony Cardno* plunged through the heaving waves of the planet Stormy's salt-and-cinnamon sea. The sky was as brown as the water, the color of whipped chocolate with too much cream and nutmeg. Captain Thanny stood braced on the foredeck and watched the ocean desert slap itself into froth. Worlds away, he knew, skies were blue and seas were gray, but not here.

Not on Stormy.

His ship creaked under the force of the waves. This was a world settled for generations. Few here knew anything of Earth, fewer still carried personal memories of the home world. Humanity on Stormy lived aboard a million boats and made port at a hundred islets and eyots where the talltrees clung to the rocks and soil was a thin accident of windblown plankton shells and what passed for terrestrial life.

Like most of Stormy's working ships, the *Anthony Cardno* was a trawler. She laid down nets with long, deep lines and pulled up pelagic life by the streaming, writhing ton. Even those vessels that bore important people from island to island drew from the sea as they traveled. Never waste food. No one here flew, except the odd survey or rescue mission, and those very rare leaps from ground to orbit

and back down again. No one here stood on dry land, as almost everything was almost always damp. Thanny himself had been born in a fo'c'sle during an especially violent storm, and his feet had been wet ever since.

But *Anthony* herself was another thing entire. She'd been birthed lifetimes ago, under a sun so distant as to be unimaginable to any of her officers and men except for Thanny himself. Through the shaking wooden rail, he could hear the old, slow thoughts of the vessel's keel and braces.

She'd come down to the sea from on high in the earliest days of shipping on Stormy, and had sailed ever since. A settler's conceit, old family loyalties, justified as template and grandmother to fleets of ships ever since. The *Anthony Cardno* worked as hard now as ever she had, and matched her descendants measure for measure even now.

Thanny watched her keel break open the power of these ocean waves and thought about the past.

Andrew, Thanny's first mate and also the ship's navigator, approached. The mate was wrapped in oilskins against the weather, which was oddly chill for the latitude at which they were currently sailing. "We're coming right near to the Reefs of Ariadne, sir." His voice was hoarse over the wind.

"Any danger from our present course and heading?"

Andrew's face drew close to Thanny's ear. "Not unless the current pushes us too far west. We'll still make Port Riot within fifteen hours on the sailing plan we got now."

"Leave it, then," Thanny said.

"The Reefs, sir ..."

The captain looked at his mate. Concern, regret, maybe even distress, lurked in Andrew's gray-green eyes. "I'm fine."

"Come on back to the wheelhouse," Andrew urged.

"No. You go. One of us needs to."

Andrew took his arguments and retreated through the horizontal blowing mists of brown spume. That left Thanny alone with his thoughts and memories, and the slow, wooden mind of the ship herself.

:: **you don't need to do this** :: said the *Anthony Cardno*. Her words came slowly, like satellites falling from a great height. :: **you may live or you may die, and they will still be gone** ::

That was unusually coy for the ship's mind, Thanny realized. She tended to be more direct, albeit more reticent as well.

"Don't you worry about me," he told the wind. He'd never gotten the hang

The Many Tortures of Anthony Cardno

of speaking silently to the ship.

A great swell of love washed over him, the kind regard of two thousand tons of wood and metal and silicon and plastics and slow neural progressions crab-walking through the mind that thrummed beneath his feet. He knew there was so much more that the *Anthony Cardno* would never tell him. He knew there was so much more he would never say.

❈

Dinty, Thanny's father, had been a born landsman on a planet with precious little of the stuff. His mother Sandy had taken Dinty into her bed and on board her ship. He'd followed for love, for lust, or possibly simply for a warm, dry place to sleep. Thanny had never really understood which, if any or all of those reasons, had been first in his father's mind.

Marine biology was perhaps the most critical intellectual discipline on the planet. Stormy's biosphere was nothing like Earth's, but the majority of pelagic life was sufficiently protein-compatible with human life to be at the least digestible, if not necessarily tasty. Understanding the exceptions, and what to do about them, was part of the life and death of everyone in the world.

For all that he was a born dirt walker, Dinty had made himself one of the pre-eminent marine biologists in the world. In the end, perhaps it was that which had first attracted Sandy to him. He made a special study of the planet's reef systems, which undergirded the widespread littoral seas and provided some of the most bounteous and most accessible fishing grounds. Much like the reefs of Earth, Stormy's reefs were home to an astonishing variety of ecological niches and body forms. Everything from electric crabs to the retiring kidneyfish could be found there, in an array of colors that would have shamed a drunken chameleon.

All those, and Dinty.

His father and Sandy harbored an especial love for the Reefs of Ariadne. Thanny was fairly confident he had been conceived there, though that was not a question he'd ever cared to examine overmuch.

When Thanny was seven, the *Anthony Cardno* had taken them back to the Reefs of Ariadne to study a pelagic species so rare its very existence was little more than a rumor. At the time, Sandy had been captain of the ship, Dinty electing to remain supercargo while focusing on his scientific and marital duties. Thanny couldn't recall anymore the name of the man who had been first mate,

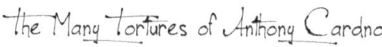

but he remembered a short, stocky fellow with hair so black it was almost blue, covering his head and neck in brief, wiry curls over skin pale as ocean foam—unusual on a planet where most people were as brown as the seas and the sky.

They'd anchored off the Reefs of Ariadne. Sandy and Dinty had done a lot of free diving, both snorkeling and with the costly scuba gear. There were no ore veins accessible from the islands of Stormy, so everything metal came down from orbit, where an entirely different human civilization pursued its own concerns in habitats and ships of another sort, though having much in common with the thalassic civilization at the surface. Those orbiting cousins held their metals dear, or at least held dear the cost of tossing them down the gravity well. As a result, things like pressure tanks were rare. Most metal went into electronics or engines. Everything else was made do with wood or ocean biomass, by preference.

Down they went, his parents. Thanny played on the deck or studied his school books or went swimming close to the ship, inside the shark nets. The reefs of Stormy had a rich ecosystem, including apex predators for whom a human, especially a small one, was the classic size of a preferred prey item.

He'd met his mother and father on the deck one day just after sundown. The orbital arcologies beaded the sky like a string of jewels, while a pair of Stormy's three small moons chased one another down to the horizon. Storms walked on lightning legs in the distance, rendering the waters of the Reefs of Ariadne choppy and restless.

"Thanny," Sandy had said, wringing water from her waist-length braid. "Greetings, child. We had a good day. How did you fare?"

Dinty had grinned at him over her shoulder, looking very satisfied indeed. Two of his father's students were hauling up canvas sampling buckets and smiling as well.

"I finished the block on sets and combinatorials," Thanny recited dutifully. He hadn't really *understood* it, but all tests were the same once you understood *them*. "And I swam for an hour. Spotted one loggerhead, but it never came near our nets."

Through his feet, the *Anthony Cardno* signaled warm approval. Even so, Thanny knew perfectly well the ship's slow-moving locus of attention was focused on Sandy and Dinty.

"Good, good." His mother' tone of voice indicated she hadn't really been listening at all. "We believe we've found our target organism."

"Stoneleaf," added Dinty. "There's a doctorate or two to be had in that silica-integrated biochemistry." Behind him, one of the students chuckled.

These were happy adults. Happier even then when they'd been into the sea-wine or aquavit of a slow, calm night.

"What did you learn?" That was a question Thanny had long known was guaranteed to draw a detailed response, taking the pressure off him.

"Exactly where it grows," his father had said shortly. "Which is a great learning indeed. That means we will be able to find it again elsewhere in the future."

After what happened the next day, the adults aboard the *Anthony Cardno* were never happy again.

❁

:: we should chart a different course ::

Thanny ignored the ship. He stared across the pitching waves. The weather being what it was, the sky displayed nothing but low, sullen clouds nearly invisible in night's darkness. The orbitals weren't as glorious as when he was a child. The Short, Kinetic War had seen to that, in exchange leaving the night sky decorated with a fine, glittering spread some people called The Veil. It was beautiful until you realized how many lost lives those thousand points of light represented.

Warmth rolled through him, making his joints tingle. *Anthony Cardno*'s equivalent of a hug. **:: not good waters ::**

"Waters are neither good nor bad," he said aloud, bracing harder against the rail. "The ocean knows no morality. Waters just are."

:: not good waters for Thanny bar Dinty ve Sandy, then ::

"I'm just a man, ship."

That brought him no answer.

In time, the mate Andrew made his way forward again. The deck wasn't pitching so badly now. The littoral waters around the Reefs of Ariadne were calmer than the depths they'd been cruising over previously. "We ain't dropping anchor here," the mate said.

"Was that a question or an order?" Thanny kept his voice mild, though a swell of anger threatened to crest and break over him like a million tons of cold, brown seawater.

"You the captain, you tell me. I just know what I see to be right."

"You. The ship. Everyone."

Even Andrew wasn't fully comfortable with Thanny's relationship to the

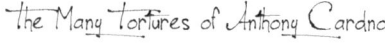

Anthony Cardno. Most people didn't understand it at all. The ship made them nervous, Andrew very much included. But the mate knew when he had an ally, so he patted the rail and looked around, as if there might be eyestalks protruding that he could exchange a meaningful glance with.

"It doesn't work that way," Thanny almost snapped. "*Anthony Cardno*'s is the only ship on this ocean who crossed the stellar gulf. She came from a place where people build, and think differently. So she's built, and thinks, differently."

"Ships shouldn't ought to think," Andrew whispered. "It ain't right."

"You know better. This one does. Always has. I figure you'd be used to it by now." Another surge of warmth shot through Thanny. "We're dropping anchor," he added.

"With respect, sir, I—"

Overriding his mate, Thanny snapped, "No respect, just anchor us in place."

:: **not good waters** ::

"Not *Anthony Cardno*'s problem, either."

✸

The next afternoon he'd been swimming inside the shark nets again, chasing a polo ball, when one of the students had come up from below ahead of schedule and apparently in a tearing hurry. "Get up the ladder, now," she'd gasped. Tee, her name had been, though he couldn't recall her lineage or home island.

Even with saltwater beading her face, Thanny could tell she was crying.

Still, he went. Shipboard discipline was shipboard discipline. You obeyed immediately, and asked questions later.

So he scrambled up a ladder, Tee close behind him, now openly sobbing. The wire-haired mate met them on the deck, his face closed and red. "Where's the captain and them?" he'd growled.

"Lost," she gasped. "Not coming back. Not ever."

The mate had glanced at Thanny, then shot Tee a hard look. "Enough. I'm sending men down to help."

She grabbed at his arm. "Don't ... I think ..."

"I don't give a good God damn what you think, missy. My captain's down there, and her husband, and we aren't going to sit up here like a bunch of kids waiting for their exam results."

By sundown three more sailors had been lost, including the wire-haired mate himself. Thanny hid weeping in the forward rope locker, and no one thought to come for him until the following day.

His parents would never have left him that long. But they also would never come for him again.

◉

Thanny stripped to his trunks as the clouds thinned, opening up enough to offer glimpses of The Veil. Taking nothing with him but his wits, he dove overboard to a last, interrupted protest from the *Anthony Cardno*. A wordless and indistinct sense of loss followed him into the water, but he shrugged it off.

If there were any loggerheads down here tonight, it was their lookout.

He swam deeper, moving with powerful strokes. The bottom was less than fifteen meters here, plenty of time for him to get down and back up again. It didn't matter what he found. The night above left no light at all below the surface except for a few ghostly streaks of bioluminescence, the hungry and the hunted each on their own prowl.

Even in the darkness, the Reefs of Ariadne were unmistakable. By touch he found the fans, the rope coral, the sessile pipeworms. Though he'd never taken academic credentials, Thanny could give most field biologists a run for their money out in open water. He'd spent years learning everything he could about stoneweed and the perils of the reef ecosystem.

There was nothing there but him, the reef, and scattering clouds of surprised fish. What had he expected? Already his chest was pounding, and his head beginning to hurt from anoxia. Careful not to let his fingers or feet stray into any inhabited holes, Thanny kicked for the surface.

When he broke through, there was perhaps even more light. The seas seemed almost calm. Andrew stood along the rail staring straight at the spot where Thanny had surfaced.

"You're almost two kilometers off," his first mate called. "We got to move along a heading of one hundred forty degrees."

Thanny didn't have the heart to smile, but he appreciated the thought. "Been talking to the ship, have you?"

"We'd rather have you back."

"I'm going to swim it," he said.

Even in night's shadows, Andrew looked depressed. "Got you a shark knife?"

"Nope." With that, Thanny oriented himself and struck out swimming.

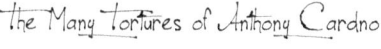

◆

As an orphan boy, they'd made him live on the eyot of Little Skua until he was fourteen, of age to sign on for crew. He was a ward of the Far Bridge Islands council. That group of tarred and salted old fisherman forced Thanny to be a landsman like his lost father, instead of letting him be a waterman as Sandy had been.

Thanny had struggled with his studies, gotten into a remarkable number of fights, and generally resented everyone and everything until he'd managed to sign on aboard the slow trawler *Quasar Forest*. Her captain was an old friend of Sandy's, and had seen more in Thanny than the Far Bridge Islands council ever would.

So he worked the waters for years, slowly gaining his certificates and ratings, until the day that Andrew had found him drinking in a nameless shebeen at Port Rollingwater.

The place stunk, as all those little places did. Built out over the water, the reek was compounded of ocean wrack and rotting kelp beer, plus whatever odors that night's anonymous drinkers had brought in with them from their days on the water.

A tall man with gray-green eyes and skin the same tan as the sky pulled up to the bar next to him. "You Thanny?" he'd asked without preamble.

"More like I'm drunk." He stared at the newcomer through the suds-riddled bottom of a seaglass tumbler.

"Andrew," said the man. He seemed uncomfortable, words drawn out of him as if under duress. "A ... friend ... of yours sent me."

So far as he knew, Thanny didn't have any friends. At least besides the one's he'd made aboard the *Quasar Forest*. Not many there, either, truth be told, but at least they all got along. He settled for asking, "Anyone I know?"

That drew a short, barking laugh. Then: "*Anthony Cardno.*"

"Mom's ship?" Tears stood in Thanny's eyes. He hadn't so much as seen the *Anthony Cardno* in almost two decades.

"She's asking for her family back."

And so his life had begun the process of coming full circle.

◆

The circle came nearly to a close when Thanny swam up to a lighted buoy bob-

The Many Tortures of Anthony Cardno

bing in the night-dark sea. The *Anthony Cardno* was already anchored nearby, her lights dimmed but not out. Her big bioelectrics had beaten him handily across the open water distance, of course. Thanny was sure everyone aboard was watching him, as was the ship herself.

He didn't bother to wave. Instead he dove, grasping the buoy's tether and kicking himself toward the reef and the sea bottom.

There was stoneleaf down here, Thanny knew. And he knew he'd need to avoid it. The stuff killed. He'd spent half his life learning what little was known about stoneleaf, much of it from Tee's carefully collated publication of his parents' working notes on the plant and its unique silica-integrated biochemistry. Stoneleaf's radical differentiation from the rest of Stormy's observed biosphere was either an argument for panspermia or for multiple, independent geneses of life on this world, depending on who you believed. Exciting stuff either way, but such a thin thread of evidence to hang so much speculation on.

Tee never had got her doctorate. She became a landswoman herself, working in Stormy's tiny Orbital Operations Group. A tinier group, that, since the Short, Kinetic War had reduced space travel to almost nothing.

Lights sparkled below him in a reef bottom reflection of The Veil. Was all life doomed to be fragmented? Thanny realized he was seeing bioluminescent glitterdots dropped overboard from the *Anthony Cardno* when the buoy had been set. They'd been busy in the forty minutes it had taken him to make the swim.

The glow was faint, eerie, like an incomplete sketch of someone else's life. Three shapes loomed nearby. Three more beyond them stretched in attitudes of supplication or horror. There never had been any bodies the day Tee had come up panicked from the reef. Thanny had never said good-bye to his parents, never kissed their cold lips, never tucked those last few hairs into place before stitching shut the sailcloth and sending them back to the ocean which they both had loved, each in their own way.

His father was closest to the stoneleaf colony, of course. Dinty had become contaminated trying to cut a sample. Or so Thanny imagined. Sandy's arm was on her husband's, the two of them bound together until tidal erosion and materials attenuation would someday render them both to gravel. The other graduate student—another forgotten name from his childhood—had reached in to help as well. Only Tee had wised up and headed for the surface.

They were cold statues, these three, turned to a crusty mass focused on a single plant. That rocky triptych was guarded at a slight distance by their would-be rescuers. All six had been left for dead on the sea bottom, victims of the

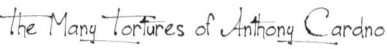

stoneleaf and its strange magics. His chest already ached. His heart had always ached, ever since that day.

Thanny wanted so much to hug his parents one more time, tell them he would be all right. That life went on. It would be fine, he longed to say. The *Anthony Cardno* waited above, with Andrew and the rest of his crew. The Reefs of Ariadne were as fitting a sea grave as he could ever have picked for them.

But in touching them, would he be picking this same grave for himself? Or had the effect attenuated over time? Perhaps the stoneleaf had been disturbed here. Perhaps it had died off.

He reached out, fingers spread in one last good-bye. His parents' ship waited above him, its keel patient as ever, radiating love for his family all the days of their lives.

Just one little touch, Thanny thought. *Just one.*

The Many Tortures of Anthony Cardno

Author Biographies

Day Al-Mohamed is co-editor for the anthology, *Trust & Treachery* from Dark Quest Books and hosts the multi-author blog http://unleadedwriting.com/. In addition to speculative fiction, she also writes comics and film scripts. Her recent publications can be found in *Daily Science Fiction*, Crossed Genres' anthology *Oomph - A Little Super Goes a Long Way*, and GrayHaven Comics' anti-bullying issue *You Are Not Alone*. She is an active member of the Cat Vacuuming Society of Northern Virginia Writing Group and Women in Film and Video.

When not working on fiction, Day is Senior Policy Advisor with the U.S. Department of Labor. She has also worked as a lobbyist and political analyst on issues relating to health care, education, employment, and international development. She loves action movies and drinks far too much tea. She lives in Washington, DC with her wife, N.R. Brown, in a house with too many swords, comic books, and political treatises.

She can be found online at http://www.dayalmohamed.com/ and @DayAl-Mohamed on Twitter.

My wife is just now recovering from surgery (i.e. we brought her home Thursday). At her last annual visit, the doctor found abnormal cells and discovered Stage 2 uterine cancer. So obviously this is very recent and very raw and very important to me. She was fortunate; so many others are not. I am so very glad you invited me to submit and hope that this one small thing I can do will help.

✸

Neal Bailey grew up in Tacoma, Washington, which is why he lives and works in Portland, Oregon. A meretricious poetaster by day, a writer by night, he really needs to get some sleep, but the baby keeps asking for Cheerios. Pray for his soul.

When my brother told me that he had cancer, the bottom dropped out of my world and I realized how truly helpless I was in the face of the dispassionate nature of the universe. When my brother beat his cancer, I learned the meaning of gratitude. True gratitude. I feel quite fortunate to be one of the lucky ones who haven't had a loved one die yet, but the nature of cancer being what it is, I know we will always have to fight, with words, with strength, and with hope.

❊

Eric S. Bauman is a database developer currently residing in Virginia. This is the first story of his to be seen by an audience outside of his family and small circle of close friends. He can be found on Twitter @InfinityLtd and, if he ever gets the time to build it, he will have a website at www.InfinityLtd.net.

I wanted to contribute to this anthology mainly because I wanted to torture Anthony. But also, cancer has done a number on my friends and family. I got back in touch with two high-school friends after at least fifteen years of silence and within a year, cancer had taken both of them. Also, we found out the day before my dad died in 2009 that he had lung cancer that had spread to his glands. We knew he had other problems (pulmonary fibrosis, diabetes, etc.) but we had no clue that cancer was in the mix as well. Hopefully, this minor contribution will help eradicate this evil disease.

❊

Steve Berman has been a finalist for the Andre Norton Award (*Vintage: A Ghost Story*), as well as numerous times for the Golden Crown Literary Awards and Lambda Literary Awards. He released a new collection of his own queer and fantastical YA stories in February of 2014, *Red Caps*, as well as editing the 2014 editions of Wilde Stories and Best Gay Stories (both out in June 2014). He resides in southern New Jersey.

I grew up with cancer on the living room wall. Not the tiny 'c' sort of cancer that belies its size and robs so many folk of dignity and life. The large 'C'—a brass trivet showing the astrological sign. It hung besides another trivet, this one of Virgo. One for my father, one for my mother. Wedding presents, I think. Almost two decades later, the trivets had disappeared. Real cancer came then. One afternoon, my elderly parents sat me down and told me that my father had been diagnosed with prostate cancer. I took the news stoically, which surprised them. But a man in his early 70s was bound to get something malignant growing inside of him—it's as if, after my mother went through three pregnancies, Fate wanted my father to suffer labor pains but the mass inside of him was no little brother I wanted.

❊

The Many Tortures of Anthony Cardno

Anthony R. Cardno's first published work was a "hero history" of *Marvel Comics'* *The Invaders* for the late, lamented *Amazing Heroes* magazine back in 1986. His short stories have appeared in *Willard & Maple, Sybil, Space Battles: Full Throttle Space Tales Volume 6, Beyond The Sun, OOMPH: A Little Super Goes A Long Way,* and *Tales of the Shadowmen Volume 10: Esprit de Corps.* In addition to a full time job as a corporate trainer, Anthony is a proofreader for *Lightspeed* magazine, writes book reviews for *Chelsea Station* and *Strange Horizons* magazines, and interviews authors, singers, and other creative types on www.anthonycardno. com, where you can also find some of his other short stories. In his spare time, Anthony enjoys making silly cover song videos on Youtube. You can find him on Twitter @talekyn.

My first dim memory of cancer was in reference to the passing of my Aunt Connie, whom I barely remember. Then my maternal grandfather Anthony Bukowski, various cousins, my maternal grandmother Victoria Bukowski, my parents Rosemary and Raymond Cardno, and close friends (M. Denise Barnoski, Karen Jenkins, Kristina Meyer) who left us at too young an age. In between my mother's and father's deaths, I was diagnosed myself. I'm one of the lucky ones: surgery, comparatively light chemo, and no recurrences yet, knock wood.

✸

Christopher Paul Carey is the coauthor with Philip José Farmer of *Gods of Opar: Tales of Lost Khokarsa* and the author of *Exiles of Kho*, a prelude to the Khokarsa series. His short fiction may be found in anthologies such as *Tales of the Shadowmen, The Worlds of Philip José Farmer, Tales of the Wold Newton Universe,* and *The Avenger: The Justice, Inc. Files.* He is an editor with Paizo Publishing on the award-winning Pathfinder Roleplaying Game and has edited numerous collections, anthologies, and novels. "With Dust Their Glittering Towers" is the first story written in his projected Fly-Leaves series, centering on members of the nineteenth- and early-twentieth-century Baconian movement and their dealings with a supernatural conspiracy. A novel related to the Fly-Leaves series is also in the works. Find him online at www.cpcarey.com and on Twitter @cpcarey.

I recently lost my Aunt Becky to lung cancer. No one should ever, ever take up smoking.

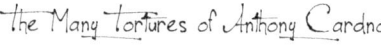

✦

At just 15, one of Australia's fastest rising singer/songwriters **Frank Dixon** has spent the last two years travelling between Melbourne and Los Angeles. His wild ride has seen him recording with Grammy Award-winning producers First Born, Devine Evans and Grammy-nominated producer Dre Knight. This all happened after being scouted on YouTube by a Canadian talent scout and producer when Frank was 11. Frank already has a string of songwriting successes under his belt. At 13 Frank won the Australian Songwriter of the Year Award (U18's) - Youth Category of the Australian Songwriters Association. He was the winner of the 2013 My Song Award and a Semi Finalist in the International Unsigned Only songwriting competition. Recent single releases over 2013 "Dream Brigade," "Toorak Girl," and "Step Into the Dark" have received significant airplay across Australia. Frank is currently recording and producing his debut album "Proof of Concept," due for release in 2014 with Lee Bradshaw and Michael Stangel (Finalist on *The Voice* 2013). The second single "Gold" (Featuring Kelebek from *X Factor*) hit radio in May 2014.

When I was asked to write about my experience with cancer, I found it challenging as I am not sure that I have anything relevant. Of course I hear stories of people's friends and family but it hasn't been something in my immediate family, although one of my close friends recently lost her grandmother to pancreatic cancer. I do know from watching what my friend and her family went through that cancer is very traumatic and can be very sudden. I know that there is lots and lots of research in all different areas, and I would hope that in my lifetime cancer is pretty much eradicated!

✦

Adam P. Knave is an Eisner and Harvey award winning editor and writer who co-writes *Amelia Cole* and *Never Ending* (with D.J. Kirkbride) as well as *Artful Daggers* (with Sean E. Williams). He edits Jamal Igle's *Molly Danger*, Sam Read's *Exit Generation*, and was one of the editors on Image's *Popgun* anthology series. He also writes prose and short comics and edits all sorts of things. He recently moved to Portland, OR after spending his first 38 years in NYC.

One of my best friends' mother passed because of cancer just a few years ago. I'm lucky enough no direct family members have done so for myself, but watching her go

The Many Tortures of Anthony Cardno

through that and supporting her where I could is one of those things that brings home how horrible, and pervasive, cancer is and how much it needs to be stopped.

●

Hugo-award winning author **Mary Robinette Kowal** is a novelist and professional puppeteer. Her debut novel *Shades of Milk and Honey* (Tor 2010) was nominated for the 2010 Nebula Award for Best Novel. In 2008, she won the Campbell Award for Best New Writer, while her short story "For Want of a Nail" won the Hugo for short story in 2011. Her stories have appeared in *Strange Horizons*, *Asimov's*, and several Year's Best anthologies, as well as in her collection *Scenting the Dark and Other Stories* from Subterranean Press. Kowal is also an award-winning puppeteer. With over twenty years of experience, she has performed for *LazyTown* (CBS), the Center for Puppetry Arts, Jim Henson Pictures, and founded Other Hand Productions. Her designs have garnered two UNIMA-USA Citations of Excellence, the highest award an American puppeteer can achieve. When she isn't writing or puppeteering, Kowal brings her speech and theater background to her work as a voice actor. As the voice behind several audio books and short stories, she has recorded fiction for authors such as Kage Baker, Cory Doctorow, and John Scalzi. Mary lives in Chicago with her husband Rob and over a dozen manual typewriters. Sometimes she even writes on them.

●

Jay Lake lives in Portland, Oregon, where he works on numerous writing and editing projects. His books for 2013 and 2014 include *Kalimpura* and *Last Plane to Heaven* from Tor and *Love in the Time of Metal and Flesh* from Prime. His short fiction appears regularly in literary and genre markets worldwide. Jay is a winner of the John W. Campbell Award for Best New Writer and a multiple nominee for the Hugo, Nebula, and World Fantasy Awards. He blogs regularly about his terminal colon cancer on his Web site at jlake.com. (I've left Jay's bio in first person because his presence will always be present for us. ˜AC)

Jay Lake spent the last of his health participating in clinical trials through the National Institutes of Health. He passed away on June 1, 2014.

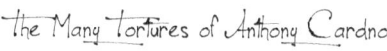

✱

Barry Mangione is a singer-songwriter, life coach, and an all-around creative guy. After overcoming many obstacles in life, he enjoys writing music and lyrics about struggle, hope, and redemption. Barry is also a fledgling biohacker and an avid martial artist. He even has a job where they tell him he's a physical therapist, but he's not sure if he should believe them or not. For several years, he worked with The Musical Geniuses to write an original song each week in just an hour. Barry is also the creator of the interactive musical stage experience The Graft (www.applythegraft.com), lead singer/guitarist for The Dalliance, and the author of No Easy Answers.

As you can see, I wear many hats, mostly to cover my bald head, which I first started shaving over a decade ago to support a friend who was dealing with breast cancer.

✱

Dennis R. Miller is Director of Public Relations at Mansfield University. He is the author of *The Perfect Song* under the pseudonym Damon, as well as *One Woman's Vengeance* under his own name. He is working on a sequel to "Vengeance" entitled *One Bullet Beyond Justice*. Over the years his father, several relatives and many friends have succumbed to cancer. Many have also beaten it.

Over the years, my father, several relatives, and many friends have succumbed to cancer. Many have also beaten it.

✱

Michelle Moklebust Moklebust grew up in New York playing make believe and writing short stories. After high school, she attended SUNY Buffalo and then moved to California, where she earned a teaching credential. She worked as a special education teacher in Southern California from 2000-2012. She's also been a bank teller, a paralegal, a school photographer, and a teacher's aide. In 2012, she returned to the East Coast with her son and their neurotic Border Collie mix. In her spare time, she can be found reading, drawing, taking pictures, and staying up way too late. Her first YA novel-length ebook, *Ghost Whispers*,

The Many Tortures of Anthony Cardno

was released in July 2012, followed by *Descendants of Amphitrite: Riptide* in the fall of 2013.

Cancer has touched many of my friends and family, taking several of them from us way too soon. In May, 2011, I found a lump in my left breast, which turned out to be breast cancer. My mammogram in February 2011 had been clean. My new mantra: If you love 'em, check 'em.

❧

Joseph Pittman is the author of the beloved Linden Corners series: *Tilting at Windmills, A Christmas Wish, A Christmas Hope,* and *The Memory Tree.* A fifth book is currently being written. Other novels include reader favorites *When The World Was Small, Legend's End,* and *Beyond the Storm.* His crime fiction includes the acclaimed Todd Gleason series, including *London Frog, California Scheming,* and *Two Todd Tales,* a collection of two novellas. In early 2013, he released the three-part serial novel, *The Original Crime,* as an exclusive eBook: *Part One: Remembrance; Part Two: Retribution; Part Three: Redemption.* A print edition is available exclusively from the Mystery Guild and Quality Paperback Book Club.

Cancer is an unforgiving organism, but the spirit of human resilience can be much stronger. My mother has battled and beaten cancer not just once but twice. She is the living example of how our minds can sometimes overcome the physical. Strength comes from somewhere deep within our souls. Cancer comes from the outside and can be excised.

❧

Jen Ryan was born and raised in New Westminster, BC, where she lives with her husband, two children, and two cats. She is the acting Secretary of New West Writers, and former Director-at-Large for the Royal City Literary Arts Society. Jen has self-published two chapbooks, *Inspiring Minds,* and *Self Help.* She writes picture books, adult and young adult short stories, and poetry. She is also working on her first novel. When not writing or working her day job, Jen enjoys quiet time with her family, noisy time with friends, and everything in between. Music, movies, TV, poker, and beer are among Jen's many passions.

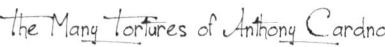

When I was a new, young, single mother, I became involved with a local women's centre and a family service centre. We lost both a family service centre's child care worker and a women's centre director, within about five years, to brain cancer. These ladies were so helpful and important to my development as a woman and a mother; I was deeply saddened by the losses. We need to fight the unfairness that is cancer.

●

Bryan Thomas Schmidt is an author and editor of adult and children's speculative fiction. His debut novel, *The Worker Prince*, received Honorable Mention on Barnes & Noble Book Club's Year's Best Science Fiction Releases for 2011. His first children's books, *102 More Hilarious Dinosaur Books For Kids* and *Abraham Lincoln: Dinosaur Hunter—Land Of Legends* appeared from Delabarre Publishing in 2012. His short stories have appeared in magazines, anthologies and online. He edited the anthologies *Space Battles: Full Throttle Space Tales #6* for Flying Pen Press, *Beyond The Sun* for Fairwood Press, *Raygun Chronicles: Space Opera For a New Age* for Every Day, and *Shattered Shields* with coeditor Jennifer Brozek for Baen Books (forthcoming). He is currently working on *Gaslamp Terrors* and *Mission Tomorrow: A New Century Of Exploration*. He hosts #sffwrtcht (Science Fiction and Fantasy Writer's Chat) Wednesdays at 9 pm ET on Twitter. Bryan can be found online at Facebook, on Twitter as @BryanThomasS and @sffwrtcht and via his website: http://www.bryanthomasschmidt.net/.

I've lost several people to cancer: two grandfathers, an uncle, my mother, and family friends. I've watched others struggling. It's the worst kind of war—one we just can't seem to win any time soon. But we should always remain determined, because the cost is too high to give up.

●

David Lee Summers is the author of seven novels and over sixty published short stories. His writing spans a wide range of the imaginative, from science fiction to fantasy to horror. David's novels include *Owl Dance*, a Wild West Steampunk adventure, and *Vampires of the Scarlet Order*, which tells the story of a band of vampire mercenaries who fight evil. His short stories and poems have appeared in such magazines and anthologies as *Realms of Fantasy*, *Cemetery Dance*, *Human Tales*, *Six-Guns Straight From Hell*, and *Apocalypse 13*. In addition to writing,

David edits the quarterly science fiction and fantasy magazine *Tales of the Talisman* and has edited three science fiction anthologies. When not working with the written word, David operates telescopes at Kitt Peak National Observatory. Learn more about David at davidleesummers.com.

Perhaps the most frightening moment of my life was when my wife told me she had breast cancer in May 2011. Six months later, after surgery and chemotherapy, she was declared cancer free and continues to do well. I am thankful for the research that allows Kumie and me to be together, still, and hope for more happy endings in the years to come.

❋

Sabrina Vourvoulias is the author of *Ink* (*Crossed Genres*, 2012), a speculative novel that draws on her memories of Guatemala's armed internal conflict, and of the Latin@ experience in the United States. It was named to Latinidad's Best Books of 2012. Her short stories have appeared in *Strange Horizons*, *Crossed Genres* and a number of anthologies, including the upcoming *Long Hidden: Speculative Fiction from the Margins of History*. Follow her on Twitter: @followthelede.

My father had pancreatic cancer. I lived with him through four years of highs and lows: the Whipple surgical procedure; the initial harsh and hopeless prognosis by a clinically brilliant but inhumane doctor; the hunt for the right doctor; the chemotherapy; the all-clear and then the heartbreaking recurrence. My father was a quietly brave and resilient man—he had survived kidnapping, psychological torture, the hardship and stresses of keeping his family safe during a violent undeclared civil war—but even he was worn down by this unrelenting disease. But what remains these 10 years after his death isn't the disease but the memory of what it never could touch. In Latin America, at gatherings, we toast the departed with words that indicate that those we love are never gone: Jason Vourvoulias ¡Presente!

❋

Damien Angelica Walters: Writing as Damien Walters Grintalis, Damien's short fiction has appeared in *Lightspeed*, *Strange Horizons*, *Beneath Ceaseless Skies*, *Interzone*, *Fireside*, *Daily Science Fiction*, and others, and her debut novel, *Ink*, was released in December 2012 by Samhain Horror. As Damien Angeli-

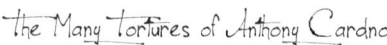

ca Walters, her work has appeared or is forthcoming in *Apex, Shimmer, Shock Totem, Strange Horizons, Daily Science Fiction, Nightmare, Drabblecast, Pseudopod*, and the anthologies *Glitter & Mayhem* and *What Fates Impose*. A collection of her short fiction will be released in spring 2014 from Apex Publications.

Cancer. It's an ugly word, summoning the image of cells waging an unseen battle. When we found out my husband had Hodgkin's Lymphoma, I was terrified. How dare those renegade cells invade his healthy body. What right did they have? As I watched my husband and his doctors wage their counterattack, I feared it wouldn't be enough. How can you fight an enemy you can't see? But they did, and the day my husband went into remission was one of the happiest in my life.

❋

Shirley Jackson Award winner **Kaaron Warren** has lived in Melbourne, Sydney, Canberra, and Fiji. She's sold many short stories, three novels (the multi-award-winning *Slights, Walking the Tree* and *Mistification*) and four short story collections. Her most recent collection, *Through Splintered Walls*, won a Canberra Critic's Circle Award for Fiction, two Ditmar Awards, two Australian Shadows Awards, and a Shirley Jackson Award. Her stories have appeared in Australia, the US, the UK, and elsewhere in Europe, and have been selected for both Ellen Datlow's and Paula Guran's Year's Best Anthologies. You can find her at kaaronwarren.wordpress.com and she Tweets @KaaronWarren.

We lost the incredibly talented horror writer Paul Haines to cancer in 2012. To read his livejournal, especially if you start way back, if you start BEFORE, is heart-breaking. Another writer we lost was Alinta Thornton, who also kept an ongoing livejournal.

❋

Bear Weiter is an illustrator, animator, artist, and writer. His fiction appears in a number of magazines and anthologies, including *Black Static, Miseria's Chorale*, and *Of Devils & Deviants: An Anthology of Erotic Horror*. He previously published under the pen names Virginia Ray and Jacob Ruby, but he has locked them all away and now those voices labor for Team Bear. You can find him on Twitter @bearthw or his personal site: www.bearweiter.com.

I don't think anyone can be untouched by cancer, and I'm no exception. There are

several people I know who have had it, or are still fighting it, but perhaps the one that touches me the most is my cousin—she was never diagnosed, but because of the death of her mom and her grandmother before her (both from breast cancer), she took the proactive step to have a double mastectomy. I'm proud of her courage.

❋

Brian White is the editor of *Fireside*, a multigenre fiction magazine with a focus on great storytelling and fair pay for creators. He's also a newspaper copy editor, bourbon lover, and curmudgeon. He lives near Boston with his wife and two cats, only one of whom is actively plotting his death.

As for my connection to cancer? I have been lucky, no one in my family in my lifetime has had it. I did however, have a friend in college. He was a gifted sportswriter, and we all thought he had a promising career ahead of him, and he developed a brain tumor. They removed it, and he was ok, got a job at a small paper, was doing well, and the tumor came back, and it killed him. It was really a punch in the stomach. Jason Haslam. Fuckin a.

❋

Christie Yant is a science fiction and fantasy writer and Assistant Editor for *Lightspeed Magazine*. Her fiction has appeared in anthologies and magazines, including *Year's Best Science Fiction & Fantasy 2011* (Horton), *Armored*, *Analog Science Fiction & Fact*, *Beneath Ceaseless Skies*, *io9*, *Wired.com*, and China's *Science Fiction World*. Her work has received honorable mentions in *Year's Best Science Fiction* (Dozois) and *Best Horror of the Year* (Datlow) and has been long-listed for Story-South's Million Writers Award. She was also the Guest Editor of the "Women Destroy Science Fiction" issue of *Lightspeed Magazine* in June 2014." She lives on the central coast of California with two writers, an editor, and assorted four-legged nuisances. Follow her on Twitter @christieyant.

I've been fortunate enough to not lose anyone close to me to cancer—yet. Because it's really a "yet," isn't it? As I watch acquaintances and colleagues in their fights against cancer, and get to know more survivors year by year, I can't help but be aware that it's only a matter of time. And when the time comes, what I hope to hear is that we've advanced enough that it's curable and survivable, and we have less to fear.

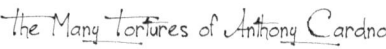

Acknowledgments

First and foremost, I must thank the authors who donated their stories and lyrics (original and reprint) for what was originally supposed to be an e-book only enterprise, and then also for their willingness to extend those rights to a print edition. You are all amazing. Thank you from the bottom of my not-nice heart.

Immense thanks to Bear Weiter, who only offered to handle the formatting and to investigate going to a print edition about a dozen times before I took him up on the offer, including the cover. He has gone above and beyond, and his belief in this project astounds me.

Thanks also to Michelle Moklebust and Lee Bloom (and BJ, Jake, and Miranda) for The Afternoon of the Unending Photo-Shoot that provided the raw images Bear used in creating the cover and which Marlyse Comte used to create the internal artwork. Many thanks, Marlyse!

Thanks to the folks who have been down this road and offered thoughts and advice on the process of anthologizing: Brian White, Bryan Thomas Schmidt, Steve Berman, Bart Leib, Kay Holt, and Constella and Nikoda at Critical Mass Rocketworks.

Thanks to the editors who have published and/or inspired me: The aforementioned Brian, Bryan, Bart, and Kay, as well as John Joseph Adams, Steve Berman, J.M. Lofficier, Jennifer Brozek, Michael Croteau, and Ellen Datlow. I've learned much from each of you, whether you knew you were teaching or not.

Last but not least, I must thank my family, both blood and extended, too numerous to even attempt to name, and leaving any one of you out would torture me forever. You all helped me through my own cancer journey and all the ups and downs since, and I hope this project makes you proud.

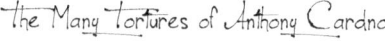

Copyright Notices

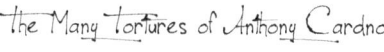

The Many Tortures of Anthony Cardno